MW00879489

PART THREE

DRAKE THOMAS

THE DEAD MOUNTAINS

TYLER SVEC
JORDAN SVEC

DRAKE THOMAS
THE DEAD MOUNTAINS

Cover Image © by Tyler Svec
Cover Design © by Tyler Svec
Interior Design by Tyler Svec

ISBN: 9798863759999

Other works by Tyler Svec

The Kingdom

I. Alliance

II. Rebellion

III. Redemption

DRAKE THOMAS

Rise of Grimdor

Deception of Merderick

Super-Hero Stories

Crunch

Boom!

Bang! Pow! Slat!

More at svecbooks.com

PART THREE

DRAKE THOMAS

THE DEAD MOUNTAINS

TYLER SVEC
JORDAN SVEC

DRAKE THOMAS
THE DEAD MOUNTAINS

Chapters

SYNOPSIS

This is the third part of Drake Thomas

Drake Thomas woke by the side of the river. After a few moments, it became clear that he had no memory of his life before that moment. The only thing he had to his name was an unusual mark on his hand. His new companions thought that the mark might indicate some ancient legend and pertain to a certain prophecy. Within a matter of days, Drake and his companions found themselves running to the Elven nation of Ariamore.

After being pursued by the Sorcerer to the borders of Ariamore, the threat of war was inevitable. Misinterpreting the mark on Drake's hand, they put him and his companions in charge of the battle. That decision proved disastrous, though they did achieve victory.

Some days after the battle they met a strange shopkeeper named Isabel, who seemed to know many things but never revealed how she knew them.

The enemy's power grew and in the middle of the night, Gwen was kidnapped. As the days progressed, they became better trained and became aware that the Sorcerer was looking to start a full-blown war.

As the war drew closer, a confrontation involving, Isabel, Rohemir, and Merderick (the Sorcerer) revealed that Gwen was the child of Isabel and Rohemir.

The battle ragged and the Sorcerer was overthrown. The land was restored and Drake and Gwen were chosen to lead the new nation of Rhallenin. However, Drake and Gwen appointed Ellizar and Lily as the intern King and Queen. During the night they left, heading north.

Chapter 1

RUMORS

It was early and already Pilas dreaded the day. The sun illuminated the mountains to the west, their snow caps glistening in the light. It was a beautiful sight, one that Pilas generally enjoyed. It was morning, and few in the city of Avdatt had yet to wake up.

His wife lay in their bed, still fast asleep. He moved past her and then stepped into a long and grand courtyard. To his right was the main courtyard. To his left were guest rooms for people of importance who may be visiting the city of Avdatt. Whether it was to meet with him or to observe the city he governed, it was his pleasure to give them lodging.

His men had contacted him before he had gone to sleep, reporting that a man named Cornelius wished to speak to him at first light. Pilas had been immediately filled with disgust at the thought of the name.

He hated the Elves and their religion. His loyalty was to the empire and the emperor himself. The Elves and their ancient religion were a waste of his time. For years he had asked the emperor to order the execution of both the Farsees and the Elvish religion.

However, in a strange way, the people of Thrace following an ancient religion was helpful. If the people of the nation kept praying and sacrificing animals to their gods then they wouldn't think about trying to revolt and win back their freedom.

Every week he was forced to meet with Cornelius, the highest of all the Farsees, and talk about things that he could care less about. The only good thing about Cornelius being the high Farsee was that he had been the high Farsee for almost fifteen years, and would usually give in to whatever demands the

Goshen government wished.

Being the high Farsee was an elected position and every year it had to be voted on by the other leading members of the religion. With Cornelius being the head Farsee for so long, it had allowed Pilas to get to know him a little bit and figure out just what he had to say in order to push all the right buttons and get what he wanted.

Pilas only hoped that he would be as successful this morning with whatever Cornelius wished to speak to him about. The fact that he had requested a meeting so early in the morning was unusual. Usually, Cornelius would be off, butchering the lamb for whatever sacrifice the law required of him.

He reached his chamber and entered into the lavishly decorated hall meant for the Emperor himself. When the emperor was not here, it was Pilas's meeting room.

A large doorway was on the far side, leading out to a balcony that overlooked the sleeping city. He moved past the guards without saying a word to them. He was met at the window by one of his advisors, who motioned for his weapons to be brought.

Pilas strapped his sword to his side and put on some of his armor as well as a cape. He had never needed the weapons, but he couldn't take any chances when meeting with Elvish folk. If they were going to start any kind of an uprising then he would be sure to squash those ideas while they were still that.

"Aramis!" Pilas boomed. Moments of silence passed before the head guard came running up to him bowing.

"Yes, my governor."

"Order the servants to get me my breakfast, also I was curious if we have any idea what Cornelius wishes to speak about?"

"He did not specify. We do not think he's here for ill intentions if that's what you're asking."

"Very good. Now get me my meal."

"Yes sir," Aramis replied, vanishing from the chamber leaving Pilas with only his thoughts for company. Minutes passed and finally, his food was brought to him. He sat at the head of his table in the middle of the large chamber and began eating, noticing the guards were starting to shift towards the door. A moment later the doors opened and Aramis led a man forward. He was older, likely in his fifties, with a long graying beard. He wore long robes of purple and burgundy, supposedly the 'official' colors of the religion.

That was enough for Pilas to laugh at. What kind of a god would demand that the high Farsee only wear certain colors? It wasn't for him to figure out and he didn't care as the slightly rounded man came forward. He stood tall and proud, which was one trait that seemed to plague the Farsees worse than any other group of leaders that he had ever met.

They walked through the city square spouting off the ancient scrolls and prophecies and acting as though they were better than everyone else. The way Pilas saw it, the whole system of them being above everyone made the Farsees not too different from the emperor he served.

Despite the similarities between the Farsees and the Goshen government, the Farsees thought of themselves as better and more wise. They awaited their rumored king, (Sherados as they called him) to come and free them from the bonds that kept them in the position they were in. Aramis and the man stopped ten feet from the table with Pilas only looking up from his food long enough to acknowledge their presence.

"My lord, Cornelius of Gadara to meet with you."

"Thank you, Aramis." Aramis walked back to his post while Pilas took another bite of his food before looking up at Cornelius. "Would you like something to eat?"

"No that won't be necessary my lord, I am not allowed to eat before the morning sacrifices are made."

"So I thought," Pilas retorted. "Speaking of which, what is it that brings you to the palace at such an unearthly hour? Shouldn't you be starting with your endless list of things to do for the day, as dictated by your religion?"

"Indeed I should, but I'm sure even Lathon wouldn't mind me putting them off for a little while. What I have come to speak with you about is a very great threat!"

"Threat? What threat could harm both you and me?"

"That is the very reason that I've come. There is great danger brewing in the nearby cities. We've even had reports of dangerous behaviors as far down as Grimdor," Cornelius said.

"I thought Grimdor was destroyed?" Pilas asked. "Isn't that what you told me several years ago?"

"Indeed it was, and once again that's the very reason I have come to you. The fact that Grimdor was destroyed is more disturbing than I once thought. I'm not saying I'm disappointed that the Sorcerer and his nation were toppled. They certainly were out to do evil, but the one who overthrew them is the one I am talking about."

"You think he is a great threat?" Pilas laughed. "What makes this man so evil and dangerous? He did the world a great favor, he saved your people from certain death. Does the fact that he toppled a great nation like Grimdor scare you? Because the Goshen government did the same thing to the fine nation of Thrace did it not?"

"It did my lord, and I'm not here to deny your government's lordship over these lands. But it is the one who leads these people into battle that is foreboding. Do you know who it is? Who he says he is? He's been traveling this countryside for almost five years now, talking and allowing his poisonous words to destroy the minds of those he comes in touch with.

"Furthermore his fame and popularity have skyrocketed due to those cursed Taruk races. We've been watching him very closely and there's something about him that's not right. He walks with a confidence that puts us all on edge. No matter what we, or anyone else does, we can't seem to figure out what his purpose is. He is gaining a large number of followers, and at any moment he could turn violent and threaten this government."

Pilas laughed. "I assure you, no matter how great his numbers, he is not a threat to *this* government. Have you forgotten that I have a number of legions at my disposal? Furthermore, a mere day away there is a large fortress that I could call troops in from if they were needed. I know of who you speak, for my scouts and spies have watched him too. He appears to be no threat to me or the government."

"But my lord! What if he did become a threat?" Cornelius pleaded. "It wouldn't take much for him to storm this place and kill you in your sleep!"

"I see, so you are here on my behalf because you fear I could lose my life?" Pilas asked.

"Yes, my lord."

"You are not fooling anyone Cornelius, you're here because you're intimidated by him. The people like him more than they like you. You are afraid for your status and nothing else."

"That is not true!"

"Oh, but it is, my friend. A person like the one we're talking about could easily rise through the ranks of your religion, and if he got to the point where he wanted to run for high Farsee, he might not get your vote, but if there was a vicious mob of his followers outside your temple then you might elect him after all. Am I calling this correctly or am I exaggerating too much?"

"You may be right on some of it, but you are completely off to the side on other parts of it! Every Elvish child is brought to the Farsees and examined carefully to see if the child has what it takes to become a Farsee themselves. I've researched and looked at the papers where he first came from and he was denied. He cannot become a Farsee."

"Any logical or dangerous reason why he was denied?"

"The reports do not say and many of the people have since died, but I do not doubt that they denied him becoming a Farsee because he was too hard to teach. He spouts these ideals to people, yet he appears to have a different focus in mind."

"I have watched this man and I have seen nothing wrong with him. Tell me Cornelius, what does he teach that makes him so dangerous?" Pilas taunted.

"That's not the point!"

"If I am going to be involved in any way, then it is a very important piece of information," Pilas warned. "If this man has spoken any kind of rebellion and war against the Goshen government then I must take action swiftly. Now I want the truth."

"What else would I tell you?" Cornelius defended.

"Anything that might get me to bow to your wishes. Remember, my dear friend, what happened the last time I found out about a lie you had told me? Do you remember what happened? An entire village was butchered in the daylight by troops under my command. The emperor had no problems with it. I told him it was the beginning of a savage uprising. Now tell me what this man teaches that you fear so much."

"He speaks of rebellion. Though, admittedly, it is not against the Goshen government. This rebellion he speaks of is directed at us. He deliberately leads people from us! From the ancient religion. This is treachery and action must be taken."

Pilas laughed heartily. "Treachery? Against who? I assure you that unless there is a direct threat to me then I will take no action. So, he is causing an uprising amongst your people? The affairs of Elves do not matter to me as long as you keep yourselves in line."

"I know that, and I will do what I can, but some people are having a hard time staying quiet. He defies everything that we teach and hold dear to us. Even as a person, you must be able to identify with that feeling of hopelessness and confusion that overwhelm people in situations like this."

"Indeed I know what you feel, and I am sorry for you. In each case in my life, I managed to get through it okay and I'm sure you will too. Although I may have had my fair share of ale to help ease the passing."

"Some people have mentioned killing the man, and you are the only person who can legally do that!" Cornelius argued. Pilas knew he was right. "It is against our laws to execute people. However, you being Lord over these lands can, on our request, sign the papers and get this man executed can you not?" Pilas shifted.

"I can. But he must have an offense against you *and* this government. I don't care what he preaches! I need hard solid proof that he's denied or broken any of your laws. If you can do that then perhaps we'll talk again," Pilas replied.

"So we have a mutual understanding then?"

"For the moment. Do whatever you want to trap or bait him, I could care less, but let me warn you ahead of time, that if you take any kind of action that could look dangerous, I will be forced to release troops on this city and take control of the riot."

"Just arresting this man will cause a riot!"

"I know. I suggest if you're going to trap him, you should do it quickly. This weekend would likely be the best time. After the festivities this weekend, I will be leaving for a couple of weeks. Now go away. I will speak of this no more!"

"I would like to try and persuade you to come to a special meeting for the Farsees. We would like to discuss with you in more detail the threat this man poses to us all."

"Cornelius, I have given you my deal and I shall stick to it. I have looked at this man and I see nothing wrong, but if you can get him to do something that would be worthy of the death sentence, then we will talk. Now get out of my sight and back to your temple. The people might worry if they don't see you there preparing the sacrifices."

"As you wish, my lord. Thank you for meeting with me." Pilas didn't respond as Cornelius left the room. He stood in the center of the room, staring into the open space in front of him for a moment or two. Aramis moved closer, abandoning his usual spot.

"Can you believe him?" Pilas asked. "He gets more laughable every day. The whole lot of them do, really."

"If I may say so, it is their ignorance that surprises me," Aramis said. "After all, don't their ancient scrolls refer to Sherados as one who would come and save them? Yet they seek to kill the first person who claims the name of Sherados."

"Do you know the man Cornelius speaks of?"

"Aye."

"And your opinions were?" Pilas questioned. "Do not be afraid of me my friend, you do not have to worry about what you say when you are here." He turned and looked at the rest of the guards. "However let it be known to the rest of you that if any words of this conversation are breathed to anyone, I'll have your heads on platters!" He turned back to Aramis. "What were your opinions?"

"I see him as no military threat. His ideals are admirable as far as I'm concerned. Having a person like him around could be useful, even our own people could stand to listen to what he has to say."

"So you have come to that conclusion as well?"

"Yes, my lord. For once, it appears the Elves have someone they can be proud of. It's a shame that they want to run him into the ground."

"They do it because they're afraid that he will reveal their darkest secrets and point out their hypocrisies. They don't like that people are respecting him. He is quite different."

"Indeed he is, he handles things like no man I have ever met. He has never lifted a finger against anyone in these parts. He can shut up the Farsees in his sleep. I find it amusing to see Cornelius so flustered."

"As do I. What else do you know about this man? Perhaps you've heard something that I have not. I can only learn so much in my position without someone coming to the wrong conclusions."

"He did topple Grimdor and the Sorcerer. From what I am told, he has many friends down in that part of the world. He's a Tarukai and a good one at that. From what I understand, he keeps little to nothing for himself. Always does what he can to help others with the money he makes from the races. As I said earlier, the way our culture is so driven towards status and power, we could all stand to take a lesson from him."

"All who have power are afraid to lose it, Men most of all. I don't deny that I feed off the power that I obtain every day I have this job." Pilas replied. "Aramis, I am about to ask you to do something that might seem unorthodox, and I would appreciate it if you would carry this order out yourself."

"It will be done, my lord, whatever your wish is," Aramis said.

"Find out all you can about this man and keep a close eye on him. I want to know exactly what happens when the Farsees try to trick him. I have a feeling that whatever report I get from the Farsees will be a little slanted."

"It will be done, my lord."

"Very good. Then be on your way and keep an eye on things. I suspect that if they try to trap him, it'll be during the festivities this weekend."

"Do you think he'll be here?" Aramis asked. Pilas smiled.

"He's probably here already. Now go." Aramis left the room and Pilas was left to wander in his thoughts. His mind reeled through all the knowledge he knew about this man.

What was it that made him dangerous?

Pilas had watched him when he was here earlier in the year. Something about him was different. The Farsees seemed to even fear speaking the man's name and strangely enough so did he. He pushed the matters from his head, knowing full well that by the end of the weekend he would know the truth, whether it be from Cornelius or Aramis.

Chapter 2

SPLENDOR AND GLORY

Gwen put a single lily in her auburn hair and stood in front of the mirror. She smiled at the woman looking back at her, both overjoyed and terrified by what the day would bring. Already the city was bustling with anticipation, everyone making their way to the stadium, waiting for the gates to open and the festivities to begin.

Gwen flipped her hair behind her ears and put on her nicest shoes, which complimented her sapphire blue dress. She made her way down the stairs to the expansive living room that was built below her and Drake's bedroom. She stood, admiring all the work they had put into it over the past few years.

Finally, she had gotten everything just the way she had wanted it to look. The house was ordinary for the most part, with a few flowering vines along the walls and ceiling, creating beautiful arches. The flowers changed their colors every day, not as much as her mother's (Isabel) flowers would have, but it was a place to start.

Gwen hurried to the front door, greeted by the sunshine that came through the windows above her. She stepped out into the beautiful day, feeling her heart race and her spirits soar. She walked a few steps from the front door and then looked at the plants to either side.

The plants, as if acknowledging her presence, seemed to move slightly in the wind that wasn't there. A moment later they grew and expanded wrapping their leafy vines around the door handles, keeping them shut.

Gwen smiled and gracefully strode down to the lavish carriage that was waiting for her. She nodded to the driver, who at once started towards the mountains near Avdatt. As many times as she had been to the mountains, they had never made her as nervous as they did today.

It was a half-hour carriage ride until she finally reached the familiar setting she had seen so many times before. The Taruks were all in their cages, lined up for the people to observe. Gwen watched the parents and their small children admiring the Taruks, keeping sure to maintain their distance.

She finally spotted Destan, sitting calmly in his cage, gazing at the people as they passed by. She called for her driver to stop and as soon as she approached, she was allowed beyond the barriers. She reached through the bars on the front of the cage and touched Destan's soft skin.

The Taruk rumbled in pleasure as he lifted his head and looked into her eyes. Gwen lost herself in the Taruk's three eyes, knowing that there was nothing quite like it.

The Taruk seemed to smile at her and she smiled back. A few of the people who had been passing by had stopped to watch her. It was rare to see a Taruk that would let anyone other than the rider touch them at all.

"You be safe, and make sure and keep my husband safe too, you hear?" Gwen said. The Taruk rumbled in agreement, holding her gaze. "Are you going to win today?" As usual, the Taruk didn't answer and held her gaze for another moment, before getting up on its massive feet. Destan looked up at the bars that were overhead and then looked back at Gwen before looking to the crowds beyond. The Taruk roared, the sound carrying through the open fields.

"Race hard Destan!" The Taruk bowed his head and Gwen went back to her carriage, which steadily led her to the stadium. Her heart raced faster as she approached the large structure. This was the largest stadium that had ever been built for Mezutor.

The stands were carved into the mountains, the race course nestled in between. Torches burned, letting off their smoke; lush green trees rose up from behind and around the structure. The starting platforms had been built in between the two sets of stands, built above endless arrays of trees and greenery. Some of the trees were filled with blossoms and flowers of all different colors, making it one of the most beautiful things she had ever witnessed.

At the top of the stands, more stands had been built, with large bridges spreading the gap between either side of the stadium. Flags hung from the bridges, representing the different nations and riders that were present in today's race. She stepped up to the large iron gates that were keeping the spectators from taking their seats.

Several guards walked inside the gates, checking over everything and making sure everything was ready for the throngs of people who were waiting to enter. Bells sounded through the air and the crowds cheered as the guards opened the gates and everyone paid their money and entered into the stands. She moved past the guards and reached the booths where they collected the money. She was stopped by a touch on her shoulder.

She turned to see a Farsee standing behind her. He stood five and a half feet tall with thick black hair that was neatly cut and trimmed and had a few grey hairs in it. His skin was dark, made obvious by the white robe and purple sash that all the Farsees were required to wear.

"My, my Gwen, I think if it's possible, you get more beautiful every day." Gwen blushed.

"You're too kind Nickolas."

"What on earth are you doing at the booth? You're not actually going to pay money to watch this race?"

"As a matter of fact I was," Gwen replied.

"Nonsense, you don't have to pay a thing," Nickolas told her, looking towards the ticket agent. "Count her as one of my guests Odar." The man nodded and Nickolas took her hand and led her past the booths. "One of the perks of being a Farsee is that you get to have a certain number of people in your section and they get in free."

"And how many people are in your section Nickolas?"

"Including you? Two." They smiled and made their way to the end of the stadium, past another gate that only the Farsees and guards would have been able to get passed. They walked down a long staircase until the trees were above them. They reached the bottom, entering into a long covered bridge, which passed several small waterfalls that sent showers of mist through the air.

Finally, they reached a tall building that was built directly beneath the stands. Several guards stood at the front. They nodded their greetings and let them pass without question. They entered a large hall, which looked as if it was meant for a king. Dozens of rooms were to either side, one given to each of the Tarukai in the race today.

Nickolas led the way to the fifth room on the right. He opened the door and Gwen pushed by him, jumping into Drake's arms. Smiles spread across both their faces as they greeted each other with a kiss.

"You ready for the race today?" Gwen asked. Drake smiled at her.

"Of course, I'm ready, although this time I must admit I'm a little nervous."

"What do you have to be nervous about?" Nickolas asked. "You're one of the greatest Tarukai there's ever been."

"I think some of it has to do with the fact that *all* the best Tarukai have come here today."

"Forty of the best," Nickolas commented.

"Just relax honey, I'm sure you'll win today."

"We will see. There are a lot of Taruks in the race that are a lot older than Destan is," Drake pointed out.

"Don't worry about it," Gwen told him.

"If it means anything, I'm rooting for you because it would cause the rest of the Farsees to get all bent out of shape if you won again," Nickolas said. They laughed.

"But wouldn't that mean you would be called in for more meetings?"

"An unfortunate downside to you winning, but it's one I could live with. They have so many things backward that I don't even know where to start trying to fix them. I must admit, however, that I find them somewhat amusing at times."

"It's funny to hear you, a Farsee, say that."

Nickolas shrugged. "I know we have flaws, but my heart is in the right place."

"Is anyone from Rhallinen in the race today?" Drake replied.

"Yes, although I'm not sure who it is," Nickolas answered. "The entry was a late one, yesterday morning. I heard he only had a few minutes to spare when he showed up. Cornelius was bent out of shape, mainly because he was looking forward to not having to register anyone else."

"Cornelius is an interesting character," Gwen said. Nickolas nodded his approval.

"You should probably get to your seats, so you don't miss the start of the race, I know that it's a little bit of a walk back to your seats."

"See you after the race," Nickolas replied. Gwen kissed him once more and they left, returning the way they came.

They reached the stands which were now nearly bursting at the seams with endless amounts of people. They moved up to the second level and to the center of the grandstand. Finally, they reached the roped-off area for Nickolas and his guests. As Nickolas had said there was no one in his section, which had twenty seats in it.

"Isn't there supposed to be one other person?" Gwen asked. Nickolas nodded.

"There is, but she hasn't shown up yet. I'm sure she will though." They took their seats watching the thousands and thousands of people settle into theirs as well. Finally, a young woman appeared at the roped-off section and was let in.

Her hair was black with a streak of green going down one side and a streak of purple coming down the other. Her skin was of lighter complexion. Her eyes were green and sparkled in the sunlight. She stood five and a half feet tall in a dark red dress that would've caught any man's attention. Nickolas stood and took her hand, gently leading her over to the chair next to Gwen. He smiled at her and then looked at Gwen whose eyes were filled with questions.

"Nickolas, are you holding out on us?" Gwen asked, playfully. He shrugged.

"Gwen I would like you to meet a friend of mine, Rachal of Laheer. Rachal this is a very good friend of mine, Gwen Thomas."

"Two names?" Rachal asked. "That's a bit unusual isn't it?"

"Hardly anything about my life has been ordinary," Gwen replied.

"I know the feeling," Rachal said. "May I sit next to you?"

"I'd be honored." Rachal took her seat while Nickolas remained standing for a few moments. "Nickolas, where have you been hiding this beautiful gem?" The woman blushed.

"I can honestly say our meeting was a strange but welcomed one. She moved from Laheer and I fell in love with her the moment I laid eyes on her."

"You are too kind my dear," Rachal responded. Nickolas kissed her hand and took his seat. They turned their attention to the massive crowds, which had filled the stadium. A guard appeared at the roped part of Nickolas's section.

"Excuse me Nickolas, but would you be willing to open up your seats to the public, if you're not expecting anyone?" the guard asked.

"Go right ahead Barnof," Nickolas replied. Barnof nodded and undid the rope leading in people until the rest of the seats were filled, each person bubbling with excitement. It was one thing to come to the Mezutor, but to sit in one of the Farsee's private boxes was another honor altogether. Gwen small-talked with several of them, while Rachal remained quiet looking at all the sights and sounds, seeming to have something on her mind.

"Don't worry you get used to it after a while," Gwen told her.

"I'm not so sure," Rachal replied. "It's much bigger than where I'm from."

"I bet it is. The village I grew up in was a lot smaller than Avdatt is, trust me."

"So how do you know Nickolas?" Rachal inquired.

"He was a friend of my husband when we first moved here. That was before my husband was a Tarukai."

"You are married to one of the Tarukai?" Rachal asked. Gwen nodded and smiled. "Which one?"

"Drake Thomas."

"The famous Drake Thomas?" Rachal asked. Gwen smiled weakly. "Lucky girl. I guess that explains why you have two names." They fell silent, watching as the rest of the seats were filled.

Nickolas stood and moved to the front of the balcony area that was his. All around the stands the rest of the Farsees did the same thing, standing and pulling a horn from their belts.

They cach blew a note from their horns, one after the other until the entire mountainside was filled with the music. The crowds roared enthusiastically and began chanting as the notes continued. The notes stopped and the crowds fell silent. Rachal and Gwen looked forward to the largest of the Farsees sections, filled with a hundred guests, reserved for the high Farsee Cornelius.

He moved forward and held his staff in one hand. He thumped it on the ground once and then spoke, his voice magnified by Elvish magic allowing him to be heard anywhere in the stadium.

"Welcome to the five hundredth Mezutor ever held at this magnificent stadium!" The crowds erupted into cheers, soon settling down by the motion of his hand. "I am honored to present to you forty-one of the greatest Tarukai to grace the skies!" The crowds cheered. "Now, please join me as I introduce the prestigious Tarukai who have come today!"

* * *

The Tarukai all paced anxiously in the wings, waiting to be introduced. Only five of them were in this room, the rest were spread out in rooms that would bring them to the different land bridges that spread the gap between the two sets of stands. Drake looked around at the other Tarukai and then listened to the chanting of the crowds, begging for the race to start. Drake couldn't suppress a smile.

It had seemed like an ambitious goal when he had decided to become a Tarukai but, he had accomplished it and had done quite well for himself and Gwen in the five years since they had left Rhallinen. The time may have changed some things but the one thing that hadn't changed was the excitement he felt every time he stood waiting in the wings.

Fear, excitement, love, and competition, all flowed through his veins, joining with the adrenaline already coursing through him. Drake looked around at the other Tarukai, one of them a good friend of his, but also his closest competition.

"Did you ever think we'd be invited to participate in an event of this magnitude?" Peter asked. He stood barely five feet tall, which was on the small side for a Tarukai. He had shoulder-length black hair and dark brown eyes. What his size lacked, his Taruk made up for in speed.

"Never in my life. It's incredible," Drake replied.

"It must be twice as amazing for you? You've only been doing this for five years and already you've become greater than me."

"I haven't become greater," Drake retorted. "I've just beat you more." They both laughed.

"Well, perhaps today I shall finally defeat you? Wouldn't that be something, to beat the great Drake Thomas in the final Mezutor of the season?"

"That would be quite magnificent," Drake agreed. "Then again, perhaps I can just beat you one last time."

They laughed again. "Maybe neither of us will win. Perhaps we'll be blindsided by someone we've never heard of before. Think that's a possibility?"

"Anything is possible. In this business of racing, I've found it is best not to say anything until you are across the finish line."

"Especially, when we're starting at the back of the pack like we are," Peter agreed.

They fell silent, each thinking about the race ahead and trying to strategize the best they could. Drake usually didn't strategize too much. After all, anything could happen, and you had to be loose and ready to change your plans at any second. The magic attacks that frequently happened during the race were just another unpredictable aspect of the race. They were wild and would have some effect on you, but they were never life-threatening.

"They're about to start introductions," the guard at the front told them. They stood and moved closer to the door, hearing Cornelius finish his final remarks. When he finished he moved to the side and a herald came forward to introduce the Tarukai.

The beating of drums began as one by one the Tarukai were introduced. As the names of the Tarukai were announced, they would exit from the chambers, and their Taruk would perform a solo low pass over the masses, before heading back to the cages for the start of the race.

"Representing the nation of Farndor, riding the great black Taruk, Duvan, please welcome Peter of Masada!" The crowds erupted as Peter stepped out and joined the others who stood on the land bridges spanning the gap between the stands. A great black shadow passed in front of the sun for a moment as Duvan came swooping out of the sky and passed overhead before flying off into the distance.

"And now, here to defend his near record-breaking run of ten straight wins and third consecutive World Cup, the one, the only, Drake Thomas!!!!" The sound was unlike any that Drake had ever heard as he stepped out into the sunlight, looking at the throngs of fans cheering for him.

He made his way out onto the bridge, getting a glance from Peter as he did. Drake nodded in reply and then watched as Destan came swooping out of the sky at a slower pace than the rest of them had. Destan made eye contact and then pulled up vanishing into the distance.

Drake stood tall and proud, searching the crowd for Gwen. Finally, he looked to the familiar spot and saw Nickolas sitting near her. Drake looked at the other people in the box, always finding it interesting to see who Nickolas would have sit with him. A flicker lit in his mind as he looked at Nickolas, and then at the woman whose hand he was holding.

Her black hair caught and held his attention as he watched her for several long seconds. She was beautiful and Drake couldn't help but wonder where she had come from.

It was usually a strange day when the Farsees were married or even had girlfriends, to begin with, let alone someone as attractive as she was.

The music stopped and then it started again, playing a more dramatic tune this time, grabbing everyone's attention.

"And now a very special guest who really doesn't need any introduction, so without further delay please welcome Aiden!!!" The stadium thundered as Elohim appeared over the horizon, swooping over the grandstands. Aiden dropped off his Taruk before Elohim left. Aiden waved to the crowds and stood in his place looking to Drake who was smiling uncontrollably.

Chapter 3

A SECRET CONSPIRACY

It had been two years since Drake had last seen Aiden. The people welcomed him longer than any of the other Tarukai. Drake smiled, knowing that Aiden truly was one of the best. He also couldn't help but wonder what had brought Aiden to the area now.

After several more long seconds, Cornelius stood up and walked back to the front of the balcony that he was on. He held up a hand and the people silenced themselves. For a moment or two you could have heard a pin drop it was so quiet. Only the breeze moved through the mountains. Drake looked to the dark chasm that awaited a hundred yards after the end of the stands.

He had raced at this course a dozen times, yet now that Aiden was here he was suddenly nervous. He didn't know why, and for the moment, he tried to push all the distracting thoughts out of his head.

"Let the race begin!" Cornelius announced. Horns echoed in the distance, signaling that the Taruks had been released. The crowds roared with excitement as the sky was filled with forty-one dark shapes racing towards them. The Taruks swooped down at different intervals, each one headed for its rider. Destan and Elohim both swooped down in unison, with Duvan right behind.

Drake sprung into the air, catching Destan's massive claw and pulling himself up until he could sit on his back like usual. Drake focused on the area in front of him as they sped by the grandstands and then entered into the dark mountainside.

His vision was clouded for a couple of moments, his eyes adjusting to the minimal light. Torches burned here and there. In addition, large square holes had been cut into the mountainside above them letting natural light in. Drake felt the adrenaline race through his veins as they made him feel like he was moving a hundred miles an hour.

Peter and Duvan pulled ahead of him twenty feet or so, while Aiden and Elohim were nowhere to be found. Drake pushed Destan ahead as they gracefully flew through the corner. It was another couple of sharp bends and crowded spaces before the first surprise came to them.

Up ahead the cavern split, which was something that Drake didn't remember. Three tunnels were before them. Peter moved his Taruk to the left vanishing from sight into the tunnel. Drake and Destan kept moving straight, descending sharply. Large Stalagmites blocked the way, forcing the riders to maneuver through the best they could. One of the Taruks in front of him touched his tail to one of the Stalagmites, and for a moment all sound disappeared.

Sparks appeared in the sky and the Stalagmite exploded. Drake and Destan moved through the debris as did the rest of the Tarukai. They exited the twisting tunnels and merged back together, but were now stacked on top of each other with large bridge-like structures all built one on top of the other.

To either side of the opening were stands filled with even more people. Large pillars stood in neat orderly rows, supporting the new addition to the track. Drake had to admire that they had done all this work in secret and had even kept it a secret from all the riders.

Drake's heart stopped for a second as he pushed his Taruk lower, avoiding two Taruks that had collided in the air. He missed them by inches, watching as they crashed into the ground. Drake took a deep breath and tried to calm his nerves, setting his sights on the Taruks ahead of him.

The light blinded him as they entered back into the outside world. Drake tried to clear his vision, searching the horizon, making sure to keep in between the towers that were laid out along the course. If at any time, they went on the outside of the towers, they would be disqualified. They raced up to the top of the mountain in front of them and passed between the towers.

Drake looked at the distant stadium, the thunder of the crowd unable to be heard so far away. He glanced around at the riders near him, looking for any sign of Aiden. Drake was sure that Aiden was the one he would have to watch out for this time.

They all turned sharply to the left. Drake ducked as he pushed Destan under a pack of Taruks and passed them. They sped towards a small canyon that was carved into the mountainside. Drake pushed Destan faster, descending into the canyon, as several riders began to show their unease.

Drake paid them no mind as he flew in between all of them, making his way to the front of the pack that he was in. He was maybe halfway through the field, but knowing for sure was next to impossible. Drake peeled his eyes to the course in front of him as Destan unexpectedly swerved to the left and a single stream of fire came flying towards them. The group scattered and then joined back together as they jostled for position.

Drake urged Destan forward as they flew through the gap that had opened in front of them. He soared into the lead as the course twisted and turned until finally, they entered the final stretch. The grandstands were in the distance, their cheering and chanting now ringing loudly in the valley.

A Taruk swooped low in front of him, the edge of the Taruk's claw snagging Drake's shirt. Drake quickly noticed that it was Peter who waved at him as he passed. Destan roared.

"What do you say we go get him Destan?" Drake asked. They entered the main stretch and Destan roared as they passed by the stands. They easily passed by the next two Taruks, as this time they were directed up over the mountain instead of into it.

Unlike the courses when he had first started racing, the course wasn't the same every lap. It would be changed, forcing the Tarukai to always stay on their toes and be alert. They climbed up the mountains, finding a row of towers filled with people enthusiastically cheering them on.

Drake looked to the left, where flashes of light raced towards them. Destan noted them too and slowed down as the light raced to intercept them. Drake dropped back through the pack and watched as the light hit the Taruks who had passed them and brought them and their riders almost to a stop allowing Drake to go overhead and pass by all of them.

The effects of the light would only last for a few seconds and then everything would go back to normal as they took chase after those who had managed to avoid the attack. They raced around the mountainside, weaving and turning as the course required. They circled to the right heading away from the mountains and back over the open fields. They passed over the people who were carrying out their normal tasks, taking a quick break to stare at the Taruks as they passed overhead.

The stadium came back into view, with them approaching from the east this time. They turned north, heading into the stadium once again. Drake and Destan shot up over the horizon, greeted by cheers and enthusiastic fans.

Drake looked to the tower noticing that only two torches were lit. Whoever was in first place would light the torch at the beginning of each lap. A smile came across Drake's face as Destan raced towards the torch, ready to release fire from his mouth. A Taruk swooped overhead and in front of them.

Peter passed in front of him, his Taruk lighting the last torch. Drake pushed Destan harder, pulling up alongside him as white light came racing at them from on top of the stands. They carefully maneuvered through the shower of light, not getting slowed down any as they reached the end of the stadium.

They entered into the darkness, following the tunnels which twisted and turned, and eventually came into the long area with the grandstands once again. They both raced side by side, their Taruks roaring with excitement. Drake looked up, seeing through to one of the other levels, wondering if he had heard another Taruk. The paths eventually merged and they exited the mountainside with no one but him and Peter in sight. They both smiled at each other and turned their Taruks to the left, the course leading them in a different direction than they had expected.

They passed between the pillars which had fires burning at the top of them. They raced up the next mountain and then up another, taller and more menacing than the previous one. This one had snow at the top of it and Drake could easily guess that they were headed for the peak. Drake briefly noted a gold fleck in the distant sky. Destan flicked his tail, kicking up snow and ice and sending it into Duvan's path. Duvan easily maneuvered through it as the Taruks continued to race each other.

"What do you say, Drake?" Peter asked. "We going to give them a finish to talk about?"

"Yeah!" Drake yelled, "And it'll end with me winning!"

"I'll take that bet!" They pushed their Taruks higher into the mountain until light snow drifted through the air, leaving a white plume of fluff snow from the air they displaced. Soon they were racing through well-carved ice tunnels. Flames flickered in them as a few people, who lived up here, stood watching. They exited and immediately found that the ground beneath them had opened up to a steep drop, nearly a thousand feet down.

Drake quickly scanned the area, spotting the next set of towers jutting out from the steep cliff. He sent Destan into a dive faster than Peter did, gaining a little distance between the two of them. They both cleared the towers, not being disqualified. They leveled out and followed the course, one final mountain resting between them and the finish line. Already Drake thought he could hear the thunder of the crowds as they were told that they were approaching.

They entered the tunnel in the side of the mountain, with only torches along the side of the wall to illuminate the edges of the tunnel. Flashes of light flew through the air as their Taruks sent magic attacks at each other. They were both easily avoided as they rushed towards a wall of light on the other side.

Waterfalls fell from the top of the mountains, creating a curtain of water for them to fly through. They did so, only getting a little wet due to the speed they were carrying. The crowds immediately created a thunderous roar as they approached the finish line, neck and neck.

Drake looked over at Peter and then to the finish line pushing Destan faster, Peter doing the same to his own Taruk. A shadow appeared overhead of them. A white Taruk dropped out of the sky, having passed them from behind. Drake couldn't help but hide a smile as Aiden looked back at him and smiled. The crowd thundered as they crossed the line. Aiden had beaten Peter to the line by only a couple of feet.

"Your winner is Aiden!!!" the announcer yelled. They flew out of the stadium, circling overhead and watching the other people finish the race as they normally did. The crowd cheered on everyone until they were finished and then slowly started to disperse. Drake landed Destan in the open fields just to the left of the stone courtyard outside the stadium that was reserved for the Tarukai. Aiden and Elohim were already in the place of honor, waiting for the stream of people that came out of the stadium. The guards kept everyone away from Aiden so the presentation ceremony could take place. Drake waved as they were led past, a large smile already across his face. Aiden saw him and nodded in acknowledgment.

The Farsees approached with the trophy and the money that Aiden had earned in the race. Nickolas and his girlfriend who Drake still hadn't met, came up and stood with them, watching the scene that would play out in front of them.

"This could be an interesting conversation," Nickolas told them.

"Why's that?" Drake asked.

"Because he's Aiden, having been a friend of his I thought you would have heard the stories by now. He and the Farsees have quite a history of not seeing eye to eye. Trust me, every time he does something I end up being called into special meetings. I doubt today will be any different."

"What do you mean?" Drake asked. Nickolas just pointed to Cornelius, the high Farsee who turned to face the masses.

"It is my great honor today to present our winner Aiden, not only with this sizable amount of money, which was greatly earned, but with this chalice of champions, that shall forever be a symbol of today's victory!" Cornelius motioned for a couple of the Farsees to come up as they brought up a large item that required two of them to carry. They pulled the canvas off of it, letting the sunlight hit the ruby and emerald-colored glass. The glass sparkled in the light, dozens of other gems and colors being illuminated in the sunlight. Words were carved into the gems, the words shining a different color than the rest of the trophy. It said 500th race, and then Aiden's name.

Drake was taken by its beauty wishing that he had been the one to get it. A large bag of money was placed in Aiden's hand. He looked at it for a moment or two, before putting it in his pocket.

"That's surprising," Nickolas said. "I would've thought that he would've done something a little more dramatic. Then again the day's not over is it?"

"No, it certainly isn't. If there is one thing I know about Aiden it's that you always get more than you plan on," Drake said. "Now, who is this beautiful woman that you haven't introduced to me?"

"Forgive me for not introducing the two of you earlier. Drake Thomas this is a very good friend of mine Rachal of Laheer."

"It's a pleasure to meet you," Drake said shaking her hand and looking into her eyes. They seemed to glow with a light that Drake hadn't seen before, both intriguing him and scaring him.

She pulled her hand away after shaking his, looking as if she was at war with herself. Eventually, the look of conflict faded as quickly as it had come, making Drake wonder if he had been the only one who had seen it. "Will you two be joining us for supper tonight?" Drake asked.

"Afraid not," Nickolas told him. "I have a meeting I have to attend so we'll have to take a rain check today."

"Very well, it was nice to meet you, Rachal," Gwen said. Rachal only nodded her reply as she and Nickolas started into the crowd and vanished from sight. "She's beautiful."

"Nickolas certainly got a good one, but she still isn't the most attractive woman I've ever met," Drake said. "That honor belongs to you." Gwen gave him a kiss, interrupted by Cornelius who pulled out a large bag of money and handed it to him. Cornelius moved on without saying another word.

All the prize money was soon handed out and the crowds slowly began making their way back to Avdatt. Aiden and Elohim remained standing where they were, talking to the last few people who were still hanging around in the area. Eventually, even they dispersed leaving only the three of them standing in front of the empty stadium.

"Drake Thomas, are you just going to stand there looking like an idiot or are you going to come say hello?" Aiden asked. They broke into laughter and ran to their old friend, each of them embracing Aiden, glad to see him again.

"I may not have planned on being defeated, but I certainly don't mind being defeated by you," Drake said. They both smiled.

"It's good to see you again Drake, it's been a long time. And of course the enchanting Gwen, as beautiful as ever," Aiden said.

"You're too kind," Gwen said."

"What have you been up to the past couple of years?" Drake asked.

"In due time my friend, first let's head back into the town, I've got some things to do. Then we'll eat and I'll tell you everything."

"Don't we even get a little hint of what you're going to tell us?" Gwen asked. Aiden smiled knowingly.

"Let's just say I am looking for some people who might be interested in an adventure."

"Another one?" Drake asked. "Wasn't the last one big enough?"

"It was a big adventure, but it was necessary. The new adventure is no different. In fact, this one should be a little simpler I should think."

"Once again we ask what the adventure is," Gwen asked.

"And again I shall deny you for the moment," Aiden answered.

"No matter what this adventure you speak of is, or isn't, it's nice to see you again."

"It's nice to be back Drake Thomas," Aiden said. "Very nice to be back. Now let us head into the city. I have some things to do with this money before we eat. By the way, I would very much like to try a new restaurant that just went in a couple of days ago."

"Do you live around here?" Gwen asked. "If you know of a restaurant that opened you must."

"No, I don't live around here, but the owner is a friend of mine. For now, let's go into the city, then I'll tell you everything."

"It's a deal," Drake replied as he and Gwen began walking towards their carriage before noticing that Aiden wasn't following.

"Will you not ride with us?" Gwen asked. Drake watched curiously. Aiden's eyes were filled with a strange light.

"Why don't you walk with me?" Aiden countered. "It is quite a lovely day after all."

"It's nearly half a mile," Gwen muttered to Drake, though not loud enough for Aiden to hear. A moment of awkward silence passed before Drake looked at the carriage driver.

"Head back and take the rest of the day off!" Drake cried. The driver waved his hat and yelled back his thanks. The Taruks took flight and vanished to the Taruk stables where they would find rest and food.

* * *

Nickolas had to hold his tongue as the meeting dragged on. How long could they sit here and debate amongst themselves and still not come to any conclusion? It had been two hours since the Taruk race had ended and they had been sitting in the stuffy hot council chamber since then.

Cornelius paced the center of the floor; the rest of the Farsees were seated in chairs in ascending fashion like he was. Overall, there were thirty of them. Nickolas watched Cornelius with interest, wishing he was more knowledgeable about the topic they were discussing. He may have heard stories, but he had never personally seen anything, which made it hard to make any kind of real decision on the matter.

"We must do something quickly!" Cornelius urged.

"And what would you have us do?" Nickolas asked. "He has broken no laws, here or anywhere else from what I've gathered. He's only been in this city for a day at most. He couldn't have broken any laws, especially none that are written in the ancient scrolls."

"Don't you understand Nickolas? Just having Aiden in our city for any length of time is dangerous to our cause. He has defiled the name of Lathon, filling people's heads with countless lies that basically say that we aren't needed anymore."

"It might as well be called treason against our creator," Another of the Farsees interjected.

"Now hold on people," Nickolas started. "I've read the ancient scrolls just as much as you have. I have been trained in the same fashion, I was one of Cornelius's disciples when I first started. There are a lot of rules and regulations that aren't written in the ancient scrolls. I'm not arguing the reasons for which they were made a part of the religion, but what if this man is just trying to make it easier for people to come to know Lathon?"

"Blasphemy!" Cornelius exclaimed. "To speak such words, you must yourself be one of his followers."

"With the exception of what I've heard within these walls, I've never even met the man or heard what he preaches," Nickolas defended. "And furthermore, because he has so many people who adore him, it makes it even harder for us to touch him without looking like the bad guys. Isn't it what we're all afraid of? I've dedicated my life to following the codes and rules and teaching of Lathon as written in the ancient scrolls. I would hate to be viewed in a disparaging way. All I'm saying is that if we, as a body, are going to do anything, we have to proceed with much caution."

"Thank you for that very obvious statement, now can the meeting continue?" Cornelius asked. "What we have to ask ourselves, is how *can* we get rid of him without looking like bad people? Does anyone have ideas?"

"The amount of things we can do is limited," another Farsee said. "He is so popular right now."

"Another perfect reason to not go after him," Nickolas pointed out. "The Goshen government is not afraid of him otherwise Pilas would have handed out a death sentence himself. Maybe the best thing we can do is nothing."

"Have you lost your mind?" Cornelius asked.

"I'm just saying that people like him have popped up before. They've given their speeches and gotten their followers and in a few months or a year at most, their cause dies and life continues on the same way that it has this very past day. If you're asking my opinion, we should just let this one run its course and die out like the rest of them."

"Not a completely unreasonable idea Cornelius," one of the other Farsees replied.

"Perhaps not, but he's been doing this for five years. Five years! Every day that passes he gets more people to follow him. His fame grows, and he seems to always be targeting us. It's enough to make anyone nervous, even the Goshen government."

"Perhaps we get him to say something that might get him in trouble to where we could trap him?" another Farsee suggested.

"Finally, an idea worth talking about. I'm sure we can do that. We have to make sure he's with people and that we do it in public because then he'll be forced to do as the law requires. If he breaks it, we can arrest him and ask Pilas to sign his death order."

"Exactly," one of the Farsees said. "He breaks the rule and looks like the bad guy, while we just do our job, keeping and enforcing the rules and regulations as recorded in the ancient scrolls."

"Intriguing idea. Which law do we use first?"

"The holy day is tomorrow, nearly anything would work then. We just have to get him to trip up for a second and we can arrest him." Nickolas zoned out of the meeting, which continued for another fifteen minutes, as they discussed amongst themselves how they could trip up Aiden without looking like the bad guys.

Something about the whole situation was rubbing Nickolas the wrong way. He was cut from the same cloth as Cornelius and the rest of them. He had been raised to be a Farsee and there had been nothing that could stand in his way. Now, however, he wondered if he had done the right thing or not.

His heart cried out for answers. Despite what he wanted to admit, it appeared as though greed and pride ran deep in the Farsees blood. They claimed otherwise, but their wanting to kill this man because he would offend their honor and because he was gathering so many followers was too much for Nickolas to accept.

What was he to do? He had never met Aiden before in his life, but even the sight of him had been intriguing. While everyone else had been dressed in nice clothes during the race and after the race, Aiden had been dressed, looking like he had just stepped out of a battle.

His clothes had been worn and looked like they hadn't been cleaned in ages. Did he really enjoy dressing like that? Or was there something more behind this action? It was always said that actions spoke louder than words, and for the first time in his life, Nickolas was starting to realize just how true it was.

The rest of the world measured success by the clothes that were worn. The Farsees had their own system of how they dressed, the different levels or statuses required different clothes to be worn in public. Was Aiden just trying to point out the flaws in their system?

His mind was filled with questions and curiosity as he pondered the situation. It was almost ironic that Drake and Gwen were friends with Aiden when they seemed nothing alike. Drake and Gwen were always nicely dressed and lived in a nice house, only down the street from his own. What was their history? Once again he was filled with questions that he couldn't begin to answer.

The meeting ended and they were finally able to escape the hot muggy room they had been stuck in. They took the stairs down to the main temple which was setting up for the afternoon and evening sacrifices as were demanded by the ancient scrolls and Lathon. Nickolas's mind was in a fog as he left the temple, wandering through the streets.

If the Farsees were really going to try and trap Aiden, should he warn him so that he could have a chance to prepare? He decided against it, knowing that the only way to discover Aiden's true motives was to catch him off guard. Still, his mind worked overtime, trying to think of how they would catch him.

Nickolas walked for another five minutes until he reached his house and disappeared inside, thinking about everything that had occurred. He sat down in one of the nice chairs that he owned. A few moments later a knock came at the door. His servant answered it and Rachal stepped in.

"How did your meeting go?" Rachal asked.

"Interesting to say the least," Nickolas replied. "Tell me, have you ever met Aiden before?"

"Not personally. He came to the town I was in once. He's a nice person in my opinion."

"The Farsees want to try and capture him, but I fail to have heard of anything that he did wrong."

"That I know of he hasn't done anything wrong," Rachal said. "That being said I'm still not sure about the man."

"Really? Why not?"

"Because he is so different from everything that is normal in this world. He stands up for the weak and the oppressed and seems to live a selfless life, not worried about status or fame, even though he is famous. He is very different."

"Do you think it's a good difference?" Nickolas asked. Rachal nodded.

"Yes, I do. I think the whole culture has gotten off track and that it is a very good difference. Not good for you or the rest of the Farsees, but I believe it's good for the rest of the people."

"I've never met this man before but I think I am going to be forced to find out all I can about him before I make up my mind."

"You know that's not going to be an easy thing to do right?" Rachal asked. "I fully support your decision, but if you're seen in public talking to him, someone's going to find out, and then you'll be accused of being in league with him."

"I know," Nickolas replied. "I have to figure out the truth, but I have to do it safely, so it doesn't endanger anything I love. I think I'll start by asking Drake about him. They supposedly knew each other in the past."

"There's something about Drake that's just as refreshing as Aiden, if I may say so," Rachal said.

"You may say so," Nickolas replied. "He's a fascinating guy, interesting past from what I hear."

"Where is he from?"

"Rhallinen, as far as I know, although he always says there is always more to the story than that isn't there? I don't know what it is because I've never inquired about it. He's been a good friend for many, many years though."

Rachal fell quiet as each of them drowned in their own thoughts thinking about what lay ahead.

Rachal was right, if he was seen publicly meeting with Aiden then he would be expelled from the Farsees. Suddenly, it seemed everything was a danger. There was more to the story than what he knew, and he was going to find out what it was. He would watch him and think about everything and then he would confront Aiden and find out the truth for himself.

Chapter 4

THE TARUK'S PUB

The streets were still filled with excitement, as everyone talked about the race and the things that were going to be happening in the next few days. Drake and Gwen walked on either side of Aiden.

It didn't take long to figure out that Aiden hadn't changed much, if at all, in the past five years. His hair may be a little longer and his eyes a little more brilliant color, but at the heart, he was the same person who had led them on their great adventure.

It was hard to believe that so much time had passed when in reality it felt like only yesterday. Drake replayed the events of the past war through his head. Drake had certainly gotten more than he had bargained for the last time he had been with Aiden, but a great evil had been overthrown and he had come out of it a different person.

It was almost disturbing to Drake that there could be *another* adventure on the horizon. He had spent the last five years thinking that he would live happily ever after and now he was finding out there was more? The Sorcerer had been defeated, justice restored, and the world had been saved. What more was there to do?

Drake struggled with the question. Was he supposed to pick up his sword and abandon everything he had worked for? He had worked so hard and had accomplished so much. He loved the life that he led right now, he was happily married and perhaps someday a few kids would come along. He felt as though his part in the story was over.

It was someone else's turn to draw swords and run headlong into the battle.

Drake and Gwen followed Aiden down the streets. Aiden walked with a sense of purpose, seeming to know where he was headed. Drake studied their surroundings, aware that they were in the slums of Avdatt and he had never been to this section before.

Aiden stopped, pulled out the money that he had won in the race, took out a couple of large coins, and put them in his pocket, before walking into a nearby building. The building was small, dirty, and seemingly insignificant compared to the more prominent buildings in other parts of the city.

"Good afternoon can I help you?" The person behind the desk asked as they approached. Aiden smiled warmly.

"Yes, I believe you can. This is the mission correct?"

"Yes sir. We supply food and clothing for those who are less fortunate than ourselves, not just here but everywhere in the nation of Thrace. How can I help you?"

"I'd like to make a donation," Aiden said. He pulled out the bag of money and set it on the counter. The man opened the bag and his eyes went wide as he saw the valuable coins inside.

"I don't know what to say," the man replied after a few moments of silence. "We've never received such a large donation before!"

"Just make sure you use it to feed and clothe the poor!"

"What can we ever do to repay you? This is a fortune! Are you sure you gave me the right bag of money?"

"I am positive," Aiden replied. "As far as repaying me is concerned, just help someone in need and do something nice for someone."

"I most certainly will. Thank you!" the man said. They said their goodbyes and left the building.

"That's definitely the most money he's ever seen," Drake said.

"Not too many people are that charitable, especially in this part of the city."

"I don't think I had ever been there before," Gwen said. Aiden smiled.

"I always try to donate to the ones who don't get as many donations."

“The Farsees would say that you could’ve donated the money to the temple, which would have gone to support good works.”

“I’m sure they would’ve said that,” Aiden agreed. “However there are many flaws with the Farsees and a lot of the money gets divided among themselves, specifically when it is a large sum. Nothing short of hypocrisy in my book. They put on a good face for the public, but inside they are nothing but dead people walking and taking everything they can get.

“If there is one flaw with the Elves, and really with all races, it’s that they desire power far too much. Although power ultimately is a good thing, and can accomplish great feats, it can also secretly destroy a person until they’re only shadows of the people who once lived.

“You can fall into the trap of power without even realizing it. You can plan on doing great things with the power, while also looking for it to do great things for you. It might be a fair compromise in the beginning, but over time, the lust and desire for power corrupts and very little of it goes to help others. The Farsees have very much fallen into those traps. At least the majority of them.”

“They are still respected leaders of the religion though.”

“Once again because of their desire for power,” Aiden said. “How many people outside of the well-educated and Farsees can read the ancient scrolls for themselves? The number is very, very small. That alone gives the Farsees the power they desire. For example, there are tons of rules that they claim are part of the ancient religion of Lathon that aren’t written anywhere in the ancient scrolls. They made them up. I’m determined to set the record straight for everybody.”

“I guess that would explain why so many of the Farsees don’t like you,” Gwen replied. Aiden smiled.

“The world is filled with many injustices and I merely wish to help fix one of them. If I were to take all of the ancient scrolls and the teachings of Lathon and condense them into two statements it would be this. Love Lathon, and love others. If you don’t do those things you have missed the point in life.”

"I imagine the Farsees would be pretty opposed to that teaching," Drake said.

"A lot of people would. Even you. Being Sherados, I think it's fair to say that I know the ancient scrolls better than most people." Gwen laughed while Drake pondered what he had said.

"What do you mean I would be opposed to the teachings of love Lathon and love others?" Drake asked.

"To realize where your real loyalties lie, look at how you spend your time or your money. What do you do with it? Some people put it into their houses and their possessions, trying to climb up the ladder so they can do more *good.* Others hide it in the ground and secretly hoard it to themselves. What do you do with your money? Money can become an idol and pull people from Lathon very quickly." Drake fell silent thinking about what Aiden had said as they turned around the corner and paused for a moment.

"I'm guessing this must be the religious district of the city?" Aiden asked. They nodded as they began walking past all the temples that were lined up on either side of the street. People streamed from the temples, offering their sacrifices and following the codes and rules of the different religions.

"Very interesting place I must say," Aiden started, looking around. "What are all these other temples? I was here many years ago and I only recall the temple of Lathon."

"I guess the world has changed a lot in the past years," Drake said. "The people have very different opinions on religion, so many more were created. Not ideal, but it keeps them happy and there haven't been any wars or battles since then."

"So, all these people are wandering into the abyss, yet they're completely oblivious, and no one cares to point it out?"

"Tolerance is preached these days," Gwen started. "If you say anything that could even be interpreted as saying you're right and they're wrong, you could end up in jail."

"Probably true," Aiden said. "Then again, if one is truly right, what does it matter what happens to you?"

"They could kill you," Drake reminded.

"Again I ask, if one is truly right, what does it matter what happens to you? The worst they can do is kill you. That may not seem very comforting to anyone else in this world, but for me, life begins after this world."

"Now you're losing me a little bit," Drake admitted. "There's another world?"

"You believe that Lathon was the creator and greatest king to have ever lived on this earth correct?"

"Yes."

"You believe that I am the heir of Lathon, Sherados, an elf, born into a nation of Men and a family of Men."

"Yes, although I've always wondered how that's even remotely possible," Drake replied.

"By human understanding and human knowledge, it isn't possible, but with Lathon it *is*. I have been sent here to save this world from the destructive paths that it is headed down. Trust me, Drake Thomas, far beyond the reach of any ship you may sail...there is something more. This life is not all lived out in vain. You have a purpose beyond just one great adventure or the next Mezutor. There is something more you are supposed to do, and something more to learn."

"I'm a little confused though," Gwen stated. "When we defeated the Sorcerer, didn't you say the days of fighting with a sword were over?"

"Yes, I said that," Aiden answered. "But I did not mean that they would never have to be picked up again. There are other forces than those of good out there in the world and they will not be stopped any other way than by a sword. In the same token, there is plenty of fighting to be done in Avdatt alone, as well as the surrounding nations, that does not have to be done with a sword."

"Like what?" Gwen asked. Aiden looked around.

"Like this street, for example, dozens of temples of all sizes line this street. Is this not worth fighting over? There is only one person worth putting any hope in and that my friend is Lathon. Will you so easily let people be led astray? The Sorcerer is at work in the minds of people, creating all these different gods and goddesses for people to worship. The Sorcerer does not seek only to physically kill the followers of Lathon, but in this day and age, he seeks to religiously kill us. Merderick has poisoned the minds and hearts of people, making them hateful and resentful toward each other. It was through those tactics that rules and laws in the land made it illegal to say one belief is right over the other. It is through these very sneaky and deceptive means that he wishes to destroy us. The other religions will not get blamed for anything, because he created them and I assure you, nowhere in their belief systems is it written to try and save people from the other beliefs."

"That's why you've come back isn't it?" Drake asked. "The Sorcerer wasn't defeated was he?"

"He was destroyed physically, but I assure you his spirit has lost none of its potency. There is more work to be done in this world. I have come to save all of the clutches of evil, not part of it. I realize at the time we overthrew Grimdor from the Sorcerer there were no maps of these northern countries to be found. But now there is, and we must be prepared."

"Don't suppose this has anything to do with the adventure you are teasing us with?" Gwen asked. Aiden smiled.

"I guess you'll just have to wait and see," Aiden said. They walked down the street a little further past a couple more temples until finally, they stood next to the temple of Lathon. People streamed in and out and the temple was filled with people. Aiden turned to face them. "What are they doing in there?"

"Raising money for the temple. Every third Saturday of the month they have sales in there. All the money goes to charity, at least that's what we are told. A friend of ours says differently."

"A Farsee by chance?" Aiden asked. Drake nodded.

"He doesn't like it, but he's outvoted."

"Well Drake, I think this is a perfect time to take a stand for something, don't you? None of the other temples have to *raise* money. The Farsees without realizing it are making a laughing stock out of Lathon. He's apparently the only *God* who hasn't provided for his people."

"What are you going to do?" Gwen asked. Aiden thought for a moment.

"Why don't we go have a look around?" Aiden said, leading the way.

They followed him up the temple stairs. They reached the top, Drake watched Aiden carefully as they walked past several Farsees with donation baskets held out. Nickolas nodded at them and then stared at Aiden who nodded at him. Nickolas grabbed Drake's arm.

"What are you doing here?"

"We were walking around the city and decided to come up to the temple," Drake asked. "Is that bad?"

"Well, no it's not bad, it's just-"

"A very good thing that I came up here," Aiden said, having come back to them. "Forgive me, I don't believe we've met. My name's Aiden. Yours is?"

"Nickolas," Nickolas managed. "Forgive me, it's not that I don't want you to come to the temple it's just that-"

"I understand perfectly Nickolas. You do not have to worry about anything I do being reflected badly on you. We walked by twenty other Farsees before we got to you. I must say this is a very interesting place. Usually a place of worship isn't it?"

"Supposed to be," Nickolas admitted. "The Farsees want to do more of these events as a way to bring people into the temple. I'm seriously starting to rethink everything that I was told was important. It's completely different when you become one of them."

"Well said my friend," Aiden said. "I must say, I've been to a lot of marketplaces but this one has to be one of the most interesting. Perhaps my eyes are cheating me, but are those oxen and sheep available for purchase?"

"Yes they are," Nickolas answered, regretfully. "It was Cornelius's idea that for those who do not own a farm or don't want to visit one, they could buy their own, pre-approved animal at the temple to be sacrificed for their sins." Aiden laughed. "My thoughts exactly. I'm sure you'll find the other things they sell just as amusing as the ox."

"Let's see what they have," Aiden said. They followed him as he walked around to the different stands and vendors. "Wine for the ceremony, doves to appear peaceful, and charmed pendants to help raise money for their charities. Amusing to some, but not to me. Money that is raised this way might as well be given and taken by thieves. This is not money that Lathon would want. Followers of Lathon are being portrayed as a laughing stock and as superficial, judgmental children. I am not amused by this. I am angered."

"What are you going to do?" Gwen asked. Aiden smiled at them.

"Take a stand," Aiden whispered. He turned from them and headed to the front of the temple, where Cornelius stood reading one of the ancient scrolls. The others went with him, with the exception of Nickolas who stayed back fifty feet from them watching everything they did.

Drake followed, wondering what was going to happen. Aiden walked up to the front of the crowd that was listening to Cornelius read the ancient scroll and stood there, watching him intently. Drake watched as Cornelius looked over the top of the scroll only long enough to note that Aiden was standing there. He was visibly shaken as he continued reading while glancing at Aiden every thirty seconds or so. Finally, Cornelius lowered the scroll.

"I'm sorry people for the interruption," Cornelius said turning to Aiden. "Is there something that I can help you with?"

"Oh, don't mind me, I was just here to listen to the ancient scrolls being read and to worship Lathon. I guess I missed the memo that today was a profitable day." Aiden smiled at Cornelius who looked as though he was struggling to keep his emotions in check. Finally, he suppressed all of them and smiled.

"You don't have to worry about anything Aiden. You see. all this money goes back to the temple and the charitable work that the temple does."

"Of course, how silly of me. What kind of charities do you support? If I'm going to buy something and donate to the cause I want to know what my money's going towards."

"It goes towards many things," Cornelius answered. Aiden looked around at the others.

"Many things?" Aiden said. "On behalf of everyone here, I think we would very much like to know what these 'many' things are."

"Keep yourself in line or I shall have you forcibly removed from the temple!" Cornelius ordered. Aiden looked at the other people again.

"All I did was ask a question," Aiden defended, turning back to Cornelius. "What kind of work do you do with the money?" Cornelius looked out to the sea of faces that were now watching him.

"We do many things," Cornelius said, stumbling over his words. "We use some of it to fix up the temple so that people who wish to worship in it are comfortable. We also give some to the poor."

"And how about yourself? You take some of the money too right?" Aiden asked.

"Leave now or I will have you forcibly removed!"

"I was merely curious about where the money went. Although since I'm bringing up concerns I have, and it is your job as high Farsee to listen to these concerns, I might say that I don't think Lathon would approve of you turning his temple into a marketplace."

"This is not a marketplace. We are simply providing services for those who may not have everything that they need to be a part of this religion. As far as you thinking that Lathon wouldn't approve of anything, who are you to say? I've heard your stories but the only one who could say such things is Sherados himself."

"Perhaps he is standing amongst you even now and you fail to realize it." Cornelius laughed.

"You're delusional. Now go bother someone else!"

"It's good to see your people skills are up to par," Aiden retorted. "I will say something now that few people up this far north have heard. I am Sherados and the things that are going on in this temple are appalling to me."

"You're not Sherados!"

"Yes I am," Aiden replied.

"Leave now!" Cornelius ordered, and guards began approaching. Aiden bowed.

"If I must," Aiden said. He turned and joined Drake and Gwen again before heading to the first table he came to.

"Would you like to buy anything sir?" the man behind the table asked.

"No I wouldn't like to buy anything, but could I request that you move aside just for a second?" The man did as he said. Aiden turned back to Drake and Gwen for a moment and spoke in a low voice that only they could hear. "This has gone on long enough."

Without warning, Aiden grabbed the edge of the table and flipped it off the ground, overturning it. The money and goods scattered everywhere and clattered noisily over the hard floor. People yelled out as Aiden continued to go down the line, flipping over all the tables. Guards came rushing towards them.

Aiden jerked to the side and grabbed a torch from the wall, swinging it through the air. The fire kept the guards at bay and slowly pushed everyone out of the temple until not even Cornelius was left inside. The crowds' emotions were mixed. Some of them were happy about what had happened while some of them were yelling threats. Aiden looked unbothered by them, facing the crowd.

"A temple is supposed to be a place of worship, not a place of profit! You've done nothing but turn it into a place for thieves to gather. I know the ancient scrolls and I guarantee that it never says anything about this in there. Am I wrong? Or do I paint an accurate picture?" Aiden asked, directing his question towards Cornelius.

"You'll pay for this!"

"You never answered my question!" Aiden pointed out. Cornelius seethed.

"Guards, seize this man." The guards started to move.

"That won't be necessary my friends, I was just leaving," Aiden said. The guards stopped approaching and Aiden walked through the crowds with Drake and Gwen slightly behind him. The people looked at them, some of them approving and some not, still others eyes were filled with questions, wondering about this man they were with. They reached the back of the crowd and finally came to the end of it. The crowd started to move back into the temple to clean up the mess. Nickolas stood watching them. Aiden handed him the torch.

"It was a pleasure meeting you Nickolas. Next time they try to create a marketplace or anything else that's not in the ancient scrolls, take a stand." Nickolas stared into Aiden's eyes for a moment.

"Yes sir," Nickolas answered. Drake and Gwen nodded and said their goodbyes. They started walking away but stopped when Nickolas began speaking. "Thank you for doing it. It was a risky thing to do, offending all of them like that."

"Don't mention it," Aiden said with a smile. "I'm only sorry it was necessary. I have no room in my heart for hypocrites. Unfortunately, it's always the good-hearted followers of Lathon that get thrown into the same category as the hypocrites. In reality, we are nothing alike."

"Once again I must agree with you. You are very different from them."

"Good day, Nickolas." Aiden said. They walked away. Drake's mind was reeling from everything that had happened.

* * *

"Clean up the temple!" Cornelius snapped. A crowd had gathered around the spectacle and now watched, every eye boring directly into his soul. Several of the Farsees as well as some of the vendors entered the temple and began cleaning up, clearing everything out as fast as they could.

"Are you seriously going to let this man get away with this?" one of the Farsees asked him.

"The last thing we need is a mob. He wins this round, but I want him trapped and captured by the end of the weekend, or else we'll all be in trouble!" Cornelius told them.

"Why not just go after him now?" one of the people in the street asked. Cornelius recognized him as one of the people who had been selling animals in the temple.

"If anything that was done got out of hand, the governor over Thrace, Pilas, would be forced to call in troops to handle the situation," Nickolas said. "Remember what happened last time?" The man nodded. "It's best for all of us if we let him go."

"For now anyway. I assure you he will pay for this treachery!" Cornelius announced to the masses, getting mixed responses from the crowds.

"Treachery? What Treachery?" Nickolas asked. "He was right to say that nowhere in the ancient scrolls does it condone the things that were going on."

"He has offended our honor and that is all that needs to be said! He *will* pay for this."

"He didn't do anything wrong!" Nickolas argued.

"He does not follow the ancient rules and regulations and he said the heir of Lathon, Sherados, is among us! The man is not right in the head," Cornelius said.

He turned away from Nickolas and motioned for a few of the Farsees to follow him. He led them through the temple to a set of stairs and then up to a large meeting room that they had been in earlier. "I want this man dead."

"But your highness he has done nothing wrong," one of the others said.

"Then we make him do something wrong!" Cornelius exclaimed. "We trick him, we capture him. This man will be the demise of us and everything we hold dear. For all we know, he was hired by the Goshen government to cause this trouble among us! If we can't trap him by the weekend we'll have to take other action."

"What action is that?"

"A hit man, someone to run him out of town; anyone that might take him out in private. Then it doesn't reflect on us and there's no mob that might cause Pilas to send out his troops," Cornelius explained.

"That just might work. Do you know of any assassins?"

"I *might* know of a couple of them. Are we agreed on this course of action?"

"Yes," the other two replied.

"Very good. Now, make sure the temple is put back to normal, if we're supposed to have any kind of dignity we can't have him coming back in here to humiliate us again."

The other two left, leaving Cornelius alone to drown in his thoughts and try to think of how he might be able to trap Aiden. There was something about Aiden that was unnerving. He knew things before they happened. He was smart and devious at the same time. Trapping him would not be easy.

* * *

"Where are we headed now?" Gwen asked.

"To that restaurant, I was telling you guys about," Aiden answered. "It's just up the street a little ways. Have you ever been to this part of the city before?"

"Once, but not in a long time," Drake answered.

"And it's been a long time since we've walked so far," Gwen lamented.

"I can't believe you flipped all those tables," Drake said.

"Something had to be done and it was obvious that they weren't going to change their ways without a little persuasion."

They fell silent, walking past dozens of little shops and merchants that were selling their goods until they finally came within sight of the only restaurant on the street.

It was a nice little building, with two stories, although the top floor appeared to be very small and if Drake had to guess, only had one bedroom. Tables and chairs were sitting outside underneath a large covered porch. Drake stared at the building, unable to shake the feeling that there was something familiar about this place.

They walked closer, the house appearing more rustic and different as they approached. Unlike the other buildings, which were mostly built out of dried mud bricks, this one was built out of stones, looking like it belonged in the mountains. The stones were all different shades of color, varying from dark green to light brown with moss growing between them. Fancy woodwork made up the trim on everything that wasn't stone.

He looked to the sign, which hung out past the balcony. The sign was painted but looked as if it was made out of wood. Daises covered the edges of the sign and a black featherless bird sat on top, watching them.

Aiden looked at the sign. "This is the place."

"The Taruk's Pub?" Drake read.

"It just opened a day ago," Aiden answered.

"I don't even remember anyone talking about a construction project in the area," Gwen said. Aiden smiled.

"I think if we go inside, you will find the place very much to your liking," Aiden said. They walked past some people who sat eating their food on the porch and entered into the small house. The inside of the house was covered in different plants, all of which grew on the walls, with long beautiful vines that created arches. Despite the difference from most buildings, Drake and Gwen both found that they liked it. The plants moved as they entered, as though there was a breeze from the door opening.

"This is kind of nice," Gwen commented. Aiden smiled. They walked further into the house, finding it modestly decorated with wooden artifacts and other strange knick-knacks. Drake looked around the place, confusion running through his heart.

"Are you sure we are in the same building we saw from outside?" Drake asked. "It looks much larger in here than is possible."

Aiden laughed. "Not everything is as it seems."

"How do we get someone to take our order?" Drake asked. They looked around, hearing sounds coming from a backroom just to their left, but not seeing anyone. Finally, they spotted a hand-carved sign over the front counter.

"It says push for service?" Drake asked. Gwen and him both shrugged.

"So you just touch this?" Gwen asked pointing at a small bright red gem that shone beneath the sign. Drake shrugged his shoulders and she pressed the gem in until it clicked. She let it out and they waited in anticipation.

The plants stood on end, a rumbling noise emitted from them. The rumbling moved to the left and then sped up as it went around the corner into the backroom, almost like a fire being lit. A moment later thunder was heard as well as the sounds of water being loosed and cascading onto the floor. Some of the water came out onto the floor before washing itself back into the room it had come from. The plants now went back to their normal positions.

"Blast that doorbell!" A woman exclaimed from the back room. The sound of a person sloshing through water was heard until finally a swinging door opened and a woman stepped out, soaked to the bone as though she had been caught in a rain storm. A plate of food was in her hands as she tried to shake herself off. The food on the plate was beautifully presented and dry despite the soaked condition of the woman.

She stood with her back to them, putting the final touches on the plate of food. Her hair was golden with a couple of blue streaks in it and her dress was a pale green with yellow lace. She turned to face them and froze in her tracks, her eyes wide with excitement as she saw the three of them. Drake squinted at the woman in front of him.

"Mom?" Gwen asked. Isabel put down the plate of food as Gwen rushed to her arms and embraced her. Isabel laughed, a light shining in her eyes.

"The one and only," Isabel answered.

"I didn't know you lived here!"

"I was going to enter the race for myself and surprise you, but Aspen got lost trying to find this place. Seems she's only really familiar with the former Grimdor nation."

"What a nice surprise!" Gwen said, embracing her mother again.

"Well I figured I only have one daughter, I wanted to live as close to her as I could. For once in my life I don't have family members wanting to kill me," Isabel said a smile stretching from one end of her face to the other. The smile disappeared and her head jerked towards Drake.

"And as for you, I've got a bone to pick with you!"

"I'm afraid to ask," Drake admitted.

"I've been standing here for a good thirty seconds and my son-in-law hasn't given me a hug yet?"

"You're soaking wet," Drake pointed out. Isabel looked at him and smiled.

"Who cares?" They embraced each other and then separated, Drake's shirt drenched as was Gwen's dress. Aiden embraced her, ending up just as wet.

"Maybe I shouldn't ask, but why are you all wet?" Drake asked. "Is there a water leak somewhere?"

"No, there's no leak," Isabel stated, pausing for a moment and looking back at the kitchen. "You rang the doorbell."

"So you get wet every time?" Gwen asked.

"Yes," Isabel answered.

"That seems a little strange, even for you," Drake stated. "Why would you make it do that?"

"Oh trust me, Drake Thomas, I didn't make it do that." Isabel started ringing out the skirt of her dress. "That was a lovely little housewarming gift I received from Ellizar and Lily before I left. Of course, I had no idea what it would do. If I had known I was going to get caught in a Grimdorian storm every time it was pushed I would've put it in the castle and let them take a shower."

"So Ellizar and Lily did it?" Aiden asked.

"Yes, it was Ellizar's idea. Blasted dwarf, if he ever comes to visit me, I'll have to hang him by his beard and sell him to local fur traders." They laughed.

"I think Lily might have something to say about that one," Gwen replied. Isabel looked undeterred.

"So, she's only one person. I can take her." They laughed together. "Just kidding, I would never do anything that cruel to the vertically challenged dwarf. However, that doesn't mean I wouldn't send a retaliatory gift in return."

"What are you going to do to him?" Drake asked. Isabel shrugged her shoulders.

"Don't know yet, it'll be something unique though."

"Would you like some help?" Gwen asked.

"Sounds like a good mother-daughter activity to me. Trying to sabotage a dwarf!"

Drake looked at Aiden. "I certainly have an interesting mother-in-law."

Isabel shot him a look. "That's a good thing, but just to clarify, every time someone pushes the gem you get soaked."

"Yes," Isabel answered.

Drake stepped back and pushed the button. The plants went crazy and a rumble went through the shop back to the kitchen as it had the last time. They all laughed as a column of water appeared above Isabel and crashed down on her. The sound of water falling came from the kitchen as well, apparently hitting the cook. The water soaked her even more and the rest of it fell onto the floor until it retracted and went into her soaked dress.

"Great, now I have a dress that weighs fifty pounds instead of twenty-five," Isabel said. "Was I seriously saying that I wanted to live *closer* to my family?"

"Yes that was what you said," Aiden replied. Isabel shook her head and looked out the window where customers were waiting anxiously for their food.

"Well, I must have been out of my mind for saying that," Isabel said with a smile on her face. "Now if you'll excuse me for a moment, I have a plate of food to deliver." She turned around to grab the plate of food, noticing at the same time they did, that the plate was now empty.

"Where did the food go?" Drake asked. Isabel stared at the plate for another second or so.

"I wish I could say I didn't know, but the plant ate it."

"The plant eats food?" Aiden asked. Isabel nodded and looked at the plant which had shrunk back to the wall a little more.

"He's not supposed to, but that hasn't stopped him today!" Isabel exclaimed to the plant. "This is the fourth plate of food that he's eaten today, and don't even get me started on this one." Isabel pointed to a small tomato plant right next to the window.

"What did that one do?" Gwen asked.

"He will only produce rotten vegetables! It doesn't matter what I tell him, that's all I get." She looked back to the kitchen. "Another plate of food is needed!"

"Alright!" the cook's voice boomed.

"I've started to have plants at my place, but what I don't understand is where you come up with such beautiful and *unique* plants," Gwen started. "Is it a specific spell that gets put on them?"

"They are special seeds. Bought them off a gypsy traveling through Cos many years ago."

"You don't by chance have any more of them do you?"

"I do, but I would be hesitant to give them to you. There are a few things you must remember about these plants. First thing is that they grow crazy fast. I just planted these plants yesterday and they've already expanded quite a bit. Second, the first three weeks are nightmares, because no matter what spell you put on them, it won't work. Once they're done growing though, you'd better watch out, because every spell or charm you've had put on them, they'll magically listen to, which can make even more of a mess.

"And last, but not least, they have incredible appetites when they're growing and will eat whatever they can. They will literally eat you out of your house and home if you let them. If I give you any of these, I should stay with you for a couple of weeks until all the quirks are worked out."

"Sounds like an adventure," Drake commented.

"You have no idea."

"Since we're on this subject, I do have a problem. I had a spell on this rare rock and now I can't get it removed," Gwen said.

"What is the rock and what did you try to do to it?"

"It's a Formite Rock, and I was trying to make it glow and then we could imbed it in the arch above our doorway, but it ended up so bright that we can't stand within twenty feet of it without shielding our eyes." Isabel nodded.

"I remember having a situation like that many, many years ago."

"So how did you fix it?" Gwen asked.

"I didn't, I sold it to a gypsy in return for some strange plant seeds." They laughed. "Well, don't just stand there, have a seat. Morgrin will be back soon. I sent him to the Market for some supplies." She turned to the kitchen. "How is that plate of food coming?" The noise of crashing plates and pots came from the kitchen.

"I'm alright! I'm alright!" a deep voice boomed. They all sat down at the table, each of them falling silent as she poured some hot tea into glasses that were already on the table.

"I'm glad to see that Aiden brought you here. Did he tell you what he is planning?" Isabel asked.

"Not yet," Drake replied. "Has he told you?"

"No, but I am going."

"So, you're going on whatever adventure he has planned, just like that."

"Yep," Isabel replied. "Life's too short to just sit around and do nothing. I like the adventure."

They were interrupted by a horse galloping up out front. Morgrin came to a stop and dismounted his horse, marching up the steps with a couple of baskets of fruits and vegetables. He entered and smiled when he saw them.

"And I thought we were going to surprise them?" Morgrin said to Isabel as he embraced all of them, putting the baskets of fruit and vegetables on the counter next to him.

"They came early," Isabel replied, swatting at the vines that had crept closer to the baskets. The vines retracted, seeming to get the hint.

"So what do we owe the pleasure that all three of you are here at once?" Morgrin asked.

"Well, you know how it is," Aiden started. "I came to kick Drake's butt at the Mezutor."

"I'll bet he did that didn't he?" Morgrin asked. Drake nodded.

"That's not why he came," Isabel told him. "He came to ask us to go on an adventure with him."

"Great! I love adventure!" Morgrin exclaimed, smiling for a few moments before looking confused. "What adventure?"

"The one he hasn't told us about. But we're going," Isabel said. Morgrin smiled weakly.

"Great!"

More crashing noises were heard from the kitchen and this time a deep voice mumbled as the cook came out into the main space. A large Gog crashed through the swinging door, soaked to the bone from the rain and looking frustrated as he tripped out the door.

"Everyone, you remember Shavrok?" Isabel asked. Shavrok stood tall and proud as he bowed.

"Not too many people forget meeting someone as fierce as a Gog," Drake replied.

"If someone forgets what a Gog looks like I might just be tempted to refresh their memory!" Shavrok boomed, laughing nearly uncontrollably, containing himself after a moment or two. "So what's new with you?"

"Are you the cook?" Gwen asked. Shavrok shrugged his shoulders.

"It seemed like a fun thing to try."

"Speaking of which Shavrok, where's the apron I made for you?" Isabel asked.

"Before you say anything, I would like to say that I resisted my urge to maliciously destroy the apron. It would've been an accident, I assure you," Shavrok said. "However, the vines took it."

"They took it?" Isabel nodded. Shavrok nodded.

"I'm pretty sure they took a spatula as well," Shavrok answered. Isabel stood up, her dress still soaking wet.

"If you'll excuse me, I have to go knock some sense into these plants." She got up and walked to the kitchen door, staring at it for a moment. "If you do anything to me I'll turn you all into shriveled-up prunes!"

She vanished into the kitchen, leaving them to talk amongst themselves. A couple of minutes passed before she came tripping out of the kitchen as Shavrok had.

"Fine! Have the kitchen you stupid plants!" She came and sat down at the table as though nothing was out of the ordinary. She smiled at Morgrin and then everyone looked at Aiden.

"So what is this great adventure that you keep teasing us with?" Gwen asked. Aiden smiled and sat forward.

"Well, it's ambitious, but there is a great amount of evil that is in this world and is trying to grasp more and more power all the time. My goal is to stop it, or at the very least slow down the events that will transpire, so more people may come to know Lathon. Are any of you familiar with the nation of Goshen?" Aiden asked.

"They're the governing power over Thrace are they not?" Shavrok asked.

"Yes they are," Aiden replied. "Have any of you been there?"

"Yes," Isabel answered. The rest of them shook their heads no and looked at Isabel. "I had a friend who lived there many years ago. Or at least lived near there. A small village near the border."

"So, you've at least been near the nation?"

"Oh, I've been in the nation. I have no idea what you want to do in this nation but I am all the more interested seeing that Goshen's involved."

"That's good. It's common knowledge that the Goshen government has nearly every nation this far north under their rule, but that is not what I wish to fix."

"What then?" Morgrin asked.

"Despite Goshen's control of nearly everything, the thing that irritates and angers me more than any other is that the nation has a very large number of slaves. They were once free people that lived in the nation before they were overtaken. Most of them Elvish, but there are large numbers of Men and Dwarves who were also taken into slavery. Anyone who was living there at the time got thrown into slavery. My goal is simple. I seek to free them."

"Which ones?" Drake asked. "The Elves? The Men?"

"All of them." Silence covered the room.

"All of them?" Gwen asked. "How are we going to do that? We don't have an army. There are only six of us, against an entire nation."

"I'm in," Isabel said.

"Count me in too!" Shavrok said. "We'll show those little shrimps how a Gog fights!"

Aiden smiled. "I'm sure you will. How about you Morgrin?"

"You've never led us astray before, and I don't think you'll start doing so now. You have my sword. Though my skills may be a little rusty, I'm sure they will shape up in no time."

"Good to have you on board," Aiden said shaking his hand. Aiden turned to face Gwen and Drake. "What about you two? Are you in?"

"Maybe," Gwen said. "It's just the numbers that are boggling me at the moment."

"If it's any comfort to you, I expect there to be a couple more additions along the way," Aiden said.

"Still though, there are so many of them, how will we ever survive?"

"Are numbers really that important to you?" Aiden asked.

"Shouldn't they be?" Drake asked. "This is not a small foe."

"No it is not, but it is the one I've chosen to do battle with. Remember Drake that numbers don't hold a candle to a few good people with a passion and a conviction about what they're doing. Numbers don't win a war. It is faith that drives people to do things beyond their wildest imaginations if they are willing to sacrifice themselves for the greater good. All I'm asking is that you risk everything to give others the life that you and Gwen have, or the life that Isabel and Morgrin, Shavrok, and I have. Who knows, you may just find yourself along the way."

"I think I know who I am," Drake said.

"Yes, but you might discover who you are at a more intimate level. Does anything about this life you lead right now stir your heart? Do you hear voices in your head that are telling you there's something more to be discovered about yourself? If you're truly honest with yourself, if we're all honest with ourselves, deep in the chasms of our hearts, there is something.

"No matter how much you learn, or think you know about yourself, as well as the world around you and the ancient scrolls, even Lathon for that matter...you should never stop learning. You will never have learned all the secrets. So what do you say, Drake Thomas? Will you be able to risk it all, or have the material possessions in your life taken too deep of a hold?"

Drake fell silent reflecting on the words that Aiden had spoken. As much as Drake wished he could dismiss the words Aiden had said as a lie, in his heart he knew Aiden had gotten it right. He had gotten too comfortable. He had gotten caught up (on some level) with the fame the Mezutor had given him. He hated himself for a moment.

"Can you promise that we will come back?" Gwen asked.

"You won't be the same if you do," Aiden replied. "So what do you say?" Drake and Gwen exchanged glances for a moment, each confirming what the other had been thinking.

"You can count us in."

Chapter 5

TRAVELING COMPANIONS

Nickolas crept into the shadows, trying to make sure that he wasn't being followed. Aiden walked ahead of him. The rest of the city was fast asleep, still dreaming about the events of the day.

Even Nickolas was amazed by the events of the day. First, he had witnessed a race, and then, despite being called into several meetings, he had gotten to meet Aiden for himself. He had only heard stories up until today.

There was something different about Aiden and he could easily see why the Farsees didn't like him. Still, Nickolas thought that Aiden wasn't a bad person and maybe that's why he was following him through the city streets in the middle of the night.

Nickolas had been patiently waiting outside a restaurant for the past couple hours, watching as everyone inside, which included Drake and Gwen, talked and laughed like old friends. Nickolas knew that Drake and Gwen had known Aiden previously, but he never would've guessed that they were such good friends.

He had carefully watched the group of people, surprised by the variety of people that Aiden hung out with. A Gog, a Tarukai, and then an Elvish woman named Isabel and her husband.

Aiden's choice of friends alone was enough to make the Farsees hate him. If you wanted to impress the Farsees, your friends had to have a certain level of propriety. Nickolas felt the pressure too but had to some extent tried to resist it, although he had never been completely successful.

Aiden stopped walking and Nickolas did the same, holding his breath, hoping that he hadn't been discovered. Aiden finally turned towards a small building, which was some sort of an inn. Presumably where he was lodging. Nickolas moved closer.

"Good evening Nickolas," Aiden said. Nickolas's heart nearly beat out of his chest as he realized that Aiden had stopped and was now looking right at him. "What are you doing up on a night like this?"

"Could ask you the same thing," Nickolas pointed out.

"Indeed you could," Aiden said, letting the silence hang in the air. "Can I help you with something?"

"No," Nickolas lied. "I think I can figure it out on my own."

"I'm always here to talk about anything if you want to," Aiden said. He started to turn and Nickolas's mind screamed at him to forget the rules of status that plagued the Farsees and talk to this man for himself.

"Can we talk?" Nickolas asked nervously. Aiden stopped moving and looked at him. "Can we talk privately?"

"Certainly. Follow me." Nickolas followed Aiden to a back alley and then grabbed a ladder that was lying along the building. He set it up and they climbed to the roof. Nickolas set his feet on the rooftop, feeling relieved that no one would likely be able to hear them up here. "What can I do for you, my friend?"

"Friend? I've only talked to you once, does that constitute me as your friend?" Nickolas asked.

"To my knowledge, you are not my enemy; even if you were I would act the same way towards you."

"That is something we Farsees don't usually do."

"You should always love your enemies. If you don't, then why would they ever think of believing in the same things you do? They would look at you and say, he is so full of hate that I hate him. I don't think Lathon hated anyone. In fact, I know he loved all his enemies."

"Does that mean you have to like what they do? Because that's what I've been taught my whole life. It's their sins that are evil and so we hate them for that."

"You can love someone without loving everything that they do. You love the person, not the sin. If you do this, eventually their hearts will change and they'll be more open-minded to you. It takes far more courage to befriend someone who doesn't believe in everything you do."

"Is that why your friends are so different in culture?" Nickolas asked.

"To some extent yes, but mostly I find the average everyday person is more honest with themselves and with me than someone in a high-up position. They don't put on a face for people. They are who they are. There is something beautiful about being honest."

"It seems all the Farsees do is put on a face. I'm no different. I have a nice house and lots of money, yet I am miserable. My life eats away at my soul, consuming me one day at a time."

"It's hard to wear a mask all the time, and then there's always the fear that you will forever become the person you've pretended to be."

"You are very different from everyone else, you know that?" Nickolas asked.

"All I can say is I'm living my life in a way that would make Lathon proud."

"The Farsees do the same thing, at least so they say."

"I'm sure they do, but most, not all, but most, are like white-washed tombs. They look good on the outside, but inside they have nothing but rotting corpses and decay. It's not what one does when people are looking that makes them an honorable, great person. It's what they do when no one is looking."

"It's things like that that are boggling my mind," Nickolas said, amazed by this man's compassion and heart.

"What do you mean?"

"You are like a teacher, but like no other teacher I've ever met. I myself am a teacher, yet you seem to teach with far more authority than I ever could. You speak as if you've read the ancient scrolls and have met Lathon himself."

"Perhaps I have," Aiden suggested. Nickolas didn't know what to think of that one.

"It's no wonder that all the Farsees want to have your head. They are afraid that you will overthrow them."

"I do not seek to overthrow them, but I do wish to help them be honest with everyone by pointing out their hypocrisies," Aiden replied.

"Currently, they are talking about trying to kill you."

"I had the general feeling," Aiden replied. "I'll be leaving on Monday, and I won't return for some time. It seems some things need to be done. Would you like to come with us?"

"Us?" Nickolas asked.

"Drake and Gwen are coming with me as well as Isabel and Morgrin and Shavrok, friends of mine. You are welcome to come with us. No guarantee that we will return, however, as is the case with most adventures."

"What are we going to do?"

"Good," Aiden answered. "We're going to do some good in this world. However, I might warn that you have to become a new person to come with us."

"I'm not sure I understand. How can I become a new person?" Nickolas asked. "I can't be born again."

"Yes, you can, just not in a physical sense. I'm talking about something deeper, something at the soul level. To truly be born again you must leave your old ways and your old self and try to the best of your abilities to change and become the person Lathon wants you to be. It is not easy and for some people, it takes a lifetime, but Lathon will send his spirit to help you."

"Again, speaking with authority! I admit that my mind is boggled, but the more you speak with authority, the more I think the Farsees and everything I've been taught is fraud."

"Not everything they taught you is bad," Aiden said. "But in many areas, they have made it impossible for people to reach up to Lathon. I believe that Lathon is trying to reach down to us. That's why I'm here, to help people see through the fog of lies and pre-conceived ideas that have filled their heads.

What do you say, Nickolas? Will you join us on our quest to do good? Be warned ahead of time that it might just cost you everything."

Nickolas fell silent, unsure of what he should do. Inside, his heart yearned to go with Aiden and Drake, but he was afraid to do so. To leave everything he had ever known and risk it all? It was something he had never done and he could only imagine what the Farsees would think if he were to do something like that. He struggled with himself.

"Take your time and think about it. If you want to come with us, meet us at the Taruk's Pub on Monday morning, about ten o'clock. That's when we will leave."

Nickolas nodded and Aiden got off the roof and left Nickolas to think by himself. There was a lot in this world that he didn't understand and with the authority that Aiden seemed to speak with, it made Nickolas wonder just how much he could learn from Aiden. Nickolas stayed on the rooftop in thought and prayer for nearly an hour before finally leaving and heading to his house, his heart still drowning in conflict.

* * *

Isabel was already up and preparing breakfast by the time the sun even thought of peaking over the horizon. There was something she loved about the sunrise, it put her at ease and soothed her soul, giving her strength to continue through the day. She swatted a couple of vines away and then moved the plates out to the table where two places were set.

She walked down the hall and then entered a room on her right, which was filled with countless floating orbs. Everything had finally arrived from her place in Belvanor. She walked up the stairs like she would've in her old shop and then grabbed one specific orb which was black and darkened.

It lit up at her touch as she pulled it closer to her and stared at it. The orb came to life and lit up in a display of colors that filled the entire room. It died down a moment later allowing her to look into it. Mountains filled her sight and a tower stood atop one of the peaks.

A lantern bobbed as someone walked towards the tower. The person stopped and looked back, as though she knew someone was watching her. The person hurried inside and vanished.

Isabel released the orb and it floated back to its place, joining all the others that floated in the air. She walked out to the kitchen where Morgrin had now made his way out from their room. She greeted him with a smile and then sat down as they began eating their breakfast.

"Sleep good?" Morgrin asked.

"Except for the person who stole all the covers, yes."

"Sorry."

"There could be worse things," Isabel teased. "Are you looking forward to the adventure?"

"I am, but somehow I don't think I'm looking forward to it as much as you are." They both laughed.

"That is probably true," Isabel admitted. "I can't wait."

"All the years I've been married to you and I still don't completely understand what you love so much about adventure. I love it, but not in the same way that you do. What is it about adventure that moves your heart so much?"

"I love what they stand for. They make you reconsider everything you could ever hope for. To risk it all for something more than yourself, or to help those less fortunate than you. For me, an adventure is filled with hope and love and the unknown."

"A lot of people are afraid of the unknown," Morgrin replied.

"Make no mistake, I am afraid. Many turn back, but I never have. The best thing about the future *is* the unknown. In the unknown you find that you are made of a different material than everyone says. You find faith and love within yourself."

"Nonetheless, my dear wife, I am very glad that I met you. For that matter, I'm even gladder that you said yes when I asked you to marry me."

"That makes two of us," Isabel said. "I've had few things constant in my life, you and Aiden have been the most constant and have helped me pull through. In the midst of it all, I found that Lathon has had protection over me and my family. I feel very blessed. I'm especially happy that my daughter didn't end up marrying some freak or going evil like her brother and father. I'm not sure what I would do if she turned on me also."

"Yes, and it is a good thing that Gwen found Drake."

"Yes, it is…Drake has many secrets," Isabel said.

"I'm still surprised he's never remembered," Morgrin said.

"There are strange things in the world, make no mistake. Five years of research, trying to piece together the puzzle that has eluded me. I don't have all the pieces yet, but I am getting close." They both reflected in their thoughts.

She and Morgrin prepared everything they would need. Shavrok was already getting ready for the first customers of the day. Hope lingered in her mind, filling her soul. The mysteries of the past and the future, beckoned to her, calling her to the adventure that lay ahead.

* * *

A knock came at the door. Drake yawned and rubbed his eyes, trying to find the energy to get up and answer it. He stumbled out of the bed and managed to get to the door, opening it.

"Good morning Drake. I was starting to think that you were in a coma," Aiden greeted. Drake half smiled.

"I felt like I was. Come in." He let Aiden in and tried to gain his bearings. "What are you doing here so early?"

"Early? It's nearly noon."

"Noon? I guess yesterday really wiped me out." Drake replied. "I'll get Gwen up. There's a lot to do before we leave."

"You can say that again. I have a couple of more people I want you to meet."

"Anyone I know?" Drake asked. Aiden shrugged his shoulders.

"Probably not; you've probably seen them and just never talked to them before."

Only ten minutes passed before they entered out into the streets, which were emptier than they had been yesterday, which was to be expected. Drake knew that celebrations of any kind in this city went long into the night.

The people were about, going their separate ways and heading to the temples for the daily sacrifices if their religion required it. They continued past, Aiden leading the way. They walked for a few more minutes and then turned down another street that Drake recognized. Many of the financial businesses were along this street.

"Who are we looking for?"

"We're looking for the right people to come with us on our adventure."

"We'll need someone who's good with a sword then. I wouldn't think you'd find the best swordsman here," Gwen said. Aiden smiled.

"We are not looking for the best people, we are looking for the right ones," Aiden replied. They continued farther until they were stopped by Aiden, who looked at all the people. "Good news, I've found one of the people I want to come with us."

"Who?" Drake asked, searching the alley.

"The Goblin over there," Aiden said, pointing out a Goblin sitting at a tax collecting booth.

"A tax collector? Seriously?" Drake asked. "Why him? Tax collectors are thieves. As far as I can see no good can come from having a Goblin with us."

"All the more reason why I would like him to join us," Aiden said. "He is despised by the culture, if not for his appearance, then for his job. Tax collectors usually get a reputation for ripping people off, particularly those who don't know any better. However part of being a follower of Lathon is befriending people like this. Don't let them corrupt you though. Instead, you can love them and be a light shining in the darkness." Drake fell silent.

They walked up to the Goblin and Drake thought about everything Aiden had said in the past twenty-four hours. Had Drake really gotten that much wrong? Had he really been pulled astray from what he had believed?

"Excuse me, can I have a moment or two of your time?" Aiden asked. The Goblin looked up, questions and suspicion dancing through his eyes.

"Are you here to pay taxes?" the Goblin asked.

"No," Aiden answered.

"Then get out of here," the Goblin said. "You stay here too long and people will begin to think that you're just as bad of a person as I am."

"You're not a bad person. That's just a lie that the world has told you. That's not saying that you haven't made mistakes, and don't have areas you can improve in. We all have those, but that doesn't make you bad. Not if you want to fix it."

"What are you talking about?" the Goblin asked, sounding interested. Drake watched in wonder as the Goblin seemed to transform a little bit. The hard-edged mask he had been wearing when they had approached seemed to have been stripped away with one reply on Aiden's part.

"I'm leaving for a long journey tomorrow and am in need of another traveling companion. These are two of my friends Drake and Gwen Thomas, they'll all be traveling with us. If you're interested, why don't you drop by a small little restaurant called The Taruk's Pub, in about an hour? There I can answer all your questions. Are you interested?"

"Yes I'm interested!" the Goblin exclaimed, a new light shining in his eyes.

"Excellent. My name's Aiden; yours is?"

"Diderus at your service!" the Goblin exclaimed, shaking all of their hands.

"Thank you for your time. I'll see you in an hour," Aiden said. They said their goodbyes and they walked further into the city.

"I would've never guessed that he would have agreed so easily," Gwen exclaimed.

"So many of the social barriers, among other things, can be undone with a simple act of kindness. Too many people reserve those for their friends and not for strangers. Everyone wants to be accepted, and there are so many people who are rejected by one part of society or another. Some of them put on different masks and pretend as though they are completely fine, yet on the inside, they're rotting away into nothingness."

"I would have never guessed that it would be so easy," Gwen said. Aiden smiled.

"So many people pass up opportunities because they don't think of it. Remember it's not great power that keeps evil at bay, as much as it is the heart of those who take a stand. Acts of kindness can melt the heart faster than anything. You do not have to be famous to be great, which is exactly what the world doesn't tell you." They fell silent as they walked, soon interrupted by a person running up behind them. Drake turned to see Diderus running up to them.

"Do you mind if I come with you now?" Diderus asked. "I know I still have an hour left of my job, but I feel as though I should leave it."

"You are most welcome to join us," Aiden said. "Now we have to find one more person to come with us on our quest, and this one requires that we look to the ocean."

"The ocean?" Gwen asked.

Aiden nodded and led the way down a couple more streets until they were headed toward the ocean, which was still hidden behind the walls of Avdatt. A loud commotion echoed through the street, grabbing their attention. Cornelius led the group of Farsees, while a throng of people followed behind.

"This is something you don't see every day," Drake said.

Aiden nodded. "Indeed. This should be interesting."

The entourage stopped and Aiden stepped forward. "Hello Nickolas, are you having a good morning?" Aiden asked. Drake spotted Nickolas to the side of the crowd watching with interest. "What can I do for you gentlemen on a nice day such as this?"

"Don't mock us with your snobbery," Cornelius said. The crowds hung on every word.

"At least I'm not a hypocrite." The crowd gasped and even Drake had to wonder if he had heard Aiden correctly. Saying anything against the Farsees was never a good idea, especially with so many in front of him.

"We are the religious leaders of the land and I assure you there is no hypocrisy among us."

"Then you're only fooling yourself. Everyone knows what you guys are. And those who don't, don't know because you give them a list of things that they must do when in reality none of those things are required in the ancient scrolls and none of them are required after today."

"I should have you arrested for blasphemy!" Cornelius thundered. "Are you saying that the ancient religion is going to be destroyed after today?"

"I'm saying the answer to your prayers is right in front of you, under your nose and you fail to see it. I am Sherados." The crowd gasped.

"You are a fool! However, we have a dilemma amongst ourselves right now. As you know, the law requires anyone caught in the act of adultery to be stoned to death immediately. Is this not true?"

"In the ancient religion that was true yes," Aiden admitted. "What of it?"

"We have caught a woman in the act," Cornelius said. The rest of the Farsees parted and a couple of them grabbed the woman they had brought with them and threw her to the ground between them. The woman was dressed in only a robe and kept her head down in shame, unable to look anyone in the eye. All eyes were on the woman for a moment or two until finally they turned back to Cornelius and Aiden. "What should we do?"

Cornelius pulled out a large rock from a chest that they had brought with them. Aiden smiled and then crouched down to his knees, looking at the ground and then drawing lines in the sand.

Drake watched in anticipation as the time went on until finally five minutes passed as Aiden sat and drew in the sand. Drake tried to look at what he was drawing, but it was hidden from his view. Aiden finally looked up, holding a hand out to the woman's chin. He gently lifted her head, looking into her tear-filled eyes. He held her gaze for several long moments, before finally looking up to Cornelius.

He stood and brushed himself off, the people still silent, waiting to see what his reply would be. Drake watched in wonder. No one had ever dared to leave a Farsee waiting this long for an answer. Cornelius looked flustered but forced a smile on his face as though he had won.

"If you are so perfect and have the authority by Lathon's standard to take a person's life, then let he who is without sin throw the first stone!" Aiden exclaimed. All eyes turned to Cornelius. He stood silent, glaring at Aiden in both wonder and rage. A fake smile stretched across his face and he began laughing.

"Very clever, Aiden. Very clever," Cornelius said, still gripping the stone in his hand. Aiden stared at him intently, a knowing look on his face. Cornelius and Aiden stared at each other unmoving for several seconds. Cornelius's resolve seemed to melt away.

"She's waiting," Aiden said, motioning towards the woman. Cornelius pulled the stone back and then stopped, every eye drilling into his skull. Cornelius struggled with himself, his arm getting tired from holding the rock. Finally, Cornelius lowered the rock and dropped it on the ground. The crowd murmured amongst themselves as Cornelius pushed his way through the crowd and vanished from sight. One by one the Farsees left, except for Nickolas, who remained. The rest of the crowd slowly dispersed until only they were left in the street. Drake looked at the woman who was in the street, her head still bowed low as she cried uncontrollably. Aiden moved closer and stooped down next to her.

"Woman," Aiden said. Her crying finally subsided and she looked up. "Where are your accusers?"

"They've left," the woman answered. "They didn't condemn me?"

"No they didn't, and I'm not going to condemn you either." He helped her up as she tried to pull herself together. "You've been given a second chance, and with a second chance comes an opportunity to lead a different life. Go and sin no more." The woman hesitated. "Go." She turned and slowly walked away. Nickolas approached them.

"That was amazing!" Nickolas exclaimed. "I've never seen anyone stand up to them like that before."

"Maybe it's time someone did," Aiden said.

"It's one thing for *me* to say something, but I don't have any authority. If I said half the stuff you said I'd be arrested immediately," Drake said.

"Exactly!" Nickolas agreed. "Even I would be in the same boat, and I'm one of them. You speak with an authority like I've never seen! They don't seem to see you as a common ordinary person, even though according to your background and where you are from, you are."

"You don't have to be born into fame to be great. The average ordinary person can do just as much as the next person."

"I've never really believed that until now," Nickolas replied. "You speak with authority and you said you were Sherados! No one has ever said that before."

"Do you believe me or am I just a crazy person?" Aiden asked. Drake watched with interest as Nickolas and Aiden exchanged glances. Finally, after a couple of moments, he spoke.

"I believe you are Sherados, although by believing that. I am saying that most of what the Farsees teach is wrong. There is no doubt in my heart that we are standing in the presence of Sherados, the heir of Lathon." Nickolas began to lower himself to one knee.

Aiden stopped him. "My friend, all the rules of the past religion are gone. What I want from you is far more important than publicly bowing to me. I want you to bow your heart and your mind; to live in a way that is worthy of being a follower of mine. So that when people look at you, they can see that you are different. Being a follower of Lathon means that through the hard times and the good times, you'll remain true in thought and action. It is the heart I'm worried about, not all the petty stuff the Farsees currently hold as important."

"I look forward to learning from you," Nickolas said.

"You must have an open mind and heart if you are to learn anything. Do you have that?" Aiden asked. Nickolas nodded. "Will we see you tomorrow?"

"Is it strange that the thought of leaving everything plagues my heart and tells me I shouldn't do it?" Nickolas asked.

"Other voices will always be present. Do not love this world nor the things it offers you, for when you love the things the world offers, you do not have the love of Lathon in you. For the world offers only a craving for physical pleasure, a craving for everything we see, and pride in our achievements and possessions. These are not from Lathon but are from this world. This world is fading away, along with everything that people crave. But anyone who does what pleases Lathon will live forever. Decide now where your true loyalties lie. We may not return from this adventure that I have planned," Aiden said. Nickolas fell silent.

"May I ask why you didn't condemn the woman?" Diderus asked. "She *was* guilty."

"Yes she was, but as much as condemning the evil is important, she needed grace. She knew what she had done was wrong, so I let her try again. That's the nature of Lathon. But be warned that mercy does not last forever, eventually everyone will be judged. Now come, we have much to do before we leave, which includes finding one more person to take with us on this trip!"

* * *

Nickolas left and then they followed Aiden down the empty streets and then out of the city to the ocean. A light breeze blew and the smell of salt water crashing up onto the shores reached them. They looked to the left and saw a couple of boats sitting, full of fish.

The fish were being counted by three people who worked vigorously, not noticing that they were approaching. Finally, the youngest of the three looked up and noticed them. It was the first Elves he had seen who were fishermen.

"Good afternoon my friends," Aiden greeted. Drake watched as they dropped their nets and came over to them. "It is a fine day isn't it?"

"Indeed it is," the oldest, who was probably their father, answered. "What can we do for you? Are you in need of some fish?"

"Yes, but we are also in need of a strong man who might accompany us on our next adventure. We are leaving tomorrow morning and I realize that it might be short notice but if one of you would like to join us you are welcome." The three stared at each other, their faces showing both confusion and joy.

"I would be honored to be included in your adventure. My name is Thaddeus." He held out his hand and they all shook it and introduced themselves. Thaddeus was taller with long black hair and shining green eyes.

"Bring some fish and we will make ourselves a meal. You can meet the others who will be coming with us and find out what we will be doing." All three of them picked up their things and followed the group of them until finally, they made their way back into the city and into Isabel's kitchen.

* * *

They prepared the food and Drake watched their newfound companions with interest, not understanding their thought process. They were dropping everything without question, and for what?

"This is an interesting group of people that are going on this trip," Thaddeus said. Drake nodded.

"Tell me about it. I'm not even sure I completely understand everything that has happened. Tell me though, because I'm curious. Why are you just picking up and dropping everything, is it for glory? Or for something else?"

"It's not for glory. It's just that no one has ever asked us to go on any kind of adventure before. I'm only a fisherman, I'm not special by any means."

"The same goes for me," Diderus stated. "I've been despised my whole life because I'm both a Goblin and a tax collector, yet here I find myself being asked to come on an adventure. How can I refuse?"

Drake fell silent as he pondered what they said. The world was rather judgmental and he could easily see how even he wasn't fit for going on an adventure. The door opened and Cornelius entered, looking at the group of them, malice in his eyes.

"This is the worst group of people that I've ever seen. A Gog, a Farsee, a tax collector, a fisherman, a Tarukai, and a Sorceress. What kind of group do you call that?"

"I call it a group that is fit for every scenario," Aiden said. Shavrok moved closer and Cornelius backed away.

"Why do you eat with such scum?" Cornelius asked.

"Because they are the only ones who know what they are," Aiden answered. "They are the ones who are constantly reminded of the people they've become, or the people they'll never be able to become. Whereas people like you know who you are, and you're exactly like you want to be. They are the ones who need hope given to them when the rest of the world wants to steal it from beneath their feet. I choose them because they *are* important; if only people would sit back and see them for *who* they are and not what they are." Cornelius fell silent, not saying much as they cooked the food and then sat down to eat.

"Would you care to join us, Cornelius?" Shavrok asked. Cornelius's eyes went wide and then he ran from the building, to all of their amusement. "Was it something I said?"

They laughed again.

"I guess he's just not used to seeing a Gog in Avdatt, let alone talking to one," Isabel said.

"I know the feeling," Diderus replied. "I'm still getting used to it. Cornelius did have one thing right, we are an unusual bunch."

"Yes, but a group full of unusual people, and unlikely friends are sometimes the best ones," Aiden said. "Where one is weak another is strong. Together we shall set out and try our hardest to rid the world of an evil that is growing."

"I'm not sure what kind of adventure this is going to be, but I don't have any weapons, I'm only a fisherman," Thaddeus reminded.

"Don't worry about it, we can either buy you some or I think Isabel might have a few you can borrow."

"You might have to show me how to use them as well. I've never done any fighting," Diderus said.

"Don't worry about it," Aiden assured. "You'll learn as we go. So let's raise our glasses to a toast." They all grabbed their glasses. "To Friendship." They raised their glasses and then drank.

* * *

"It's amazing what your mother thinks up," Drake said, walking further into the twisting maze of halls and corridors that stretched on inside the restaurant of sorts. Gwen walked with him and looked at everything with interest and curiosity.

"There is so much I can learn from her. Pretty soon we'll be just as eccentric as she is," Gwen joked.

"Lathon help us all," Drake kidded. They smiled and then shared a kiss.

"Don't do that in front of strangers!" Isabel said, coming up behind them. They all smiled. "I'm just kidding, at least Gwen's married to someone normal and not Rohemir."

"Was there any good in my father?"

"At one point in time yes," Isabel said. "I did love him when I married him, but he changed and went down a path that I couldn't follow. There are many things I don't understand, but one day I will understand them."

"You have quite a place here and lots of interesting things to look at as usual," Drake said.

"Indeed there is, however, I've kept the owls in a separate room so that if a certain dwarf ever visits he doesn't know they're here."

"Probably a good idea," Gwen said. She was called away to one of the other rooms leaving just Drake and Isabel in the long hall.

"How did you become the person you are?" Drake asked. "I think you know more about me than I know about you."

"There are many secrets that I still possess Drake Thomas and I shall only reveal them when the time is right."

"When is that?" Drake asked. Isabel shrugged. "I'll know when it is. Come, I need some help bringing up some supplies for our trip." Drake followed her to a small door that he hadn't noticed before. It led to a small winding staircase, which led down to a small ten-foot by ten-foot cellar. The walls were lined with shelves, the contents of which were coated with dust and countless items that Drake couldn't recognize.

Despite all the beauty and elegance the rest of the house held, this room held none of it. Just dusty shelves, with dusty cloths covering whatever items lay beneath. Drake watched her as she slowly moved along each shelf as if carefully searching for something specific.

Drake's eyes were drawn to a table in the center of the room. A picture was propped up on a stand and was covered with a thick black cloth. Next to it, a small wooden chest, old and worn, yet vaguely familiar. He had seen something like it before at one of the vendors that were along the streets.

"What is this room?" Drake asked, starting to move to the table in the center. She put another cloth over the items on the table. Drake took a hint and backed away, following her to the shelves.

"A very special room that few have ever seen. Consider yourself lucky. In this room lie many mysteries that have not been solved, and for that matter, might not be solved. Many things in here are both good and evil. This is not a room you want to visit every day."

"Then why are we down here now?" Drake asked. "I thought you said we needed something for the trip."

"We do. It's right here," Isabel said. She reached past Drake and removed the cloth that covered the item she was headed for. Dust flew in the air and she waved it away with the cloth. A single piece of parchment lay in front of them. She took it and blew the dust off of it. In the dim lighting, Drake could only make out faint lines drawn on the paper but it was enough to set his mind racing.

He looked back to where the parchment had been sitting, noticing that there was something where the parchment had been. She grabbed it and also dusted it off. It was a small broach, with a single white diamond in the middle of it. The sight of it captured Drake's attention as he stared at it, unable to look away. She put her hand over it and the sensations faded until he was back to normal.

"Do I dare ask what these things are?" Drake asked.

"This is a map of a set of mountains that I grew up in. They are called the Dead Mountains. I'm not sure if we'll have to go into them, but if we do I'm not being caught without a map."

"And the broach?" Drake asked.

"It's a broach. Why would you think there's anything *different* about it?"

"Because I looked at it and couldn't look away," Drake said.

"Let's just say that if we should run into any trouble, it could be our saving grace. Now come, let's get us some weapons before everyone gets here." Isabel led the way as they exited the cellar and locked it, sealing off Drake's curiosity for the moment. They moved down the hall now rejoined by Gwen who came running up behind them. Isabel had hidden the broach and the map was folded up in her hand, but Gwen seemed to not notice anything out of the ordinary.

Isabel brought them to a room on the right. The room was full of different weapons, some of which were covered in dust and others looked like they had just been put there yesterday.

She grabbed a weapon, which Drake recognized was her sword and she put it on. She grabbed a couple of swords and daggers from the next shelf and handed them to the two of them. Drake put his hand on the pommel of the sword, slowly pulling it out, recognizing the blade that he had been given.

"I didn't know you had our weapons," Drake said.

"Yes you did, hon," Gwen said. "Remember we gave them to her for safekeeping?"

"I guess I do remember that now," Drake replied after a moment or so. "It feels different than before?"

"How?" Isabel asked.

Drake studied the sword. "Did you do something to it?"

"Made it twice as strong as it was. Shouldn't break for anything, and I can guarantee you it can stand enormous amounts of heat. The metal has been coated with a special compound I created. It's been modified to not melt unless it reaches a sustained temperature of three thousand degrees for about ten minutes or so. As far as everyone else is concerned you have an indestructible weapon."

"How do you discover these things?" Gwen asked. Isabel smiled.

"A lifetime of study and research."

They put on their weapons and then followed Isabel down the room as she came to a separate shelf. A couple of bows with quivers of arrows were in front of them, as well as several different strange weapons, including what looked like a walking stick.

"We need some weapons for our friend who might not have them. A bow for Thaddeus, as well as several different knives. For Diderus we have two jagged-edged swords, and for Nickolas, should he show up, we have something special." She grabbed the wooden staff and pulled it into plain sight.

"Looks ordinary, but this is far from it. If you tap it on the ground three times fire shoots from the top of it. If you hold it sideways for ten seconds it'll shine a light brighter than any the world has ever seen, protecting you from your enemies; and lastly, if you happen to get hit by the staff when you are fighting the staff holder, you'll regret it.

"How do you mean?" Drake asked.

"The wood will become as sharp as any sword, cutting your enemy. Further, it has been known to cause extreme boils; very deadly and not much fun."

"Did you create that?" Gwen asked. Isabel laughed.

"No, I didn't create this. This was created by the Sorcerer himself. I *borrowed* it from him when I left Iscariot when I was pregnant."

"How much did you take from him and Rohemir?" Drake asked.

"As much as I could. I didn't want the weapons, or anything else for that matter, to be used against people. It was very dangerous and a couple of times I barely escaped with my life, but I managed. Every risk was worth it."

"You don't by chance have something we can send to Ellizar do you?" Gwen asked. "You know to get him back for the gem."

"I think this should do the trick," Isabel said, reaching into a pocket and pulling out a small rock that to Drake looked like a small paperweight.

"What does it do?"

"Let's just say it should give him a headache, if he says the right thing," Isabel answered. They left the room and made their way back to the main entrance where everyone was standing outside waiting. Nickolas was the only one who hadn't shown up yet.

-

Chapter 6

A NEW ADVENTURE

Aiden leaned up against the railing of the stairs. His double-handed broad sword that the elf kings had given him, hung by his side.

"We'll wait a few more minutes and then we'll have to be off," Aiden said. They nodded and small-talked. They began to get to their feet, interrupted by the sound of a person running up to them. It was Nickolas who stopped just short of them and tried to catch his breath.

"Looks like I made it just in time," Nickolas said. Aiden smiled and embraced him.

"Where's your girlfriend?" Gwen asked. "Is she coming too?" Nickolas's face clouded over with hurt and confusion.

"I wish I could say yes, but I wasn't able to find her anywhere today. I went to her place and it was picked clean! Nothing of hers was left. I guess she didn't like that I was going to give up everything."

"Not everything is as it seems," Isabel said.

"I hope you are right, but I'm not sure that you are," Nickolas said.

"Don't worry about it," Aiden said. "Welcome to our company of people. It'll be a great honor to have you with us," Aiden said. "You did what few in this world could do, you left everything behind."

"I didn't just leave everything, I sold everything," Nickolas pulled a large bag of coins from his pocket. "I figure the money should more than fund our trip."

"Here, this is for you," Isabel said, presenting him with the staff. Nickolas took it. "A walking stick?" Drake couldn't help but smile at Nickolas's dumb face.

"More dangerous than you think, I'll explain on the way," Isabel said.

"Sounds...good...who are you?"

"My mother-in-law," Drake answered. Once again Nickolas was speechless. "Okay…"

"You'll get used to it," Isabel said, happily skipping next to Morgrin. "Now let's go on an adventure?"

"Couldn't have said it better myself!" Aiden exclaimed. The group began walking through the streets, drawing attention to themselves due to the large variety of races with them.

"I still stand true to my offer Aiden," Gwen said. "Drake and I could easily and swiftly hire fifty carriages to take us wherever we're going."

"I have no doubt you could," Aiden said. "But the true adventure is the things that happen along the way. There is much to learn, and much of it cannot be done by sitting on our butts in a fancy carriage." Gwen half kicked the ground in frustration, mumbling under her breath.

"Why can't we just take horses?" Nickolas asked.

"They will be too easy to track if we are being followed by anyone," Aiden answered.

"We're being followed?" Diderus asked.

"I suspect it is so," Aiden answered.

"The Farsees have been furious with you lately," Nickolas said. "In our meetings, they were openly discussing to have you arrested or killed. I wouldn't put it past them to have you ambushed once we're outside of the city."

"Ha! Let them try!" Shavrok said, laughing heartily. "If they pick a fight with one of us, they get the rest of us."

Drake laughed. "I certainly wouldn't want to pick a fight with a Gog."

"The Farsees would be watching the main roads, most likely," Aiden replied.

"It would make more sense to go completely in the other direction," Morgrin suggested. "Head south perhaps."

"Or at the very least make them think we went another way," Aiden said.

"We will send the Taruks south."

"That would work," Isabel said. A couple of minutes later all three Taruks (Elohim, Destan, and Apsen) landed in the street. People took cover momentarily but then came out, admiring the Taruks. "We can send them to Mera Runa first, I have something for Aspen to deliver."

Isabel reached into her pocket and pulled out a small package, and took it over to Aspen dropping it into a little bag that was mounted on her back. "Why don't you deliver that to our short little friend?"

The Taruks seemed to nod and then flew into the air, vanishing into the south.

"We will head through the Mezutor stadium, stay off the main roads, and hopefully go unnoticed," Aiden said.

"There are foul things in the mountains beyond," Diderus commented.

"Yes indeed," Aiden said. "With Sheol being so close, it's not just someone's imagination coming up with the stories you hear now and then. We will make for Gadara and then figure out our next course of action."

They left the city and with it everything that Drake had come to know. After everything he and Gwen had accomplished, it was hard for him to leave everything. Still, something in his heart knew that it was time to put aside his efforts and follow someone else's lead.

Aiden had never led him astray before and he knew that Aiden wasn't about to do that now. Drake put all of his trust into the person that had saved his life again and again, without thought of reward. There was something they could all learn from Aiden if only they weren't too proud to humble themselves.

True love, no matter what the circumstances, never looked for anything in return, it only hoped that you would notice the kind gesture.

The further Drake was the clearer everything was becoming to him. He may have gained great fame during the years as a Tarukai, but he had done nothing with the money. He knew in his heart, that he had been deceived by the world and gotten pulled into the lie that status equaled success.

The people watched them as they left, some with confusion on their faces and others glad to see them leaving, although most of those stares came from the Farsees.

"They won't even look at Nickolas," Drake whispered to Aiden. Aiden nodded and looked at Cornelius who was standing in and behind the rest of them.

"They say they are full of love, but their actions do not prove it. Actions do speak louder than words."

"I wish I could grab them by their robes and shake them," Isabel said.

"Those who show no mercy will receive none. If you see a person in need and do not help them you might as well join the Sorcerer," Aiden said. Drake and everyone else fell silent. "A follower of Lathon must be filled with love to the point that they cannot sit back and do nothing."

They let the silence linger as they left the city, which soon was lost from sight. They turned west towards the Mezutor stadium, which was now looming before them. Drake had never been to the stadium when there wasn't anything going on.

The entire area was as silent as a tomb, only interrupted by the thundering falls at the south end of the main stretch. They went around the side of the stadium, finding themselves climbing up the steep hill where the Taruks would have normally entered the first tunnel. Drake looked at everything with interest and a newfound curiosity. Something was different.

Drake pushed on as the company of travelers snaked their way over the first mountain and then began descending. They kept their eyes peeled and their ears alert. Drake found himself looking over his shoulder, feeling as though they were being watched.

The sun drifted further through the sky. Drake zoned out, a strange sensation coming over him. He looked to Isabel who walked up ahead with Gwen. Isabel was hiding something from all of them, but what it is Drake couldn't even begin to guess.

He thought about asking but had decided against it, knowing that when Isabel wanted to tell them she would.

His mind drifted to her story and the Sorcerer, remembering everything that had happened during the last few battles six years ago. He had never done anything like that before, but he had grown through the experience and had endured testing by the Sorcerer.

The testing still plagued his mind. The memory of the vision the Sorcerer before him, was just as real now as it had felt in that moment. Drake had never shared with Gwen, about that moment. Instead, it festered in his mind and demanded his attention.

The mountains rose up all around them, the snowy peaks glistening in the sunlight that fell from the bright blue sky. They walked on no particular path but followed in Aiden's footsteps.

He led them through the valleys and along the cliffs, only a foot or two ledge separating them from a long deadly fall. Drake watched the path ahead, wondering what secrets these mountains held. He had lived near them for five years and still, he knew nothing about them.

The farther they walked, the more the forest seemed to change, their course becoming easier and the air seeming to become lighter. A stream was heard flowing somewhere in the distance and after another ten minutes of walking, they finally came to it. A small bridge was to their left, leading to a small, modest house.

"We will stay here for the night," Aiden announced as they crossed the bridge. They put their bags down and collapsed on the ground, while Aiden gathered some wood for a fire and lit it. The house appeared to be abandoned.

Thaddeus moved to the stream, pulled a small fishing line out of his pack, and swiftly caught several fish, which were cooked with some vegetables that were growing nearby. The meal satisfied their hunger and they soon fell asleep, lost to their dreams for the time being.

The next day they set off just as the sky was beginning to grow pale with light. They covered the ashes from their fire and traveled further into the mountains, preventing their sound from carrying too far in one direction. The day passed without incident as the traveling became a little easier. The paths became wider and better traveled, although they still hadn't seen any people or towns. The only things that Drake could see that he even remotely recognized were the large towers from the Mezutor, which were built into the mountains.

The group was silent, except for Isabel who walked along whistling as though nothing was out of the ordinary. The simple tune brought joy to all their hearts as they traveled further into the mountains.

"When we get out of the mountains how close will we be to Gadara?" Diderus asked. For a moment Drake envied the Goblin who was easily using his talons and claws to pick his way through the tough parts of the trail.

"When we exit tomorrow morning, we should be within a couple of hours walk of Gadara," Aiden replied. "If all goes well and there are no surprises that is."

"Do you think we'll see any surprises?" Thaddeus asked. Aiden shrugged. "There's no way to know for sure until we end up in the middle of a trap," Aiden said with a smile on his face. "We're getting closer to Sheol so it's always a possibility."

"What exactly is in Sheol?" Drake asked.

"I've heard many tales of that land from the northern settlements of the Gogs," Shavrok replied. "Strange things have I heard. Never seen them for myself though."

"Many strange things dwell in Sheol," Aiden stated.

"You said Gogs from the north? Are there more?" Morgrin asked.

"There are three settlements of Gogs, the largest settlement is on the Negev River in Ariamore. Now that Atruss is back in charge of the nation we are allowed to live there, though I would love for them to try and challenge us. Ha! The second settlement is in the nation of Edon, hidden far to the east among the hills and ravines that make up the far east border. Then the last is to the northwest, on the other side of Sheol. They live on the sea with a navy nearly as impressive as those that my settlement built. Other than that there are a few camps of them scattered throughout the world, perhaps even in these mountains. Hard to say really."

"Maybe if we get into a bind they will be able to help us," Drake suggested. "Perhaps," Shavrok replied. "We lie in secret, waiting for the day to rise up and destroy all evil forever, though the Sorcerer is gone we know his spirit still walks the earth doing evil deeds."

"The Sorcerer can't come back can he?" Drake asked. Aiden shrugged.

"There are many dark ways he could come back if he wanted to. But he will not prevail either way. He didn't prevail the first time, he certainly won't the second. Though that doesn't mean he won't give a hard fight."

They walked for a couple of more hours until the light was fading and they couldn't continue any further. They stopped in a little valley, climbing up as far as they could so they would be able to better defend themselves if something were to attack them. The others quickly fell asleep while Drake was unable to sleep.

Lights shone in the distance, hidden in the forest beneath them. He watched the lights and thought for a couple of minutes that he even heard drums being beaten. The ground shook lightly, but other than that there was no sign that anything usual was occurring. Drake finally fell asleep.

* * *

Drake woke to the feel of cold steel being pressed to his throat. His eyes focused on the torches burning around their camp. Shavrok was missing. The rest of them were tied up in the center with him being the only one who was still free.

He looked to his captors, easily identifying them as Goblins of some sort. They had the general build and shape of a Goblin, but they were different from any that he had seen. Their teeth were long and pointy, almost like fangs and their skin was dark black and shone like the thick skin of a Taruk. Trails of orange ran over them. Drake studied them for a moment, noting that it was their blood veins he was seeing. The veins bulged out of their bodies, a thin mesh covering the blood veins. Wisps of hair were on the top of their heads and the rest of their body was covered in armor which was coated with dried blood.

The creature yelled harshly in his own tongue. The knife was pulled away from Drake's throat and he was taken over to the others. His weapons were taken from him and put in a pile with all the other weapons.

The strange creatures argued and spoke harshly to each other for several minutes.

“What's going on?” Drake asked.

“They can't find Shavrok,” Aiden said calmly. The leader turned and cursed and spat at them. Drake and Aiden both sat back taking the hint. They would be quiet.

Wood was brought and laid before them, and was soon ignited, the flames licked high into the sky. Howling was heard in the distance. The hideous creatures all let out strange calls and moved to the perimeter of the camp, drawing their weapons.

“What’s happening?” Drake asked. Rumbling filled the ground and shook the trees.

“That can’t be good,” Diderus said. Twigs and branches began falling from the trees as the rumbling intensified. A roar filled the forest around them. Gogs crashed into the opening. Shavrok was with them, as they easily swept the creatures aside, with their powerful arms.

Two of the creatures came running at Shavrok who picked them up and hurled them down the mountain, where they crashed into the forest below. Shavrok twisted and backhanded another creature, his powerful spikes on his knuckles lifting the creature in the air and sending him flailing into the rocks behind him.

Another of the Gogs tossed the creature into the fire. Flames consumed the creature as he tried to run off the cliff, only to be backhanded by one of the Gogs. He flew up into the trees and then collapsed to the ground where he was consumed by the flame.

Shavrok ducked to the left as one of the creatures threw a large spear at him.

He caught it with one hand, snapping it as though it was a twig. He threw the pieces back at the beast, hitting his target.

The fight continued for several more minutes until finally there was only one creature left, and he was surrounded by the Gogs. The creature shivered and shook with fear. He sprinted towards a small gap between Shavrok and another Gog but was smashed by Shavrok's hand as it came down on him. Shavrok picked up the twisted pile of bones and flesh and threw him over the edge of the cliff where he met the forest below.

"We are glad to see you," Morgrin exclaimed. Shavrok just smiled as he walked over to them and started undoing their ropes.

"I thought I remembered hearing that some of the Gogs from the northwestern shores were tailing some creatures in these mountains, so I went and found them."

"What were they anyway?" Thaddeus asked.

"A form of Rantwart, although in some ways they look nothing like Rantwarts. For the most part, Rantwarts live in the Dead Mountains, but some have separated and have blended themselves with several other twisted dark creatures. It's hard to say what they are anymore."

"We've been tracking them for five days, following their pile of bones and blood," another Gog answered. "Shavrok tells me you are headed to Gadara?"

"That's correct," Aiden said. "Would you like to join us?"

"There are many dark things in these mountains. We will escort you to the edge of the mountains and then go on our way," the Gog replied.

They put out the fires that were burning around the camp, as a result of the firewood being scattered and then laid down on the ground. They all grabbed their place on the ground and then easily fell asleep and this time were able to stay asleep.

Drake was lost in his dreams, which were strange and weird. He was baffled as the dreams persisted, it wasn't much of a dream and for that reason, he couldn't explain it to anyone. It was mostly sights and sounds all the while the world around him seemed to be a blur. Drake studied each sight with interest, not recognizing them at all.

The rest of the night passed without incident and they were soon on their way early the next morning, following the company of ten Gogs and Shavrok. The paths they were on today were different from the other ones they had been on previously.

The paths wove in and out of the mountains. There were parts of the path that were surrounded by tunnels, as though some ancient city had once thrived. The sight was interesting but was soon behind them as they descended from the mountain to a narrow path between the two mountains behind them.

They walked for a while longer before reaching a darkened cave with intricate carvings all around it. The Gogs lit torches and then everyone pushed into the darkness, having to try not to gag on the smell of rotting flesh that reached them.

“What is this place?” Drake asked.

“This is the dwelling place of the Rantwart-like creatures that attacked you,” one of the Gogs answered. “They’ve been hunting small villages and traveling groups that come into these mountains. We tracked them here and then fought them, before coming after the group that got away and captured you.”

“So we would’ve been eaten if you hadn’t shown up?” Gwen asked. Shavrok nodded.

“The Rantwarts are all part of a pagan culture that believes they must not simply defeat their opponent but feast on their flesh. It’s disturbing.”

They walked for a little while until they reached a large wall of rock that went hundreds of feet in the air. Attached to the wall was a long rope ladder. The Gogs motioned for them to start climbing first which they did, with the Gogs pulling up the rear. Finally, they reached the top and came to a landing which then opened up to a large area, carved into the rocks.

“The main barracks,” one of the Gogs told them. They walked past the tomb-like surroundings until they reached a large gate that was opened, allowing the sunlight and fresh air to penetrate the darkness. They stepped into the pleasant surroundings. A waterfall thundered to their left and ran into a pool down below. They took a break when they reached the pool, taking turns to bathe and refill their canteens before they continued. Strangely enough, the pool of water didn't go anywhere, with no river or stream connecting on either side.

They continued through the forest which was becoming both more pleasant and more annoying. Large vines and more brush grew in their way, making them have to cut a path for themselves. They finally exited the brush, coming out onto a ledge that overlooked a standing body of water. Stairs were to either side, leading down to the forest floor. Beyond that Drake could see grassy plains and a city lying in the distance.

"This is where we leave you," the Gogs said. Shavrok as well as the rest of them said their goodbyes and the other Gogs disappeared into the forest. They continued down the stairs and out of the forest, the sight of Gadara being a welcome one.

They entered the town, melting into the people who walked through the streets. They followed Aiden, who led the way to the local hotel to try and find rooms for all of them, but came up empty with no one having any room. Instead, they moved to one of the back alleys and started a fire, sleeping on the ground for the night.

* * *

Drake lay awake wondering what the next day would bring. It had only taken them two days to end up in a life-threatening situation, Drake could only imagine what would happen in the coming days. He stopped his thoughts and reminded himself why he was doing this. He was doing this because it was the right thing to do, and it would continue to be the right thing to do no matter what happened to him or his belongings.

"You awake Drake?" Nickolas asked. Drake sat up and the two of them moved closer.

"I'm awake. I'm surprised you are."

"I find it hard to sleep, but not out of fear, out of amazement!" Nickolas exclaimed.

"Amazement of what? You'll have to be more specific than that. There's a lot that's different."

"Aiden. I may have only met him a couple of days ago, but already I feel as though I'm a new person. He speaks with such authority and dignity that I am left speechless by what he says and does."

"Dignity?" Drake asked.

"Yes dignity, or rather he treats everyone with dignity. It doesn't matter your station or your stature he still cares about you. We are on our way to free slaves for crying out loud! No other person in history has ever cared this much about slaves or anything."

"He is incredible. He gives without thought of reward and challenges the people around him to live the same way. Maybe if the world did operate the way he did, the world would be in better shape."

"I'm starting to think so," Nickolas said. "Never have I heard of a man setting out on a journey with such an eclectic group of people. A tax collector, a Gog, a fisherman, a Farsee, you, and an eccentric woman who most people wouldn't touch with a hundred-foot pole."

"That's what love does," Isabel said from the other side of the fire. Drake and Nickolas both noticed she was knitting something. "Love doesn't care about anything, except proving that the love is real. I can think of no better way of doing this than humbling yourself and coming to choose him. He's a great teacher, but he's far more than that. He is Sherados."

"Why does my heart have a hard time believing that?" Nickolas asked.

"Because it's human nature to believe that he isn't. It's human nature to believe that we can save ourselves and do our own thing and be alright. We question everything, even when the truth is right in front of us," Isabel said.

"One of the biggest reasons people wouldn't be able to believe that Aiden is the heir of Lathon is how he came. He was born of a virgin and into a nation and family of humans. For two years he was virtually unnoticed. Then the elf kings came and found him. I'm just guessing, but do the Farsees think that a man like him would possibly be Sherados?"

"The belief has always been that Sherados would be more magnificent. A strong leader as far as the military is concerned. Someone who would kick the butts of our enemies and destroy them. Someone who likely would work with the Farsees instead of against the Farsees," Nickolas said. "He is very different from what everyone thought, but the more I think about it, the more the character of Lathon has been demonstrated by Aiden."

"We should all model our lives after him," Isabel said.

"I'm still amazed at how he treats other people. I don't know how many times I could say it, but he has lowered the Farsees and raised up the poor and underprivileged. It's as if he's saying that the first shall be last and the last shall be first. That we must serve other people."

"The opposite of how the culture works these days," Drake said. "I must admit that although I've done some traveling with him before this and fought alongside him, several times, he does seem quite different from what he was. I don't know what it is."

"I look forward to finding out," Nickolas said. Isabel agreed. They all drifted off to sleep.

* * *

Gwen followed Aiden blindly as they walked down the streets of Gadara They passed by a small café. Gwen couldn't help but notice all the stares their traveling group was getting.

"I think our plan worked," Morgrin said. "We wanted to get here late enough that the Farsees wouldn't be here and they're not."

"I'm not sure I would say that they aren't here," Aiden replied. "I have a feeling a couple of dear friends of ours are waiting to surprise us with some kind of a trap."

"What should we do?" Thaddeus asked.

"If they show up just let me take care of it," Aiden said. They all agreed. Gwen pointed to a couple of robed figures coming in the distance. Aiden turned to greet them, a large smile spreading across his face. Cornelius was at the head of the procession and looked to the ground when Aiden looked at him.

"Good morning Cornelius," Aiden greeted. The only greeting Aiden got was a cold hard stare.

"Teacher, we know that you are sincere, and teach the way of Lathon in accordance with truth, and show deference to no one; for you do not regard people with partiality. Tell us, then, what you think. Is it lawful to pay taxes to the emperor, or not?"

"May I see one of the coins?" Aiden asked. Cornelius reluctantly pulled one out of his pocket. Everyone around them watched with interest. He handed the bronze-colored coin to Aiden who carefully inspected it, looking at both sides as if studying for the answer that was written somewhere."

"I'm not sure why you constantly try to catch me, but I have a question for you. Whose face is this?" Aiden asked, holding the coin out for Cornelius to see.

"It's Ahab's face. The emperor of the Goshen empire, which rules over us."
"Well then give to Ahab what belongs to Ahab and give to Lathon, what belongs to Lathon. It's that simple my friend." Aiden handed the coin back and they continued.

They left the city behind them and were soon into the countryside, which was dotted with small houses and farms, surrounded by countless fields of crops and livestock. For a while, all their fears and their trials were forgotten and they were allowed to enjoy the beauty that surrounded them.

The sun shone high in the sky, which was blue with faint white streaks in it. The wind was light and refreshing, taking Gwen back to Fiori, where she had been raised as a slave.

Although she had lived in many different places in her life, none of them had ever felt like home. Not in the same way. She loved her and Drake's home in Avdatt and she had loved the palace in Mera Runa, but she felt as if something was missing.

She looked at Isabel, wondering if there was any place in particular that her mother would go to if she had the chance. She knew her mother had lived in more places than some people had their entire lifetime and she also knew that her mother had more secrets and enemies than she could count. Still, the question occupied her mind. Drake walked next to her and held her hand as his eyes drifted towards her. Drake's hand became cold and he jerked it away as he looked to the horizon.

"What is it, Drake?" Gwen asked. Everyone else looked to see Drake holding his hand. The scar was filled with ice. Her mind flashed back to the first couple of times it had happened years ago. He opened his mouth to speak but no words came out.

"You alright Drake?" Aiden asked. Drake looked at him, and the ice melted from the scar.

"I am now," Drake answered. "What happened?"

"The Sorcerer, though he's not physically able to attack us, will attack us in our hearts and our minds. All wars are won or lost in the heart, but the head is equally as deceptive. Cling to Lathon and you will find your strength," Aiden said. Drake nodded and they continued.

"It's been a while since that's happened," Gwen pointed out.

"I know. I wonder why after all this time it's just starting to give me problems again," Drake replied.

"Probably because you're trying to do something," Isabel said. Aiden nodded his agreement.

"Really?" Drake asked.

"Why would the Sorcerer need to attack you if you weren't trying to do something that might hinder him?" Morgrin asked. "If you are doing nothing, he would have no reason to try and get you. Take it as a compliment. The more you try to do good in this world, the more you're going to be attacked by one person or another."

"Makes sense to me," Thaddeus agreed. "However, my heart is uneasy just by the talk of this Sorcerer. I have heard what he did in the South. Is this the enemy that we rush to face?"

"Yes it is," Aiden answered. "He may have a different face or name, but at the heart of all of this, his spirit is living in the souls of people, corrupting their morals, and filling their hearts with lies that aren't even close to the truth."

“What kind of lies?” Diderus asked.

“Many different kinds, there are all the different religions of the world, that help pull people away,” Aiden started. “But at the heart of the issue, there are three lies that are more destructive than anything else. The first lie says that if you have a dark secret you can hide it. I can assure you that hiding it does no good, for eventually everything will be revealed. Plus it instills in a person both power and greed which can corrupt the soul faster than anything else.

“Secondly is the lie that you can handle it. Don’t get me wrong there are many things that you can handle, but there are some struggles that go too deep, that leave long scars on your heart.

It is in the midst of those struggles that you must get help from someone else, if only just so they can hold you accountable for your actions. A person's will can be very weak at times.

“And the second lie leads into the third one. The lie is that you can halt something and heal it without help from anyone. The third lie removes Lathon from the equation, even though he desperately wants to help make you the best person you can become.

These three lies are corrupting the world and destroying all that is good. That is why it is a good thing to have good close friends that you can talk to about anything and confide in.”

“We are not meant to do this life on our own,” Isabel said. “I would’ve never made it through all that I’ve endured without Lathon.” An arrow flew through the air and struck the ground a couple of feet in front of them. Seconds later another arrow was heard.

“Run!” Aiden urged them. They sprinted across the field. Diderus had no problem keeping up, despite the size difference between him and everyone else. Goblins were naturally fast. More arrows flew overhead.

Hooves thundered in the distance as twenty horsemen came riding over the top of the nearest hill. They turned around, and twenty more horsemen appeared behind them. The same was true to the South.

"Into the field!" Morgrin yelled. They all disappeared into a large cornfield, running as fast as they could until they broke free on the other side. They ran past several warning signs and sprinted towards the forest in the distance.

"They won't follow us into here!" Aiden exclaimed as they reached the tree line. The men pulled their horses to a stop when they reached the first warning sign.

"Why are they afraid of this place?" Diderus asked.

"Better question, what is this place?" Thaddeus asked.

"Fellow travelers and friends I would like to welcome you to Sheol," Aiden said, turning to face the forest in front of them. "I can assure you that in these hills are the darkest and most foul of creatures in all of the world. Keep your swords close and your wits about you."

Chapter 7

SHEOL

The horsemen vanished from view as they continued into the forest which was already strange from any other forest they had been in. The ground was made of rock, some of them loose pieces that were only the size of your hand, and some of them were so large it took a couple of minutes to walk over them. No dirt or vegetation could be seen on the ground, just dark solid rock, which echoed every sound they made. The trees were covered in leaves, yet not a sound was heard except their heartbeat.

Hours passed and the ground began to descend, slowly and gradually at first, but eventually becoming so steep that they couldn't go down it without a rope of some kind. The country became filled with steep ravines and cliffs and remnants of old towers and buildings.

"How far down does this go?" Drake asked.

"The entire nation is a large bowl," Aiden replied. "Enjoy the downhill while we can, eventually we'll be going uphill. Also don't drink the water in this nation. I've heard many strange stories and it all happens because they drank the water. So be cautious."

They continued, watching their surroundings carefully as the trees became closer together and the path continued to get steeper and more dangerous. They held onto the trees as they tried not to lose their footing on the steep side. Roots of the trees jutted out from the rocks. The roots were so large in places that they had to find alternate routes because they couldn't cut through them.

"What's the story behind this place?" Diderus asked. "Looks like a Goblin paradise with all of this rock."

"That's because it was a Goblin paradise," Isabel said. "It was once the Goblin's homeland. But eventually, it was deserted for whatever reason. As many scrolls as I've read, I was never able to completely discover what drove the Goblins out of here."

"Probably don't want to know," Thaddeus replied. "Let's just hope we get out of here with ease."

"I wouldn't count on it," Aiden replied. "Evil never rests. They are always at work trying to come up with evil plots and plans to capture and deceive people. There *are* things in this nation, but I will not speak of them unless I have to."

"Is there any hope in a place like this?" Gwen asked. "Is there even the slightest bit of hope that there will be something good?"

"There is now that we have entered," Aiden answered. "There is only hope if you don't give up and keep pushing forward. In both books, ancient stories, and the ways of Lathon, it's the people that keep on going, despite the overwhelming odds, that are remembered. Lathon continues to love this world even though there is much evil in it. So you should follow his example. You'll be seen as a symbol of courage and how a person should act when dark times come crashing in. No matter what, we will keep going and keep pressing forward, rushing into battle to do what must be done. The day we stop doing something is the day the Sorcerer wins."

They continued descending into the steep, unending bowl-shaped landscape they were in. Diderus took the lead, creating footholds in the steep rock, with his razor-sharp claws. They eventually came to a stop for the night and camped on the edge of a large cliff, which descended further than they could see. A sea of black and fog awaited them below as they each claimed their spot, some of them sleeping higher than others.

"No fires tonight," Aiden said. "We don't want to alert anyone to our presence."

"What is out there?" Gwen asked.

"Borags?" Drake suggested.

"There are Borags. Then there are other beasts we don't want to associate ourselves with," Aiden replied. They all lay down and closed their eyes hoping to fall asleep. Gwen's mind ran a hundred miles an hour, every sound registering in her brain until she felt as though she would go insane. Rustling was heard in the trees above, but when she opened her eyes she could see nothing. After a long while she fell asleep.

Distant methodical clicking echoed through the hills, alerting Drake and arousing him from the sleep he had been enjoying. He opened his eyes and looked down, still seeing the fog and the darkness that had been there the evening before.

He slowly crept from his spot next to Gwen and made his way to Aiden who stared into the fog, as if it held the answer to life's questions. Aiden said nothing to him and instead stared up at the trees. The distant clicking that had awoken Drake was heard again.

"What is that noise?" Drake asked.

"Someone knows we're here," Aiden answered. They both searched their surroundings. Aiden pointed up to the trees where a pair of beady eyes could barely be seen, glowing yellow in the darkness. The eyes vanished a moment later.

"What is that?" Drake asked.

"Hard to say," Aiden said. "Get the others up, we have to leave immediately. The tapping that was heard was likely a coded message alerting every creature to our presence." They moved back to the camp and woke the others motioning that they should be quiet. They left their camp and headed down a small narrow path.

Light nearly vanished, forcing them to walk in the darkness, despite the rising sun above the trees. Isabel pulled a torch out of her pack and it lit itself, allowing them to at least see a little bit in front of them. An hour later they finally reached the bottom of the ravine they were in. A glance to the left however told them that it descended even further if they chose to go that direction.

Buildings sat scattered here and there, abandoned and falling apart, with not a soul to be found anywhere. Rustling was heard in the trees far above them, not comforting them any. Aiden continued to lead the way, seeming to have no fear.

Eventually, they exited the ravine they had been stuck in and found themselves on a landing that was only large enough for all of them to stand. In front of them, a large gorge split the nation as far as the eye could see. Another staircase went down to the left, carved out of the rock.

"How are we going to get across?" Thaddeus asked. "I'm not sure I want to go all the way down. If something goes wrong it's that much further to go up."

"I agree," Aiden said. "If we have a rope and one of your arrows we should be able to cross it." Thaddeus pulled out one of his arrows and Morgrin pulled some rope out of his bag. They tied the rope to the end of the arrow and then handed it to Thaddeus who put it in his bow and pulled the drawstring back. Thaddeus aimed and released the arrow, which hit a tree on the other side. They tied the other end of the rope to a large bolder, creating a secure rope for them to hang onto.

"Who's first?" Aiden asked, smiling at all of them. Finally, Thaddeus came forward and grabbed onto the rope, pulling himself along the underside of the rope. Aiden went next, easily moving across the first half of the gap. The sound of a bowstring releasing reached their ears. Aiden heard it as well, twisting away as much as he could on the rope. The arrow grazed him in the side and he lost his grip, falling to the darkness below. Thaddeus also slipped off the rope, falling into the darkness below.

Drake cried out and quickly moved to the edge, looking down into the dark chasm, trying to see any sight of them, but was unable to see the bottom. Isabel threw her torch into the gorge, the light swallowed up by the looming darkness. Screeches cut through the silence around them. They drew their weapons.

Borags leaped down from above, while other creatures flooded out from the cracks between the rocks. They were tall and skinny. Their bones were visible and fangs came from their mouth. Their hands and feet were covered in sharp talons and claws. Their grey skin was covered with bloodstains and matted in fresh blood. Hair hung off them in clumps.

"What are these?!" Gwen cried.

"Dreeds!" Isabel yelled. "Now fight!"

Drake ducked the first sword and then spun around and struck the dreed from behind. The creature yelled out and then dropped his sword, lunging at Drake, claws and fangs ready to devour him.

Drake leapt back, avoiding the talons that had been coming at him. He tripped and fell as the dreed bounded over top of him. Drake kicked the creature backward. The dreed stumbled and fell over the edge, tumbling into the darkness below.

As quick as he got to his feet, Drake was knocked down onto the hard rock. Drake tried to move but was pinned down by a Borag. The Borag paused and stared into Drake's eyes. Drake lost all feeling in the hand where his scar was, as it turned to ice. Drake willed himself to remain conscious, trying to think of a way out of this.

"Drake!" Isabel cried.

A loud shout came from behind, as Nickolas came and swung his staff, beheading the creatures with one swing. Drake rolled out of the way as Nickolas swung the staff several more times. Drake watched in amazement and horror at the staff that Isabel had given him.

Drake grabbed his weapons, following Nickolas's gaze as they stared at the rope that spanned the valley. The rope was covered with dozens of Dreeds and Borags alike, all climbing their way across the gap.

Before Drake could think of a solution, Nickolas had already run up to the rope and slashed it with his staff. The foul creatures cried out as the rope fell loose. They crashed against the wall and then tumbled into the great pit below.

Drake swung his sword at another Borag that had attacked him. The Borag soon slumped to the ground, life fading from his eyes.

"How are we going to get across now?" Nickolas asked.

Drake's attention was momentarily diverted to the space above them. A single black featherless bird flew and nestled itself on one of the branches. Nickolas followed Drake's gaze, seeming to see the bird.

"What is that?"

"I don't know," Drake admitted, a sense of familiarity coming over him.

Suddenly, a loud explosion filled their sight and flames licked the air above them. Each of them took cover.

Drake looked up to see that Isabel had swung her sword at a tree that was standing near the gap. The tree had caught fire and fell over, now spanning the gap. Burning debris and branches plummeted to the ground far below.

Isabel sprang down from the rock she had been standing on and stuck her sword into the tree. The fire that had engulfed the tree went out, and any branches that were in their way, flew to the sides of the massive trunk, creating a railing for all of them.

"Only the power of Lathon could display such a miracle!" Nickolas exclaimed.

"Then let us not waste it!" Drake replied.

Gwen cried out. Drake and Nickolas both rushed to her as she fought two Dreeds who had pressed her against the rock. They quickly slew their unsuspecting enemies who joined the others on the ground.

Without another word, they rushed towards the bridge where everyone else was waiting. Shavrok was the last one to reach the bridge followed by dozens of Borags and Dreeds. They sprinted across and made it across the gap.

The moment that Shavrok's foot left the tree it caught fire again, fully engulfing anything on it in flames hotter than any Drake had ever felt. Within seconds the tree bridge crumbled and collapsed into the pit taking with it all their enemies.

"We have to go find Aiden and Thaddeus!" Diderus said, starting to move toward the edge of the crevice, staring into the darkness. The others followed his lead but froze seconds later as they heard the sound of rock breaking. They looked behind them and felt their hearts drop.

All around them, the rocks were being moved from their spot as more of the twisted creatures came to the surface. Dreeds rushed towards them and scores of Borags descended on them as well.

"Fight!" Isabel yelled, swinging at the first creature to reach them. Shavrok bounded in front of the group and grabbed one of the creatures, throwing him through the air. The creature crashed on the rocks, rolling and flipping wildly.

Gwen was knocked onto her back by a Dreed. Shavrok grabbed the Dreed by the leg and then wielded the beast like a club, using him to destroy and mangle any other creatures that rushed towards him. Snapping of bones could be heard every time the creatures were struck by Shavrok's force.

Drake pulled Gwen to her feet, watching as Shavrok continued to pummel enemies with the creature in his hand. Eventually, the creature in his hand became as limp as a fish, having so many broken bones that it was like swinging a dish rag.

"Drake! Shavrok!" Morgrin yelled. They both turned to see a narrow crevice they had discovered two hundred yards away. Nickolas stood at the opening, while everyone else had already entered. The three of them sprinted towards the opening, jumping over all the dead bodies and avoiding the smoldering remains as they entered the crevice, which was barely wide enough for Shavrok.

Screeches and cries were heard above them as their enemies clawed their way down the sides of the steep crevice. Their claws dug into the rock, sending small chucks of it down to meet them.

"Nickolas your staff!" Isabel yelled, holding her hand out.

Nickolas tossed it to Isabel who held it sideways for several seconds. It began to glow with a white light. She thrust it into the ground and the light became brighter than anything they had ever seen. It flooded into every crack and crevice, blinding all of them. The crevice to either side of them was leveled and the creatures were thrown through the air, their bodies decomposing before they even struck the ground. Their skeletal remains hit the rocks and exploded lighting the entire forest with fires.

When finally they were able to open their eyes and see again, Drake saw only Isabel standing on her feet, holding the staff in her hand. The staff had lost its glow and a deep crater had formed where it had struck the ground. The entire nation for at least a mile had been completely leveled by the shockwave and was now dotted with flames and smoke that rose into the deep forest.

"What kind of a staff is this?" Nickolas asked as Isabel handed him back the staff. She smiled, though nearly everyone had to stifle a laugh as her hair now stood on end.

"It was made by the Sorcerer, it's bound to have special abilities," Isabel said.

"Is she for real?" Nickolas asked Drake.

"Yes she is," Drake said, standing again.

"We should keep moving," Isabel said. "We might have defeated those who were attacking us, but I'm sure there's more on the way. The sooner we make it out of this nation, the better off we'll be."

"What about Aiden and Thaddeus?" Gwen asked.

"We must leave them for now," Isabel replied. "We'll wait for them once we escape this infernal nation."

"They can find their way out right?" Diderus asked. "There are other ways?"

"Dreeds live underground," Isabel said. "That means there are underground tunnels that should allow them to escape. It's a two-day march to the nearest edge of Sheol, and thankfully the staff made our traveling a lot easier. Hopefully, we don't have to use it again," Isabel said. The others fell silent as they followed Isabel through the nation. Drake looked back, first to the black featherless bird who took flight and went ahead of them and then at the crevice where Aiden and Thaddeus had fallen.

* * *

"Get up!" Aiden urged. Thaddeus was pulled from the rocks, his head throbbing endlessly. His bones were stiff as he tried to get them to move. The crevice in front of them was littered with dead and smoldering bodies as well as pieces of wood that burned.

Aiden led the way, moving into the crevice, with Thaddeus following close behind. Thaddeus stumbled for a little ways before finally managing to get his bearings back and continue at a normal pace. They walked through the deep crevice until nightfall, unable to go any further. They both collapsed on the rocks gathered what sticks they could find and built a fire.

"Quite a day!" Thaddeus exclaimed. Aiden just nodded. "I don't think I've ever seen that much action."

"Don't worry, you'll get used to it," Aiden said.

"I'm not so sure. Right about now I'd love to be back at home eating a nice home-cooked meal."

"When we get out of here you can go back home if you wish," Aiden said. "I would completely understand if you did. Not everyone is cut out for this life I lead."

"My heart is torn," Thaddeus replied. "I always wanted to be on an adventure, but I also would have liked to have stayed home. Have you ever experienced that feeling?"

"No. The heir of Lathon has no place to hang his hat because there is always something to be done. I never stop trying to help people no matter what the cost to myself. But I do understand your position and many people are like that."

"Is that a bad thing?" Thaddeus asked. Aiden shook his head.

"No. It's not bad to be divided, but neither will it bring you peace if you understand what I'm saying?"

"I'm not sure I do."

"When you look at and study all the people of the earth, you will find that there are four hearts that make up the masses of people. There are what I call hard hearts, those are people who know all the knowledge in their heads, but their heart doesn't feel anything. They're just going through the motions, much like the Farsees do.

"Next is the shallow heart. These are people who hear that Sherados have come, spring up, and are so excited, but they don't have deep roots and the first time they are persecuted, they desert and run away.

"Thirdly there is the divided heart. They are people who want to serve

Lathon and do great things for him but don't want to fully give up everything they have. It's a natural response of human nature, whose natural instinct is to grab everything that can be grabbed and cling to it. However, I have found that sometimes these people are the most miserable out of any of the groups because they are trying to serve two masters and it just doesn't work.

"And finally there is what I call a surrendered heart and that is people who drop everything and follow Lathon without looking back, no matter what happens to them. The surrendered heart is ideal for serving Lathon, but it is also quite rare. The divided heart is the most common I find. So the question is which one are you?"

"Is it possible for your heart to change over the years?"

"If it wasn't possible then why would I have come? Inside all of us is the longing to do something great, but only with Lathon is it possible to do the impossible. Only when you surrender everything you have for something greater can you even begin to understand what it really means to follow Lathon. He who gives up everything will have everything, he who clings to his life will lose it."

"How will you have everything if you give up everything?" Thaddeus asked.

"Because you will have far more in your heart than any of the other people, and that's what makes life so worth living. I'm not interested in winning people's allegiance by what they do for a living or by who they know. I'm interested in winning their heart, because only then will true change take place. They will reap courage, compassion, humility, dignity, love, and character. There is so much to be gained by choosing to risk it all to help other people."

"I wish I had a heart like that."

"You can," Aiden replied. "It just takes a little time and a little prayer to Lathon to help you become the person he wants you to be. Now let's get some sleep. We'll be off at first light." They both lay down on the rock and closed their eyes. Thaddeus struggled to fall asleep, his mind on fire with everything that Aiden had just told him. There was truth in all of it. Even if he didn't want to admit it. After a long while he fell asleep.

"How do we get out of this place?" Thaddeus asked. The night had passed too soon for the both of them and now the day was beginning to grow long. Weariness overcame them, but they continued.

"I imagine if we keep looking we'll find a staircase, or a cave system that will take us somewhere closer to where we want to go," Aiden answered.

"What were those creatures that attacked us?"

"Dreeds," Aiden said. "Mythical creatures of the underworld, at least according to ancient legend. Little does the world know they actually do exist. It's almost ironic in some ways that people turn real things into mythical ideas and convince themselves that they don't exist. There are more dark forces at work in this world than people are aware."

"There are?" Thaddeus asked.

"People become quite desensitized to things. It's like a squeaky door. After a while, you don't know it's there anymore, but it still squeaks."

"What else lives in this nation?" Thaddeus replied.

"Keep your eyes peeled for any kind of a cave. That might be our only way out of this hole." They searched the area they were in, finally discovering a staircase that descended further into the ground. They followed it, soon coming out on a carved path that wound and twisted much like the previous one had. This one was also accompanied by a massive wall of rock on each side. Thaddeus looked up as the path continued to descend seeing the tops of the trees so far above them.

Aiden stopped and put a hand on his sword, and motioned for Thaddeus to get into the shadows. They both did, as two Dreeds came up the path. They muttered in their own language, hauling a dead body behind them.

Thaddeus shifted and the sound echoed. They remained perfectly still as the Dreeds stopped and sniffed the air. After several long seconds, they dragged the dead body into the shadows. They stayed in their hiding spots for a couple of minutes before slowly inching back onto the path.

"If we're lucky they'll lead us right to the entrance to their underworld. Then we'll be able to pass through and come out on the other side," Aiden said. Thaddeus tried to control his nerves as they slowly inched forward. "Just try not to make too much noise."

They walked for another ten minutes, the path getting more twisted and confusing as they descended further into the nation. They carefully crept to a corner and peered around, seeing an arched gate and doorway. Torches were to either side of it, and strange markings were along the edge of the entrance. Thaddeus looked at the text for a moment and gave up trying to figure out what it meant.

"We found it," Aiden said. Running his hand along the runes and symbols that were along the edge. Thaddeus smiled weakly, feeling all the joy drain from him. "This is the entrance to the underworld."

"Are you sure?" Thaddeus asked. Aiden nodded pointing to the text.

"It's an ancient language long forgotten by the world," Aiden started. "It says, 'Here lies the gate of the dead world. The dead are contained and the living shall perish.' This is where we need to go."

"How?" Thaddeus asked. "It said the living shall perish."

"Yes, but the Sorcerer who forged this gate many years ago did not expect the heir of Lathon to be going through it. I do not fear death and death will not conquer me! The only thing we have to fear is the voice in our head that tells us we cannot do it." Aiden drew his sword.

"Do you fear death?" Aiden asked. Thaddeus trembled and tried to get his mind to focus.

"Yes, but I trust you." Thaddeus pulled out his knives, trying to hide his fear."

"We will make it out of here!" Aiden quietly exclaimed.

They moved closer to the gate which creaked and groaned as Aiden pushed it forward. The walls of the cave were filled with cobwebs as they moved further in. Aiden grabbed a torch from the wall and held his sword by his side as they descended yet further into the earth. The cave sloped downwards and eventually, all light except the torch was lost.

The air was musty and smelled of rotting flesh, threatening to make them gag as they pushed forward. Thaddeus briefly looked around at the cave that surrounded them, seeing strange drawings and markings on the walls that he couldn't begin to understand. Skeletal remains lay scattered along the floor and against the walls. Thaddeus shivered as a voice entered his head. It was soft, seductive, and beautiful all at the same time. Aiden continued forward as though he didn't hear it.

The world around him faded and changed, shapes seeming to melt out of other shapes until finally, his home village was standing in front of him. To his left was the Fair Havens, his hometown. To his right was a person he did not recognize. He was tall with no hair on his head. The person stared off into the distance and looked around as though he didn't know that Thaddeus was right beside him.

"Hello there," the man finally said, looking towards him.

Thaddeus froze.

"Hello," Thaddeus finally managed, struggling to form the words. From the town, he could hear music being played as though there was a festival of some kind. "Who are you?"

"I am whoever you want me to be. My name is Merderick. A lot of people don't like me, but that doesn't mean that I'm not good. Good after all is a point of view and some people tend to get that part pretty screwed up these days. They think that one way is better than all the rest."

"I'm not sure I understand," Thaddeus said. Merderick smiled.

"I'm sure you wouldn't. Not that it's your fault, but the people you've associated with lately have led you astray. You travel with Aiden, do you not?"

"I do."

"There is your problem. He's nothing more than a rebel out to make himself king of the world. He will rule over everything and destroy people like you. If I were you I would get out while you still can," Merderick said.

"He's the first one who ever accepted me, why would I get out?"

"Perhaps you should think about the very fact that he did accept you. I know you Thaddeus, you have a wonderful life. Why would a stranger whom you've barely known this past week come out of the blue and ask you to go on an adventure with him? He must have a different motive.

"He will say he doesn't, but he is lying. That's what he does, he lies and deceives the world telling them that their religions are worthless. He's the worthless one I can assure you. He's trying to kill you. Why else would he have led you to the underworld?"

"You know about the underworld?"

"I know more than the normal person could ever hope to know about the underworld," Merderick answered. "You're still in it as a matter of fact. I just have filled your vision so that I might warn you of the danger that awaits you if you continue to follow him. Do you think it was an accident that those Rantwarts found you in the mountains outside Avdatt? Do you think it was an accident that you were forced to go into Sheol in the first place? Furthermore, do you think that it was an accident that you and Aiden were separated from the rest of the group? Face the facts, he's leading you into the trap. He is the leader of the underworld and has many dark creatures that work for him. After he kills you he will destroy the world."

"I don't know," Thaddeus said. "In my head that makes sense, in my heart I don't believe it."

"Above all the heart is the most wicked and deceitful thing. Who's to say that it's telling you the truth?" Merderick asked. "Aiden's deceptive skills are far beyond anything that this world has ever seen. He can affect people's minds and ways of thinking until they no longer know right from wrong. When that happens he can do whatever he wishes and get away with it."

"Who are you anyway?" Thaddeus asked, pulling out one of his knives.

"I told you who I was. I am someone who can save you."

"No," Thaddeus said. Merderick shifted and looked at him knowingly. "I don't believe you. I don't know who you are, but I don't think you can help me."

“I’m the only one who can get you out of here.”

“I don’t think so,” Thaddeus said. Merderick stared at him.

“Very well then. Enjoy the rest of your journey!” Merderick and the vision that he had been in faded and a stabbing pain filled his side. He screamed out as he found himself staring up at the ceiling of the cave. Aiden was over top of him, torch in hand.

“You alright?” Aiden asked, helping him up. Thaddeus looked to his side where he had felt the pain, seeing no sign of any weapon striking him.

“I am now,” Thaddeus answered.

“Keep your head about you,” Aiden said. “Be careful of your thoughts. There are many evil forces at work in this part of the world. In here who knows what they’ll do.”

“Who is Merderick?” Thaddeus asked. Aiden looked back at him.

“He is the Sorcerer. He was killed, but his spirit moves in the world. Now come, we must keep on the move if we’re to make it out of here in any good amount of time.”

They fell silent, walking through the cave which appeared to get more rough and grim with every step that they took. The darkness was thicker. Signs of death were to either side of them as they picked their way through the tunnel.

“What kind of a place is this?” Thaddeus asked. Aiden didn’t reply as they continued forward and eventually came to a place where the cave rose up hundreds and hundreds of feet above them.

“It probably goes right to the surface,” Aiden said. The torchlight only reached so far, but at the distant top, they could see a small dot of light.

“We should keep moving,” Aiden said. They moved further down the hall, seeing more and more strange holes like those that had been in the shaft. They were about three feet wide and about five feet tall.

“What are these holes?” Thaddeus asked.

“Dwelling places of the dark creatures that live here,” Aiden replied. “Don’t look in any of them. They might be in there, they might not. I don’t want to find out.” They kept walking until finally, they heard something approaching from in front of them. Aiden stopped and they listened intently, noticing a new sound.

"Fire?" Thaddeus asked. Aiden nodded.

"Stay close and be ready to fight. If there is fire, then we are at the deepest and darkest place in Sheol. Actually in all the known world. Not even the Dwarves have tunneled so far." Aiden drew his sword and Thaddeus drew his knives as they walked closer to the location the sound was coming from.

The heat began to build as the path descended towards another large gate. Beyond the gate was darkness, but the heat and sound grew with every step they took. Screaming also joined in with the sound of the fire, sending chills up his spine.

"The chamber of Sorcerers," Aiden read, pointing to the markings around the arched doorway. Thaddeus shifted uncomfortably and tried to calm his nerves as Aiden pulled the gate open. Light flooded in their eyes, as the darkness was immediately gone, replaced instead with fire.

Thaddeus cringed but Aiden ran headlong into the hall of fire. Thaddeus found the courage to follow, his heart nearly beating out of his chest. The chamber was carved out of the rock, with thousands of holes as far as the eye could see. Dreeds and other unidentifiable creatures lingered in the area. Running from place to place, moving large piles of weapons.

The walls of rock were filled with fire, glowing like lava, unlike any heat Thaddeus had ever felt. Sweat formed. More fires and furnaces burned all around them adding to the heat. The ground sparked where it struck and a wall of flames rose and encircled them, preventing them from going any further.

"What's happening?" Thaddeus asked. The fire that surrounded them grew hotter and more uncomfortable. Fire rained from the top of the cavern, creating billowing flames as they struck the ground.

"How are we going to get out of this?" Thaddeus asked.

"Have faith!" Aiden yelled above the rumbling of the fire. The heat stung Thaddeus's skin. Aiden appeared to be just as calm as ever, which unnerved Thaddeus.

"I'm not sure how much longer I can take this heat!" Thaddeus yelled above the noise of the fire, which was growing in strength.

"This is where many people fall astray!" Aiden exclaimed. "They can't take the heat! I ask you again Thaddeus what kind of a heart do you have?"

Thaddeus fell silent. He had thought he had understood what Aiden was all about beforehand, but now he suddenly saw things so much differently than he had before. He knew what kind of a heart he had, and he also knew what kind of a heart he wanted to have.

Suddenly the heat didn't seem as bad, even though it moved closer to them and appeared to grow hotter. The blades of their swords glowed red from the intense heat, as though they were in a forge, but they were cool to their touch. Thaddeus looked at his skin in wonder and amazement, noticing that he wasn't sweating anymore.

Aiden thrust his sword into the fire. The fire recoiled and split in front of them. They sprinted through the opening expecting to find enemies waiting for them. Instead, the entire cavern was empty except for the fires that burned and one person who stood at the far end of the room.

The person stood in his place, his bald head shining in the firelight. Aiden slowed to a walk as the man came closer. Thaddeus recognized him immediately as Merderick from his vision.

"You have entered my domain?" Merderick asked. Aiden remained silent. "Does this mean that you surrender?"

"Hardly," Aiden answered. "I came here because it was necessary and you will let me pass!"

"I do not let anyone leave this place, surely you must know that."

"You could not kill me before, and you will not kill me now!" Aiden boomed. Merderick let a yell escape as the fire around him rushed to the spot in front of them. The fire took form into a massive Taruk, with three heads, each billowing in flames. Thaddeus looked behind the creature noticing that Merderick had gone.

Had he even been there in the first place?

"I do not fear you!" Aiden yelled. Thaddeus felt his heart stir. "I do not fear death! Death is powerful and dark only to those who cling to their life. If you want my life come and take it! You will not conquer the world."

"I'm afraid for your sake I will." They turned to the voice, seeing Merderick coming from behind them. He vanished a moment later and the three-headed creature opened its powerful jaws and spewed flames.

Thaddeus yelled out as they struck Aiden and knocked him twenty feet away. Thaddeus rushed to Aiden seeing that he wasn't breathing. Thaddeus felt his heart sink and then felt it soar as Aiden's eyes opened and he began breathing again. Aiden stood back to his feet, grabbing his sword and holding his arms out to each side.

The three-headed creature let a roar escape, flames circled all around them. A moment later the flames backtracked and struck the creature. Aiden held his sword up and then struck it into the ground.

The ground trembled and the entire cavern shook. Fire rained down from the ceiling far above. The three-headed Taruk roared and tried to attack again, but found that the fire only recoiled back at itself. Finally, the Taruk took flight and was lost into a distant tunnel.

A path cleared for them, the flames creating an archway for them to pass under. Thaddeus followed Aiden, looking into the flames, thinking for a moment he saw faces. Dark shapes moved and shifted in the fire, drilling fear into his soul.

"Don't delay!" Aiden yelled. "Run to those who need help!" Thaddeus followed Aiden as they came to a large iron gate. They exited the cavern of fire, finding themselves immersed in darkness. Cool air flooded over them, chilling them due to the drastic difference. They stood for several seconds, letting their eyes adjust to the lack of light.

Neither one of them spoke a word as Aiden led the way. A breeze swept through the chamber, bringing with it screams from somewhere in the darkness. Thaddeus and Aiden both stopped.

"What was that?" Thaddeus asked. Aiden looked around for a moment or two as if trying to figure it out for himself.

"A trap," Aiden said. Thaddeus gave him a strange look. "This is the hall of visions. The Sorcerer uses places like this to trap people. If they manage to make it out of the fire chamber then they are forever stuck in here trying to help people that don't exist. Trust me when I say we could search the chamber high and low for a lifetime and still wouldn't be able to find anything but the rock walls that surround us."

"So this Sorcerer? Is he stuck down here? Or is it possible for him to live on the surface?"

"He is stuck down here until someone can figure out how to free him from the chains that he's created," Aiden said. "Eventually someone with a corrupt heart will come along and figure out how to free him, and when that happens the world will be in trouble once again. That's when people like us shall rise up and give everything we have to save the people of the Earth."

"Are you sure that I'm the person you want traveling with you for this mission?" Thaddeus asked. "Who am I, but a fisherman?"

"In the world's eyes, you are just a fisherman and nothing else, but it's not the world's eyes that matter. Never believe the lies that you are someone who *can't* make a difference. Lathon looks down, sees a willing heart, and smiles, watching over you as you combat the evil that is loose in this world."

They continued walking, finding that the cave that they were in was slowly moving upwards, instilling hope that they would soon leave this place. The rocks became a light grey color like they once had been, instead of dark black.

The cave opened up above them until they were in a crevice like the one they had started in. Stairs were carved into the rock and they slowly began ascending towards the surface. It was another hour or two of climbing before they entered into the cool grey air. The trees were still above them and the forest was silent.

They stopped when they reached the surface and Aiden studied their surroundings, the edge of the forest loomed on the horizon but never seemed to get any closer as the rocks, cliffs, and gorges, slowed their travel.

Thaddeus trembled as they walked through an area with bones scattered everywhere, the rocks stained dark red with blood. They continued until the light faded, forcing them to stop for the night.

Thaddeus curled up on the rock but was unable to fall asleep. In all his life Thaddeus had never in his wildest dreams imagined that he would be doing anything like this. His life had changed in just a short while and it was all he could do to not smile. His mind quickly drifted to everyone else, wondering where they were.

* * *

Drake lay staring up at the stars. They had escaped Sheol, only barely, having to fend off another vicious attack by the tormented creatures that called Sheol home.

Now they lay in the cool grassy fields just outside the forest, talking and laughing and having a good time. The fire burned and Morgrin and him sat on the far side of the fire.

Drake let his eyes wander to Gwen and Isabel who sat talking and laughing on the other side of the fire. Drake couldn't hide a smile. There was something in Gwen lately that he hadn't seen before. It was a light in her eyes when she was with her mother. Isabel had always had a special quality, but the fact that Gwen seemed to be developing it as well scared him.

Isabel seemed to have more secrets than anyone he had ever met and he doubted he knew what half of them were. His mind wandered to the room in the basement where the items that had intrigued him still lay.

The memory was burned in his mind, like a parasite waiting to devour him. There had been something about the table that had called out to him. The impulse had been far stronger than he had ever felt in his entire life.

"You're quiet Drake," Morgrin said. Drake sat up and smiled weakly. "Got something on your mind?"

"Maybe."

"If you want to talk about it I'd listen."

"It's just a question really," Drake started. "Does it ever bother you that Isabel has so many secrets? You don't know everything about her do you?"

"Not even close. I know I love her more than anything, except Lathon of course," Morgrin said. "What can I say? I find her both intriguing and frustrating, beautiful and haunting, exciting and dangerous. There's so much I don't know about her and I probably never will, but you can bet I'll spend the rest of my life trying to find out!"

"She's very unusual to a lot of people," Drake said.

"And that's perhaps why I love her as much as I do. She is scorned and despised by everyone because of her past, yet she still chooses to love them. She isn't bitter towards her enemies, she wasn't even angry or bitter at Rohemir, even though most people would have been. In some ways, I feel she is closer to truly following Lathon than any of us ever could hope to be. She lives differently from everyone else and is still nice to talk to, not concerned about herself. Inspiring to me, to say the least."

"Can't say I thought of it like that before," Drake said. "I'm starting to think that Gwen has just as many secrets as Isabel does."

"You say that as if that's a bad thing."

"It just makes me uncomfortable."

"Love is patient Drake," Morgrin said. "Always remember that. We don't have to know everything right now. Love does not push anyone, but rather brings them to the point where they *can* tell you everything."

"I'm not sure I like it."

"Don't worry about it, Drake. As far as secrets are concerned, She probably has just as many as you do."

"What secrets do I have?"

"That remains to be seen doesn't it?" Morgrin asked. "We know the truth, because we're your friends, but to everyone else who doesn't know that you have no memory of your past, they likely think you're just being mysterious and that you don't trust them. You have a past but no one knows what it is. To me, it sounds like you have a lot of secrets."

"I wish I didn't," Drake replied. "I wish I was able to know my past and figure out everything for certain. If my parents hadn't died I might have been able to put some pieces of the puzzle together, but for the most part, even I am in the dark about my past."

"I wouldn't worry about it Drake, I'm sure you'll find out when the time is right. We're always learning about ourselves and no matter how much we learn there's always more."

"I won't argue that one," Drake replied. They fell silent for a few moments until their thoughts were interrupted by the sound of footsteps coming up alongside the camp. Drake grabbed his sword, and the others all did the same.

Two figures became visible and then came into the light, smiles stretching across their faces. Aiden and Thaddeus both stood in front of them, smiling. They looked worn and tired and appeared as though they had walked in the war zone.

"Good evening everyone!" Aiden exclaimed. They all put their weapons away and took their turns welcoming their lost friends.

"You look like you saw some action," Shavrok said, grinning.

"I think that's putting it mildly," Thaddeus replied, laughing. "I don't think I've ever come as close to death as I was."

"Have a seat, we still have some food left from supper," Nickolas said, moving to the pot over the fire and scooping out some of the soup that had been made. "We were starting to think that you were dead."

"Came close," Aiden said. "But we made it out alive and now we must press forward as fast as we can. The longer we linger the more likely it is that our enemies will be waiting for us, and trying to kill us. Where are we exactly?"

"With all the farmland around here, the best I can figure we're about twenty miles from the town of Edrei," Isabel answered.

"I take it Edrei's a farming community?" Diderus asked. Aiden nodded.

"It is also popular with travelers," Aiden started. "Usually, they look better than we currently are, so I'm not sure what kind of a welcome we will get. We will make for Edrei tomorrow, and stay the night. From there we'll find our course heading north I should think."

"North?" Nickolas asked. "Into the Dead Mountains? Why on earth would we want to go in there? They say any who enter those mountains never come out."

"Indeed that's what they say," Aiden said. "But unknown to you, there has been someone following us. They won't likely follow us into the mountains due to the myths and legends. We'll be relatively safe in there."

"He is right about that," Isabel said. "But I warn that there are many dark things in the mountains."

"Comforting," Thaddeus remarked.

"Don't worry, I do know a couple of people in the dead mountains."

"Of course you do," Drake replied, laughing. "How do you know people in the Dead Mountains?"

"After the death of my parents, I lived in the Dead Mountains for many years," Isabel said. Trust me when I say there are many dark things in the mountains. Great place to disappear though. We should be able to go undetected."

"That settles it then," Aiden said. "We will leave at first light tomorrow morning."

They said nothing else. Drake eventually laid down next to Gwen, his eyes feverishly scanning the horizon, unable to see anyone following them as Aiden had said there was.

Chapter 8

ISADON, AARON & SAUL

The Dead Mountains waited to their north as they traveled towards Edrei. The mountains were brown, covered with dead vegetation and fog creating an aurora of mystery that both excited and terrified Drake. A town appeared on the horizon, chills swept through Drake as he looked at it.

"What's wrong?" Gwen asked. He looked at Gwen noticing that she seemed to have noticed that he was paying more attention now.

"Is this Edrei," Drake asked.

"Yes it is," Aiden answered.

"I recognize this town," Drake said.

"You recognize it?" Gwen questioned.

"I've been here before."

"You have?" Morgrin asked.

"It seems familiar to me."

"Maybe, you are finally starting to remember your past," Aiden suggested.

Drake's heart cried out for the answers as they neared and then entered the small town. The buildings were all built out of logs and looked old and weathered. The locals watched them with suspicious eyes. Disapproval already evident in the atmosphere of the town. At the center of the town, they found a small inn and tavern. They entered and were swallowed into the crowd as they pushed their way to the front desk.

"The owner's name is Isadon," Drake said, only in a whisper loud enough for Gwen to hear.

"We would like accommodations for the night if you have any available," Aiden asked the man at the front desk.

"We have some available," the man replied. "We rarely get travelers like yourself in here, especially in your shape. I can get you all separate rooms, or a room together. Your choice."

"Together please," Aiden replied.

"You have money?" the man asked. Nickolas pulled a bag of coins from his pocket and set them on the counter. The man's eyes went wide when he opened the bag.

"Is that enough?" Nickolas asked.

"That's more than enough, I'll throw in meals and hot bath water, free, for the price you paid."

"Thank you," Aiden said. The man picked up a key from underneath the counter. "You are in room five, I'll have some of my people prepare your baths. If there's anything you need just give me a shout. My name is Isadon."

"A pleasure to meet you," Aiden said shaking Isadon's hand. They left the bustling dining hall and found their room. True to his word, Isadon, sent for more than enough hot water. It was carried in large clay jars and then poured into a large tub where they all took their turn getting clean. Drake was silent almost the entire time as he pondered everything that was happening.

Once they were all cleaned up and put together, they returned to the dining hall. Which now had music piping through it. People happily danced on a large portion of the floor that had been cleared on the far side.

They were shown to a large table right in the center and Isadon himself, came and took their order, giving many orders for their drinks to be refilled as many times as they wanted.

The food was ready and brought out to them. They thanked Isadon and dropped a couple more coins in his hand as thanks. They gave thanks and then ate, receiving occasional stares from the locals who seemed to look at them funny. Shavrok put down his plate looking at it strangely.

"What's wrong?" Isabel asked.

"This is what they call a portion of food?" Shavrok asked, looking at all their plates which were still fairly full. "That doesn't even begin to satisfy the hunger of a Gog, especially after such a long journey."

"Something tells me they're not used to having Gogs dine with them," Nickolas said. The others smiled.

"If you're still hungry order some more," Aiden suggested. Shavrok nodded his approval and stood up, shoving the chair into the table behind him. Shavrok carefully pushed his way through the crowds and up to the front of the bar once again.

A minute later, Shavrok returned with a large serving tray, which was filled to near overflowing with chicken wings. Shavrok sat down smiling widely.

"Now this is a Gog-sized portion!" Shavrok exclaimed, with a laugh.

"I'm almost afraid to ask how many are on that tray," Diderus said.

"Eat well tonight, because it might be the best meal that we have for a very long time. This is only the beginning of our travels," Aiden told them.

"Hopefully we don't come as close to death as we did in Sheol," Thaddeus said.

"I wouldn't count on it," Drake said. "We always seem to find trouble." They all chuckled.

Drake looked over the people, noticing two cloaked figures standing in the corner. They both held glasses of ale and talked lightly. One of them looked his way, drilling him with a stare.

Determined to ignore them he turned to look at Gwen. "The music in here is quite nice, would my wife like to dance?"

"She would love to!" Gwen answered. They joined the other couples enjoying the music and quickly catching onto the rhythm and dance.

"You're doing much better at this kind of dancing than I am!" Gwen exclaimed happily. Drake smiled at the compliment but didn't say anything else.

He remembered this dance.

Soon Morgrin and Isabel also joined, and for a moment it seemed like the world was perfect. When the music finally ended, a great shout went through the crowd and the music started again. The four of them excused themselves and made their way back to their seats.

"I'm going to get a refill!" Drake cried above the music. The others all nodded and Drake moved to the large bar. Drake gave the glass to the bartender who went to the back room to fill it.

Drake nearly jumped when he noticed one of the cloaked figures that had been watching him, was now sitting on the chair next to him. His cloak was still up, but Drake could see he had a beard that was light brown.

"Mr. Thomas. I was wondering when you'd be making your way back up here."

The man's voice was deep and if he was standing, he would've been as tall as Drake. He stared ahead, taking a drink from his cup.

"You were?" Drake asked. The man shook his head and took another drink.

"I would advise against going back," the man said.

"Who are you?" Drake asked. The man looked towards him, his eyes were barely visible through the dark shadows that fell across his face.

"You don't know?" the man asked. Drake shook his head. "Perhaps, then, this is divine intervention. I need to speak with you."

"I'm afraid I can't. I have to get back to my friends."

"Trust me, your friends will understand!" The man put his drink down on the table. A loud commotion was heard from behind them. Drake turned to see the other cloaked figure making a fool of himself, clearly drunk. The man next to him grabbed Drake by the arm and pulled him through the crowd. A moment later he was shoved inside a darkened room lit by a single lantern.

"Who are you?" Drake asked.

"It's best if we don't reveal ourselves. What do you know of the northern lands? Specifically the lands east of here?" Drake hesitated. The man was armed only with a knife. For a moment Drake considered taking him out but decided against it. "What do you know?"

"Nothing. Except that we are traveling there."

"Where exactly are you going?"

"Tell me your name and I might be a little more forthcoming!" Drake shifted his hand to his sword, hoping to intimidate his opponent if he could. The man seemed unaffected.

"My name is Aaron. Outside, making a fool of himself is my brother Jacob. Do those names sound familiar to you?"

"No," Drake replied.

"You know how long we've searched for you? We've been called everything under the sun thinking that you still existed."

"I'm so confused. What are you talking about?"

"The woman with you? The auburn-haired beauty? Who is she?"

"She's my wife."

"How long have you been married?"

"What business-"

"Answer the question! How long have you known each other?" Aaron yelled. The sound of his voice was covered by the commotion in the bar.

"Six years, I think. Married for five." The man thought for a moment, pacing in front of him. After a couple of moments, the man smiled and then began to laugh. He rushed up and embraced Drake. Drake had to restrain himself from grabbing his sword. Confusion swarmed over him.

"You have my sincere apologies, my friend, for holding you like this. You can go as you wish." Aaron moved to the side of the door and motioned to it. Drake remained where he was, too confused to move.

"I don't understand."

"You've just made me the happiest I've been in a long, long time. My brother and I are not crazy! Though we might never convince the others of that, at least now my brother and I can live in peace knowing that we have learned the truth for ourselves."

"The others?" Drake asked. "Who?"

"Don't worry about it. Go and continue on your journey. My brother and I have our own to make, as do all who live on this green earth." Drake hesitantly stood up and moved to the door, watching Aaron carefully.

He made no move to attack Drake or do anything that might harm him. His hood had come down and now he could see light brown hair and pointed ears. His face was hard and his hands were calloused. Drake reached for the handle.

"Can I ask one question?" Drake asked. Aaron shifted.

"Technically you've already asked one question, and I answered it. However, I guess it's only fair to let you ask one more."

"Have we met in the past?" Drake asked. Aaron shifted uncomfortably and looked away, staring out the window.

"I think Jacob's getting tired of acting like a fool." Drake started to object but thought better of it when Aaron shot him a look. Drake slipped out of the room and let the door close behind him. The entire hall was still a chaotic scene as Drake slipped back to the counter and grabbed the drink that the bartender had gotten for him.

Drake made his way back to the table where the others were sitting, trying to stifle a laugh, even though the rest of the bar was caught up in a skirmish. Shavrok still sat eating his food as though nothing was out of the ordinary. Drake watched as the man, apparently named Jacob escaped the bar and vanished into the darkness.

"I was wondering if you were ever coming back," Gwen said, a playful smile on her face. "Where did the bartender have to go to get your drink?"

"Apparently, a very long ways away," Drake answered. Two horses in a full run, galloped past the window. Drake assumed the riders were Aaron and Jacob, who once again were hidden in their cloaks.

Drake slipped further and further into his thoughts, trying to solve the mysteries the night had presented. His heart and his mind were at war with each other as each tried to come up with possible explanations for everything that had transpired.

"Can I buy you people a drink? You look like you could use one right about now." An elf stood at their table, tall with shorter brown hair.

"No, I don't think we could use any drinks, but you are most welcome to join us if you wish," Aiden said. The man pulled up a chair.

"Don't mind if I do."

"Do you have a name, or do you just go around buying drinks for random travelers?" Thaddeus asked. The man smiled.

"Forgive my manners, I have done much traveling myself, and notice fellow travelers when I see them. My name is Saul. I would ask all of your names but I have a feeling that might take a while." They laughed.

"In that case, I'll introduce myself and *if* the others wish to introduce themselves then they may do so. My name is Aiden."

"A pleasure to meet you," Saul replied shaking his hand.

"Likewise. What kind of traveling brings you out this way?" Isabel asked.

"I'm kind of a jack of all trades, and I love to travel so I've always figured, why not just go from place to place doing job to job? It suits me well and I can make a pretty decent living at it. It's probably not a life just anyone could lead, but I enjoy it."

"It's always a good thing to do what you enjoy," Isabel said. "It makes your life a whole lot easier. If you're happier it's likely to show on the outside as well as the inside."

"I'm sure that's true," Saul replied, glancing around the bar for a moment. "Now, I must say, out of all the traveling fellowships I've seen, you are probably the most diverse I've come across. What brings you up this way?"

"Just taking a little trip," Aiden said. "You are welcome to join us if you wish. We're headed for Goshen. Are you familiar with the nation?"

"Perhaps," Saul admitted. "Unfortunately I have a job I've got to get to. I do appreciate the offer though, and I must say I'm a little thrown off by it. I'm a stranger to you and yet you offer for me to come along? That is a rare thing these days. Did you mean it or were you just being polite?"

"I wouldn't have offered it if I hadn't meant it," Aiden said. "I don't do anything by accident or just to satisfy people. The approval of people is not my main concern."

"Peculiar," Saul commented. "Most of the world is very consumed with status and pleasing others."

"Which is why the world is in the shape it's in," Aiden said. Drake watched and listened intently. Something about this conversation wasn't right.

Saul seemed to take more of an interest. "In my book, the first shall be last and the last shall be first. If you want to be great, first you must be a servant." Silence followed for a moment.

"Not too many believe in that, especially the Farsees if you take my meaning," Saul said after a moment.

"I know exactly what you mean and I agree with you!" Aiden exclaimed. "It is rather annoying to me, people who put on a false face for everyone to see. When people really find out who you are it creates a lack of trust you know?"

"I suppose I do," Saul admitted. "I guess to some extent we all have done that at times in our lives."

"Yes, but that doesn't make it right," Aiden said. "Our group of travelers here is wholly devoted to Lathon and making sure our lives are honoring him in every way."

"Lathon? The ancient religion that the Farsees claim to be a part of? I thought that only applied to Elvish folk."

"The Farsees have made many rules that don't apply," Nickolas said. "I would know, I used to be one of them. The heart matters more than the body. As long as you dedicate yourself to Lathon and do all you can to please him then you're good."

"I've never heard it like that before," Saul said. "The Farsees seem to hate any who don't fit into their perfect little mold."

"Indeed," Aiden said. "And that is one of the most infuriating things for me. I've come to cast aside the old tradition. Show the people what it's *supposed* to be like because they've been led astray."

"I can imagine with a mission like that you're not the most popular person with the Farsees," Saul said. Drake pondered his words, suspecting that Saul was here for some other purpose than just talking.

"If pleasing people were my goal, I would not be Lathon's servant."

"Couldn't you do both?" Saul asked. "Please people and be Lathon's servant?"

"Have you ever tried to serve two masters?" Aiden asked. "Done one thing, but also wanted to do another? If you have, you will find only that it causes you more pain and heartache than it's worth. It's not possible to serve both fire and water."

Saul didn't speak for a moment. "You are interesting folk. I hear it from good authority that the Farsees are looking for you."

"I'm sure they are," Nickolas said.

"Aren't you afraid of what they might do to you?" Saul asked. They all shook their heads.

"What can they do to us?" Morgrin asked. "They could imprison us, they could kill us, but even if we are imprisoned, we can still live our lives in a way that people see a difference and are curious."

"It seems though we just met, I'm beginning to agree with you and not the Farsees. It was a pleasure to have met you." Saul stood to leave.

"And a pleasure to meet you," Aiden said shaking his hand. "Perhaps we will meet again."

"I'm sure of it," Saul said, with a smile. "Good night everyone." Saul left the table and then made his way out into the night walking off to the left. Drake lost himself in thought and then looked to Aiden.

"We will be seeing him again," Aiden said.

"How can you be sure?" Gwen asked.

"He's Aiden that's how he's sure," Shavrok replied. They nodded their approval and the time went by faster than they would have liked. Weariness overtook them and they made their way to their room where they all grabbed a place on the floor or wherever there was room. They talked lightly for a few minutes and one by one fell asleep. Drake slipped into his dreams, watching them play before his eyes. The dreams seemed familiar.

He stood looking down at a village. The dream changed and eventually, it played back the events of the night. The two men who had wanted to talk to him. His heart stirred as he studied the faces in his dream.

He had seen them before.

* * *

"Are we liars or not?" Jacob asked, dismounting his horse. Aaron dismounted his horse and then grabbed some wood from the saddlebags.

"We are not liars, though I still don't think anyone would believe us."

"Only one person would, and we have a long ways to get there," Jacob pointed out.

"The point is, he hadn't met his wife at the time he ran away," Aaron said. "There was no lie in his eyes. Now that I've met him, I'm sure I've heard of him someplace else other than in the past."

"Probably the Mezutor," Jacob said. "That's where I first heard the name Drake Thomas. I've certainly never met anyone else with that name!" They both chuckled.

"If he was truly trying to run away he would've adopted a new name."

"Was he the same that he was before? Drake I mean. Or was he much changed?"

Aaron nodded.

"Changed? Yes, but not in a bad way," Aaron concluded. "Granted, kidnapping a person probably isn't the best way to judge anyone's character. He is now just like he was, a kind person with a big heart. Did you take notice of who he was traveling with?"

"Which one?" Jacob asked. "Forgive me, I was busy making a fool of myself, I didn't get a chance to see who was with them."

"Two people specifically caught my eye. One was a sorceress, whose name escaped me at the moment. She was an Elvish woman with blond hair. I heard them mention they were heading into the Dead Mountains. I don't know much, but I know if she's with them they'll be safe. However, the one I was excited to see him with was Aiden."

"The Aiden we've heard so much about? How did I miss that one?" They both laughed.

"Well you were a little preoccupied with the scene you were making," Aaron pointed out. They both laughed. "Aiden's a good soul, better than any I've ever come across. I've heard a lot about him, and of course, it all depends on who you talk to whether it's good feedback or bad feedback."

"The world's a bit screwed up these days. Bad has suddenly become good and the line between black and white has turned grey. I wonder just how the world got the way it is? It's certainly not the way Lathon intended it to be!"

"If there was to be any specific reason why our world is the way it is I would say it has to do with pride and power."

"Pride can be the defeat of every man. It blinds him to all that is corrupt in himself and from there, it spills out into the world. How though does power fall into it? I can't see how having power would be a bad thing."

"I didn't say it was altogether bad," Aaron corrected. "I implied that it could be bad. Power is great, and inside all of us I feel there is a great desire to be powerful, some to do good and some to do whatever they wish, but what does one have to focus on to get the power they desire? Greed and pride run hand in hand, and both contribute to power in their own seductive ways."

"Part of me wishes I never get to be powerful," Jacob said. "Nor any of us."

"All we have to remind ourselves is that we are not the high and mighty people we think we are. Compared to Lathon, who created everything from nothing…we are nothing. We are mere specks in the grand scheme of things, a grain of sand on a beach. Yet, Lathon still cares about us and will send an heir to save us."

"*Has* sent an heir. Have you heard the news that has slowly drifted up from the south?"

"Aye. Do you think Aiden is Sherados?" Jacob bowed his head for a moment, searching his heart. He looked up a new light in his eyes.

"I don't think he is Sherados. I *believe* he is Sherados." They both smiled.

"Me too," Jacob replied. "Aiden is Sherados."

"What now?" Jacob asked.

"First light tomorrow we'll make for Avdatt and see what we can accomplish there.

Chapter 9

INTO THE MOUNTAINS

"You are quiet this morning," Drake said. Nickolas took a deep breath and stood up from the floor.

"Something about last night isn't sitting right with me."

"What do you mean?" Drake asked.

"That person we talked to? I'm sure I've seen him somewhere else."

"Do you have any idea where you might have seen him before?"

"No," Nickolas answered. "Not the slightest clue."

They joined the company that was waiting for them as the morning sun flooded into the town. The mountains to the north beckoned to them and sent fear into Drake.

They soon left the village behind them, walking on a small path that slowly wound its way around dozens and dozens of small farms. Drake envied them for a moment, being able to live in one place and not have to worry about anything or go on any adventures.

Nickolas still checked over their shoulders every now and then, seeming to be on edge. If anyone had reason to be on edge it would be Drake. He had been temporarily kidnapped by a stranger. Drake replayed the conversation through his head again and again.

The hours passed and the Dead Mountains grew taller and more ominous in front of them. Their peaks were grey and covered in brown as the rest of the mountains were. The dead vegetation crumbled when they brushed up against it and crunched beneath their feet with every step that they took. Not a single animal was heard anywhere in the mountain range. Not even the wind moved through the area, just the sound of their breathing and their footsteps echoed through the mountainside.

"What kind of things are in these mountains?" Drake asked.

"Not likely things that we want to think about," Aiden said. "There are many dark things in these mountains but don't worry, I think we're safe enough for the moment."

"How can you be sure?" Thaddeus asked. "What if we're being hunted right now?"

"Then we'll have to fight," Aiden said. "Most of what is dark and evil in these mountains lies beneath the mountains, not on top."

"Beneath the mountains?" Nickolas asked.

"He's right," Isabel said. "Under the mountain live large numbers of Rantwarts, similar to the Dreeds. They have large furnaces for forging weapons and other things. That's why it's so hot in these mountains and that's why all the vegetation is dead. They've been cooked alive by the heat that comes from the mountains. If you touched the rock with your bare hand you could feel the heat. Drake reached down and touched his hand to a rock, pulling it away after a few seconds. It was hot.

"Didn't you say you grew up in these mountains?" Diderus asked. Isabel nodded.

"After my parents died I lived here with a woman who took me in. Haven't spoken to her in years."

"Why not?" Morgrin asked.

"Lost touch. I came back on a couple of different occasions and tried to find her but I was unable to find her house. These mountains, if you'll notice, are all completely identical. Every rock, every crevice, is the same on one mountain as it is on the next. Though they might sit in different directions, they are all the same."

"That's strange," Gwen said. They all nodded in agreement.

"There are many strange things in this world. These mountains house unthinkable evil, and great perils, the likes of which even I've never seen, but

I'm sure we will at some point," Isabel assured. "Sound carries through here the same as it did through Grimdor. Be careful of how much noise we make. If someone's following us then we might just give ourselves away," Isabel advised.

hey didn't speak for three hours as they began ascending one of the tall mountains in front of them. They climbed higher and higher, the heat growing more and more immense.

"What kind of fog is this?" Nickolas asked. "It seems thicker, but it isn't moist like fog usually is."

"It's an unusual kind of smoke. Doesn't burn the eyes and acts more like fog," Isabel answered. "I've never been able to figure out exactly what it is made of. However, I know where it comes from." They walked further up the mountain until suddenly the smoke disappeared from their view and they could see a hundred miles in every direction. In between the mountains and in the deep valleys, they could see the smoke.

They looked in wonder as the mountain tops glistened in the sunlight which was as clear as day. The mountains in the distance let off plumes of the smoke which then drifted down and filled the valleys. Drake tried to wrap his mind around what he was seeing and to understand it but was unable. Isabel watched their faces in amusement.

"It's quite fantastic isn't it?" Isabel asked. They just stared into the horizon, speechless.

"I've never seen anything like it," Gwen said. "Is that a city I see?"

"Ah yes!" Isabel exclaimed. "The all-famous Maurivian Tower! The only city in these mountains you'll find above the mountain. It was built for the prince of the great King Hemold in the days of old. Though, Ironically the prince perished in the battle of Tinev three years before it was completed. It is a beautiful city, even if it's full of filth."

"It looks beautiful, I guess growing up here wouldn't have been that bad after all" Gwen said. They all nodded their agreement.

"Yes it's quite beautiful, but it's also a lie," Isabel said, stooping down to the ground. Drake watched as her hand neared the surface of the rock, noticing that something seemed to move when her hand neared it. She reached down and grabbed a handful of the material and held it up for them to see. Drake took it in his hands.

"Metal?" Drake asked, showing the metal shavings to everyone else. "This is metal?"

"The mountains are real, but this spectacular view is nothing more than metal shavings covering everything. They get blown out of the mountain tops, almost like a volcano erupting. The smoke drifts down and these get thrown up into the air and then lazily float onto the mountain tops. This is the only proof that I have for supporting my theory that the Rantwarts are forging weapons beneath the mountains."

"Have you ever thought of trying to get below the mountains and see if your suspicions are right or not?" Shavrok asked.

"It would take more time than I have to do it," Isabel said.

"Why's that?" Drake asked.

"They're Rantwarts Drake," Isabel said. "Not much of them is known in the world outside of the mountains, but Rantwarts can create things to look real when in fact you're looking at nothing more than open space. If they have any bridges or buildings beneath the mountains that are not real, you could easily walk to your death or right into a trap. My mentor, last I knew, was trying to map the world beneath the mountains but I don't know if she was ever successful or not."

"There are always dark forces at work, trying to hinder those who wish to do good. It's too bad so many people are afraid of these mountains. If they saw this they might not be so scared of them," Morgrin said.

"Indeed," Aiden started. "But the smoke drifts down and creates the vision that people have of these mountains. People are usually afraid to go within twenty miles of them for that very reason. It is in places like this that Men's courage runs out and evil is allowed to run free, to plot and plan as they wish. This is more of a threat than the Sorcerer in physical form ever would be."

"Why's that?" Diderus asked.

"Because he can go unchallenged here," Aiden answered. "Who would stop him? This is the Sorcerer's plan and I do not doubt that his spirit is finding new power and soon will be ready to make his war."

"I thought he already made his war?" Gwen asked.

"Evil never rests. With me being here, he realizes that the people of the world are not as weak as he hoped. He is building and building. The thought of me leading nations into battle unnerves him," Aiden said. "And so it should."

Silence overtook them for a moment. They watched as another of the great mountains spewed out its smoke and metal shavings. The metal glistened in the air, looking like snow as it fell.

"We should go," Isabel said, studying a map she had brought with them. "We need to head east and stay off the mountain tops. If there is anyone that would see us it'll be on top of the mountains."

"I doubt there are that many people in the mountains," Thaddeus said. "Who would want to live here?"

"Those who don't wish to be found," Isabel replied. They headed down the mountain and back into the fog like they had before, finding that their hopes were pulled away from them. They walked in silence, each mindlessly following Isabel and Aiden who led the way.

The path was rough, carved into the mountains. They passed by several clearings in the mountainside where remnants of large buildings still stood, their ghostly towers reaching into the foggy air. They skirted those areas, deciding they didn't want to risk it in case anyone was in the mountains.

The time passed and Drake began to feel as though they were running in circles. He brought the subject up but was quickly reminded that every mountain looked the same. The longer they traveled the more Drake noticed that was true. The fog disappeared at the same level, the trees grew or leaned in the same direction, and even a small stream that had been flowing down the first mountain flowed down any other mountain they came to, and along the same natural rock formations.

"Why do I feel as though a part of me belongs in these mountains?" Diderus asked.

"Goblins do usually live in rocky mountainous areas," Drake suggested.

"I know that, but I don't think that's the reason," Diderus said.

"You feel that way because a part of you does dwell in these mountains," Aiden said. Drake was taken aback by the certainty in Aiden's voice. "These mountains are very much where we are at some point in our life. We are lost, and confused, and can't help ourselves out of the situation we've gotten into. We are helpless. In the dark mountains of our hearts, we travel in circles, to destinations that lead nowhere. Then you find the truth and it becomes your map and your lifeline. It saves you and brings you to the top of the mountains to show you where you are and where you need to go. It shows you the big picture."

"Lathon," Diderus answered. Aiden and the others all nodded.

"Lathon," Aiden said. "What people often forget is that Lathon isn't just a set of rules to follow. It's a choice and a lifestyle. Many will not grasp this concept and will deliberately defy Lathon and expect everything to be alright. They shipwreck their faith and find themselves once again stranded in the dark mountains of their hearts. Following Lathon is not easy. It's a choice."

"As much as I wish I could deny what you said, it is the truth," Diderus replied. "I have been a tax collector for many years and I've never found the purpose in life. It didn't matter how much I had it was never enough. I'm coming to realize that the road I was on would have led me to my death."

"All roads on this earth lead to death," Aiden said. "But it depends on how much you cling to this earth as to whether it will hurt or not. For those who follow Lathon, there is more after death. There is more to life, a life full of serving and love. With it comes purpose and compassion, which can save the world. With all other roads, it leaves Lathon-sized holes that can never be filled by the things of this world. In the absence, greed and lust take hold and send you into the endless pit of selfishness."

"I want to have a life of purpose and of giving. It's just something I'm not used to," Diderus stated.

Aiden smiled. "Ignore all the voices that say you will never amount to anything or you're doing the wrong thing. Serving others in love is never wrong. Only by serving others will people see that you are not as hypocritical as some people in the world."

They continued, growing weary with each step they took. They traveled through the great mountains, slowly moving over the path that had started to twist in unpredictable patterns.

Though the path had started pretty straight and narrow, it now had several branches that went off to either side every now and then. Drake looked up to where the path went only able to do so from a distance. When he looked he thought he could see more ruins, just like there had been on the previous mountain.

"You are quiet," Drake said to Gwen. They now walked at the back of the company, only a couple of feet behind Shavrok.

"Just thinking," Gwen replied.

"What about?"

"I think my mother's hiding something from me."

"I know she might be full of secrets, but I'm sure she wouldn't keep anything from you."

"What if she was?"

"You're not considering this as a serious possibility, are you? What's making you come to this conclusion all of a sudden?"

"I don't know Drake!" Gwen exclaimed as quietly as she could. "I've had this feeling for a long time, I just didn't know how to approach her about it. She comes and she goes, vanishes for months at a time, knows something about everything, and doesn't usually offer any explanation for how she knows it. I'm starting to lose my trust in her a little bit."

"I don't see what the big deal is," Drake said. "Are you saying she might be a villain?" Shavrok looked back and dropped back even with them.

"I don't know what I'm saying, all I know is she's hiding something!"

"If I may offer my opinion on this matter, I think it might help you out some," Shavrok said. Gwen nodded. "The Gogs have known your mother for a very long time, I think the first time we met her was after she had given birth to you. Never in our long history have we found a reason to not trust her. She has a tremendous heart and a tremendous amount of secrets, but so do the Gogs. I do know that your mother only tells things when it is important and when you need to know it. Not before, and not everything. Over the years I've come to think that she does this so that we aren't surprised by what she tells us."

"How does that make sense? If she told me her secrets now I would believe her."

"I don't think you would," Shavrok countered. "Think back to when you learned that she was your mother. What did you feel?"

"I believed her and I felt loved."

"That's right. Now, if she had shown up in Fiori one day and told you she was your mother and told you everything she knew…would you have believed her?"

"No. I would've thought she was lying."

"You see, trust your mother. When it's time for you to learn more of her secrets I'm sure she'll tell you." Gwen fell silent again as they continued walking. Drake could understand her frustration but he didn't mention it again. He was starting to feel as if he had nearly as many secrets as Isabel, the only difference was he didn't know what his were.

"We should stop here for the night!" Isabel announced. They stopped and put their bags on the ground. "We don't want to head into the next mountain anywhere near nightfall."

"I'm almost afraid to ask why," Morgrin asked.

"It'll be a lot safer if we don't. Many years ago I was almost killed on the next mountain. I'd like to go around it all together."

"The mountain looks the same as all the others, what could possibly be so bad about it?" Gwen asked.

"Trust me, it's nothing we want to mess with," Isabel said not offering any more information. Gwen threw her pack on the ground and Drake knew she was upset that Isabel hadn't told them more.

"Can we start a fire?" Gwen snapped.

"Yes, the fog that surrounds us should hide any light and smoke it may give off," Aiden said. A couple of them immediately went off into the mountains to find something burnable but were careful not to wander too far off and never by themselves. Soon everyone returned with brush and some wood they had been able to find. It lit easily enough and soon they had a roaring fire in front of them.

They cooked their meal and found that they were renewed by the food that they ate. Drake watched both Gwen and Isabel with interest. Gwen seemed to be more and more quiet with every second that passed and Isabel seemed to be growing more and more talkative with every second that passed. Aiden was nearly as talkative and for that matter so was everyone else. Shavrok laughed jovially while keeping a lookout for them.

"We will leave early in the morning and head south for one mountain. Then we'll head back north and continue east. That mountain scares me too much to continue on our present course," Isabel said.

"I don't suppose you'll tell us what's on the mountain?" Drake asked, knowing that Gwen was going to ask that question.

"It's not what's on the mountain that scares me, it's what's under it. There used to be an entrance to the Rantwarts cities. They sometimes stand guard outside, watching carefully for any stray travelers that they might attack. And in case you're wondering they don't imprison captives, they sacrifice them to their gods."

"I vote we go around the mountain," Diderus replied. They all smiled and nodded their approval as they drifted off to sleep.

* * *

Saul carefully crept around the dying campfire in the middle of their camp. He was just as familiar with these mountains as Isabel was, but only because he had used these mountains as an escape several times during the past couple of years. The entire company slept peacefully, not paying him any mind. He grabbed a small branch and lit it in their fire, heading north into the darkness.

He walked along an old worn path, cutting any of the dead vegetation that might be in his way. He walked for nearly an hour until he came to a large valley in between two of the mountains. A large gaping black cave sat at the far end.

Saul continued to cut the vegetation all the way up to the cave entrance. He trod carefully, cutting the final ten feet, hopefully making it look like a well-traveled path. He put his knives away and moved away, heading back to the trail he had been walking on. He cut more of the vegetation and put it in several piles on his way back to the camp.

He reached the camp and then passed through it as he cut more of the dead vegetation from the south side of the mountain. He piled it high, bordering the camp on all sides, and then made a long pile to his hiding spot.

Saul finished making his trail of dead vegetation and then moved further away from the camp, reaching a tree he had been to on many other occasions. The tree was large and old, likely the largest of the trees in the mountains.

A large "S" was engraved on the trunk. It was dead, the branches hung low, creating a canopy. He moved beneath the canopy now able to stand upright and not worry about being seen as the branches created a solid cover from the outside world.

Dozens of crates waited for him. He moved to a longer crate and undid the latches. He grabbed the bow and quiver of arrows that were inside and strapped them on before moving to the next box. This one contained several knives. The next crate produced more weapons.

A sword with a jagged edge and a couple of daggers that were just as deadly. None of them needed to be sharpened, because they were Elvish-made and for reasons beyond his comprehension, this type never went dull. He left his hiding place, taking his torch with him.

* * *

Isabel woke suddenly. Fire raced through the fog, igniting a pile of brush that had been unspotted earlier.

"We have company!" Isabel exclaimed. Everyone immediately sprang to their feet and drew their weapons. "Get your bags, let's go!" They did as she said, blindly following her. The fire had now split and was racing ahead of them, giving them only one way to run.

"I thought we needed to go south?" Drake asked. As best as he could tell they were headed north.

"We did!" Isabel exclaimed. "Whoever is behind this is smart. We don't have an option."

"There has to be another option!" Gwen yelled frustrated. A single arrow came through the fog, grazing Gwen in the side.

"North!" Aiden yelled. They sprinted down the path on the north side of the camp, having to run single file as the path narrowed. Isabel followed at the rear of the company, looking over her shoulders for the person who had attacked them. She searched, finally thinking she saw someone in the fog. The figure vanished a moment later.

Her mind scrambled to come up with a place to hide. If there was someone following them they were sitting ducks. Anyone close enough would be able to pick them off the mountain. She searched her memories, trying to think of a way out of this.

Her thoughts were interrupted as a flaming ball of debris fell from the cliff above them. It hit the rock behind her and flames spread out in every direction, the heat stinging her skin. They ran faster, with another flaming ball of debris landing behind her.

"Jump!" Isabel yelled. They dropped off the ledge falling fifteen feet, hitting the ground in a roll as one final ball of flame hit the ledge where they had been standing. Flaming debris fell all around them. Aiden kept his hand on his sword searching for any sign of the person that had been chasing them. Isabel helped the others back to their feet.

"I knew someone was following us!" Nickolas exclaimed, grabbing his staff.

"Unfortunately they want us deep-fried," Morgrin said.

"Don't worry, it'll be alright," Isabel assured. "What we have to do now is figure out how far off course we are and get back on track."

"Do you remember any of this place?" Shavrok asked. Isabel studied their surroundings for a moment. The two mountains met in a steep valley with a massive rock formation arched up over a large chasm that offered nothing but darkness.

"It seems familiar, but I can't remember for sure. I have to get somewhere, where I can see more," Isabel replied, beginning to walk to the dark chasm. "I think the ruins of Bargen Ur are on the other side of this arch."

"Looks like a cave to me."

"It is. The entrance to the city was an underground tunnel. The walkways we were on, and the mountainside beyond this were used for defensive positions," Isabel explained. "You might notice the ruined guard towers to either side of us." Isabel moved from the main group, who were still trying to get their bearings. She walked up next to Aiden who stood just in front of the gaping hole.

"Who do you think was trying to kill us?" Isabel asked. Aiden shrugged his shoulders.

"Hard to say," Aiden replied. "Likely someone hired by the Farsees."

"Whoever it is, they are a coward."

"Indeed."

"So you know what lays in the cave?" Isabel asked. Aiden nodded. "I've watched this earth long enough to know the dark secrets. I know what's in that cave. My bet is we'll be forced to battle it before the day's done."

"You're probably right, but I hope you're wrong," Isabel said. She grabbed the first rock she could and pulled herself up, until she could put her feet on steps that had once been carved into the rock. She walked up across the arch until she stood on the ruins and looked beyond.

"What do you see?" Morgrin asked.

"I was right, these are the ruins of Bargen Ur," Isabel said. "We can either risk going south and running into whoever, or we can try and go through the ruins and get back on track. That will likely take us an extra day though."
They froze in their tracks as a loud rumble filled the valley they were in. The rocks shook and the mountains trembled. Then the sound stopped.

"What was that?" Diderus asked.

"Nothing good," Aiden said, moving towards everyone else. "Isabel get down from there!"

The silence was shattered as another arrow was loosed, flying directly into the dark chasm in front of them. Immediately a rumble was heard and the earth trembled again as a roar came from inside the cave.

Isabel jumped to the ground. Now the trembling was rhythmic and fear flooded into her soul. The others backed up and tried to flee to the south but were stopped as fire appeared like it had at the camp, blocking off any hopes of leaving. Isabel stood to her feet and drew her sword and a small dagger, moving as close as she could to the edge of the opening.

"Draw your weapons!" Aiden yelled. All the others did as he said, standing ready to face their opponent. Finally, the creature began to come out of the dark cave. Isabel tried to clear her mind as she laid her eyes on a creature she had only ever heard of before.

It stood twenty-five feet tall, its muscles rippling as it walked on all four legs. It had two necks and two heads and its skin was a dark brown color, with a dull glimmer to it. Large spikes protruded from its back and its razor-sharp claws dug into the ground, over twelve inches before its foot touched the ground.

Their hope dwindled.

"What is this foe?" Morgrin asked.

"A Ronish," Aiden answered plainly.
Isabel rushed forward, catching the Ronish by surprise. Her blade pierced the flesh near the legs. The beast let out a fierce yell and thrashed violently as it

whipped one of its heads around to her.

Isabel tried to move out of the way but was unable, as the creature knocked her out of the way with his powerful head. Isabel was thrown from her spot. She crashed into the rocks on the far side, the wind knocked out of her, and her head throbbing.

For a moment, all Isabel could do was lay there and try to get her bearings back. She could hear Morgrin calling out to her. Everyone found their courage as they attacked the Ronish.

Morgrin pulled his blade back and swung, only to find himself sideswiped by one of the massive feet of the creature. He flew to the other side and was knocked unconscious. Isabel struggled to get to her feet, feeling the back of her head and pulling back her hand when it became wet with her blood. She blocked out the pain and joined the battle once again, running up alongside Diderus who had ascended onto the creature's back, using his Goblin claws to climb the creature.

Isabel moved directly underneath the creature and thrust her sword into the belly of the monster. The creature ran to the left and spun around, knocking Diderus off and nearly trampling the rest of them. Isabel ripped her sword free. Chills ran through her as horns echoed through the valley. She looked back towards the cave entrance.

"Borags!" Isabel yelled. She swung her sword at the first one, decapitating it. Two dozen Borags rushed from the dark chasm in front of them.

"Thaddeus! Get your bow and get to high ground!" Isabel yelled. Thaddeus nodded and retreated from fighting the Borags, heading to a spot where he could aim. He released arrow after arrow, each one seeming to have no effect on the monster.

They quickly defeated the Borags, allowing them to turn their attention to the strange beast that still advanced towards them. Aiden pulled out two large knives and hurdled towards the creature.

The knives dug deep into the Ronish's tough skin, blood streaming from the wounds. Aiden gained his footing on the arrows that were stuck in it and used the knives to climb up the creature, which shook and stomped wildly as it tried to get Aiden off.

Isabel rushed forward as the creature let out another roar. She found it harder to move and harder to react to what was happening around her. The roar stopped and she could think straight again. The creature was rearing up on its back legs.

It thrust itself towards the ground, the front legs striking the earth. A crater was formed where its feet had struck. A shockwave twisted around from the impact point. Ripping through the ground and throwing everything in its path into the air. Nickolas screamed out as the shockwave struck him, but was caught by Shavrok, preventing any serious injury.

Aiden, who had been nearly to the top of the creature was thrown off, landing only a few feet in front of the massive claws. Aiden rolled out of the way, and Isabel pulled out a throwing knife. She hurled it through the air, striking one of the creature's eyes.

The monster convoluted and let a fierce roar escape, stomping the ground and sending another shockwave through the area. Isabel tried to run but wasn't able to escape as the shockwave went under her feet and threw her into the air. She crashed into the vegetation that was now trampled.

She pushed herself to her feet but was knocked down immediately as a Borag blade met her in the arm. A Borag pressed his foot on her chest and stood over her with his swords drawn. She glanced towards the cave where more Borags were coming out.

"I'm ready," she whispered. The Borag screwed up his face for a second but then swung the blade at her neck. A roar filled the area as Shavrok threw himself at the Goblin, twisting sideways as he flew through the air.

The Goblin looked, impaled immediately by Shavrok's spikes. They rolled across the ground and finally, Shavrok stopped himself. The Goblin was thrown from his spikes and crashed into the rocks.

"Thanks Shavrok!" Isabel said. Shavrok nodded and then turned his attention back to everyone else. The beast, once again, reared up on two legs and came down on the Borag, opening his gaping jaws and roaring. Fire erupted from the shockwave, this time, setting fire to anything the shockwave touched. Several Boraags were caught up in the fire and ran around as they burned, still trying to kill them.

"We can do this!" Aiden yelled. Shavrok hopped up to the rock ledge and then onto the creature, using his spikes to grab on. Isabel and Aiden quickly scaled the archway and then dove to the creatures' back, swinging their swords at the necks. They both hacked at one of the necks until it fell to the ground.

The Ronish thrashed violently, throwing them off. Shavrok charged but was swept away by the massive foot that struck him. Isabel quickly regained her footing. Gwen and Thaddeus were shooting as many arrows as they could, managing to take out two of the remaining eyes.

The beast charged towards her, the ground shaking as the shockwaves ripped the ground apart to either side of her. Isabel gazed into its one remaining eye. The creature stopped for a moment and held her gaze. Isabel reached to her neck and pulled on the golden chain and pendant, bringing it into view. She let the pendant hang in view of the creature.

The Ronish looked at it confused and then swung his powerful foot at her. She quickly darted to the left and ducked away from the creature which was following her. She grabbed a dagger on her right and closed her eyes.

The gem in the pendant around her neck began to glow and sparkle, further angering the creature as it relentlessly pounded the ground with its feet. Shockwaves ripped everything apart as it came towards her. She drew a large knife and rushed at the creature. The creature opened its powerful jaws, purple flames spewed from them. The flames split when they reached the dagger, as though they had hit a wall. The flames changed direction and followed the track of her dagger as she whirled it through the air.

All the fire raced towards the creature and consumed it. The flames went out moments later, and Isabel panicked, someone had enchanted the creature.

Morgrin, who had gained consciousness, came up to her but she pushed him away as the creature took another swing at her. Aiden and Shavrok both climbed up on the rock ledge, jumping down on the Ronish once again.

They swiftly climbed up the spikes on the neck of the great beast which began to open its mouth to release more flame. The creature thrashed and growled fiercely as Shavrok moved to the long snout and wrapped himself around it, clamping the large mouth shut. Aiden raised his sword and thrust it into the skull of the beast.

The Ronish thrashed and threw them off, staggering a few feet. The beast tried to rush them but instead collapsed on itself. They collapsed on the ground, exhaustion taking over them as they tried to come to grasp everything that had happened. The valley had been destroyed by the battle.

Aiden was the first to stand, moving to the dead creature and pulling his sword from its head. He cleaned the blade off and slid it back into its sheath. "I was starting to think it was impossible to kill that creature!" Morgrin said, finally standing. Isabel slipped the pendant back inside her dress and slowly stood.

"With Lathon anything's possible," Isabel said. "Helps even more when he's with us." They half smiled. Isabel searched the area for Shavrok. She spotted his massive body lying motionless on the ground, ten feet from where the head of the creature had fallen.

She limped over to Shavrok, her limps suddenly feeling all the pain that had been inflicted. The others raced over to him as fast as they could, helping to roll him on his back. Shavrok lay motionless, with his mouth open. He coughed a moment later and he sat up.

"That wasn't fun!" Shavrok exclaimed.

"Either way, you fought like no other Gog ever has!" Isabel said. He stood up and they embraced each other, each helping the other to gather their weapons and belongings which were scattered everywhere.

"I hope we don't meet any more of these things along the way," Drake said, having to support Gwen's weight. Gwen's leg was mangled and deformed.

"Let me do something about that leg," Isabel said. Morgrin helped her as they bandaged Gwen up the best they could. "I'd heal you with one of my special tools, but I left most of them at home."

"Be healed," Aiden spoke. Immediately, Gwen's leg cracked and snapped as the bones began to rebuild themselves and the skin joined together. Within seconds, her leg was back to normal. They felt overcome with amazement as the healing power of Aiden's words took effect on all of them, each of them healed of their numerous injuries within seconds of each other. They stood, still feeling weary and weak, but more at ease knowing their injuries wouldn't kill them now.

"Thank you Aiden," Isabel said. "It's much better than I could have done."

"It was nothing," Aiden said. "I came to heal, not to destroy. But if people do not wish to be healed then they will be destroyed by themselves." They fell silent.

"We should get moving. The longer we wait the more susceptible we are to attack," Shavrok said. They grabbed what they could find, as they prepared to leave the valley. Isabel's mind went on high alert as the pendant in her dress began to grow hotter.

"Someone's here!" Isabel whispered to them. They all scurried to wherever they could hide. Isabel looked around the pile of rock that she and Morgrin were hidden behind, seeing a silhouette appear above the black chasm where the Ronish had come from. The person was cloaked and held a sword in one hand and a long staff in the other.

"Well, well, well…what do we have here?" the person asked. The voice was a woman's voice. Another smaller silhouette appeared next to her, no larger than a dog. "I knew there was some excitement going on. Something powerful is here."

The shadows moved to the stairs and walked down to the battlefield, sniffing. Isabel studied the dog, which was as large as a small cow and as nimble as a cat. Isabel shifted her attention to the woman. She stood and the dog came back to her, looking in their direction and growling. Isabel tensed up as the woman muttered something under her breath.

Slowly the valley began rebuilding itself, the fires went out and the dead vegetation went back to the state that it had been in before the attack. The craters that had been created by the Ronish rose back up and the rocks that they hid behind began to go back into place. They stood, knowing it would be useless to try anything at this point.

"I must say you are a strange group of travelers," the woman replied. Isabel's heart stirred.

"And you are?" Drake asked. The woman looked at him and then gazed in Isabel's direction.

"An old friend to some and an enemy to others," the woman said taking down the hood on her cloak. Isabel felt her heart nearly leap out of her chest. "It's been a long time since you've come around Isabel."

"Perhaps too long," Isabel said with a smile. The others all relaxed as the two of them embraced. "Everyone, I would like you to meet Enya. She raised me after my parents died."

Enya was a tall slender woman with a black dress and red hair colored with green streaks running through some of it. Enya was covered in weapons wherever she could put one on, certainly making her look like one of the most intimidating people they had ever seen.

"I've never seen anyone take down a Ronish before," Enya told them. "I only wish I had been around to see the battle. You look remarkably unscathed for having fought a battle that must certainly be remembered in tale and song."

"Trust me, we certainly feel it," Gwen said. "Plus, we were just healed of our injuries before you got here."

"Not many people travel this deep in the Dead Mountains, even in the most desperate situations. Where are you headed?" Enya asked.

"We're heading for Goshen and we've been followed. Someone set this whole thing up as a trap," Morgrin said.

"I see. Come…you will stay with me for the night and then if you wish I can lead you out of these mountains, safely and without raising any alarm. I guarantee whoever is following you won't follow where I take you," Enya said.

"That alright with everyone?" Aiden asked. No one objected and they began walking towards the dark cave and then up the stairs to the left. They scaled them and looked out into the ruins that were on the other side.

"Follow behind me and don't touch anything that is off the path that I lead you on," Enya warned. "There is a safe way to pass through here without alerting anything to our presence and it'll save us a lot of time if we can pull it off."

None of them spoke for the next hour and a half as they traveled through the ruins. With the dog-like creature in the lead, the rest of them followed single file behind. Enya picked her way through the ruins with ease and care.

Isabel studied the area, having no memory of this place from her younger days. She thought she could see dark shapes moving in the shadows, but she wasn't sure.

The ruins were soon behind them and they were able to rejoin the identical mountains that surrounded them. Fog still dominated the landscape, the lifeless trees like skeletons with their bare branches visible through the fog.

After another hour of walking, they came into the sight of a large tower with a small house adjoined to it. Isabel half smiled at the sight of the old house. There were many secrets in this tower and even though she had grown up here, she knew she didn't know half of them. Enya pulled out a large set of keys and threw open the lock.

The door creaked and groaned noisily as it opened to darkness. Isabel grabbed the lantern on the far wall and it came to life at her touch. The light flooded into the darkness, showing dark grey stone walls, covered in moisture. Isabel watched curiously. It had been years since she had been in here, and it had changed considerably.

"I imagine you are used to Isabel's place and the flowering vines," Enya said, closing the door behind them, and grabbing another lamp. "I force myself to keep my house looking as much like this as I can, in case someone happens to come across it."

"Does that happen often?" Thaddeus asked.

"Now and then," Enya said, leading the way. They all followed and found themselves walking for thirty seconds until they reached a large opening. A fireplace roared in the far wall, and a small kitchen and table set filled the circular-shaped room. Several doors were seen in the wall, each one of them branching off in different directions, heading down into the ground.

"Grab yourself a chair and make yourselves comfortable, I'll get some supper cooking in just a couple of minutes. I just have to go down to the cellar and put some of these weapons away. Not all of them are safe to have on me all the time."

Enya pulled out another large key and opened one of the doors, which led to a steep staircase. Isabel watched as she vanished from view. She looked to the others who all looked uncomfortable. Aiden was the only one who seemed to be at peace.

"Relax everyone, we are among a friend of mine. There's nothing in here that's going to harm us."

"How can you be so sure?" Diderus asked. "You said yourself it's been a long time."

"I know my friend," Isabel replied. "She takes just as much precaution as I would in her situation. Living here is like living on the run like I did for so many years."

"Yeah but even you still found a way to make your place beautiful," Gwen said.

"Just different tastes. The only reason I have the flowering vines in the first place is because I came into possession of the seeds. As you know by visiting the restaurant before we left, they can be both a curse and a blessing."

"So you grew up here?" Morgrin asked. Isabel nodded. He half laughed. "That explains a lot."

"Does it now?" Isabel asked. They all laughed lightly.

"It explains why you're so amazing," Morgrin said.

"Suck up," Shavrok said. Morgrin smiled.

"If it keeps me out of trouble."

"I'll get some food started," Enya said plainly, coming into the kitchen with a large pot. She sat the pot down and locked the basement, before making her way to the fire. "I wasn't expecting any guests, so all I can make you is stew."

"That's perfectly fine," Aiden said. "Is there anything I can help you with?"

"Offering to help a woman in the kitchen, that's rare," Enya said. "Nonetheless you are my guests, sit back and relax, tell me all about your adventures and why on earth you are in these blasted mountains."

"Trying to go undercover," Diderus said. Enya raised an eyebrow at him. "They why don't you go under the mountains rather than over them? It'll save you both time and headache."

"Isabel seemed to think that it would be more dangerous," Thaddeus answered. Enya shrugged.

"It depends on how you get into the cave systems below the mountains. If you use one of the many caves you come across, you might as well jump off a cliff now. Your odds of survival would be better."

"You've discovered a safer way then?" Isabel asked.

"I have been attacked at their entrances more times than I can count. Barely escaped with my life on several occasions. I figured it was worth the risk and the danger to my life to try and find another way in and map the caves down below."

"So you did it then?" Isabel asked. Enya nodded.

"Yes, I did. I finally mastered the puzzle of the Rantwarts, how to get in and out without being detected, and which paths are real and which aren't," Enya answered.

"Can you could lead us through the mountains?" Drake asked.

"I can get you wherever you want to go."

"We'll take you up on that offer," Aiden said.

Enya smiled and nodded. "We'll leave at first light. That's when the Rantwarts are usually sleeping. They are nocturnal beings, which is of course why living in the mountains suits them well. They don't know one day from the next."

"How long will it take us to reach the caves?" Gwen asked.

A long time, because we're not going to enter through the caves. We're going right through one of the volcanoes, or rather where they vent all their smoke and metal. There's one less than an hour from here. If you climb in there they'll never suspect you. It takes nearly three days to get to the edge of the mountains, then from there I imagine you could go into the plains in Vonlaus and make decent time," Enya said.

She moved back over to the pot over the fire and grabbed some dishes from the cabinet, dishing them up some stew and handing it out to them. Isabel took a bite and cringed, suddenly remembering that there were only two things Enya knew how to make and the stew was the worst out of the two options. She tried not to laugh as she watched the others take their first bite.

"What is this?" Shavrok asked, screwing up his face. Enya smiled.

"It's very interesting, isn't it? To be honest with you, I'm not sure what's in it, I found barrels of it in the cellar when I moved into this place."

"Are you serious?" Isabel asked. "All these years and you didn't tell me that? No wonder this stuff tastes so bad. It's probably contaminated." Enya and Isabel both laughed.

"It hasn't killed me yet. I doubt it's going to now," Enya replied. They laughed and tried to finish the stew the best they could before being shown to rooms for the night. Isabel laid down next to Morgrin and felt uncertainty well up inside of her.

She tried to fall asleep and finally succeeded. She lay there, lost in her dreams, before waking a little while later. Her mind drifted to past events. She finally pushed them from her mind and fell to sleep again.

Chapter 10

UNDER THE MOUNTAINS

Light moved past the hallway, catching Drake's attention as he lay awake in the darkened room. Gwen lay next to him, breathing gently, unaware of the world around her. Drake climbed out of the bed, stepping onto the cold bricks and wincing before slipping on boots. He quietly crept to the doorway, looking up and down the hall as the light vanished around the corner that led into the main room. Drake turned and walked in that direction.

The air was cold and damp as it greeted him, bringing his mind alive in the middle of the night. He reached the main room. The fire had gone out and all the dishes were still dirty and in the small basin. Two torches burned on the wall, giving off light and two of the doors were open.

Drake slowly moved towards the doors, realizing that one of them led to the cellar like before and the other met a set of spiraling stairs that went up into the tower. Drake slowly proceeded, finding his curiosity taking hold of him. He walked up the stairs, which were filled with light from torches that hung along the wall.

Drake looked to the top of the stairs, seeing a different light glowing on the walls. There was no torch, yet something was giving off light, its rays bending and reflecting off the walls. The light slowly changed from one color to the next. He had to half smile. Maybe she was Isabel's mentor after all.

He looked at the pictures along the wall, studying each of them as he passed by. He paused when he reached a picture that seemed familiar to him. He looked at the woman in it, unsure of where he had seen her before.

He continued going forward until he reached the landing at the top of the stairs. The stairs opened up to a large ten-foot radius circular-shaped room. No windows were in the room.

Drake looked around the blank and vacant walls and then finally at the source of the light he had seen. He laid his eyes on a circular stone pool that stood three feet high. The water in the pool moved in wave-like patterns as though it had a mind of its own and it was its own ocean. The water changed color and seemed to radiate light. The small waves crested, creating the interesting light patterns he had noticed as he climbed up the stairs. Drake put his finger into the water and then pulled it away when the water felt hot.

He looked at the rock border around it, fascinated by the ancient writing on the side. Drake wondered for a moment what it said, as he was unable to identify the text. He ran his hand along it and then looked at the water again, unable to look away from the water.

"Curiosity is not a sin Drake Thomas, but I would exercise caution," Enya said from the stairs. Drake's attention was pulled from the pool of water as he looked in Enya's direction.

"Sorry, I didn't mean to come up here. I just couldn't sleep and it interested me."

"You don't have to apologize Drake. I know where your heart was and it was in a very good place. I suppose there's no hiding what this pool of water is, now that you're up here. Am I right?"

"I am rather curious," Drake replied. "Why is there a pool of water in the upstairs of your tower?"

"This is no ordinary pool of water. If it was, the water would not even catch your attention. There were once nine of these all across the earth. They are called the pools of Wuralon. Of course, you realize that Warlon is the ancient Elvish word for-"

"Prosperity," Drake finished.

Enya smiled. "Very good."

"Who created them?"

"No one really knows."

"But why is it here in a tower?" Drake asked.

"According to all the parchments I've found on things of this nature, they were hidden to keep them out of hands that would use them for ill plans. I have spent much time and energy to locate all of them. I have destroyed eight of them."

"So this…"

"Is the last one," Enya replied. "However, I have not been able to destroy this one. I just can't seem to find the right combinations of spells and magic to do it. I wish I could though, and I'll keep on trying until the day that I die."

"What do they do?" Drake asked. Enya began pacing.

"What did you feel when you touched the water, Drake?" Enya asked.

"I'm not sure. I guess it felt hot, but at the same time, it didn't feel hot. I know that doesn't make sense logically-"

"Oh, but it does make sense! You see these pools of water, like I said before, are unusual. The water has an incredible ability. I probably shouldn't even say what the water does. The very thought of what they might do might be a temptation to you."

"It doesn't look that dangerous," Drake said. "What could possibly be harmful about these?"

"It offers you power beyond what you can imagine. It'll give you whatever you ask for."

"Anything?"

"Anything," Enya answered.

"That's not possible," Drake said.

"Test it. Put your hand in the water and think of something. Anything." Drake took a deep breath and lowered his hand to the water already feeling the power of the water overtaking him. He let his finger slide into the water. Energy coursed through his veins. Drake thought of something. He looked at his hand, confused as nothing happened. He pulled it out of the water and his hand dried up.

"You see it didn't work," Drake said. Enya pointed beside him. The water had run off his hand and landed on the hard rock. Where it had landed, a golden chalice sat, exactly like Drake had thought of.

Drake's hand trembled as he reached out and grabbed it. His hands closed around the chalice, his heart and mind racing. He stared at the water feeling power ripple through him.

"I told you it would work," Enya said. "I can see in your eyes that you long to use this pool. Many would desire to use this as you would, for good. This pool does far more than just offer golden cups. It has the power to affect the minds of people and the land around you. You can create whatever you want with this pool. That's why I've destroyed all of them."

"Power is the one thing everyone desires," Drake said. "It's also the one thing that can destroy faster than any other. Only one person in all the world is capable of using this power and not having it corrupt him…and I'm not him."

"Who do you speak of?" Enya asked. Drake looked into her mysterious eyes, confused and fascinated by what he saw. In some ways, he could tell that Enya had raised Isabel, but in other ways, they were nothing alike.

"Lathon."

Enya raised her eyebrow. "Lathon? So he's who you put your trust in?"

"No one else. Isabel does as well, is that bad?"

"I have a hard time believing in a king who deserted his people and hasn't returned."

"He has returned, but people's hearts are hard and they don't hear or see the truth, even when it's right in front of them."

"If he had returned he would have done so by now. The fact that Lathon left thousands of years ago and hasn't returned means only that he never cared about us," Enya said.

"Have you read any of the ancient scrolls?" Drake asked. Enya shook her head. "There is a scroll of Lathon and it says 'you must not forget this one thing, dear friends: A day is like a thousand years to Lathon, and a thousand years is like a day. Lathon isn't really being slow about his promise to return, as some people think. No, he is being patient for your sake. He does not want anyone to be destroyed, but wants everyone to be saved.'"

"The words of a fool who was only trying to deceive people into believing that Lathon cared about anything," Enya replied.

"I'm sorry you think so," Drake said.

"I don't hold anything against you. I will do whatever I can to help you, no matter what the cost."

"What do you think will happen to us when we get below the mountains?"

"If we're lucky, we'll go unnoticed," Enya said. "But if we're not lucky and we have to fight, then you'd better hope your skills are up to par. Next to Borags, the Rantwarts are the second most fierce creatures that are loyal to the dark forces that lie beneath the surface of this earth."

"Great," Drake said. Enya looked at him for a moment, a light shining in her eyes.

"Where are you from Drake Thomas? Originally that is?"

"I have no memory of my past."

"Really?" Enya asked. "No memory at all?"

"No," Drake replied. "Just remember waking up one day on the side of a river. I wish my memory would come back to me. For whatever reason my heart has been telling me that I would find out my past on this trip. So far I haven't figured out very much."

"Sometimes the heart deceives you," Enya said. "Best to live in the moment if you ask me."

"But the moment passes so quickly," Drake pointed out. "Live for the moment, but also work for the future. Living in the past doesn't do you any good."

"Then why do you wish to find out your past?"

"So I can know where I've been and learn from it," Drake said. "It would put my soul at ease to know where I'm from and what my life was like. I might look back and not like what I see, but even if that were the case I would be happy that everything had happened like it had."

"You are a very strange person, you know that Drake Thomas?" Enya asked. Drake half smiled.

"I had a feeling."

"What else do you think learning your past will profit you?"

"Nothing," Drake said. "I'm not looking to profit by knowing it. I'm just curious about myself. Also, my heart tells me that I'll have to know my past for the future."

"A bit odd if you ask me."

"What do you believe in Enya?" Drake asked.

"I believe everyone has a right to believe what they believe, even if they're wrong. What I believe, I believe to be true and I prefer to keep it to myself."

"I meant no disrespect," Drake said. Enya smiled at him.

"I live in these mountains because the people of the earth seem to always unite against me. These mountains are my home. I can believe what I want without anyone telling me I'm wrong. That is just their opinion anyway. My dream is to someday create a land or dwell in a place where people of all kinds can live and not have to fight amongst each other about who's right."

"Nice thought," Drake admitted. "But there is only one thing that is right, and that's Lathon."

"So you say," Enya pointed out. "You see, Drake Thomas, it seems like we disagree on several things and this is one of them. You would tell people that there's only one reason worth living, and for that matter only one God in this world…Lathon. I would not do that because I believe in a peaceful world. Even if there *is* only one, who's to say they can't believe in their god? Why not just let them believe the lie they've told themselves if it keeps the peace?"

"I love them too much to do that," Drake said. "I want to tell them the truth so that they aren't destroyed when the end comes."

"The end won't come," Enya replied, half laughing. "You say that Lathon is full of love. Maybe I'm reading it wrong, but doesn't that mean there will always be another chance? Lathon will never destroy the world, because he loves everyone in it too much. He is weak and that's all there is to it."

"Once again, I disagree. His patience will run out, and when that happens the world and all who don't belong to Lathon will be destroyed, while those who believe will live forever."

"That's another reason not to believe in your religion," Enya said. "Do you realize how crazy it sounds? Living forever in a world that has known death during the countless wars."

"Love is crazy," Drake replied. "It is crazy to believe that Lathon sent an heir to save us when Lathon lived so many years ago. But he did, and I believe in the truth."

"According to you," Enya said. "I still don't believe what you say. Where is the heir of Lathon? If he's coming"

"Downstairs," Drake said. Enya shifted uncomfortably. "Aiden is the heir of Lathon, Sherados."

"Impossible," Enya said. Drake shook his head.

"Not impossible. In the days to come, we will all be marked by Lathon as either his or the world's. The ones marked as his will inherit much more than we can imagine."

"Mark?" Enya said. "I've never read any scrolls that speak of a mark."

"There is a scroll," Drake replied. "It's not very well known though. As for the mark, with many people it's on the heart, for me, it's on the hand." Drake held up his hand, revealing the scar for her to see. She looked at it, a new light shining in her eyes. Drake wondered what she was thinking.

"We'd better get ready to go. We'll be leaving in a few hours," Enya said. Drake nodded and left the room. Drake knew there were a lot of people like Enya in the world and the question was how to get them to see the truth.

Drake knew that some people's hearts would be too hard to see the truth in the matter. They would hear the truth, see the truth, and still not believe it. For a moment Drake thought he understood the pain that Lathon must be feeling every time someone chose to ignore him.

He began waking all the others, knocking on their doors and hearing them stir inside their rooms. He finally reached his and Gwen's. He looked in, seeing her sleeping peacefully. He looked into her face feeling his heart stir. He loved her more than anything, yet something still gnawed at his heart, telling him that there was still more to learn about love.

He really didn't know much about love, except that he was in love with her. What was love really? Drake thought about it for a moment unsure of the answer. Love was far different from the fairy tales and predictable endings that people always wrote in stories. Love was more than the superficial things people often considered to be love.

It was humble, patient, not easily angered. The list went on and on and Drake couldn't help but notice that he still had a lot to learn about love. He gently shook her awake and they both got ready. Drake followed her out where everyone else was ready and waiting.

I was starting to wonder if you had gotten lost," Enya said.

"I guess everyone else just moved a little faster than I am today," Gwen said. "I'm ready now though."

"We've got an hour hike due north, from there we will enter the mountains and make good time," Enya said. They followed behind as she briskly picked her way through the mountainside as though she could walk it blindfolded. Drake's mind drifted to the pool of water in the tower.

Maybe people who made their way into these mountains weren't meant to make it out?

People in need would be easily seduced by the power of the water once they found out what it did. He shivered, imagining the evils that could be accomplished with sinister intentions.

The path they followed was now only a foot and a half wide and steadily spiraled up the mountain. Screams pierced the silence. They all quickly glanced over their group, confirming that no one had fallen off.

"Where's that noise coming from?" Thaddeus asked.

"Pay it no mind," Enya said.

"Someone's out there!" Gwen exclaimed.

"Yes, and sound travels like it's nobody's business in these forsaken mountains. The source of that scream could be a hundred miles from here," Enya said. Gwen and Drake both looked at Isabel.

"She's right," Isabel said. "We need to keep going. The sooner we get to the top, the sooner we'll be safe."

"Or the sooner we'll fall to our deaths in the caves," Diderus said. Aiden laughed.

"Either way our problem is solved."

They continued as the screams continued to come. Eventually, the sounds ceased leaving them in silence once again. Drake tried to forget the sound of the screams, but unease struck his heart. The screams rang out again and again as they pushed forward.

"We can't just pretend that person doesn't exist!" Drake exclaimed as the screams continued.

"Fine!" Enya yelled. "Go find them! I dare you. You'll be lost in a minute and get taken captive, tortured, or worse. You'll be dead before sunset and I'll rejoice!"

"Does it bother no one else?" Drake asked looking at all of them.

"It bothers everyone, Drake," Isabel said. "My heart is greatly troubled for the one that is suffering. But our path is not to help right now. We *can't* right now. Enya's right that we could be in grave danger to go after the voice. Many evils lie here, perhaps it is a trap prepared by the Sorcerer. First, we have to get out of the mountains, do our research then come back."

"I want to fight it though!" Drake said.

Aiden smiled. "So do I, but raising awareness or researching the source of an evil is fighting it. The day when these mountains will be rid of all that is evil is coming, but it is not this day. We must prepare the hearts and minds of the people in the world for the coming events. We will raise awareness of the problem and something will be done."

They were all silent.

"I guess I always thought that the only way to fight evil was with a sword," Drake said.

"Many people make that mistake, but there is just as much to be said of those who never raise a sword. The sharpest and most deadly weapon that can counter evil is Lathon and the ancient scrolls," Aiden said.

"Why?" Enya asked. Aiden looked at her.

"Because they are true." Aiden held Enya's gaze for several seconds before the screaming pierced the silence again.

"We need to keep moving," Enya said, breaking off the stare and leading the way up the mountain. Gradually the path leveled out and widened out as the mountain began to become more rounded. In front of them, a sharp wall of rock descended steeply into a bottomless pit of black. "This is it."

"How are we going to get down?" Nickolas asked.

"One step at a time," Aiden said. "You can't get to the finish line without crossing the start line." They followed Enya down the narrow stairs that were carved into the steep wall. They descended further until all light was lost from the sky above them.

"Nickolas hit the staff against the ground once," Isabel said. He hit it against the bottom of the next step and it glowed with light, illuminating the area they were in.

"Nice staff," Enya said. The path continued down in a spiral for at least another three hundred yards.

"When we get off these stairs you'll want to put the light away. We'll travel by torchlight. Rantwarts don't have glowing staffs, but they do have torches."

They walked until they reached a rock landing at the bottom of the winding stairs. Enya opened her pack and pulled out torches handing them to everybody. The flames illuminated the area around them, showing nothing but rope bridges that stretched in every direction across gaps where the other side couldn't be seen.

"Remember, Rantwarts can make certain things look like they are there, even when there's nothing. Just because you see a bridge doesn't mean it's real," Enya reminded. "Follow directly behind me and we'll all live happily ever after. I didn't spend years of my life figuring out the path through here for nothing."

They followed Enya onto the bridge which creaked and groaned noisily as it sagged underneath their weight. Drake looked over the edge unable to see anything in the thick darkness. Smoke reached their noses as it moved past them and up the chasm they had just climbed down.

"Is there more than just Rantwarts in these dark places?" Nickolas asked.

"These are the Dead Mountains. There are many races beneath the rocks. The Borags and Rantwarts, seem to have formed some kind of agreement."

"How do you know that?" Morgrin asked.

"The Rantwarts started stocking up on weapons a couple of years ago, but they've put them deep into territories that the Borags have long held to. They are planning for an assault of some kind, although I can't imagine the size of the army they must have, for all the weapons they've built."

"That's comforting, so if we fall and lose our weapons, we'll just be able to grasp theirs," Thaddeus said. Enya smiled.

"Only if you live that long. Rantwarts are very fast and nimble. They don't trust outsiders unless their king trusts them. We would be slaughtered before we could walk three steps," Enya started. "My advice is don't fall off the bridge."

The hours passed slower than they would have liked as the company passed through the dark caverns, walking on one bridge after another. The bridges were longer than any they had ever been on and eventually connected with large rock platforms and then branched off to three or four different bridges, only one of which was real.

They followed in Enya's footsteps as she effortlessly figured out which bridge was real and which ones weren't. Drake was amazed and looked for any kind of difference between the real and fake bridges but was unable to find any.

"How far do you think we've traveled?" Gwen asked.

"Hard to say, we might have traveled fifty or sixty miles by now," Enya answered.

"Already!" Gwen exclaimed. "How is it possible that we've traveled that far in such a short amount of time?"

"You are asking me a question I don't have the answer to," Enya said. "The Rantwarts have become skilled in their dark arts. They've put enchantments on these caves under the mountains; you can make way better time on these bridges than you can on a piece of flat ground. Never made sense to me."

"I'm beginning to think that these mountains can't get any stranger," Drake said. "They can't have any many more secrets."

"Trust me, Drake Thomas, they have many more secrets that people like yourself could scarcely begin to imagine."

"Like what?" Thaddeus asked.

"I won't trouble your good hearts with what goes on in here," Enya said. A scream came from behind him as Diderus fell through the weak old bridge and plummeted into the darkness below. Drake felt his heart drop out of his chest as the ropes on the long bridge were severed. Everyone grabbed on as they swung blindly through the darkness. Finally, after several moments they came to a stop. They dangled from the broken bridge.

"Someone must have cut the ropes," Drake said.

"Who cares, get to the top!" Enya exclaimed. They all began pulling themselves up the collapsed bridge. Shavrok was the first to reach the top, helping everyone, by pulling the bridge up, until they could get off. Drake and Gwen collapsed on the rock.

"We have to find Diderus!" Nickolas said. Aiden held up a hand.

"We will, don't worry. I'm sure he's alive."

"How can you possibly know that?" Enya asked. Aiden held her gaze.

"The voice in my heart tells me the truth, not the lies that deceive the world."

"You have a strange heart. There is only one chance that he survived," Enya said. "The Rantwarts have a lake further down. We're close to the right place, if he hit the water, then he may just be alive. Otherwise, it looks like we're going to be having a funeral for your friend."

"How do we get down there?" Nickolas asked.

"We run," Aiden answered, turning to Enya. "How quickly can you get us down to the bottom of this place?"

"As fast as your legs can carry you," Enya answered. They sprinted over the bridges, no longer caring if they were seen or heard. A large grey wall became visible to them and in the wall was a heavy cast iron gate. Strange creatures were seen on either side of it, drawing their attention.

"Rantwarts!" Enya exclaimed. She drew her sword and beheaded the first one and then the second, quickly dumping their bodies over the edge. Drake looked down, hardly having noticed that they had now been walking over a large city. Torches burned in the darkness below, and people yelled out and cursed at each other. Some of them carried large crates with special markings on them."

"What are they carrying?" Drake asked.

"Don't ask! Let's go. This is the fastest way," Enya told them." Drake looked up to see that Enya had already grabbed the keys and had proceeded through the gate. They were greeted by twenty Borags who came running up to them, swords and weapons raised. Drake ducked the first blade and then swung at the next one as they were engaged in battle. They fought relentlessly, seeing more and more of them coming every second.

Pounding shook the mountains, momentarily stopping all the fighting. Drake watched as dust and pieces of rock fell from the mountaintop above them. They took cover as the rock above them gave way. They looked up, a large head sticking through it. Two more holes appeared. Drake felt his spirits rise.

The Taruks.

Elohim opened his powerful jaws letting his roar, echo through the dark caverns and passages. Chills ran up and down his spine as the sound shook the mountainside. Rocks rained down from the sky, crushing everything they landed on.

"Follow me!" Aiden said.

"How are we going to make it through?" Nickolas asked. "The city's falling apart."

"I tell you the truth! This city will be destroyed on this day. Its evil must be punished," Aiden exclaimed. "Follow me and don't look back! The Taruks know what they're doing."

"I know another way!" Enya said.

"There is only one way and that's to follow me!" Aiden yelled as the sound continued to shake the mountains. Destan and Aspen put their heads through the other holes and joined in the chorus. The Rantwarts cowered and covered their ears as the sound reverberated. "Don't look back! If you look back, you will die!"

Drake was the first to follow after Aiden as he sprinted through the city. Destan and Aspen opened their jaws, sending fire spewing from them. The rocks that were falling towards the ground ignited and fell into the city. Heat sweltered from the city as the company sprinted through the streets, trying to avoid the panicking Rantwarts. A fire consumed the city behind them as they ran.

"Don't look back!" Aiden reminded them.

They sprinted down another level and through several more gates, finally breaking free of the large gated walls. The fire continued to stream from the sky, igniting the city in a blaze unlike any that Drake had ever seen.

Drake looked over to Gwen as they ran. Her eyes moved away from his and back towards the city. Drake stopped in his tracks as Aiden's words echoed through his mind. Drake watched in horror as Gwen's skin became as pale as limestone. The color drained from her eyes and the color in her hair and skin, flaked away as though it was nothing more than tissue paper. Her skin became hard as she slowly turned to salty stone. Drake watched as the last of her lifeless eyes hardened leaving her a shadow of the woman he once had known.

"Don't look back!" Aiden yelled to the others. Drake looked ahead where Aiden had come up to him, looking to the side of him and not towards the city. He grabbed Drake by the hand and dragged him along. Drake thought momentarily about looking back to see Gwen's body again but resisted the urge.

The city faded from the background but the glow of the fire could still be seen. At last, they came to a stop as Aiden slowed down. He looked at Drake and held his gaze, silently trying to comfort him in whatever way he could. Drake felt as if his heart was broken.

"We will stop here for a little while. It is safe for you to look back now." They all turned seeing nothing but the orange glow of fire. The Taruks had vanished, likely hiding in the mountains. Isabel came up to Drake and sat next to him. Drake looked at her knowing that if anyone would feel the same kind of pain he was feeling it would be her.

"She looked back didn't she?" Isabel asked. Drake nodded, unable to get the words out.

"Why did she have to look back?" Drake asked. Aiden came close and kneeled before them.

"Drake, Isabel. I know I might not have all the answers for you right at the moment but I can say this…Gwen is in a better place now."

"She's dead that's all there is to it!" Enya exclaimed. "Accept it and move on!"

"She is dead," Aiden conceded. "But only her body. For those who follow and believe in Lathon, there is life beyond death. A life that cannot be imagined while here on this earth. Nothing in this fallen and broken world can ever come close to the wonder and majesty of what is after."

"Sentimental hogwash," Enya said. "This is life."

"It is a sad existence my friend to put all your hopes and efforts into a world that is dying. This world will pass away in the end. For those who have placed their faith in Lathon, there will be life. For those who cling to the earth, only the bitterness of death will greet you. It's time Enya to ask yourself what you believe in."

Enya fell silent and took a seat on the ground as they mourned Gwen's death.

Drake's mind struggled to focus as the company once again pressed through the darkness. Silence had fallen over them as they each mourned Gwen's death. Part of Drake was angered that she had looked back in the first place. He quickly let go of his anger, knowing that anger was never anyone's friend.

Instead, he walked with Isabel and Morgrin who were feeling the same pain he was. Drake looked at Isabel in amazement. Even with all she had been through she was pressing on and continuing forward.

Her husband, Rohemir, had turned on her, trying to kill her multiple times. Her son, Tremin had turned evil and had also tried to kill her. Now on top of it all her only daughter, who had always loved her and remained faithful, had died and been turned into a pillar of rock.

"How do you do it?" Drake asked. Isabel looked at him, questions in her eyes. "How do you find the strength to continue?"

"Because this is not the end," Isabel answered. "We *will* see her again and there is still much for me to do here. I have to keep the faith and follow the one person who never lets me down."

"But with all that you've been through with your family, doesn't this just wreck you?"

"Yes," Isabel answered. "And no. Gwen was the one family member of mine I could be proud of, with the exception of my parents that is. She found a loving husband and made a life for herself that Lathon could be proud of. There is nothing I can be upset about when I think of Gwen's life. I'm just glad I did the right thing so many years ago when I left her in Fiori." Drake fell silent.

"How do you feel about all of this Drake?" Morgrin asked. Drake thought for a couple of minutes.

"Conflicted," Drake finally answered. "I feel sorrow over her passing, but I also feel that I must continue the journey we started on even though I want to stop and cry for a month."

"As do we all," Isabel answered. "But that is not for us to choose. Things are meant to happen a certain way to some extent."

"To some extent?" Thaddeus asked, joining the conversation.

"For everyone who follows Lathon, he has a plan for their lives and it will work out if we remain faithful. The sad reality of life is eventually everyone has to die. Those who don't follow Lathon, live their lives how they want and reach destruction on levels that we can only imagine. We will see Gwen again."

The conversation died and they walked in silence. A strange glow was seen on the horizon and soon flames came into view. Aiden motioned for them to be quiet and then crouched down as they moved closer. They quickly concluded that it was one of the forges that would vent out the top of the mountains.

They followed Aiden as he led them around the perimeter of the clearing. Drake looked at the Rantwarts, carrying out their business as they pounded the metal with hammers, making it into deadly weapons. They eventually passed by the large forge without being noticed and then rejoined the darkness on the other side.

"How much further until we reach this supposed lake?" Morgrin asked.

"About five minutes," Enya answered. They walked for five minutes, stopping when they reached a large lake. The water was still, lit from an opening in the mountain far above.

"Where do you think he is?" Shavrok asked.

"If he survived the fall he would have likely been captured," Enya said. "We'll probably all be going to our deaths if we look for him."

"Tracks," Aiden said, pointing to the ground near the water. They moved closer and studied the tracks. Clearly, there had been two people who had entered the water and three people that left, as the middle set clearly indicated that the person had perhaps been unconscious.

"We still don't know that he's alive," Enya argued.

"We don't know that he's dead either," Isabel countered.

They moved through the darkness keeping themselves as silent as possible as they followed Aiden. The tracks went on for another ten or twenty minutes and at some point there became three tracks of prints, indicating that Diderus had become conscious and was alive after all.

Aiden stopped them and they listened to the silence that followed. Voices were heard in the distance. They were strange and mutilated voices, not a language they had heard before. They carefully crept closer to the sound, approaching a pile of rocks in the middle of the vast world beneath the mountains.

Three guards stood at the bottom of the rocks. Diderus sat behind them, tied up in a small clearing in the rocks. In the distance, the fire of another forge glowed bright, and ash lazily rained down. Aiden started to move, but Shavrok stopped him.

"Let me take 'em," Shavrok said.

"Just try not to make too much noise, we don't want to attract any more attention than we have to. If you need help we'll be there in a second," Aiden said.

Shavrok nodded and then darted off into the darkness going around the backside of the pile. They all watched the Rantwarts out front, looking for any sign that they had heard Shavrok. Diderus searched the darkness, his eyes stopping when he reached them. He dipped his head to them, and Aiden nodded back.

Shavrok appeared over the top of the pile. He dropped down next to Diderus. The Rantwarts at the bottom of the rocks sprang to action, sprinting up to Shavrok. Shavrok pulled out a large knife and cut Diderus's ropes. Diderus sprang to his feet. Drake and everyone else followed Aiden's lead and drew their weapons, charging up the hill.

The Rantwarts looked around, startled and confused as they ran towards their enemies. Shavrok dropped to the lower level, smashing one of them beneath his massive body. Drake swung his sword at another. He grabbed his opponent's sword as it fell to the ground and tossed it to Diderus. Aiden sprinted to the last Rantwart and slayed him, but not before the Rantwart blew into his horn.

They retreated down the rocks until finally, they were beside the lake again. More horns answered the call. The area all around them was filled with light and sound as unknown numbers of Rantwarts came over the crests of the hills, carrying torches and weapons.

"How are we going to get out of here?" Thaddeus asked.

"I don't know!" Enya replied. "I've only entered and exited through the paths we were on."

They had no more time to plan as the wave of Rantwarts crashed upon them. For several minutes they were consumed in battle, with their enemies falling at their feet. Aiden pointed to the water where a dead Rantwart quickly flowed past them

"Drake!" Aiden yelled. "The lake has a current to it! I'd be willing to bet that there's a river that branches off of it. If there is then it might lead us out of the mountains."

"And if it doesn't?" Enya asked.

"Tell the others to get ready to swim!" Aiden exclaimed.

"Swim?" Drake asked.

"The exit is under the water!" Drake nodded and ran to Shavrok and the message spread until everyone finally fought their way to the water's edge on the cliff that Aiden had climbed onto. The Rantwarts began to close in on them.

"Jump!"

They dove off the cliff, free-falling to the water below. They hit the water, the cold liquid chilling them to the bone. Drake turned in the direction the water was pulling and swam toward the light he could see. They stayed below the surface and swam, getting sucked into the current.

Finally, they reached the light and were pulled into it. The ground vanished beneath them and light flooded all around them. They plummeted down a waterfall, landing in a surging river that wound its way through the Dead Mountains.

They continued to go with the current of the river for several hours until they were brought out of the mountains and into a small pond. They swam their way to shore and collapsed on the ground, relieved to see green grass ahead of them.

"That was fun," Morgrin replied, laughing.

"At least we made it out alive!" Nickolas replied.

"Is everyone alright?" Aiden asked. "Are we all here?" They looked around seeing everyone but Enya."

"Enya's missing?" Drake asked.

"Yes, she is dead," Shavrok said. "I watched her as I fell to the water below. She had waited and was shot with four different arrows. Her body fell in the water but didn't get pulled out of the waterfall."

"After all these years I had been starting to think that nothing could kill her," Isabel said. "My daughter and my mentor dead on the same day."

"She killed herself," Nickolas said. "If she had jumped at the right time and trusted Aiden, then she would've lived."

"Thanks for coming after me," Diderus said. They nodded "Does anyone know where we are?"

"If my eyes don't deceive me, we are on the south side of the Dead Mountains, in the east," Aiden said. "Over to the east is Goshen and our road."

"We should be able to cross the plains easily enough without being seen," Isabel said. "There are only a few small villages, a couple of which are right on the edge of Goshen From our current position, Laheer would be the safest option."

"Have you ever been to Laheer before?" Morgrin asked. "I don't recall having ever been there."

"Trust me hon."

"Always do what the woman says," Morgrin said with a laugh. They began walking through the open wilderness. The sun faded and they made camp and started a fire.

They found some food and ate it before each of them fell into their dreams. Drake wished he could wake up as he replayed the events of Gwen's death before his eyes again and again. His heart cried out to hold her, yet a strange new peace was flooding over him. His nerves went on high alert as a sound came to his ears. He sat up and searched the horizon, seeing nothing. He went back to sleep.

Chapter 11

THE FAILING OF KINGS

Saul was crouched in the tall grass, eyeing his prey like a hungry pack of wolves. He had followed the group into the Dead Mountains. He had tried to kill them on several different occasions, yet somehow they had managed to survive. It was both inspiring and scary.

Could they die? He had led them to one of the most fierce monsters he had ever discovered in the Dead Mountains only to find that they had slain the monster. He had cut the bridge in the caves beneath the mountains, only to find that they had all survived.

He had been following them ever since they had escaped the mountains, trying to come up with something that would be unexpected and would catch them off guard. He was starting to think that they couldn't be killed, which presented another problem for Saul.

He had been hired to take out Aiden and had never failed an assignment before and even though they had wounded his pride, he wasn't going to fail now. He eyed their camp. They were all asleep.

He grabbed a large, jagged-edged knife from his side. All it would take was one stab in the eye. The blade would enter his brain and render Aiden helpless. By the time the others heard his cry Saul would have finished him and vanished into the night, lost forever.

He moved around the camp, approaching Aiden from the back. The fire was by Aiden's feet. Saul held the knife, ready to kill the man he had been hired to kill. Saul felt conflicted. It didn't seem like Aiden was any kind of a threat.

He certainly wasn't a politician.

Saul broke into a sprint, not wanting to wait any longer to strike his prey. He threw the knife towards Aiden's head. Quick as lightning Aiden twisted out of the way and the knife struck in the dirt.

Saul tried to stop and run away, but tripped and fell next to his knife. Aiden was already up to his feet, standing at the ready. The others all were awake now and drawing their weapons. Saul decided to pay them no mind, rushing Aiden with the blade once again. Aiden effortlessly ducked and darted to the left, grabbing a stick from the fire.

Saul followed his every move, rushing towards Aiden at the moment when he reached for a stick in the fire. Aiden swung the flaming piece of wood at him and Saul tried to turn around.

The fire passed in front of him and the world around him went dark as all light vanished. He fell to the ground and turned his head frantically, unable to see anything. He froze with fear as everyone approached him. Saul couldn't see them!

"Stop!" Aiden told the others. The footsteps stopped and one person could be heard coming closer. Saul held his breath and tried to figure out how close the person was as they approached. Saul still clutched the knife in his hand. A person grabbed his hand and made him release the knife and then proceeded to take away the rest of his weapons. No one spoke.

"It seems we have a visitor," Aiden said. "What brings you this far east?"

"Just a man trying to make a living in the world," Saul replied.

"What's your name and why have you been trying to kill us for the past few days?" another voice asked. This one was female and if Saul remembered correctly her name was Isabel.

"My name's Saul. I was hired to find you."

"And kill us," Aiden finished. "Who hired you?"

"Enemies of yours. I won't reveal my sources," Saul said, his heart racing.

"The Farsees hired him," Nickolas said. "I knew he looked familiar at the bar in Edrei. He's been hired before to take out people the Farsees think as dangerous to them."

"It's an honor to have you with us, Saul," Aiden said. "We'd love to stay up and chat all night, but we have a long day's journey ahead of us tomorrow and we need to get some sleep after the day we've had. Hope you don't mind but you'll be coming with us."

"Why can't I see?" Saul asked. "What kind of spell did you put on me?"

"There was no spell put on you," Aiden said. "You blinded yourself. When your heart is open you will see again."

"What are you talking about?" Saul asked. He thought he could see Aiden smiling.

"Just get some rest and we'll be on our way in no time. Let's tie him up." Saul was bound and laid next to the fire, leaving him alone in the darkness. Saul's mind replayed through everything, wondering what was happening to him. He had tried to kill them, yet they hadn't tried to kill him? Confusion swarmed over him as he tried to figure out the mystery.

* * *

Drake mindlessly followed behind everyone else. The past two days had been a blur, his mind occupied with his thoughts and sorrows at the passing of Gwen. He had found some joy in the beautiful and empty plains they had been traveling through for the past two days. For the moment though, he was lost in his thoughts and walking mindlessly.

"It might be a good idea to stop here," Aiden said. "What do you think Isabel?"

"I think that would be smart. The people of Laheer don't take kindly to outsiders who approach at night."

"How do you know that?" Drake asked.

"I had friends in Laheer. I lived there for a while" Isabel answered.

"You lived there?" Drake asked.

"To say that I lived there isn't exactly right, I've been there several times over the years. My family lived in the middle of the plains we just crossed."

"Really?" Thaddeus asked. "I didn't see any houses."

"First of all, these are my parents we're talking about, the house was far from ordinary. Second of all, it was a long time ago, it was probably destroyed," Isabel said. Aiden finally stopped and they put their things down on the ground.

"We'll camp here for the night. Let's try and find some food to eat."

"What about him?" Shavrok asked, pushing Saul forward slightly. Saul was still tied and was still blind.

"Leave him with me," Aiden said. The others began dispersing to go look for food. "Drake, I would like you to join us if you wouldn't mind." Drake hesitated for a moment and then started building a fire. Soon it was started and all three of them sat down waiting for the others to return. "I don't think these will be necessary anymore." Aiden undid the ties around Saul's wrists. Confusion was displayed on Saul's face.

"You are very different, you know that?" Saul finally asked after several minutes of silence.

"Different?" Aiden asked. Saul nodded.

"I've been trained to take out my enemies, and here you should have killed me but you've left me alive. Why? Is it to torture me?

"No Saul, it's not to torture you," Aiden said. "Hatred and killing gets the world nowhere."

"What if the person was evil?" Saul countered. "What if I was a Sorcerer?"

"We would still try and show you love."

"Why though?" Saul asked. "I'm your enemy."

"In your mind," Aiden answered. "I look at people and I see my friends. I see the potential in them, even when no one else does. I love everyone. First and foremost those who hate me."

"That makes no sense!" Saul exclaimed. "How does that even begin to make sense?"

"I could say I'm a blacksmith, I could buy a forge and open it, pretend I'm a blacksmith, but if I don't forge any tools, who would ever believe that I was a blacksmith?" Aiden asked. "I say I love people…anyone can love the people who are nice to them. It takes far more courage and character to love someone who hates them. Only by loving your enemies will others truly believe that you are a loving person. That's what love does. It loves when everyone else bails. Love is not a feeling, as much as it's an action."

"I've never heard that before," Saul said.

"I have, but I've forgotten," Drake replied. They fell silent again.

"Where are we headed anyway?" Saul asked. "If I'm going to be blind and held captive, can you at least tell me that?"

"We are headed towards Goshen," Aiden said. "More specifically we are heading to Cavil." Saul perked up.

"Cavil?"

"Yes," Aiden answered. "Have you ever been there before?"

"Depends on who you ask," Saul answered. "Yes is the answer though. I used to live there."

"Live there?" Drake asked. "How long did you live there?"

"Until six years ago," Saul replied. "I kind of grew up in Cavil. The royal palace to be exact. What are you going to do there?"

"Free all the slaves," Aiden answered. Drake watched Saul's expression carefully.

"Free them? All the slaves?"

"Yes," Aiden said.

"That's impossible," Saul said. "No one can do that."

"Has anyone ever tried?" Aiden countered. Saul looked defeated.

"No."

"Then I guess it's not impossible, it's just never been done. The evil of the Goshen empire has reigned for too long, imprisoning my people."

"They're my people too," Saul said.

"You were a slave?"

"No," Saul answered. "And yes. It's complicated, and would take a long time to tell you everything."

"Good thing we have all night," Aiden said. Saul remained silent for a couple of minutes.

"My parents were slaves for the Goshen government," Saul started. "They had three kids, two boys and a girl. Eventually. they ended up pregnant with a fourth child, me. During that time the Emperor of Goshen became concerned about the number of slaves that were in the area, so he ordered a decree that all the baby boys had to be killed. For whatever reason, my parents hid me and kept me secret for three months.

"When they couldn't keep me hidden any longer they took me to a river and put me in a large basket and set me afloat. It wasn't long until I ended up at the royal palace where the princess was bathing. She saw me and took me in, raising me alongside the princes. I lived the life of a prince my entire life, but I always knew that there was something that I didn't know about myself. I found out all of this from my sister who I met a few years ago. She had been watching me as I floated down the river. She knew that I had not been killed."

"How did you go from being a prince to being an assassin?" Drake asked. Saul looked away.

"I was out watching over the slaves doing their work, and I saw one of the guards mercilessly beating one of the slaves. I couldn't stand it anymore. I attacked and killed the guard. I hid his body and then left. I knew I'd never be able to get out of that one.

"I fled to the Dead Mountains, needing a place to hide. It was the perfect place in some respects. My sorrow turned to bitterness and rage as I decided to figure out a way to get even with the royal family and the Goshen government.

"I became an assassin in the hopes of being able to return to Goshen and kill some of the guards or anyone of importance. I was able to do that and killed many of them, though my brothers as well as the Emperor and his family live on. For years, my bitterness has raged inside of me and has been eating me alive. What am I supposed to do about it? I can't possibly change what I've done and I can't go to them and try to talk it over because it would be my death. They have a price on my head. What am I supposed to do?"

"Forgive them," Aiden answered.

"Forgive them?" Saul asked.

"Yes," Aiden answered. "It is completely necessary to survive this world.

Not forgiving people is like putting poison in your ale every day and drinking it in hopes it'll harm the other person. It only hurts you."

"Why should I forgive them? They don't deserve it!" Saul exclaimed.

"Forgiveness isn't about them. It's about you! It's about you trying to show your love for them. You forgive them whether they forgive you or not, and not just one time, but five hundred times. You forgive them as much as it takes, that they might see the kind of person you are."

"That's not what the society is like these days," Saul said. "They actually have places where you can pray to the gods for the killing of people you don't like."

"Exactly! Imagine how powerful it could be if you forgave them. It would start a shockwave. People would suddenly see you as a different person than what they thought. Those who thought of you as a heartless prince and a ruthless assassin would see a compassionate person. A loving person."

"Even if I can forgive them, I'm not sure I can forgive myself for what I've done," Saul answered.

"In time Saul, I'm sure you will."

Saul nodded and they sat in silence for a few minutes.

"Who are you guys? You are nothing like the Farsees said you were."

"One must look beneath the mask a person is given or puts on, if you are to get to truly know them," Aiden started. "My name is Aiden. I am Sherados, who has come to deliver the world from the clutches of evil. I come to correct those who need to be corrected. I come to lift up the poor and give them the strength of the kings. I have come to take the pride of the kings and give it to the poor, who oftentimes have far more courage than the kings do. I seek to live with my people in spirit and body."

"Having been a prince, I am well versed in the religions of the peoples of the surrounding nations," Saul said. "You are an unusual king, I must say."

"Unusual?" Drake asked. Saul nodded.

"What kind of a king would give up all his power to live among his people? Not in a palace or a mansion, but in the middle of nowhere? It's unheard of."

"I'm only doing what every king is called to do. Live with, fight with, die with the people I love. I do not seek power, because power is mine. Rather, I give up my powers in order to win the hearts and souls of the people. That's what love does! Love is all in. I do not want people to think of me as some angry God who is going to crush them at every turn. I want them to see me as I really am. I do not want fans; I want followers. I fight for love, not honor, glory, or power. If I was to gain the heart of only one person who walked this earth, it would still be worth it!"

"That's not how people think these days," Saul said.

"That is why the Farsees fear Aiden so much," Drake said. "He tells people they have worth, that you can be great no matter what your status. He gives the power to overthrow the dark forces that run wild in this earth."

"That's another reason I left Goshen," Saul started. "I was afraid of the power that would fall upon me someday. I've seen what it did to the Emperor and his family...I didn't want that future. So I fled."

"It seems we have something in common," Drake said. "I did the same thing."

"You are a prince?" Saul asked.

Drake shrugged his shoulders. "I was given great power and responsibility, and it scared me. What did I know about running a nation, or even watching over one for that matter? Then I ended up becoming a Tarukai and from there I also achieved great power and honor. Until recently, I was unaware of how much I enjoyed the power that I had achieved. I had thought I could do no wrong, but it had become all about me."

Silence lingered for several minutes. Each reflecting in their own way.

"Are you actually going to march into Goshen and free the slaves?"

"Yes," Aiden replied.

"Can I come with you guys?" Saul asked after a few long moments.

"Why do you want to?"

"I want to help. I want a chance to do some good in my life. Will you let me come with you?"

"It depends," Aiden said. "What do you believe? What are *you* going to believe?"

"For years I've believed what everyone else told me I should believe, but I always knew better. I believe that you are unlike any other person that has ever walked this earth. You have my sword for as long as it is mine to hold." Saul tried to reach for his sword in his blindness and finally found it and pulled it from the pile of weapons. He laid it next to him.

"You are most welcome with us Saul. There is just one thing more…do you believe that I am who I say I am?" Aiden asked.

Saul nodded. "Yes."

Aiden smiled and Saul began to sit up, his eyes becoming clear, not clouded like they had been. "I can see again!"

"You have seen the truth, you will always be able to see the right way if you open your heart," Aiden said. "Welcome to the family!"

They embraced and welcomed him as the others came into the camp with the food that they could find. Isabel held a few wildfowl in her hands. The rest of them had gathered some fruits and plants that would be edible. Shavrok had managed to find an old well where they could get water.

"We shall be off first thing in the morning," Aiden said. "We will head towards Laheer and see what progress can be made there."

They ate and drank, talking and laughing and getting to know Saul. Drake remained quiet, for the most part thinking about Gwen and then about what Aiden had said. Drake certainly hadn't done very much with what had been given to him. He had pawned his job off to Lily and Ellizar and had still fallen into the very trap that he had been trying to resist.

His mind drifted to Laheer. Something about the name struck a chord in his heart every time the name was spoken. There was something different and unique about it. It gripped his heart and begged him to rush to the town and see for himself what the town was like.

The next morning they set out for Laheer. Drake's heart pounded in his chest. The forest was in front of them. He looked around at everyone else, who appeared to have no concerns. He stopped when he saw Isabel, noticing that she seemed to be acting a little different than usual. She had been quiet nearly all morning and stared straight ahead as if there was nothing for her to be afraid of.

She and Morgrin talked lightly but Drake couldn't make out what they were saying. The forest rose in front of them until they finally entered the shade of the trees. Drake's heart rate increased further as he studied everything around him with interest and fascination.

Below them was a small town. The buildings were small and beautiful, made of stones of varying colors and shades. Drake felt his heart race a little more as he recognized it. He struggled to understand what was happening as he remembered where he had seen this place before. The Sorcerer had once shown him a vision of a village and now it stood right in front of him.

"What is this place?" Drake asked.

"Laheer," Isabel answered. "At least that's the Elvish name for it."

"It has another name?" Drake asked.

"It was first inhabited by Men," Aiden said. "In those days, which were a long time ago, it was named Trundale." Drake's heart stopped hearing the name Trundale. He replayed the word in his mind over and over again wondering if he had heard right. That's what the Sorcerer had told him. So far, the Sorcerer seemed to have told the truth.

They continued into the small village, walking past the people who at first paid them no mind and then took notice of the unusual company. It wasn't long before every eye was trained on them as they walked further into the town.

Drake looked at the ground, noticing that the people of the town seemed to be looking at him. They looked at him and scowled and then turned about their business as if he had suddenly done something wrong. Drake's discomfort began to grow as they received more stares from people.

"Where are we headed?" Drake asked, hoping to get away from the people whose judgmental glances were eating Drake alive. Had he done something wrong?

"Take a left into that alley up ahead, I've got some old friends that live there," Isabel said.

"Of course she does," Shavrok said. They all smiled.

Drake was pulled from the street by arms that held him like iron. A hand clamped tightly over his mouth as he was pulled from the others and into a small building next to the alley the others had entered. They released him and Drake spun around and grabbed his sword. The two men lowered their hoods. Drake stopped mid-motion, recognizing one of them as Aaron.

"You are pretty good at abducting people," Drake said, remembering how Aaron had pulled him aside in Edrei. Aaron just smiled.

"I don't abduct them, I just borrow them for a little while," Aaron said with a laugh and then suddenly turned serious. "Why are you here?"

"Excuse me?" Drake asked.

"Why are you here? I told you not to come here didn't I?"

"I don't think so."

"Well I should've," Aaron said. "Of all the places for you to show up, this is one of the worst for you."

"How? I don't understand."

"Thank goodness!" the other man said. "By the way, my name is Jacob."

"Why is it bad I'm here?" Drake asked.

"Where is your wife?" Aaron asked.

"She died," Drake said.

"I'm sorry for your loss. I'm sure she was quite special," Aaron said. "However, there is a silver lining to this. People might not hate all of your guts if you don't have a woman on your arm."

"I'm so confused. Why is my wife being dead a good thing?"

"We never said it was a good thing that your wife was dead because we know the truth," Jacob said. "However, since you don't remember any of your past, perhaps we can help fill in some of it without endangering you anymore."

"You used to live here once, seven or eight years ago," Aaron started. "You met a beautiful woman, who happens to be our sister. You fell in love, you were engaged. The wedding festivities were all planned and on the eve of the wedding, you vanished. You ran off."

"I did?" Drake asked.

"You made many enemies on that night Drake Thomas," Jacob said. "Broke our sister's heart. People never knew where you ran off to, but a few of them swore to find you and make you pay for the pain you had inflicted on all of us."

"I don't know what to say."

"Don't apologize," Aaron said. "We know the truth and believe you, however, the rest of the town won't believe us."

"What do you mean?" Drake asked.

"You didn't run off like everyone thought you did. You were kidnapped. I was going out one last time to make sure everything was locked up for the night when I saw a cloaked figure pulling you from the house. By the time I realized what was happening you were gone. There were no footprints, no leads of any kind to go on. Even your belongings were gone. My only conclusion is that whoever kidnapped you was a sorcerer.

"When morning came, everyone saw that you had gone and taken everything of yours with you. No matter what Jacob and I said no one would believe us. We had no way to prove our story and no way to disprove it either. You had vanished off the map. As a result, we were outcast from the town."

"So how did I end up on the side of the river?" Drake asked. The two brothers shrugged their shoulders.

"No idea." Aaron moved closer. "I wouldn't suggest staying in this town any longer than you have to though."

"We are leaving first thing in the morning," Drake replied.

"Good," Aaron replied, moving towards the door. The door was kicked in by Aiden, all the others trailing behind him. Their weapons were drawn as they rushed the two brothers.

"Don't hurt them!" Drake exclaimed.

"They on our side?" Shavrok asked, holding Jacob in the air by the collar of his shirt.

"Yes, they just wanted to talk to me," Drake said. Shavrok dropped Jacob and Aiden let Aaron go.

"Sorry," Aiden said. "We've had a rough week."

"It's alright," Aaron said. "We'll just slip on out of here like we were never here. It was a pleasure meeting you all." They disappeared out into the streets as the others moved back into the alley they had been walking down.

"Aiden, did I use to live here?" Drake asked.

"How should I know?"

"You're Lathon, certainly you would know. Those two men claimed that I had lived here and that I had been engaged to their sister. Are they telling the truth or are they delusional?" Aiden remained silent for a moment.

"You used to live here," Aiden said. Drake's heart was suddenly flooded with unexpected emotion. They reentered the alley and walked until they came to a small modest house in the middle of the village.

Isabel knocked on the door and a few moments later a knock was heard inside, as though it was answering Isabel's knock. After a moment, they heard footsteps and the sound of a door creaking. A man stood in the doorway. His beard was long and grey and the hair atop his head was a mess. He wore long blue robes, and his eyes looked as if he hadn't slept in a hundred years.

"Well, I never thought I'd see you again Isabel!" the man greeted. They embraced and she introduced everyone else first before she introduced Drake. The man eyed him warily, fascination in his eyes. "Drake Thomas," the man said before she had said his name. "It's been a long time." Drake didn't say anything.

"Everyone, I would like you to meet an old friend of mine. He was a friend of my parents when they were alive. This is Queman," Isabel said turning to Queman. "I was wondering if we could get a room with you for the night, and discuss a few things."

"Certainly, certainly, come on in!" Queman exclaimed, inviting them into his house. He snapped his fingers and servants came and took their few belongings to their rooms for the night. They moved into the main living space, taking a seat wherever they could find one. "What can I do for you?"

"We need to know what the best way to get into Goshen is," Thaddeus said.

"We're not exactly sure, we would like to cut straight east, but I can't help but think that it might be heavily guarded," Isabel said.

"The only other option is north, or through the Sea of Mar in the south," Aiden said.

"You don't want to go to the Sea of Mar," Saul said. "They have several ports and major cities along the shores of that sea. Getting in there alive without the proper papers and ships, would be a suicidal move."

"How about the north?" Drake asked.

"Also no good. Its flat lands as far as the eye can see and they have watch towers everywhere. If you're spotted, you'll be dead faster than you can blink an eye. Although it might be just as dangerous, I would suggest going straight east and entering Goshen in the forest. It has hills and trees that should provide plenty of cover," Saul replied. "It'll save time and prevent us from having to be sneaky for as long. Once we get across the border Cavil is only half a day's journey, depending on how fast you can go."

Queman laughed. "Sounds like you have it all worked out Isabel. What do you need me for?"

"Lodging for the night and if it's possible horses to speed us along?"

"It shall be done," Queman said. "I will get you the fastest horses from my stock."

"In case you guys are wondering, they are *very* fast," Isabel said. "I rode one once and almost thought I couldn't control it."

"They must be special horses," Diderus said. "How many do you have of them?"

"About three thousand," Queman answered. "I've been building up my herd so that if there is a great war, there will be great steeds as well. I figure I can cash in on it and make a contribution besides. I will give you all the food and traveling supplies you can possibly want and I will have your weapons sharpened and cleaned. As I can see they are quite used right now."

"We always see our fair share of action," Shavrok said. "I can run alongside the horses I'm sure. Besides, I doubt you would have a horse large enough to carry me any great distance."

"The herd is quite unique, but I think you might be right on that one. Due to Mr. Thomas, it might be safer if you are with someone that they know and trust. I'll personally escort you out of the village."

"So is it all true?" Drake asked. "Was I engaged to a woman here?"

"Yes, you were. She was a kind-hearted, gentle woman. Not a bad bone in her body."

"Where is she?" Drake asked. Queman shrugged.

"I'm not sure. She left a couple of years ago. She hasn't been heard from since. The town angered me greatly after you left. They treated her like a criminal that needed to be put to death. They said she had brought great shame to the family and therefore she was shunned. I don't know what happened to her. There are only rumors?"

"What are the rumors?" Morgrin asked.

"They vary depending on who you talk to. Some claim she sold herself to a man to be married. Others say she committed suicide, others say she went off looking for Drake. It's hard to know for sure unless she shows up."

"Great! I've got everyone mad at me for something I can't fix?" Drake asked.

"Patience Drake," Aiden said. "I'm sure you will have a chance to get things right before it's all over."

Drake hung on to those words as they talked a little longer and they went off to bed for the night. Drake's dreams were strange and dark, offering him nothing but chaos as he tried to figure out what they might mean.

He flinched, his hand instinctively going towards his sword as there came a sound out his window. A ladder had been propped up against the side of the house and two people could be heard talking to each other in hushed tones as they climbed the ladder. Drake quietly rolled out of the bed and to the one side of the window, ready to defend himself if he needed to. The window was carefully opened and one of the people stuck their heads in. Drake kept himself from doing anything more, recognizing the two men on the ladder.

"You guys again." Aaron and Jacob both slipped into the window. "Are you here to kidnap me again?"

"No, this time we came to get you out of here," Aaron said. The others now began to stir as Aiden woke up and then Morgrin and Isabel. "Don't ask questions. All we know is that there are about ten people in cloaks roaming the city. We haven't seen them before and we can only conclude that they are after you." Queman burst through the door, swords in hands.

"Hello Queman," Jacob said.

Queman rolled his eyes. "You! You are the miserable little thieves who stole my horses the other day."

"You have no proof of that," Aaron said, with a weak smile.

"There were two of my horses missing from my herd. I may not have hard concrete proof, but my stable masters gave me a description of the thieves and they bear a striking resemblance to yourselves."

"Really?" Jacob asked. Queman nodded. "That's amazing. We'll have to keep on the lookout for them."

"I know you are the ones who stole my horses!"

"Stole is such an ugly term," Aaron said. "Can't we say that we… borrowed…them. Because we did bring them back just now."

"Were you going to leave them here?"

"Well, we were going to need them again," Jacob replied with a laugh. By now everyone else had woken up and had come into the one room. "On another note, the people in the cloaks don't look friendly."

"What should we do?" Morgrin asked.

"We depart immediately," Aiden answered. "We will head east and make our way to Cavil and arrive a little earlier than we had planned."

"I'll alert my stable boys and get your horses ready," Queman said. He turned to leave but was stopped by Aaron who had cleared his throat.

"I'm afraid that won't be necessary, my friend. You see we already took the liberty of borrowing a few more horses from your stables because we knew we were coming here. We've got enough horses for everyone."

"The one time I don't mind thieves," Queman replied. They dressed and prepared to leave. Queman had agreed to stay behind, in case people came asking questions, he would have answers to give them. The rest of them climbed out the window, which they closed right before they took the ladder down.

They walked down the alley turning to the left where nine horses were tied up and waiting. They all mounted and followed Aaron and Jacob, who led them out of the town. Drake watched the town as it slipped from his view. A piece of his heart longed to stay there and make amends for everything he had apparently done.

"Ten minutes and then we'll be across the border," Jacob told them.

"I can't believe I'm walking back in this nation to do something other than kill people," Saul said.

"It's an interesting chain of events I must say that," Drake said, struggling to keep his mind focused. His wife had died, he had been kidnapped, told that he had been engaged to a woman before Gwen, and now was carefully sneaking through a forest. It was almost more than one person could take.

"What are we going to do when we get there?" Saul asked. "I know we are trying to free the slaves but how are we going to do it?"

"You tell me," Aiden countered.

"I'm not sure I understand," Saul said.

"They are my people, but they are your people as well. You were a prince there, therefore in their eyes, we are your assistants. You will lead us in our efforts."

"Me?" Saul asked. "What do I know? I'm a fugitive."

"All the more perfect of a reason that you should be the one to lead them out," Aiden said.

"How is that a perfect reason?" Drake asked.

"Is there not a better way for a person to prove that they've changed and started a new chapter in their life than to do something completely outside their comfort zone, not necessarily because they're trying to prove a point, but because they want to."

"Did I ever say I wanted to lead the people out?" Saul asked.

"Not in so many words, but in your heart I know you do. You said you wanted to help us. This is the task that I would like you to do."

"I'm the wrong person," Saul said.

"I'll make you a deal Saul. You lead the way to the city. If we get there and in your heart, you don't think that you're supposed to lead them, then I will do it." Saul thought hard for a moment.

"Okay," Saul finally agreed.

"Remember to be great you have to find your comfort zone, and then leave it. That is what Lathon calls all of us to do. We do the world no good if we stay in our comfort zone and don't try to further his kingdom."

"If you don't mind, we'll be taking our leave from your group," Aaron said. "We have other matters to attend to." Aaron and Jacob said goodbye and rode away.

"Drake and Isabel, I have a job for the two of you if you would like it?" Aiden said.

"Whatever it is, count me in," Isabel said. Drake couldn't help but laugh.

"You don't even know what it is he wants yet."

"So?" Isabel answered. "I prefer not to put anything off, to jump at the very will of Lathon and let Lathon take care of everything I would normally worry about. Look at the birds of the trees. They do not think about what they are going to eat and where they are going to sleep. Lathon provides for even them, why should I worry?"

"Every day that passes I'm more and more convinced that I've lived these past five years wrong," Drake said, a wave of guilt passing over him.

"Everyone makes mistakes Drake," Morgrin said.

"There is only one thing you did Drake that was perhaps not the greatest in the world. You left the throne in Mera Runa because you felt you had something to do in the northern lands. The only problem is you never returned to the position I gave you."

"I know. I felt like I should at some point, I just kept putting it off. I guess I was just afraid the power would corrupt me and destroy all that is good."

"That happens to many people," Aiden said. "Their lives become sad stories, but for those who put their trust in Lathon I think they have far more potential to be great without turning corrupt."

"I doubted myself," Drake said. "I didn't like all the attention and I was scared of where it might lead."

"I wouldn't have chosen you for the task if I didn't think you were capable of it. Saul that goes for you as well. You have it in you. I'm not saying that you won't make mistakes because everyone does. That's what friends are for and that's why they are so important to everyone. Drake, can you guess what I want you to do?" Aiden asked.

"Go back and lead the people."

"That's right. We will need you before the slaves can truly be free."

"What do you want me to do?" Drake asked.

"Fly to Mera Runa and bring back as large of a force as you can muster. Ride to Mt. Dahab and we will meet you there. Isabel, do you know what your job is?"

"Yep," Isabel replied.

"It's set then," Aiden said. They walked for a few more minutes until they came to a large clearing in the forest. The three Taruks sat waiting for them. Drake moved to Destan who hung his head in sorrow over the absence of Gwen. Drake momentarily let himself be pulled into thoughts of sorrow but soon came back to reality. She was in a better place than this.

Aspen stood in the clearing as well and Isabel kissed Morgrin goodbye and then wasted no time in jumping on Aspen and lifting off into the sky. Drake climbed on Destan and they rose high above the forest leaving everyone else behind. Isabel and Aspen flew alongside them for several minutes before heading off to the north. Elohim had begun flying to the east and had long vanished from their view.

The sun began to come up over the horizon and Drake was amazed at just how beautiful and powerful Lathon was. To have created something so magnificent that would happen every day, for them to look at was beyond his comprehension. Drake wondered what would happen when he landed outside Mera Runa. Would they be happy to see him? Would they resent him for what he had done?

He sat tall as they flew over the land below. The day stretched on and they got closer and closer to Mera Runa. Anticipation rippled through Drake as they neared the only home Drake had ever known.

Even though he had only just set course for Mera Runa it felt as if a great burden had been lifted off of him. It was a new day and with that came a new beginning. Drake thought about everything that had happened and lightly entertained what the future might hold, then he stopped himself. If there was one thing he was growing sure of, it was that life wasn't about him. It was about what he could do for other people.

Chapter 12

ALEXANDREA

The city Saul had lived in for most of his life, Cavil, now stood on the horizon as nothing more than a dot. Saul knew he was a wanted man for having killed the guard years ago, but did they know the other people he had killed over the years? Aiden rode beside him while everyone else followed behind.

Mountains lay to the southeast and the city lay just to their north. Years of anger and hatred towards the people who forced the slaves to comply came back to him like waves in the ocean. Saul's determination grew with each crack of the whip he heard. They finally reached the open fields in front of the fortress, seeing rock columns being moved by hundreds of slaves, which held long ropes.

Piles of mud bricks were being moved from one area to another and the people were forced to work no matter what their age. They were clothed in rags and beaten and whipped regularly.

The guards took notice of him and blew a couple of horns. Saul and the others continued their march towards the main gate, paying them no mind. A moment later more horns were heard and the large gates opened. Horsemen rode out, twenty in all, surrounding them and holding them at spearpoint.

"Well, look who it is," one of the guards taunted. "The fallen prince? I've long wanted the privilege of killing you."

"I'm sorry to inform you that it is not the time for me to be killed," Saul answered. The guard laughed.

"Amusing I must say," the guard said. "I have twenty men at my disposal and you are surrounded. I don't think you have any choice in the matter."

The men pulled back their spears but never got to throw them as the bones in their arms snapped. The head guard was the only one who wasn't affected by the strange injuries that had plagued his men.

"I think you should let us go, and escort us to the main palace. We have words that are for the emperor's ears only," Aiden said. The man muttered a curse and then yelled for his men to let them pass. Twenty more horsemen came out and surrounded them as they were led into the city.

They passed through the second gate, met by countless guards. They stared at him, their eyes showing surprise. They finally reached the keep and then dismounted their horses as they were led into the stronghold.

Inside, the building was dark and cold with only a few torches burning on the walls. The guards led them down the hall until they were stopped at a large set of double doors. Most of the guards remained with them, but some slipped in.

"How are we going to get the slaves out of here?" Saul asked Aiden.

"Tell the king that the longer he prevents the slaves from leaving with us, the more disasters will fall on this nation."

"Disasters?" Nickolas asked. "What kind of disasters?"

"Bad ones," Aiden answered. "Just tell him that and listen to the voice of Lathon which will come to you and we'll be just fine."

"I'm trying to find the courage right now," Saul said. The doors opened and they were escorted into the large throne room.

To either side were statues of past kings and of the gods they worshiped. In front of each of the statues were alters that were used daily by the emperor and his family to sacrifice to the gods and kings of old. Saul knew the things that they did and his heart cried out, more determined than ever to free these slaves.

The only father he had ever known his entire life sat on the throne, with his wife and all the princes and princesses, who he had been raised with, to either side of him. Saul returned their glances, holding the gaze, first with the king, his stepfather Ahab, then with the queen, who had been his stepmother, Jezebel.

"Saul, my *son*, what a surprise to see you here!" Ahab started. "I was hoping we'd get to talk soon, to discuss the contract out on your life. Perhaps we might come to a mutual understanding."

"I highly doubt that."

"You lack optimism," Ahab criticized. The others laughed and chuckled.

"I didn't march in here to have meaningless conversations with a half-witted king and his family!" Saul exclaimed. The room fell silent.

"You realize I could have you arrested for what you just said," Jezebel said. "Actually, I could have you killed."

"You could but you won't. Not until you hear what I have to say."

"I have no time to listen to cowards who run away from their duties," Ahab said.

"It takes far more courage to come back than it does to run away," Aiden said, stepping forward. "Now you *will* listen to what he has to say."

"And why should I listen to you? You're probably another one just like him, a murderer, a thief, someone I should hang and butcher. You are an elf and that means it's open season in this country! Perhaps you should go join the slaves. That is after all where you belong."

"Kill him and you'll have to kill me as well," Thaddeus said stepping forward.

"And me," Morgrin said stepping forward. "I'm not an elf, but my wife is. Does that make us villains?"

"If you're going to kill them you'll have to kill us as well," Diderus said, stepping forward. Shavrok stepped forward as well. "We are all here together."

Ahab appeared uninterested. "Do you have anything to say?"

"I have a demand actually," Saul started. Ahab chuckled. "You must let the slaves go. All of them, Elves, Dwarves, and Humans alike." Laughter filled the room.

"And how do you suppose you are going to force me to do this?" Ahab taunted. "Have you learned nothing about negotiating in all the years you lived in the palace with us?" They laughed again. Saul looked down the line of princes and princesses, which numbered ten in all. One of them caught his eye and held his gaze for a moment. Sorrow was in her eyes.

"Tell us, dear boy," Jezebel started. "Are our lives in any danger? Even if you managed to kill us you would not make it out of the city alive."

"Your lives are at risk, as are the lives of your people," Aiden said, stepping forward. Ahab looked amused.

"The elf talks again?" Ahab said, looking at his wife and then back to Aiden. "How is my life at risk?"

"If you do not let the slaves go, there will be dire consequences that will wreak havoc on your land and your bodies. You will let us go before the end," Aiden answered.

"I will do just the opposite," Ahab said. "Guards, take these people and lock them up in the dungeons! Also, double the workload for the slaves and beat them twice as hard if they do not meet their quotas."

"Tomorrow when the sun rises the rivers and waters of this land will be turned to blood, due to all the innocent blood you have shed on account of your actions," Aiden said.

"What would that profit you, my *elf friend*?" Jezebel asked. "Something of that magnitude, if it were possible, would hurt your own people as well."

"The slaves will not be affected by these plagues, Only you and your people, and those select few in your service or family who do not honor Lathon."

"I can assure you, no one in this nation worships your make-believe god," Ahab said. "Someday, I hope to get rid of that pathetic religion."

"I'm sorry to say that you won't get that chance," Aiden said. "There is no need to arrest us, we will be on our way out of here and we will return tomorrow."

"Fine, wander off into the wilderness for all I care," Ahab said. "This isn't over yet."

Aiden looked at him, his eyes filled with sorrow. "You couldn't be more right."

They turned and began walking out of the throne room. Laughter filled the room as they left.

"What's going to happen now?" Saul asked.

"We will make camp a couple of hours from the city, near the mountains. We will remain there until we return tomorrow. Each day that passes will bring another plague. It will be interesting to see how long he holds his ground."

"Probably as long as his pride remains intact," Shavrok said. "I wanted to shake him right there and then." They all smiled.

"I'm sure you did, but that is not the way things are meant to happen," Aiden said. They walked past the slaves and then through the city gates, collecting their horses and then riding to the mountains. They dismounted, quickly gathering things for a meal and a fire. Within an hour they had caught some small game and some fish from the river nearby.

"Who's going to do the cooking?" Diderus asked. "I only know how to cook Goblin food, and it's not very good, even to me."

"I'll cook," Shavrok volunteered. Thaddeus laughed.

"You're going to do the cooking?" Nickolas asked. "A big warrior like you is going to cook?"

"Just because he's a big warrior, doesn't mean he's too great to not have to cook," Saul said.

"Well said," Aiden agreed.

"Who's that?" Morgrin asked, pointing out towards a horse and rider coming towards them. They all stood up and studied the person approaching. "Looks like we're going to have company."

"That's one of the royal horses," Saul replied. "You can tell by the emblem on the front of the bridle. It's no one that's going to harm us that I know for a fact."

The horse and rider came closer and then finally brought the horse to a halt. The rider hopped off and lowered her hood, letting her long golden hair fall down. Her sapphire eyes shone in the midday sun as she and Saul ran to each other. She embraced him with a long kiss on the lips. They held each other for several seconds. Finally, Saul set her back on the ground and their lips separated as they stared into each other's eyes.

"I didn't think I'd ever see you again," the woman whispered, trying to hold back tears.

"I didn't think you'd ever want to see me again," Saul answered. Nearly as emotional.

"Who is our guest?" Nickolas asked as the company approached. Saul smiled.

"Everyone this is one of the princesses of Goshen, Alexandrea." They went around and introduced themselves. Alexandrea shook their hands, smiling from ear to ear.

"Shavrok, I think you should make enough food for another person," Aiden said. "Because she is most welcome to join us."

"I would be honored," Alexandrea replied.

"How about that?" Morgrin said. "Royalty who isn't afraid to have dinners in the outdoors with a strange group like ours."

"I'm not strange," Shavrok defended, laughing and playfully smacking Morgrin on the shoulder. Morgrin fell to the ground and they all laughed.

"Please have a seat," Saul said. He took her by the hand and led her to their fire where Shavrok was now back to cooking the food.

"So you're one of the emperor's daughters?" Diderus asked.

"Yes, I'm the last born, which of course means that I'll never be queen or anything like that, but that's not a concern to me. You will find that I don't agree with my family on much of anything."

"So I take it they don't know you're here?" Aiden asked. Alexandrea nodded.

"I left in secret and I don't plan to return unless it's with you. When I saw you walk in and I saw Saul leading the way I couldn't help but feel as if my very heart had leapt out of my chest. I guess it's no secret that I still love him."

"A little strange isn't it? Dating your brother?" Thaddeus asked.

"He's not actually my brother. The queen found him in a basket along the river. Furthermore, my father, the emperor, leads a very active social life. None of the princes or princesses are from the same mother. I was actually born from an elf slave."

"An elf slave?" Morgrin asked. "Funny, you don't look Elvish."

"Perhaps the one reason I've been kept alive," Alexandrea replied. "If I had started to show signs of my Elvish mother in me I would have been slaughtered immediately, or taken out to the fields and left for dead."

"Fields?" Shavrok asked.

"After a baby is born, if the couple does not approve of the baby, whether it has a birth defect, a flaw, or they just don't want the baby, they can take it out to the fields, which are located about a mile from here, and leave the baby there. They either die of heat and starvation or are devoured by the wolves at night. If you try to save a baby, you'll be tied up and left there as well."

"Only if they catch you," Aiden said. "I've known many people who rescued dozens and dozens of babies. Given them away to people who will love them."

"Very true," Alexandrea said. "After I was born, the emperor continued to have babies with my mother. Every one of them became visibly Elvish and every one of them was taken to the fields. My own mother was taken to the fields and left for dead. Saul was the only friend that I ever had in the palace, and certainly the only one who even remotely understood me. We aren't like everyone else."

"And on that note, you're not meant to be," Aiden said. "There are many cruel injustices in this world and the two of you will put an end to many of them."

"We will?" Saul asked. Aiden nodded.

"Yes you will," Aiden answered. Alexandrea and Saul both fell silent.

"How though?" Alexandrea asked. "Are we actually going to try and free all the slaves?"

"We're not going to try; we will free them," Aiden corrected. "Right now the Goshen government is Lord over all lands in the northern region. If we take all these slaves out, I can assure you that the government will act swiftly and violently to kill all the slaves and take new slaves to restore their power. What we have to do is get all the slaves out of the nation and then return with a force and overthrow the government. Then we can bring everyone back and give them the land that was once theirs. Once we do that, I think it would be only fitting if Saul and yourself were given charge of the nation."

"I have no desire to be queen," Alexandrea argued.

"You have no desire to change how people view the king and queen?" Aiden asked. "I can imagine that your fear of leading or standing out in front of the crowd comes from your past as a princess. You've both seen things that have appalled you and made you resistant to the idea of leading, but would you be interested in being a new kind of king and queen? The kind that the people deserve?

"A humble king is the only one that should ever rule. A king filled with compassion and can feel the suffering of his people. They are few and far between these days. You could be a light for the whole world to see." Silence followed for a moment.

"I suppose you're right about our fear," Saul said. "I'm afraid of failing."

"The fear of failure is the most destructive of all fears," Morgrin said. "It fills our heads with lies that say we can't do things, therefore, preventing us from doing them."

"I would not ask this of you if I didn't know that you could do it," Aiden said. "There will be many trials and tribulations no matter what you choose, but I promise, you will have the strength to go through it and come out a different person. What do you say?" Alexandrea and Saul looked at each other for a couple of moments.

"We'll do it," Alexandrea said. "We don't know much about how to lead a nation, at least not well. So we might need some pointers." They laughed together.

"Advice will always be given to those who ask for it," Nickolas said. Shavrok half laughed.

"That's because the ones who ask for it are smart enough to know that they need it."

"I'll drink to that!" Thaddeus said.

"How about we start by eating," Diderus said. "Is the food done?"

"What do I look like, a cook?" Shavrok asked.

"Kind of," Alexandrea said. They all laughed as Shavrok went back to the cooking.

"Is there anything we should know before we march into the palace tomorrow?" Nickolas asked.

"My father is planning to kill you as soon as you are within range," Alexandrea answered.

"Comforting," Nickolas replied.

"Don't worry, nothing will happen to us," Aiden said. "He can try all he wants, but all of his efforts will be unsuccessful. Once the plagues start hitting he will resist us more, but the last one, will crush him and he will let us go."

"I'm afraid to ask," Morgrin said. Aiden looked at them, fear in his eyes.

"It is wise to fear the last one," Aiden said.

They all went about their own business while Saul and Alexandrea sat talking to each other.

He stared into Alexandrea's deep blue eyes, falling in love with her like he had never felt before. The light in her eyes said that she was feeling the same thing. He doubted that separately they would be able to lead a nation, but the two of them combined with Aiden? That would be worth trying.

They were pulled out of their thoughts as they looked to Shavrok and the others who were all jovially laughing and singing songs, not caring if anyone heard them. Saul might not have known them for long, but he had observed them long enough to know that they weren't just putting on an act as many people did. They were real.

It wasn't what was on the outside that mattered, it was the inside that mattered. You were defined by what you did when no one was looking. That's what makes someone a great person. Watching Aiden now, Saul was confident that he was the real deal. He was the one who would save them.

"The feast is finally ready!" Nickolas exclaimed, stepping closer and looking into the pot, confusion on his face. "Where's the food?"

"What do you mean where's the food?" Shavrok asked. "It's right there!"

"That's stew!" Nickolas exclaimed. "We brought you all that meat! What did you do with it?" Shavrok hesitated.

"I might have gotten a little hungry while I was making the food and as a piece of meat was cooked, ate it?" Shavrok asked. "Might have though, you don't have any proof."

"I guess we should be thankful we even have stew, the way a Gog eats," Morgrin said. "Although, seeing your size I can understand why you eat so much."

"You see?" Shavrok said speaking to Nickolas. "His wife has taught him well, that's why the Gog's like her so much." They laughed as they ate their meals and then fell asleep under the stars.

* * *

Lily watched the sunrise. The vast green lands lay before her like a sea, filled with life. She loved this part of the morning. She sat on the balcony, overlooking Mera Runa and all the wonderful people that lived in it.

It was in this part of the morning that she found peace. So often in the everyday world, it was so easy to get pulled into the craziness of the day and forget just who had made all of this possible. She praised Lathon for making something so beautiful, and so magnificent even despite the direction everything was headed.

She listened to the sleeping city, only hearing the sound of Ellizar snoring noisily. Their marriage had certainly raised some eyebrows when it had finally taken place, but nothing could keep her from loving him. They pushed each other's buttons and got on each other's nerves, but they still loved each other more now than they had on their wedding day.

She looked down at the nice robe she was in, guilt swarming over her. The fact that she had clothes so nice and all the food she could eat, when everyday people went hungry made her sick to her stomach. Her soul cried out to change the situation she was in, but she was powerless. An order like that could only be made by the king. The real king.

She closed her eyes, trying to imagine what Drake and Gwen's faces looked like. It had been so long since she had seen them. So long since Drake and Gwen had left and vowed to return.

How long would she and Ellizar have to wait? They loved to have the opportunity to serve, and they had done many great things, but this job hadn't been appointed to them, it had been given to Drake and Gwen.

A black speck appeared in the northern sky. Her spirit rose as she recognized the sight of a Taruk flying. She marveled at the magnificent creatures, who despite their power and their might, humbled themselves and carried around people and did what they could to help in the situation.

Not many people understood Taruks, they just thought they were something you had if you were going to go into the Mezutor. Beneath the surface, there was so much more than just a fast Taruk. Lily contemplated everything, realizing how much Lathon was like a great Taruk.

People who just read the ancient scrolls, saw just Lathon, a simple name and the things that he had done. But to those who studied the ancient scrolls, they took on a deeper understanding of everything. Written throughout the ancient scrolls was the great love story of the ages, some people never got it, and some never would.

Her heart cried out for people who would never understand it, or see the truth in a world full of lies. How could they not see what was right in front of them? She and Ellizar had tried their hardest to be real and to live a life that would catch the attention of others, and it had worked.

She turned her gaze to the north seeing the Taruk, coming closer in the sky. She studied the Taruk, hoping to make out its color, so she could identify who it was. Finally, the sun caught the Taruk's hard skin at just the right angle, reflecting at her the deep green and then stripes of light green. The color of Destan. She stood and woke up Ellizar, smacking him in the side as she threw on a nice gown.

"What yeh deh that fer?" Ellizar asked. Lily threw some clothes at him.

"We have some company on the way," Lily said, unable to hide the excitement in her voice.

"Visitor? At this time ov the mornin'?" Ellizar asked. "Can't they wait another hour or so?"

"They must like to annoy Dwarves," Lily countered.

"Blasted elf kind!" Ellizar said. They both laughed and dressed heading out of the room to the main hall which stretched to both the left and the right. The guards outside their room stood at attention.

"Good morning your Highness," the guard said.

Lily laughed. "Perhaps Dwarves should be greeted as your lowness?" The guard laughed and Ellizar did too. "Send a messenger out and alert all the people of the city, that a very special guest will be joining us today. Prepare a feast, we must celebrate!"

The guards nodded and ran down the hallways carrying out the order.

"What guest are yeh talkin' about?" Ellizar asked. They walked to the left coming to a large winding staircase that would take them out of the tall tower that had been their home for the past few years.

"I spotted Destan in the sky and I think Drake and Gwen are with him."

"So, the king returns?" Ellizar said with a joyful laugh escaping him. "That is good news indeed. Maybe he'll take over fer us again."

"That would be nice," Lily said. Their five-year-old daughter and four-year-old son came running out of their rooms. Both of the children were tall like Lily was, with hardly any dwarvish in them.

Together they made their way out of the main spire and were now looking over the city, which was filled with horns blowing. The citizens of the city were awakened and the message of their guests' arrival was announced at every street corner by the royal guards. The city came alive with excitement as many of them moved out of the castle to the open fields to watch as the Taruk came in for a landing.

Destan was growing bigger in the sky, now clearly being identified as a Taruk with one rider on it. Lily and Ellizar both looked at each other, questions and joy rippling through them at the same time.

Destan and Drake flew lower, moving more to the north and coming along the mountains, flying over the city from the back. They flew low, only a couple of feet from the highest wall. The people of the city cheered and the horns were blown as Destan flew to the large grassy fields in front of Mera Runa. In the distance, more horns echoed as the farmers and villagers passed the message to the next.

It was a unique message system they had developed, having placed farms and houses in the right position so the sound would reach them. From them, they would pass it on, and the message would eventually travel all the way through Rhallinen, and even as far as Atruss who served as king in Ariamore once again.

Destan finally landed in the field and Ellizar and Lily ran out to meet him, their kids following right behind. Drake smiled from ear to ear and laughed as Lily ran and embraced him. When they separated Ellizar smiled and held out a hand. Drake grabbed it and pulled him close, embracing him.

"It's about time yeh showed up!" Ellizar exclaimed.

"It's been far too long my friends," Drake said. "Somehow I've forgotten what it feels like to be home. And who are these beautiful young people?" Their daughter and their son smiled at him.

"Drake I would like you to meet our children; this is our daughter Celine and our son Timothy. Kids, this is your Uncle Drake."

"Well I would have come home much earlier if I had known you guys were this big," Drake said to the kids. They smiled and then embraced him in a big hug.

"No Gwen?" Lily asked. Drake's face saddened.

"No. She's no longer with us."

"She died?" Lily asked. Drake nodded and Lily fell silent. Lily searched for peace in her mind, but couldn't find any.

"Many more will die if we don't act quickly," Drake said. Lily was pulled out of her thoughts. "That is why I've come back."

"Yeh, have a battle fer us teh partake in Master Drake?" Ellizar asked, a smile already on his face.

"Yes. Aiden has led us to Goshen and we're going to free all the slaves, but if we're going to do that, then we'll have to have a force to fight with once the emperor gives chase. If we can defeat them, then Gwen will not have died in vain."

"I think yeh already know that yeh can count my axe into this battle!" Ellizar exclaimed. They all smiled.

"I had no doubt," Drake said.

"I should have turned it into a candlestick holder. It would have been a better use of it the last six years," Lily said.

"A candle stick holder?" Ellizar asked. "Blasted elf kind! What kind ov a person would use it fer somethin' like that."

"Someone like me," Lily said smiling at him.

"I do have one more thing to say to you guys," Drake said. Lily and Ellizar both looked at him. He hesitated for a moment. "I was wrong to do what I did to you these past five years. Leaving you on the throne and never returning like I said I would. I was scared of being the king, so I got rid of the problem and gave it to you, and I never should have done that. I've come to be the king I never was if you'll let me?"

"Of course, we'll let you," Lily said, "And we completely forgive you for whatever you did or didn't do. You came back and that means the world to us. We will be glad to serve you once again."

"Do you think they will?" Drake asked, looking to the soldiers who had now gathered on the field.

"I think they will be just as hap'y teh serve under yer rule as we are," Ellizar said. "There is a light in their eyes that I have not seen fer some time, they still respect yeh and will gladly follow yeh into battle."

"In that case, we must leave as soon as we possibly can. Call all the troops from Phenoix and Ephesi to make their way north and rendezvous at Mt. Dahab in Edon. There we will wait until Aiden and the rest of them show up with the slaves. Use any horses you can find, we ride at noon!"

A few of the messengers and guards who had been near them immediately started carrying out the orders, spreading the word. Drake slowly started to turn from them.

"Drake," Lily said. Drake stopped and looked towards her.

"I'm sorry about Gwen."

"So am I."

Chapter 13

PLAGUES

Nickolas stared at the horizon in disbelief. The sun was overhead, quickly rising into the sky and they were left to stare at the water, which was as red as blood. The company moved closer to the water as they wandered up to the fortress in the distance.

Nickolas stole a look at Saul who appeared just as stunned. The water was red. Nickolas finally stopped and put a hand in the water, pulling it away when he realized that it didn't feel like water.

"What is this?" Nickolas asked. The animals that lived in the water were already dead, floating on top, slowly getting pushed into the shores by the current. They looked to Aiden whose eyes were filled with sorrow.

"This is but just a little bit of the terror that will come over the emperor, every day he does not let our people go," Aiden said. "This is the blood of everyone he has had a hand in killing and this isn't even all of it. It is time that this reign of evil comes to an end. We will go to the king and give him another opportunity to save himself. If he lets them go the water will return to its normal state, if he does not, then an even worse plague will ensue."

"Aiden, won't this hurt the people that we are trying to free?" Alexandrea asked. Aiden shook his head.

"The slaves are generally kept in towns just a half mile from Cavil, their water will be unaffected. Grab a handful of blood from the river." They all watched as Alexandrea bent down and cupped some of the blood in her hands. She pulled her hands from the river and the blood turned to sparkling clear water. She licked some of it with her tongue.

"It's perfect," Alexandrea noted.

"Any slave or follower of Lathon who needs to drink of the water can do so, but it will only change for them. Even if there's a jug of water and it is taken by one of the royal guards, as soon as they touch it, it'll turn back to blood. I will protect my people."

"If there was any doubt in my mind that you were who you said you were, those doubts have long since been gone," Nickolas said. "How can we ever be worthy to be in your presence?"

"Serve me with every part of your life and I will make you worthy," Aiden said. "I say it again, serve me with *every* part of your life. You cannot expect Lathon to bless you if you keep nine of the rules, but break the tenth. I'm not interested in fans, who only want to use me as a wishing well. I'm interested in people who want to change the world and follow me to the very ends of the world!"

"The ten rules?" Diderus asked. "I don't think I've heard about those before. Of course, I'm not very educated on much of anything except what I've learned from you."

"Yes, the ten rules. There are only ten rules. They are simple rules, but people have made them complicated," Aiden started. "First off, there is only one God, and that's Lathon. Anyone who tells you otherwise has been deceived by the Sorcerer. Second is in ways connected to the first, you must not let idols take a part of your life. An idol becomes a god and will consume both your time, your money, and your possessions. You can't serve water and fire, both serve their purpose but together they destroy each other.

"Third, don't misuse the name of Lathon. What I mean is many people say that they do things because Lathon has gifted them, yet they are lying through their teeth. Fourth, remember that Lathon was the one who created this great earth.

"Fifth, honor and respect your father and mother. If you think you know everything you couldn't be more wrong. They are wise and full of advice that will benefit you. Six, seven, and eight are simple, do not murder, steal, or lie.

All three defy the natural order of what Lathon both is, and intended. Those three things have likely been the most powerful forces that have destroyed the world and made it what it is today.

"Nine and ten are similar in some respects; nine says do not commit adultery. Doing this destroys all that is good in a person's soul. And finally, the tenth is don't lust after anything your neighbor or friend has. Be happy and content with what Lathon has given you and he will multiply it."

"When you think about it, after those ten rules, there isn't much more that you could do wrong," Thaddeus said.

"Those sure aren't practiced in this nation," Alexandrea said. "Many of the royal princes and princesses are because of adultery. Myself included. Ahab got my mom pregnant and then had my dad killed in battle just to cover it up. As far as idols and gods are concerned, the name of Lathon is only spoken among the slaves."

Aiden nodded. "That's why we are here. Come, we must be on our way." They rode through the wilderness, passing by the red waters and then past several pastures that were filled with flocks and herds of animals, all dead.

"They drank the water?" Saul asked.

"Yes," Aiden replied. They rode to the walls of the city, the guards blocked the way. Alexandrea rode to the front of the company and Shavrok moved up on one side of her.

"I suggest you let the princess and her friends in," Shavrok said, with a growl. "Or else I might just have to get forceful."

"In case you're wondering, you don't want to see a Gog get forceful," Morgrin said. The others laughed, and the guards looked at each other.

"Gentlemen?" Alexandrea asked. "Would you please let us pass, or I shall report you to the king?"

The guards slowly parted and opened the iron gates letting them into the city. In the streets, the scene was much like the scene outside the city had been. The majority of the livestock had died from the water and people were trying to find water that they could drink. Alexandrea led the way through the city and past the people, easily getting them into the inner gate and the palace. The guards opened the palace doors and they were ushered in. Aiden and Saul led the way with Alexandrea on his other side. The king and royal family were up front just as they had been the day before.

"So you are with them are you?" Jezebel said.

Alexandrea nodded. "Perhaps I was never with you in the first place."

"Traitor. I should have you killed right now," Ahab said.

"You would die before you touched her," Saul said, drawing his sword and a dagger.

"I highly doubt that," Ahab taunted. They all laughed but stopped a moment later when a dagger struck the chair just by Ahab's head, missing only by an inch.

"I missed my target this time, but I promise I won't next time," Saul said. Ahab went to speak.

"Don't bother wasting your breath on us Ahab," Aiden said. "You can't harm us and you won't harm us. Have you had any water today? You look a little dehydrated."

"Get this Sorcerer out of my sight!" Ahab yelled. The guards struggled to move, an invisible force keeping them in place.

"We will leave after you hear what we have to say. If you let the slaves go you can stop all of this right now. If you continue to oppress the slaves you have taken this land from then more disasters will follow you to your grave."

"You call this a problem?" one of the princes taunted. "This is not a problem, take your pointless banter elsewhere."

"Let our people go then?" Alexandrea asked. The king stared at her.

"No. I will make their lives as miserable as I possibly can!"

"Then yours too shall be miserable," Aiden said. "Tomorrow a great storm will come, raising this city to the ground."

Ahab laughed. "This is the largest city in the Goshen empire and was built a thousand years ago. No storm can level this city, not even the largest army on the earth could do it."

"I bet an army of Gog's could do it," Shavrok whispered. Nickolas smiled.

"You can save yourself a lot of pain if you let everyone leave now," Morgrin said.

"The only suffering I would save myself is the suffering from a headache caused by the sounds of your voice. Look, you are great magicians, I get that, but so what if you can turn a little water into blood?"

"They are no cheap tricks! These disasters will fall on you until you let us go. They are no laughing matter!" Aiden exclaimed.

"Says you. I say this, Guards!" The guards opened doors and a couple of people in long royal robes entered with a couple of basins and a bucket of water. They set them on the floor and stood behind them, facing Aiden and the rest of them. They poured the water into the basins and then dumped a strange potion into the water. It turned to blood.

"You see?" Ahab taunted. "Nothing special about your turning water to blood trick. I will admit it's impressive that you were able to do it to all the water, but other than that I am unimpressed and undeterred. Now get out."

"As you wish," Aiden said. The blood in the basins turned into water and at once they turned and left. Nickolas stole a glance over his shoulder at the king who stared at them, his eyes full of malice. They left the castle the way they had come, riding out to the west a half mile or so where the slaves were kept. Just as Aiden had said the water there was clear and cool, providing for the people they wanted to save.

"How did the king have clear water for his sorcerers to change it to blood?" Nickolas asked.

"It wasn't water, it was vinegar," Aiden said. "You probably didn't notice, his magicians no doubt would've had a spell to cover the odor. There were a few things that gave it away, not easy to see mind you."

"A bunch of con artists," Shavrok said.

"It would've worked on normal people," Alexandrea noted. "Most people are uneducated about things like that."

"They did have water when they were done," Aiden said. "But it wasn't their doing, it was mine. The emperor failed to notice that though."

"I'm sure he noticed, but he won't admit it," Saul said. "He's too proud."

"Most are, and like all who are proud, his kingdom will crumble around him. If he would let us go I would have mercy on him," Aiden said.

"What now?" Thaddeus asked.

"We go back tomorrow and try again. First, though we must warn everyone here about the coming storm. It won't affect them, but this way they are not afraid. We will stay here for the night and return in the morning."

* * *

Saul woke, thinking it was still the night. He knew better though as he sat up, the hot muggy air greeting him. The others were already up, waiting outside the tent for him. He dressed and stepped outside, looking at the dark eastern sky where everyone else was watching.

He stumbled through the darkness, unable to see, except for the torches that people held. The lightning raced across the sky and the thunder rolled unceasingly. The area around them was lit with lightning and thunder, while the town itself was seemingly protected. He walked up next to Alexandrea, watching the light show in front of them.

"Looks like the end of the world," Saul said.

"I can only imagine what's going through Dad's head right now," Alexandrea said. Lighting struck the ground in the distance, setting it ablaze. Cries came from the city as people rushed out to try and put out the fire which had already grown seemingly out of control, burning their homes and their crops.

"If Ahab would let us go then this wouldn't be happening," Aiden said. "Some people's hearts are too hard for their own good."

"Some people have to learn things the hard way," Morgrin said. They nodded and looked forward to the horizon that was now filled with fires and people frantically trying to put them out.

Rain began to fall from the sky, just a few sprinkles at first, but soon it had steadily picked up and turned into a torrential rain. The thunder and lightning continued as they stood. The fires still burned, despite the rain. They grew afraid in the shadow of the storm.

"We will not be harmed!" Aiden yelled to everyone. At once huge hailstones, the size of small rocks began falling from the sky. They crashed into the ground, sending mud and dirt flying. They crushed all the crops and pummeled the people who were trying to put the fires out. The city was unable to be seen in the darkness, except for the flashes of lighting.

The hail crashed through the rooftops and struck down the mighty walls. People cried out and cursed their gods as their homes and belongings were destroyed. They finally moved inside, watching the storm as it continued to pummel the city and surrounding fields.

Three hours later the storm subsided and gave way to bright sunny skies. The air was warm, melting the giant balls of hail that now covered the ground. The ground became spongy as they tried to absorb all the water. The fires were now extinguished and cries of anguish echoed through the nation.

"You would've never known that anything happened," Diderus said. "There's not a cloud in sight."

"There will be soon if the king doesn't let us go," Aiden said. "If this doesn't convince him to let us go then there will be only one choice left and it will strike him at the heart."

They didn't ask any questions and instead followed Aiden as they left the slums and villages, where the slaves were kept, and headed for the city once again.

Cavil came into view, its walls broken and battered. The roofs of buildings had been collapsed by the giant hail, and people cried in the streets, saying prayers to the gods they had created.

"Their prayers are useless," Shavrok said. "There's only one person worth praying to."

They marched to the inner gate, surprised this time when they spotted the king and his family rushing out of the keep.

"Arrest this man and his friends! They are the ones responsible for this!"

Ahab yelled.

"The only one who is responsible here is you," Aiden replied. "You will let the people go or face an even worse disaster yet."

"Or I can kill you all and be rid of your sorcerers' ways right now," Ahab said.

"Any effort against us, will be useless I assure you," Saul said.

"We'll just see about that!" Ahab grabbed his sword and swung it at Aiden's neck. The blade missed, confusing all of them. Ahab swung again. They all watched as it passed through Aiden's neck as though it wasn't there.

Screaming came from the wall behind them as one of the guards toppled off the wall, his head severed. No one spoke. Ahab looked at the sword in his hand, confusion filling him. He swung at Alexandrea this time, but the blade passed through her neck as though it wasn't there. Instead, the head of one of the guards on the walls was lobbed off and fell over the edge. Ahab screamed and threw his sword on the ground.

"Fine, you might have won this round, but I'm not going to let those slave scum go!"

"In that case I am sorry. For tonight a great terror will fall over this land and you will be helpless to do anything about it." Ahab and the rest of the royal family stormed off into the inner gate, the guards closing it behind.

Aiden led the way as they began leaving, curiosity burning in all their minds. Saul remained quiet, choosing to keep to his thoughts for a little while longer. How much could one king take before he finally let them go?

"What is the last disaster that's going to fall on this area tonight?" Saul asked.

"The firstborn of every family will die, that is unless you profess to be a follower of Lathon. You will be spared if that is true in your heart, otherwise, livestock and people alike will suffer."

"If that doesn't convince the king to let us and the slaves go I don't know what will," Alexandrea said. "Most of the princes and princesses are first born from the mothers they came from."

"It's going to be a terrible blow to the king and his people," Aiden said. "When he lets us go, we must get out of here as fast as we can."

"We could make for Laheer," Morgrin suggested. "It's out of the nation and the trees might give us cover."

"It might," Aiden admitted. "But I don't think they'd be much help for us. We will have to make our way to Mt. Dahab, where Drake is supposed to meet with us. We'll cut across the Sea of Mar and meet up with him there. Our exit will not go unchallenged."

"How are we supposed to get across the Sea of Mar, when we have no boats?" Nickolas asked.

"Faith," Aiden replied. "When we do begin departing with the slaves, I want Saul and Alexandrea to lead them, the rest of us will ride at the back, watching for Ahab and his men."

"Are you sure that we're the right people to lead the slaves out?" Saul asked.

"I couldn't be more sure. You are known in this land, whereas we are not. If they see that you have defied the king they will certainly find the courage to do the same," Aiden said. They finally reached the village and spoke with many of the slaves who were curious about the things that had happened.

The skies clouded over, becoming as dark as night. They lit torches and lanterns to see as the time passed. The land around them became deathly silent as night came. Saul was unable to get any sleep and walked out of the tent.

"Good evening Saul," Aiden greeted. "Can't sleep?"

"Can't turn my brain off," Saul said. "I just can't believe everything that's happened to me. I've gone from being a prince, to being an assassin and now I'm going to be leading a bunch of slaves out of slavery. It's almost too much for me to comprehend. It feels great to finally be able to do something worthwhile and helpful, I just never saw my life unfolding like this. I'm starting to think that Lathon laughs when he hears my plans for my life."

"Sometimes he does, we're all fearfully and wonderfully made. He has a plan and a purpose for us if we are willing to drop everything we've ever known and follow him," Aiden said. "You were born for this moment. Nothing happens by accident, there is a reason and a time for everything."

"If nothing happens by accident, was I meant to become an assassin?"

"That's what you chose," Aiden said. "Lathon will not force you to do his will, he will let you choose to do it or not do it. That is the true nature of love."

"I guess that makes sense," Saul said. "I still feel like I screwed up my life."

"Everyone screws up Saul. Mistakes are proof that you're trying. You have to hang in there, knowing that the next day will be better than the last."

"But I don't know that," Saul said.

"That's what faith is for," Aiden said. They fell silent, watching the dark skies as they cast darkness on everything. Lightning flashed across the sky, but unlike the previous night, no thunder was heard.

"What's happening Aiden?" Saul asked. Aiden looked at the city before turning away.

"It's nearly time," Aiden said. "The firstborn of every creature and family will die. This will be what breaks the king's heart and will convince him to let us go." White light slowly came down from the sky, hitting the ground and forming unrecognizable shapes. Some of them appeared on the wall and others appeared deeper in the city. The mysterious shapes faded into the city, making no sound.

"Don't worry, they won't be coming here," Aiden said.

"What are they?" Saul asked.

"Something seen in this world on rare occasions," Aiden said with a smile. "At least in their true form."

"Are they dangerous?" Saul asked. Aiden thought for a moment.

"If they need to be," Aiden replied. "We have nothing to fear from them, however."

They went back to their tents and then to their separate places where Saul remained awake thinking about everything that would transpire tomorrow. Was he really going to lead the six hundred thousand slaves out of the nation and to safety?

For years he had lived in the palace and seen how the slaves were treated and oppressed. When he had learned the truth about his origin, it had affected him more than he realized. He had been filled with a discontent that he eventually couldn't contain. That was why he had done what he had. Now in an ironic twist of fate, he was back to take everyone with him.

Then again was it fate?

The word fate was popular in the culture he had grown up in, and even in the rest of the world, but he was beginning to think that fate didn't exist. According to Aiden, people controlled their own destiny and Lathon was Lord above all of them. Both of those concepts together ruled out any possibilities of fate, which stated that everything that happened, happened by accident.

For years he had thought of himself as nothing more than an accident, he had been born by accident, been found by the princess by accident, lived by accident, but the more he thought about it the more false he found the concept.

His parents had intentionally hidden him and then released him at the river. He may not have ever met them, but he was sure that anyone who would have gone three months to hide him in the first place would've been smart enough to know what time the princess would be out by the river. Having grown up in the royal house, he knew it was always at the same time of day.

If all of those things had been carefully planned and thought out, then it meant that he was not an accident and he had been born for the moment that was fast approaching.

It was early in the morning and the sun was now rising. Saul was filled with sorrow as he and Alexandrea made their way back into Cavil. The clouds had gone and the terror that had struck in the middle of the night had now passed, leaving behind a trail of corpses. Their eyes both misted as they looked around at everything they had once known and called their home.

People wept and cried in the streets, carrying their dead out and covering them with sheets until something else could be done. The animals that had died were carried away by some of the soldiers, likely being taken out to the fields where they would be left to rot.

"I can't believe it," Alexandrea said as they walked further into the weeping city. "Somehow, my heart breaks for these people like I've never felt it before."

They fell silent, overwhelmed. Aiden and the rest of the company had chosen to stay with the slaves for the moment, preparing them to leave as soon as they could. Each step they took felt like a mile as they pressed towards the inner wall and the king who no doubt waited for them inside. They reached the guards at the inner wall, realizing that they were both dead.

"They were on duty last night," Alexandrea said. "They must have been the firstborn."

No other guards were present allowing the two of them to slip into the inner wall without anyone questioning them. The ground was littered with the bodies of those who had died. They opened the palace door and then walked in, finding the familiar hallways and passages that they had grown up in.

They walked to the throne room and entered without being questioned as the guards weren't at their posts, either they were dead or they were carrying out some other order that had been given. They looked to the front of the throne room where they saw King Ahab and his wife Jezebel kneeling on the floor, tears soaking their face. Around them, the bodies of all the princes and princesses were scattered about.

"I had no idea *all* the princes and princesses besides ourselves were firstborns," Alexandrea whispered. Saul nodded and they pushed forward, stopping when the king and queen looked up at them. In Ahab's eyes, they saw nothing but sorrow and regret, and in Jezebel's eyes, an uncontrollable malice.

"What do you want?" Ahab asked. Saul and Alexandrea stopped in their tracks.

"We can't imagine what this suffering is like for you," Saul replied.

"Why did you bring this upon me?" Ahab asked. "By what source does your power come from? My magicians can do many things, but this…this is unlike anything that should even be close to possible. Where does your power come from?"

"Our power comes from the one true God and provider in this world, Lathon," Saul answered. "He is a God of love."

"Love?" Ahab asked. "What kind of a loving god would do something like this?"

"You wouldn't let the slaves go. If we had just taken the slaves and run what would've happened? Everyone would have ended up dying, we respected your authority and asked for your permission and you wouldn't give it to us. Lathon did what he did to convince you to free our people."

"I'm convinced now!" Ahab screamed. "Get out of here and take your miserable god with you!" Jezebel drilled them both with a death stare.

"Why don't we just kill them now?" Jezebel asked. Ahab's eyes lit up for a moment and then they turned dark.

"Kill them now?" Ahab asked. "You've seen what happens when you defy their god! I will not risk further pain to myself. Let them leave!"

"We will be going," Alexandrea said.

"I don't think so," Jezebel said, grabbing the swords of one of the dead princes. She stopped Saul and Alexandrea from leaving. "I think we should kill them right now! What a fitting end for a murderer and a traitor to have been killed by the king and queen. Even more so seeing that Saul is one of the miserable creatures we've had working for us for all these years. I ought to kill him right now…but I won't." She threw the sword to the side circling the both of them.

"The way I see it, the ultimate revenge could be even sweeter. If this is what their god does to people who don't please him, then I hope you make every mistake that you can, so your god may strike you down. Live in fear and then die."

"We live in fear, but the word is used a little differently than the world does," Saul said. "We have respect for Lathon and love for our enemies. We will live our lives, serving him to the best of our abilities."

"And if your life should end now?" Jezebel taunted, grabbing the sword again and slowly pressing it to their throats.

"Then may Lathon take us home," Alexandrea said. Jezebel held her gaze. Her face filled with overwhelming rage.

"Leave!" Jezebel said. "Leave now or die!" She swung the sword at their necks. Saul pushed Alexandrea to the ground and pulled a knife from his side. Jezebel screamed and cursed as the knife found her arm, piercing the flesh, the blade protruding from the other side. He reached down and grabbed Alexandrea by the hand, pulling her off the floor and towards the door.

"I think we should go!" Saul said. They sprinted out the door as Jezebel pulled the knife from her arm and chased them. Saul and Alexandrea sprinted past the doors and threw them shut. The Queens's screams and curses were muffled behind the doors. Swords were put to their throats as a group of soldiers closed in on them.

"Give us one reason why we shouldn't kill you right now?" the commander asked.

"Because I'm the princess Alexandrea, as proved by the royal seal on my ring." Alexandrea held her right hand out to the man to see. The commander's face clouded over.

"My sincere apologies my lady," the commander said. All the soldiers bowed down to one knee in front of them.

"Rise, my friends," Alexandrea said.

"How may we serve you my lady?" the commander asked. The screaming and curses from Jezebel were still faintly heard as she banged on the door.

"Keep everyone in this room for at least the next three hours," Alexandrea said. "Do this as if your life depended on it. We will return in a couple of days and you will be rewarded."

"It shall be done, my lady!"

The commander bowed again and then moved out of the way. Alexandrea and Saul ran down the halls, leaving everything they had ever known behind them.

They didn't speak until they were back on their horses, riding as fast as they could to the village. Even from this distance, they could see that everyone was ready and waiting. The sight nearly overwhelmed the two of them.

"How many slaves are there?" Saul asked. "I didn't think the village was that large?"

"That's because it isn't," Alexandrea replied. "Father didn't want the slaves to get any ideas, so he had them split into twelve different camps, several miles apart. This way his men could have the numbers advantage on them. It looks like Aiden got all of them here. I wonder how he managed to do that."

"He's Aiden, I don't think that's for us to figure out," Saul replied. They rode faster towards the masses of people. Three horses came from the north and then one green Taruk with a woman on top. They pulled their horses to a stop and let everyone else come up to them. Aiden rode one horse, while Nickolas and Morgrin rode up on two more. Aspen landed twenty feet away and Isabel dropped off, casually walking up to them.

"Was your trip to the north worthwhile?" Aiden asked.

"Yes," Isabel answered. "Are we ready to go?"

"They have permitted us to go. Although I doubt that will hold up for very long."

"I agree with that," Isabel said.

"Once we get to the Sea of Mar the hardest part will be over," Morgrin said. "I advised as many people as I could to travel light."

"Very good," Aiden said. "Let's get these free people out of these lands." Aiden led the way to the front of the people. Saul and Alexandrea followed to either side of him. Aiden pulled out a horn and let the sound echo through the land.

Moments later several more horns answered Aiden's call, each one of them a different sound and pitch, indicating the different races of whoever was blowing them. Finally, a loud horn blast echoed through the land. This one was low and rumbled the ground as the note was sustained for fifteen seconds.

"What was that?" Alexandrea asked. Aiden smiled.

"That was a Gog horn. Shavrok was stationed with the last group in line,"

Aiden said.

Saul looked to the land in front of them as they headed south, along the eastern edge of the forest. How long did they have before they were pursued?

The question nagged at his mind and forced him to ask it over and over again, each time coming up with no answer. If the emperor was to send his army to wipe them out, the number of people who died would be far greater than Saul cared to count.

These people weren't trained fighters. They were farmers, craftsmen, and ditch diggers. Except for a couple of butcher knives, he doubted they had anything dangerous on them. Saul looked ahead, noticing that Aiden was watching him.

"Something bothering you Saul?"

"I'm just wondering how long we have until the emperor comes after us," Saul admitted.

"Don't worry about that."

"How am I not supposed to worry about it?" Saul asked.

"When you are playing a game, you don't play from the bench, you play from in front of the ball. I tell you the truth, if you focus on leading these people to the Sea of Mar, then I will take care of any resistance when it comes."

"Deal," Saul agreed, his heart more at ease than it had been before. They pressed on through the wilderness, Aiden's words echoing through his heart and soul.

You would never be able to move on and accomplish anything if you were constantly living in the past or looking over your shoulder. He looked to the path that lay before him, more eager than ever before to live his life differently than he had up to this point.

***

Ahab stared at the carnage and walked about the empty castle. Anger flowed through his veins as he looked at his shattered empire. He couldn't even begin to guess how many people and animals had been killed the night before, and for that matter, he didn't want to. This was far too much for any one person to take.

THE DEAD MOUNTAINS

The soldiers carried the dead away, while some of them tried to clear the rubble that had resulted from the hailstorm. He walked back inside the throne room looking at the bodies of his dead children, feeling an uncontrollable anger. Jezebel sat in the corner, mumbling to herself and staring into space.

The city needed to rebuild itself and quickly recover from the disasters that had crippled the entire nation, but they were unable to. Thousands had been killed in this city. How would they even attempt to rebuild the empire that had once stood tall and proud over the world? It wouldn't be long before their enemies and allies alike, got word of what happened and decided to revolt.

Something had to be done and Ahab carefully thought about all of the possibilities. The slaves that he had let go, numbered nearly six hundred thousand, no small force. Pleasure rippled through his veins as he moved past his wife and exited the throne room. A commander and his men stood outside the door waiting for his orders.

"How many men did we lose in the attack this morning?" Ahab asked.

"Not as many as we first thought," the commander said. "We still have a force of two thousand people or more."

"Very good. Gather every able-bodied man or boy old enough to fight and first thing in the morning, ride after the slaves and bring them back to me. Destroy the elderly or the crippled, anyone who will slow you down, and then bring the survivors here."

"Yes my lord," the commander said. He bowed and then he and his men left, vanishing from his sight. Ahab felt power rippling through him and his anger seemed for the moment to subside.

"It's about time you acted like a king!" Jezebel exclaimed coming up behind him. He drilled her with a death glare.

"It's time you started acting like a queen," Ahab said. Confusion was etched on her face.

"What do you mean?" Jezebel asked.

"All of my children, including our own child were just wiped out. We need to start rebuilding our line so that people don't get any ideas. This throne is ours and always will be."

"May the gods smile upon us," Jezebel said. Ahab didn't reply as he moved towards a lone troop who stood against the wall twenty feet away. The soldier took notice and stood at attention.

"How may I serve you my lord?" the soldier asked.

"Take some men into the city and bring me young women that I can sleep with and have children through. My line will not end like this!"

"Yes my lord," the soldier replied. He slipped off into the distance and then vanished down another hall. Jezebel and himself moved to the nearest balcony and looked out over the city and to the army that was beginning to form again. He could already taste the blood of his enemies as he watched his men.

Saul and Alexandrea might have a day's start on him by the time his men left, but they wouldn't get very far. They would have women and children and elderly, it would be slow going for them, which made it all the better for him. His men were on horseback, while most of them were on foot. They had no escape, except for one. Death by the sword. Tomorrow victory would be his.

Chapter 14

SEA OF MAR

"How much farther until we reach the sea?" Diderus asked. He rode alongside Saul at the front of the long trail of people.

"Not too much longer," Saul replied. "It's hard to say just what we're going to do when we get there though."

"You don't know?" Diderus asked. Saul shook his head.

"Not a clue, Aiden said not to worry about it. How can I not? We have six hundred thousand people with us."

"I'm more worried about the army that's going to come chasing after us," Alexandrea said.

"Don't remind me," Saul replied. "How long do you think we have until they give chase?"

"They're probably already giving chase. I hope they don't catch us until we are at the sea, but there is no way to foresee that one," Alexandrea said. The pounding of horses' hooves on the ground demanded their attention. They turned to see Aiden riding up past the trail of people to the front of them.

"Our enemies approach," Aiden said. "We must get these people moving faster. Our force of eight will catch them by surprise but we will not be able to win the battle."

"How many did they bring?" Diderus asked.

"According to Isabel, Aspen said around two thousand men."

"Two thousand?" Alexandrea asked. "How are we going to outrun them?"

"We start by running," Aiden said. "Diderus, raise the alarm, meet up with Shavrok, and inform the people that we must run as fast as possible because there is great danger."

"Yes sir," Diderus said. He turned his horse around and galloped down the line yelling out to the masses. Nickolas, Thaddeus, Morgrin, and Isabel all turned their horses, heading to Shavrok at the end of the long trail of people.

Aspen spun in the air, letting out a massive roar as she flapped her wings and also headed to the back. Saul, Alexandrea, and Aiden all spread out, pushing the horses a little faster. The trail of people followed suit and picked up the pace. A trail of dust flew up into the air behind them.

"They'll know where we are!" Alexandrea yelled. Aiden looked back.

"They already do!" Aiden yelled. Horns shattered the area around them as horses appeared on the horizon. They were still distant and small.

"Will they catch us before we get to the sea?" Saul asked.

"Not on my watch!" Aiden exclaimed. "Saul, lead the people. Do not stop when you get to the sea. I repeat do not stop when you get to the sea! Run right at it! Alexandrea come with me!" Saul started to object, but they had already turned their horses and spurred them faster as they flew by the trail of people.

Saul looked behind at the growing mass of black on the horizon and then looked ahead, seeing the first hint of blue, on the horizon. It was small but it was enough to offer himself and everyone behind him a hint of hope. A large shape appeared in the sky. Saul immediately recognized Elohim from the Mezutor. The Taruk swooped low, flying past Saul.

***

"What are we going to do?" Alexandrea asked. Aiden rode next to her, watching the sky.

"Get to the others, they'll tell you what the plan is," Aiden said. She turned to ask him another question, but he had slipped off of his horse, grasping the giant foot of a white Taruk. He climbed up the Taruk and sat on its back, racing ahead of her. A few minutes later she reached the end of the people where everyone was now waiting on their horses. The powerful green Taruk flew towards the army, flanking Aiden and Elohim on one side, and another Taruk she didn't recognize, flanked the other side.

"Whose Taruk is that?" Alexandrea asked as she finally brought her horse to a rest.

"Drake's Taruk, Destan. You haven't met him yet, but he's waiting for us at Mt. Dahab," Isabel answered.

"What's the plan?" Alexandrea asked. Isabel smiled.

"We attack."

Fear filled Alexandrea as she looked at their small force and then at the large army of two thousand horses running toward them. Isabel drew her sword and they all lined their horses up one next to the other.

"Charge!" Isabel yelled. They spurred their horses forward, dust flying from behind them as they got further away from the trail of people, who were now fading into the distance. Alexandrea looked ahead and drew her sword, watching in amazement as the three Taruks swooped down out of the sky and extended their feet. Their feet collected countless men and horses, shoving them back through the ranks. The chariots at the front were destroyed, crashing into the army behind them. The soldiers yelled out curses.

They formed a line again, charging only a moment before the Taruks ripped through the back section of the army, and their small force collided with the front of the army. Alexandrea reached out with her sword and swiped away the large spear that had been aimed at her. The man swung the spear, but it never reached her as Shavrok crushed the soldier with his massive hand.

Alexandrea stared at Shavrok in fear as he continued to defeat his enemies. The men cowered as he approached. Alexandrea spurred her horse forward, sticking her sword into a man passing by. The man fell off the horse and then she pulled the sword out of his stomach, blocking the next blow that had been aimed at her.

An arrow streaked by her head, hitting a man nearby. She looked, relieved that Thaddeus had been the one shooting. She fought and lost all track of time, realizing that their plan was working. The army had stopped advancing and had instead focused all of their attention on destroying the eight of them. The white Taruk swooped low and Aiden dropped off, letting out a battle cry as he did. He struck the first man he landed by and then spun around and got the next one.

She looked behind her, seeing no sign of the large trail of people, only a distant blob of blue. The fighting raged on as the Taruks continued to rip through the army. Alexandrea looked at the Taruks, amazed by their strength. She had only ever seen Taruks in the races, never in the wild like this.

"Alexandrea!" a voice yelled. She turned to see Isabel, turning her horse and beginning to run in the direction of the sea. "Let's go!"

* * *

Saul moved over the crest of the hill, beginning the downward slope to the Sea of Mar below. He looked behind, seeing the confusion in people's eyes as he raced towards the water. His heart rate began to quicken and his anxiety increased as he approached the water.

His horse reached the edge of the water, its hoof touching the first speck of water. A rumbling filled the sea. The water in front of him parted to either side, creating a wall of water nearly twenty feet high. Saul stared in wonder as the ground his horse ran on was immediately dry and tough. Saul pushed his horse into the sea, the dry stretch of land leading all the way to the other side.

Once inside the sea, Saul slowed his horse, giving them all rest from the sprinting they had just done. The long trail of people made their way over the crest and to the sea, joining him as they traveled to the other side. Saul reached out and touched his fingers to the water.

He pulled his fingers away and the hole they had made sealed itself, creating a flawless wall of water once again. Finally, he made it to the other side of the sea with the first of the free people, touching their feet to the shore. They piled onto the shore, moving back as far as they could to make room for the rest of the people who were still entering the sea.

To their west he could see Mt. Dahab, rising up on the horizon. He looked back to the shore on the other side, wondering what had happened to the others. The people finally exited the sea, with all six hundred thousand of them able to stand on the shoreline.

* * *

THE DEAD MOUNTAINS

Alexandrea's fear threatened to take hold of her as she rushed to the sea. The large army behind her had been reduced to half of its size by now, largely due to the Taruks. The remaining soldiers gave chase, flanked on either side by the remaining chariots. The Taruks still circled overhead, swooping down and destroying troops whenever they could. Eventually, though the Taruks flew on ahead, rising high into the sky and disappearing.

"Don't slow down until we're out of the water!" Aiden yelled. Their horses moved over the crest, revealing the sea. Her breath was taken away by what she saw. The sea of water had parted down the middle, leaving a dry section for them to cross through. A few arrows whizzed by her head, but she kept riding for the opening. They all entered at the same time.

The army flooded into the sea after them, beginning to close the gap. Anxiety flooded through Alexandrea as her horse touched the shore on the other side. She pulled her horse to a stop and joined everyone else as she looked at the sea. The entire sea was filled with the black uniforms of the Goshen empire, with a thousand more still on the opposite shore.

She looked at Aiden, unnerved by his calm demeanor. The army continued to pour into the sea, the walls of water to either side, remaining just as they had been when they had passed through.

Aiden moved his horse to the shore, staring down at the commander who led his army towards them. The commander's face washed white as his horse came to a stop. He looked to his men, yelling for them to continue, but their horses were unable to move. Aiden drew his sword and held it into the air, the sunlight glistening against the blade. The walls of water began to shift. Small streams of water, slowly appeared at the base of the waves, as though they couldn't contain themselves anymore.

"Magic! He's using Magic!" the commander yelled. A man dismounted his horse and came to the forefront, mumbling a spell turning the water to ice, keeping it at bay.

Aiden lowered his sword to the ground. The walls of water were shattered and they rushed in towards the army. Within seconds the water had joined back together, erasing the land bridge they had crossed, and had swallowed the entire sea of black that had been before them. Helmets floated in the water, their owners left at the bottom of the sea.

Alexandrea stared in amazement as the water, left the sea on the other side and crashed up onto the shore, taking out nearly all of the army on the other side. Only a small handful had managed to escape the oncoming tide.

"How did you do that?" Alexandrea asked.

"I don't think that's for us to know," Saul said, gently bringing his horse towards her.

"There were about twenty of them who got away," Aiden said. "They'll be back, with a force. Fortunately, they don't know that we have a force of our own. We ride for Mt. Dahab at once! We will be there by nightfall."

"What are we going to do when we get there?" Thaddeus asked.

"We will turn around and attack them before they have a chance to try anything," Aiden said. "We will return these people to their homeland and give it to them. We must not fail to bring down the corrupt leader and his wife."

They started to the west, leaving the Sea of Mar behind them. Alexandrea stole one more glance, at the watery grave, the crystal clear water seeming to shine with lights in it.

"What are those lights?" Alexandrea asked.

"The swords of our fallen enemies," Isabel told her. "They will forever be markers of the price that was paid for these people's freedom."

They rode through the plains, Mt. Dahab growing bigger and bigger with every hour that passed. Finally, the mountain towered over them. The smell of smoke from a fire reached their noses and then the smell of food being cooked. The sun was setting in the west, casting everything in shadows from the mountain. Alexandrea and Saul rode side by side among the people, casually carrying on a conversation with everyone.

The thundering of hooves echoed through the land as the silhouettes of horsemen and riders coming from the south became visible. The horsemen broke off, half of them running toward the mountains, while the other half continued making their way toward the masses of people.

The people began to murmur among themselves, all looking to Aiden who once again didn't appear to be concerned. Saul and Alexandrea rode up next to him. The horsemen to the south parted again, with the rest heading towards the camp and one lone rider coming towards them.

"You're late Drake Thomas! I thought you would've been here already!" Nickolas exclaimed. Drake laughed.

"I thought the king was always on time and everyone else was early?" Drake jested. "Besides, by all technicalities, I still was here before you."

Nickolas waved him off with a humorous expression.

"I bring almost six thousand spears. There were more of course, but those were as many as could leave when we had to. Several men rode ahead and secured enough food and water from our friends in Punair for all of the refugees. It should hold until we can get their land back."

"You've done well Drake," Aiden said.

"Thank you," Drake replied.

"I'm proud of you."

Drake smiled and they continued into the shadow of the mountain. Tens of thousands of tents had been set up, plenty for the army and the refugees.

"I know Aiden said he's impressed, but I must say that I'm even more impressed," Nickolas said. "How did you manage to get so many tents here so quickly?"

"You can thank Isabel for that one," Drake said. Isabel showed her surprise much to everyone's amusement.

"How did I contribute to this?" Isabel asked. Drake smiled and motioned to the next tent where Lily and Ellizar came out. Ellizar walked tall and proud, putting the handle of his axe on the ground and using it as a staff.

"I would like teh refresh yer memory, my dear friend, about a certain gift we gave yeh?" Ellizar started. "It soaked yeh every time someone rang a doorbell! In retaliation, yeh sent me a rock that would scream at me every half hour… *not* cool by the way. However, whether yeh knew it or not, the rock did have a side effect. When it wasn't screamin' at me it would create anythin' I wanted. So you see? All I had teh deh was say I wanted ten thousand tents and it gave them teh me. They even set themselves up. Not a bad retaliation gift if I may say so myself."

"You think that was the retaliation gift?" Isabel asked. "No my dear Ellizar that was simply a warm-up gift, now it's time for the retaliation gift."

"What are you talking about?" Morgrin asked.

"I'm talking about that," Isabel said pointing into the distance. They turned to see an owl flying through the sunset sky, nearing them. They watched as the owl turned and sped towards Ellizar. The owl landed on his shoulder and then a moment later exploded, sending a plume of smoke and soot into Ellizar's face and clothes. The bird was reduced to feathers as Ellizar choked and gagged on the smoke.

"Shuckers!" Ellizar exclaimed.

"I think Ellizar's plan just went up in smoke," Lily said.

"Blasted elf kind!" Ellizar exclaimed. They all laughed. "I should've known there was another catch."

"There always is my dear Ellizar," Isabel said. "I think the score is two to one now, my favor."

"Yer favor? Ha! I'll get yeh fer this one!" Ellizar exclaimed.

"I look forward to it," Isabel said, as she and Morgrin left the company and headed to one of the empty tents. Ellizar watched her ride away and shook his head, mumbling to himself.

"Lily, we have teh get her back."

"*You*...have to get her back, I'm staying out of this."

"Fine way teh support yer husband!" Ellizar said. They all laughed.

"This is your mess, oh and don't you touch me until you get cleaned up," Lily said. Before Lily knew what had happened, Ellizar had wiped the soot off his face and then wiped it on her dress.

Alexandrea looked to the west seeing another owl coming through the sky. It swooped down towards Ellizar and touched him as it had the first time. The bird exploded into feathers and this time left him covered in snow.

"Isabel!" Ellizar exclaimed. He took off into the camp with Lily following close behind.

Alexandrea shook her head as they walked away. "I knew you guys had an interesting traveling group, but is he for real?"

"A question we've asked many times," Drake said. They moved further into the camp, laughing when they saw yet another owl come swooping out of the sky and fly into Ellizar's tent. Feathers and a cloud of smoke and soot billowed from the tent as both Ellizar and Lily came out, looking like they had been through a war.

"Now she's gone too far!" Lily exclaimed. They could hear Isabel laughing.

"Don't worry I only told the owl to do that two more times," Isabel said.

"Thank goodness!" Lily exclaimed.

They made their way into the camp, where a large tent had been set up in the middle for all of them. They dismounted their horses and handed them off to the servants who then took them to the grazing area for the horses. The three Taruks were nestled on the mountain, relaxing and keeping watch over the masses.

Drake entered first, moving to the large meeting table and chairs that were waiting. Isabel and Morgrin entered a moment later, with Lily and Ellizar right behind. Aiden stopped Ellizar from entering.

"Would you mind waiting until the last owl comes before you enter the tent?" Ellizar shook his head as Isabel smiled at him.

"Don't worry I'll send the owls early," Isabel said. They watched from inside the tent as two owls came, one from the north and one from the south. They touched him at the same time and they exploded. A wall of water appeared over his head and soaked him, the feathers from the two birds sticking to him. The other one created loud horns that blasted all around Ellizar for twenty seconds or so.

"Ellizar, why do you look like a chicken?" Drake asked. Ellizar couldn't help but laugh.

"Very funny Drake. As much as I hate to admit it, Isabel, yeh have gotten me good on this one."

"At your service," Isabel said taking a bow.

"But yeh haven't seen the last of this dwarf's efforts!" Ellizar exclaimed.

"Yep, I'm really afraid of someone four feet tall," Isabel teased. "Don't worry, that was the last bird."

"In that case come on in Ellizar, and we'll start our preparations," Aiden said. Ellizar hesitantly came in, trying to get all the feathers off of him. Lily picked them off as the meeting began.

"Down to business," Aiden said, pulling a map from one of the side tables and spreading it out on the table. "We will start with basics, how long do you think it'll take for the emperor to learn of his loss?"

"There were some troops that got away. If they rode as hard as they could all day and didn't linger for too long, I'd imagine they could reach Cavil by early morning. There are a few shortcuts they could take that would save some time," Alexandrea said.

"We'll assume that they'll find out tomorrow morning. At least two thousand troops were wiped out today," Aiden said. "We have to go back and defeat the emperor, or else we've done all of this for nothing. I never want to put people through suffering, forcing them to leave everything and not be able to provide for them."

"We have six thousand spears at our disposal to do whatever we can to give freedom to these people," Drake said. "I say we ride right up to Cavil and try to take the city before the emperor has time to gather any forces and muster an attack."

"That is a good plan," Shavrok agreed. "We could catch them by surprise."

"How is that?" Lily asked.

"Because Ahab doesn't know we have an army with us," Saul said. "As far as his men are concerned we are the only warriors among us. I would not expect the emperor to wait at the castle for us to attack, because he doesn't know we're going to."

"Saul is right," Aiden said. "I suspect that the emperor will take all available units and set out after us, to wipe us off the map."

"This could work out better than we think," Alexandrea said. "At the castle, they would have refuge and a defensive position that could hold out for days, with them leaving the castle, they'll likely take the same course we did today, riding through the open fields and grasslands that we passed through. They will be defenseless."

"How many men do you think he'll have with him?" Thaddeus asked. Saul and Alexandrea both shrugged.

"It's hard to say really, I wouldn't think he could muster more than three thousand on such short notice, with the cities and towns nearby having already been destroyed by the plagues...he may not have fully trained soldiers with him," Alexandrea said.

"At those numbers, we should have more than enough people teh take care ov the army," Ellizar said. Aiden nodded.

"I want to split the army up," Aiden said. "I want to send half of them to meet the army straight on, and I want the other half to try and ride through the border of Vonlaus and try to get behind the approaching army. If we can do that and trap them then none of them will be able to flee back to Cavil and raise the alarm and defend themselves further."

"I like it on paper, but it's a long way for our horses to go in such a little amount of time," Drake said. "They won't be rested from the trip they had today."

"Isabel?" Aiden asked. "I believe you can help with that. You said your trip north was a success."

"Indeed I did," Isabel said. "I spoke with Quemen about borrowing his special horses for a few days and he gladly offered them. I went north to where he raises them and inspected the herd and I agree that they are very, very fast. They should have no problem carrying everyone the distance in the time that we have."

"Always full of surprises," Morgrin said with a smile. Isabel winked at him playfully. "How are we going to get to the horses?"

"Quemen had his men move them from his pastures in the north to the border of Edon and Vonlaus, in about an hour's ride you can reach these horses and go from there," Isabel said.

"We'll send Destan and Aspen with the group that is going to come up behind the army. Elohim and I will be with the army from the south. Using the Taruks we should be able to easily scout out the army and track their movements, making it easier for us to get behind them without being detected. Drake, I would like you to lead the northern army."

"I'm not very familiar with that area," Drake admitted.

"I'll come with you," Isabel said.

"You can count me in!" Morgrin said.

"And yeh'd better not leave me out of the mix or I'll have teh smack all of yeh on yer heads!" Ellizar exclaimed.

"If you can even reach their heads," Lily said. They laughed as Ellizar frowned at her.

"Blasted elf kind! If yeh weren't my wife I'd kill yeh." They laughed again.

"Ellizar, I don't think you can really call any of us blasted when you're the one who looks like you stepped out of a campfire," Isabel said. "Either that or you fell down a chimney."

"I've had just about enough of yeh," Ellizar said. "This is one dwarf that will be the one laughin' when our little contest is finally done!"

"Why don't you just surrender now and save yourself the soot," Alexandrea said. Ellizar shook his head.

"Dwarves take such abuse! At least I know Lily loves me."

"It comes and goes," Shavrok said, speaking for Lily. They all laughed and shook their heads.

"He doesn't know what he's talking about. Of course, I love you Ellizar," Lily said. She kissed him on the lips.

"Now, that we've gotten completely off topic, the rest of us will ride up from the south. We'll take out the army and leave none alive," Aiden announced.

"No one?" Saul asked.

"Show no mercy, for you shall receive none in the upcoming battle. I hate to think of having to kill so many souls, but their treachery against Lathon has blinded them beyond all hope," Aiden said. "As will be the case in the days to come. The future that lies ahead of us is ever growing dark."

"What does the future hold?" Drake asked. "What are we going to be up against?"

"Something far worse than any army the Sorcerer could ever conjure up. We will face a great physical threat, but our biggest battle will be in ourselves. It is in the heart that all wars are won," Aiden said. "I will speak of this no more tonight. We should all get some sleep and tell the men of the assignments. Tomorrow, we'll ride at first light."

***

They dispersed from the tent until only Aiden and Alexandrea remained. Aiden took a seat and pointed Alexandrea to another chair, she gratefully accepted it.

"Is something bothering you Alexandrea?"

"I know that my father and the queen have to be dealt with. I've seen the pain and suffering they've inflicted on people for years, but I'm afraid about having to face them."

"Fear can be a powerful enemy. It can keep many, many things from being done."

"What am I supposed to do?" Alexandrea asked. "He's still my father isn't he?"

"Yes, he is, but think about it for a second. If he walked into this camp right here and now, what do you think he would do?"

"He'd probably try to kill me," Alexandrea admitted. "I've always longed to have a real father, one who cared about me. He cared about the other kids more than he did me, I was always on the bottom of the totem pole, no matter what I did."

"A hard place for anyone to be," Aiden said. "There are several things to remember in this rough world we live in, the most important being that you are not meant for this world."

"I'm not?" Alexandrea asked. "What world am I meant for?"

"You were intended for this world, but this world has since fallen into darkness. This world is full of pain, but after every life, there is something more; I can promise you that there is a very different world to be lived in."

"I'd like that," Alexandrea said. "Why can't we just go there now?"

"Because we love the people of this earth too much to just abandon them," Aiden replied. "If we were to run away from the trouble, or bury our heads in the sand, then we would be no better than those who serve the Sorcerer or your father."

"Can I escape what my father is? I've always felt like I was different from him, and I guess I've always been afraid, deep down, that I would end up like he was."

"Another common fear in this world. There are two things to remember. Number one is that your relatives do not have to define you. You have to have guts and courage, but you can redefine your life if you believe you can do it. Number two is that you must always remember that no one or nothing in this world can ever complete you. You have to be complete in Lathon or else you'll end up searching this entire earth for something to complete you when there is nothing that can."

"I guess that explains why my father was never very content with any of the women he slept with," Alexandrea said.

"Exactly."

"He has banned the name of Lathon and I'm beginning to see why. He was afraid."

"He was," Aiden agreed. "Don't worry about tomorrow, everything will play out as it's meant to be played out and life will never be the same. We will give these people back their land."

"I'm just glad that we won't have to deal with Jezebel," Alexandrea said. "I've never known a more evil woman. She's made my life miserable over the years."

"We will have to deal with her," Aiden said. "But do not be afraid, for you will find the courage to face her."

"I hope so," Alexandrea said. They talked for a few more minutes before Alexandrea left and made her way to her tent where she lay down and fell asleep, dreaming about everything that might happen tomorrow. Fear grew inside of her and threatened to take hold, but she managed to keep it at bay as she slept through the night.

Chapter 15

REINFORCEMENTS

Drake looked out into the massive camp. He took a deep breath trying to keep his emotions in line. Sorrow flooded over Drake as he thought about the cowardly king and leader he had been. He had done nothing to be worthy of the title of king, but now for the first time in his life, he was actually acting like one.

He was greeted by a couple of his advisors, who handed him various pieces of weaponry for him to put on. Ellizar and Lily were coming out of the tent next door and within minutes everyone traveling with him had gathered in one spot. Drake looked at them and smiled, noticing just how much they had all changed. Ellizar and Lily, Isabel and Morgrin.

He closed his eyes, trying to imagine Gwen standing next to him. Already the image of her face seemed distant and vague, replaced instead by the face of salt and stone that she had turned into. He missed her already and doubted the pain would ever cease.

He took comfort in knowing that everyone felt the same way he did and just had a different way of showing it. Although Isabel might not have expressed in any words her deep sorrow, he could see it in her eyes and knew it was in her thoughts. Still, she found the strength to go on and do what had to be done, which in turn offered strength to him and everyone else around her.

"Everyone's ready Mr. Thomas," the commander, Matthew, said as he walked up.

"We will leave in just a few minutes," Drake told him. Matthew hurried off. He looked to the others who were waiting with anticipation. "What do you say we get this show on the road?"

"I say we have a long way to travel," Isabel said. Ellizar smiled and laughed as though he had been told a funny joke.

"Just like the old days, the five of us ridin' into battle together!"

"Yep, just like the old days," Drake replied. They walked to the left where their horses were saddled and ready. They climbed on, with Ellizar riding with Lily. They galloped to the north until they were finally in front of the entire force of three thousand people that would be riding with Drake. He glanced into the sky, seeing the Taruks waiting to fly ahead and scout out the situation.

"For your families, for their families. For Lathon!" Drake yelled. The army let a shout escape them as they began to move their horses across the plains. The thunder of the hooves shook the ground as they picked up more speed, leaving the camp and all the refugees behind them.

Drake felt chills run down his spine as they raced into the wilderness. The unknown lay ahead and with that, there was always a need for caution. They pushed their horses faster, running for almost an hour, until finally, they noticed large masses of brown and black in the distance. Isabel took the lead, the other riders following them. Finally, they slowed their horses and then dismounted, quickly removing all their saddles and equipment and placing them on the new horses.

Drake ran his hand along the horse's body, already feeling muscles that were unlike any that he had ever seen in a horse. Power and pride rippled through the horse's veins, while mixed with the adrenaline that the horses fed off.

Within a few minutes, everyone had changed horses and were ready to depart once again. Isabel looked at the horses they had just been riding. As though something else was leading them, all the horses turned and headed back the way they had come.

Drake led the way as he slowly pushed the horse faster and faster, amazed by the speed that it had to offer. It ran at least twice as fast as a regular horse, but without growing tired or weak, allowing them to keep up the pace for as long as they wanted.

The morning flew by and the land around them changed constantly until finally they reached the woods just on the open fields on the north side of Laheer.

They turned due east, and entered back into Goshen, searching the horizon for any sign of the army. The Taruks flew overhead searching and carefully scouting the land for any sign of them.

"I wonder if they've even left Cavil yet," Drake asked.

"There they are," Isabel said, pointing to a distant plume of dust rising from the road that the horsemen were coming down.

"Into the forest!" Drake yelled. They retreated into the forest, taking cover in the trees, while staying on their horses. The army moved past them without noticing. "How many do you think there are?"

"Maybe two thousand," Lily answered. "If that."

"We'll follow after them in ten minutes," Drake said. "Hopefully Aiden and the rest of them will be in position by then."

Isabel shot him a look. "This is Aiden we're talking about, of course, they'll be in position by then. They're probably already across the sea and on their way here."

"Sorry, don't know where that came from," Drake said. "There are enough people that worry in this world, I don't need to be one of them."

They sat in silence for a moment, carefully noticing that the wind was out of the south, so any noise they made would be carried to the north instead of towards the army. They led their horses out of the forest, pushing them forward as the land flew by.

They slowed their horses, having forgotten that they would likely catch the army if they kept the horses at full speed. Drake's heart rate picked up as they continued to chase the army.

It had been years since he had been in any kind of an organized battle. The Taruks climbed into the sky and flew on ahead to alert Aiden and the rest of them that the army was approaching. Anticipation consumed Drake as they rode after the army.

* * *

Alexandrea and Saul rode their horses side by side, with Aiden in the lead. They watched Aiden with interest as he led the army forward, seemingly without any fears or reservations. It was both inspiring and intimidating. They could never hope to be the leader that he was.

Still, her heart longed to be like him and to live like he did, and maybe in time she would, but right now her thoughts were distracted by the battle that they rode to face. She had never been in a battle before. Even though the princes had been, the women of the royal family were never allowed.

Two shapes appeared in the sky, instilling a sense of wonder in Alexandrea. She knew it was only the Taruks, but even they seemed different from the others she had seen over the years.

The number of differences between Aiden and the people who traveled with him were astounding to her. They were a group made up of so many different groups and races, each one defying the norm for their race. Elves were arrogant and judgmental, men were proud and easily corrupted; Goblins were greedy and unworthy of anything that was good in life. Gogs are fierce and vicious creatures and should be avoided at all costs.

The more Alexandrea was with these people, the more she began to realize that her world was changing. Everything she had ever been told had been challenged and ultimately destroyed. All these people didn't have the traits she had thought of their races all these years.

They had more love and more conviction in one act than she had felt in her entire life.

One person at a time, Aiden was forever changing the world. He spoke of mercy to the weak and forgiveness to those who had wronged you. At his core was humility in a way that she had never seen. From what she understood, he was the one who had first convinced them to go on this journey, now he was stepping back and letting other people do the leading. Even when they didn't necessarily think that they were capable.

How was she supposed to lead anything like Aiden suggested that she would in the future? The prospect scared her and she struggled to understand what Aiden saw in her.

She wasn't perfect by any stretch of the imagination, but what did he see in her that made him think that she could be a great leader? She looked as hard as she could, she couldn't find one reason that was justified in her mind. Maybe she would grow into it.

The Taruks flew overhead letting out a roar, displaying their power as they flew overhead. Alexandrea was once again humbled by the great creatures and amazed that creatures so great would do as simple a task as carry messages back and forth. The Taruks faded in the distance and the horizon in front of them began to grow black.

The black grew and became larger as dust trailed behind. Alexandrea and Saul both took a deep breath as both sides raced towards each other and then came to a stop a thousand yards from each other. The two sides formed lines and stared at each other for several moments, each of which felt like an eternity.

She searched the opposing army, looking for her father who she knew would likely be with them. Finally, she spotted the emperor's royal chariot and the armor of the emperor. Every eye turned and looked at Aiden.

Aiden lifted his sword and let out a cry. The rest of the army followed suit, charging their steeds towards the army. The opposing army let out their battle cry and charged towards them, dust filling the area around them as the two armies rushed to meet each other.

Saul and herself swiped away the blades of the enemy soldiers and attacked their enemies before they had a chance to figure out they had been blocked. Men and soldiers on both sides fell from their horses as the battle continued for some time.

Alexandrea yelled out in pain as a sword caught her in the arm. She managed to stay upright, watching as a knife sailed through the air and struck her opponent. The person fell and Saul came forward, grabbing the knife.

"We have to find your father!" Saul exclaimed.

"We'll never get there on a horse," Alexandrea yelled. "We're too easy to see." They both dismounted and sent their horses off, Alexandrea ignoring the bloody wound on her arm for a few minutes.

"Did you see the chariot?" Saul asked.

"Yes, but I don't know where it is now," Alexandrea answered.

"It's three hundred yards to the northeast," Aiden said, coming up to them. "Better act quick, I don't know how long they will let the battle go on without withdrawing, seeing all the troops they've lost already."

"I don't think you'll have to worry about them escaping!" Shavrok exclaimed as he came running up to them. He pointed to the northern edge of the battlefield where Drake and his army had now appeared.

Drake stood at the helm of the army with everyone behind him blowing into their horns. The soldiers of the opposing army looked behind them, trembling in their armor as the horns bellowed into the battlefield.

A small line of defense was formed at the northern edge as the force of three thousand horsemen rushed towards the dwindling force of the Goshen army. The horsemen crushed the defensive line, trampling all of them, plowing into the army, pushing further and further, engaging troops that hadn't yet been engaged.

"There!" Saul yelled, pointing to the emperor who was still standing in his chariot, fighting anyone who came to challenge him.

"Allow me!" Shavrok exclaimed. They moved aside, keeping up the best they could as Shavrok bounded towards Ahab and launched himself into the air. Shavrok landed behind the chariot and crushed the chains that bound the horses to the chariot He grabbed the wheel of it, flipping the chariot end over end. The emperor was thrown to the ground as the chariot crashed down onto him.

Shavrok roared and grabbed what was left of the chariot and threw it over their heads. Shavrok grabbed Ahab and threw him into the battle.

Alexandrea and Saul ran up alongside Shavrok who had found and pinned the emperor down to the ground. They both knelt, their minds confused by what they saw.

"This isn't the emperor!" Saul said.

"This is his assistant. The second in command," Alexandrea answered. "But why is he in father's armor."

"It's a trap!" Shavrok yelled.

They sprang to their feet and started to run. Alexandrea screamed in pain as an arrow pierced her side. She grabbed at the wound as she fell to the ground.

Her father stood before her, sword drawn with an evil smile on his face. He was wearing the armor of a normal soldier. He drew his sword and held it to her throat, his hot rancid breath raining down on her as she was forced to look into his hatred-filled eyes.

"Any last words my *daughter*?" Ahab asked.

"I don't think so!" Shavrok cried. He kicked Ahab in the stomach. He picked himself up and yelled as he raced toward Shavrok and Saul. A moment later Aiden had rushed in from the side, knocking Ahab to the ground, his sword lost from his grasp.

Ahab lunged for Aiden, but only got an empty plot of ground as Aiden had already climbed back to his feet. Ahab swung his foot and knocked Aiden's feet from under him, landing him on his back. Ahab grabbed another knife and brought his hand towards Aiden's chest.

Aiden anticipated the move and grabbed Ahab's hand before it reached his chest. The two of them struggled with the knife, Ahab able to force it closer to Aiden's chest. Shavrok rushed forward and brought his arm down on Ahab's, crushing the bone.

Aiden moved the limp arm to his side where the knife blade hit the dirt. Ahab attempted to launch himself onto Aiden, but Aiden was faster, grabbing a stray arrow from the ground and thrusting it into Ahab's chest.

Ahab fell back onto the ground, clutching his chest. Aiden stood to his feet as did everyone else who had fought him. The emperor's breathing was hard and labored as he looked up at them, anger burning in his eyes.

A strange dark red arrow pierced the air and struck Ahab in the throat, killing him. Alexandrea searched for the source of the arrow but was unable to find the person. Aiden stepped over the man, grabbed his sword, and slid it back into its sheath. After a moment Aiden approached Saul and Alexandrea.

He came to Alexandrea first and pulled the remainder of the arrow from her side. A momentary stab of pain shot through her body and then vanished. She put her hand to her side, seeing blood but no hole. Her mind tried to make sense of what was happening, as Aiden moved next to Saul and laid a hand on his injuries. One by one they were healed and with the exception of the blood no one could tell that they had even been injured.

Alexandrea stared at her father's body. She knew he would have never surrendered and he had never loved her, but she still felt sorrow at his passing.

Within a couple of hours, all their enemies had been defeated. Everyone who was able mounted their horses, ready for the next part of the journey. Drake rode to the front, with Aiden right beside him. No one spoke as they slowly began making their way out of the battlefield. They walked their horses for a half hour or so, allowing everyone to gather their bearings back again.

The ground flew by and her mind drifted in and out of what was going on before the castle finally came into view. The castle was still in shambles from the hail storm.

The bodies of both people and animals still littered the ground from the plagues that had devastated the land earlier. When this was all over they would have a lot of cleaning and fixing to do before they could start to rebuild the nation.

The remaining citizens took notice of them but made no move to get weapons and fight them. Instead, they let the host ride into the city. Everyone remained quiet, not waving a flag of victory nor telling everyone that they were now the ones in charge.

They moved further into the city, the pain and devastation, getting worse than it had been on the outskirts of the city. Only a few guards remained and they were all moving out of the way and bowing to them as they passed by. Finally, they came to the inner gate and passed through without any delay as the guards opened the gates.

The army moved inside, with not all of them able to get in. They were surrounded by a couple hundred troops who stood on the wall and on top of the buildings, each of them aiming arrows at their heads. Aiden stayed calm and collected, offering the same strength and courage to everyone else.

"Foolish of you to come here!" A voice yelled. They looked up to see Jezebel standing in one of the windows twenty feet above them. Her two servants stood behind her.

"I think it's more foolish of you to think that you've done good while you were queen," Aiden said.

"Good is a point of view and you are nothing but evil," Jezebel replied. "Shoot them full of arrows!" Alexandrea and everyone else watched as the soldiers never shot the arrows as they eventually lowered them.

Jezebel cursed. "You invalids!"

The soldiers took out their swords and lay them on the ground in front of them.

"Perhaps they're the ones with the brains," Aiden suggested. "Give yourself up and we will let you live."

"I will never give myself up!" Jezebel yelled. Aiden frowned, his eyes moving slightly to the servants that stood in the window with her. "You're never going to kill me."

"I don't think we'll have to," Aiden said, looking to the servants. "Do away with her." Jezebel's face showed confusion and then was filled with rage as her servants rushed her and threw her out the window. She flailed to the ground and struck the stone courtyard head first, splitting open her skull and splattering blood everywhere. Her crown had fallen off her head and rolled to the feet of Alexandrea's horse.

Alexandrea dismounted and grabbed the crown staring at the crown for a minute. A voice appeared in her head, small and strange, but somehow it seemed familiar to her.

She silenced the voice and raised the crown high above her head, throwing it onto the ground. The crown shattered into a million pieces, which turned into dust when they struck the ground and then were carried away by the wind. Alexandrea looked to the queen's dead body stepping back a couple of feet at the sight.

The entire body had already decomposed to nothing but bones. The blood had already dried on the bricks and the flies swarmed to the bones, picking off the last remnants of the queen. Finally, the bones disintegrated into nothing and were taken away in the breeze.

"What just happened?" Saul asked, sounding just as terrified as Alexandrea was. She looked at Aiden, patiently awaiting his answer.

"The wages of sin," Aiden replied.

"What do we do now?" Drake asked. "Is that it?"

"Evil never rests Drake," Aiden started. "Even now our enemy is regrouping, and reorganizing his efforts."

"Where though. There's nowhere left," Drake argued. "Grimdor isn't a possibility for the Sorcerer anymore."

"Why don't you ride with me and I will show you exactly where the Sorcerer will strike from. Though you may not believe me."

"I'm game if you guys are," Drake said. The others nodded their agreement and mounted their horses.

"Nickolas, Thaddeus, and Diderus, there is much work to be done here and we need people we can trust, would you be able to lead the slaves back into their land?" Saul asked.

"We would be honored to," Nickolas said. "We'll try to rebuild the city the best we can and prepare it for the festivities when you get back."

"Festivities?" Saul asked. Aiden nodded.

"It seems Goshen needs a new king and a new queen, and I very much would like you two to accept my appointment. Remember, I would not suggest it if I didn't know you could handle it. We'll be back in three days Nickolas, do just as you have said."

"Yes my Lord," Nickolas said bowing. Alexandrea watched in amazement as every knee bowed to Aiden. Even the soldiers that had served Jezebel and Ahab bowed down.

"Rise, my friends," Aiden said. The crowd of people who had gathered let them pass through the city to the eastern gate riding off into the sunset.

***

"I don't think I've ever been this far east and I've traveled nearly everywhere in this nation," Saul said. Drake rode a little ways behind Aiden with Isabel on one side and Ellizar and Lily on the other. Drake studied the land around them, wondering where Aiden was taking them. Something seemed familiar about it.

"Not many people in your region of the world have been this far east," Aiden answered. "But I can assure you that in the days to come there will be more and more people coming in this direction."

"Are they trying to fall off the edge of the earth?" Ellizar asked.

"They won't fall off the edge of the earth," Isabel said. "I've been further east than this before."

"Of course you have," Drake said with a smile. "Is there any place that you haven't been?"

"There's always someplace I haven't been Drake," Isabel said with a smile. "You'll just have to give me a couple of minutes to try and figure it out."

"Gog's have ventured this far east, but only on a couple of occasions in the deep history," Shavrok said.

"Deep history?" Drake asked. "What's that?"

"It's the part of the history that isn't written down in scrolls or ancient writings," Shavrok answered. "Rumor has it ancient Gogs traveled this far east."

"How much further are we going?" Alexandrea asked. They came up over the top of the hill they had been ascending and Aiden stopped his horse.

"We are here," Aiden said. They looked down at the large expanse of land in front of them, their breath taken away by the beauty that it held. Far into the east, farther than they could hope to measure from where they were standing were tall mountains, their peaks covered in snow. The mountains stretched across the entire horizon, with everything between them, and the mountains filled with rolling hills and valleys, lush with green life and flowers and small forests here and there. Drake's heart was stirred as he looked at it.

"It's beautiful," Alexandrea said, moving her horse forward. Isabel grabbed the reigns of Alexandrea's horse.

"It's deadly," Isabel said.

Drake looked at her with confusion as did everyone else.

"Deadly?" Ellizar asked. "What makes it so deadly? It looks beautiful."

"That's why it's so deadly. I've never understood it," Isabel said.

"Nonetheless, she is right," Aiden said. "This is where the Sorcerer will one day attempt to grow his forces and unleash his terror on the earth."

"From here?" Lily asked. "Why here?"

"This is an ideal place for him to grow an army. This land has no name, no king, as of yet, but I have named this land Auzing. Would you ever think that evil could come from such a place?"

"No," Morgrin replied. "It looks perfect."

"Perhaps it's too perfect," Aiden said. He drew his sword and used the tip of it to dig up some of the lush green grass. The grass hit the ground and quickly died and withered. Where the grass had been dug up the ground had turned brown and cracked as though it hadn't seen rain in months. "A dark force is at work, right beneath our noses. These lands have been tampered with to the point that they cannot sustain life except through magic."

"I still don't see how this is bad," Alexandrea said.

"It offers people the one thing that every living soul on this earth desires more than any other. Power," Aiden said. "Power in itself is not bad, but it's the reason behind wanting the power that corrupts. This land will be viewed as a place of great opportunity. There will appear to be nothing bad about it. Oppressed people will flock here, looking for a new life. With no government established, they will be able to have a new life and a new nation will rise.

However, evil can't live with itself. The desire for power in people's hearts will grow and consume them and they will fight among each other, destroying all that is good in these lands. Then, when the people are weakest they will be united by a foe far too familiar to us. Together they will unite and march on the land of others. seeking to plunder it for their gain. The darkest force the world has ever known will come rushing to destroy us, and when that time comes we *must* be ready. Our enemy grows stronger by the day. Let us hope our strength goes unnoticed."

"So the battle is not over?" Drake asked. Aiden shook his head.

"In this world, the battle is never over, the darkest days are ahead of us, but so are the days of deliverance. A good king never seeks out war, but he is always ready for it. We will be ready for it." Aiden said. "No matter what happens, even if everyone on this earth turns on each other, we will stand strong together, our faith in Lathon uniting us all, and therefore standing against all that is evil. Are you with me?"

"Yeh can count us in!" Ellizar said. Lily smiled.

"And you can be sure we're in," Isabel said. Morgrin and her both drew their weapons.

"The Gogs will stand against the evil," Shavrok exclaimed.

"Us too," Saul and Alexandrea said. They all looked to Drake who smiled.

"Drake Thomas is definitely ready to do his part in this war."

Aiden smiled. They turned their horses around, heading back the way they had come. Drake's blood flowed with a renewed energy that he hadn't felt in years. His heart and soul soared as they rode to the west. It was unclear how long it would be until the last war started, but Drake would stand against the growing threat. Even if no one else did.

Chapter 16

DEFENSE OF TARSUS

Five Years Later...

Drake flailed in the rushing water. His head was forced below the surface. His lungs burned, as he desperately wanted to gasp for air. He looked down seeing the ground rushing towards him.

The vision faded and he saw a modest two-story house. Two figures darted into the moonlight for only a second. They turned and ran the other way. Drake looked to the left seeing another figure in the shadows, this one more mysterious than the others.

The vision faded.

Drake bolted straight up in bed, his mind overrun with emotions and questions. He steadied his breathing and pushed the covers off him, trying to figure out what his nightmares had meant. These were hardly the first nightmares to have disturbed his peaceful sleep. He closed his eyes, trying to forget the sights and sounds that haunted him. He forced himself to his feet, walking out to the balcony that overlooked Mera Runa. The city lay sleeping peacefully, while he was left to his thoughts and visions.

He looked over the city, his heart and mind stopping when he spotted a lone bird sitting atop the nearest building to him. It was black and featherless, its beady eyes looking around and then cocking his head at Drake. Drake's mind was filled with more questions as he watched the bird. It sat watching over the city and occasionally looking back at Drake.

Drake opened his mouth to try and call to the bird but the second he thought of it the bird took flight and left Mera Runa, fading into the moonlit sky. Drake moved back to the bed, trying to fall asleep, but was unable as the questions flooded through his mind faster than he would have liked. Nothing made sense anymore.

* * *

The stars shone like diamonds in the night sky. The only thing that accompanied them on this suicide mission was silence and whatever animals were up and about at this time of night. Saul crouched down, hiding behind a small pile of rocks. Alexandrea was next to him.

Moments later Jacob and Aaron came next to them. They carefully listened to their surroundings, trying to make sure that they hadn't been discovered. In front of them, a gaping canyon stood waiting for them and what would be in the canyon remained a mystery that they couldn't solve.

The dry river canyon was one of the most dangerous places in Goshen. It was nearly three hundred feet deep and once you got down into it, you weren't likely to get back up in a hurry. The gap between the walls of the canyon was a thousand feet wide, making it impossible for them to get through by building a bridge of some kind. Their best bet was to enter the canyon and hope that they could find some staircase into the wildlands on the other side.

To the eye, it seemed silent, but Saul remembered Aiden's words and warnings. Aiden had warned that the wildlands, now called Auzing, would become dangerous all too soon. If action was needed, then they would have to get their army through the canyon somehow.

"Everyone ready?" Saul asked. He looked to his wife Alexandrea, who nodded, and then to Aaron and Jacob who appeared nervous, which was unusual for them.

"We're ready," Jacob replied. "There should be a small staircase leading into the canyon about a hundred yards ahead. We don't seem to have caught the attention of the guards."

"Let's hope it stays that way," Saul replied. The guards paced back and forth on the other side of the canyon. There were enough Borags nearby that they would be hopelessly outnumbered if they were spotted. Saul darted out from their hiding place.

He reached the staircase, which was no more than two feet wide and made of hard red stone. Three hundred feet later, they finally reached the bottom, darting into the shadows and trying to get their composure before continuing. Saul looked at his feet, noticing that the ground was moist and they were leaving tracks.

"Wasn't counting on this," Alexandrea said, pointing to the tracks.

"Me either," Jacob replied. "It wasn't like this the last time we came here."

"I guess we weren't undetected after all," Saul stated. "They must have used a spell to make the canyon floor wet."

"We'll have to be light on our feet and deliberate about where we step," Alexandrea said.

"Aaron and Jacob lead the way because you know where we are going, Alexandrea and I will follow directly in your footsteps that way they only see two sets of prints instead of four."

"Yes sir," Aaron replied, taking the lead as they kept to the shadows walking for a couple of miles without speaking to each other. They kept watch on the canyon around them, looking up at the canyon wall and the guards who seemed not to notice them. Each inch felt like a mile as they crept closer and closer to their destination. Aaron and Jacob came to a stop, pointing ahead to an orange glow that came from the canyon floor. Saul's spirits sank.

"Looks like they do suspect someone was here," Alexandrea stated, the others nodded their agreement. "How are we going to get by them without raising the alarm?" Aaron and Jacob both thought for a moment.

"Act natural," Saul finally answered. They began moving again, this time not caring whether or not they hid their numbers. They walked four abreast casually making their way through the canyon. The people around the fire laughed and carried on, seeming to not notice that they were approaching. Saul checked his weapons and the rest of them did the same.

"Good evening gentlemen," Saul greeted as they came into the light. "Mind if we join you by your fire?"

"Who are you?" the leader asked. Even in the dim lighting, they could see he had once been an elf, though now he was twisted and distorted beyond all recognition.

"Weary travelers…traveling," Saul said, sitting down. The others followed his lead. The others glanced around suspiciously, looking at Saul and the four of them who had made themselves at home at their fire.

"You realize we have to kill you now?" one of the men said, drawing a knife and slowly beginning to play with the blade.

"You realize that it's your choice to kill us," Alexandrea said. Saul smiled to himself. Confusion was on all of their faces.

"We have no choice."

"So you're slaves to your master's will?" Saul asked. The elf who had first spoken to them kept a watchful eye.

"We serve our master willingly," the elf answered, looking around at the others with him. "What is it to you?"

"Perhaps nothing, it just doesn't seem like you want to serve him. If you did we would be dead right now."

"You know nothing of our master!" another fired back.

"No, but I have some friends who do. They defeated him once."

"You'll pay for your treachery," the Goblin declared.

"It's not treachery if we never served the Sorcerer in the first place," Jacob said. In an instant, the Goblin lunged at Jacob.

Saul threw a knife which landed in the Goblin's neck. The Goblin kicked Saul back and then jerked the knife out of his neck. Saul stood to his feet staring down his opponent.

Saul backed up until the heat on the back of his neck told him he was near the fire. The Goblin lunged at him. Saul moved out of the way and stuck his foot out, tripping the Goblin. The Goblin fell into the fire, consumed by flames. The Goblin stood up and raced at him, still engulfed in flames. Saul pulled out his sword and quickly defeated the foul creature.

Saul darted to the other side of the fire where Aaron and Alexandrea were fighting the others. Alexandrea was knocked back on the ground and her sword was out of her reach. The elf snarled over her. Saul flew over Alexandrea and knocked him over. The elf stumbled back and swung wildly at Saul. Saul blocked the attack and unleashed his own, wasting no time dispensing of his enemy.

Saul looked around seeing only one Goblin left, and he was running from them. Jacob strung his bow and easily hit the Goblin. Saul reached down and helped Alexandrea.

"That went well," Aaron said, with a weak smile. "All things considered."

"I was hopeful that we wouldn't have to kill them," Saul admitted.

"It's as Aiden said. A wise king never seeks out war, but he's always prepared for it," Alexandrea reminded.

"Without Aiden none of us would be here, we all know that," Jacob replied. They laughed.

"Of course we wouldn't! He's Lathon after all!" Saul said.

"Indeed he is," Aaron said, sitting down and disappearing into his thoughts for a moment. "It's almost hard to believe sometimes."

"I know," Alexandrea replied. "But it is true. It's one thing to know it in your head but it's quite another to know it in your heart. He's impacted my life in ways that I never thought possible. I'm not the same woman I was. I can't imagine what life would be like without him."

"I don't think I'd want to," Saul said. "He was my saving grace." Aaron nodded.

"You alright?" Alexandrea asked. Aaron shrugged his shoulders.

"I'm fine I suppose, I just wonder sometimes."

"Wonder about what?" Alexandrea asked.

"If he's Lathon and he's all-powerful why doesn't he just destroy all the evil right now and be done with it? Make everything right?"

"His love for the world is so deep that he wants to give everyone as much chance as possible to do the right thing and choose him," Saul replied. "One day he will get rid of all the evil, but until then we must serve the people of the earth and demonstrate his love."

"I just wish I could see my family again," Aaron said. "Jacob and I are outcasts from our family, and though we initially kept in touch with some family members we've even lost touch with them."

"It's a hard place to be in," Alexandrea replied. "The only family I ever knew were killed. I may not have had much respect for them, but I do long to have that extended family. You still miss your sister?" Jacob and Aaron both shook their heads.

"Very much," Jacob answered. "She was the last one we were still in contact with and it seems that death has taken her. I can hardly remember her face let alone the sound of her voice. I don't suppose we'll ever see her again."

"If she was a follower of Lathon then you will see her again," Saul reassured. They both smiled.

"That's how following Aiden is different from following the other leaders or gods in the world," Alexandrea said. "There's life after death for those who follow him." They fell silent for a moment as they all stood up and then left the area heading further into the canyon with Jacob and Aaron once again leading the way.

Another hour passed and the pale sun slowly started to appear in the sky, it wasn't visible yet but already the darkness was giving way. Saul smiled, watching the lightening sky. Darkness couldn't hide the light.

"Here it is," Jacob said, darting over to the shadows, they did the same. He put his hand into a small crack in the canyon wall and pushed. Aaron helped him and the rock slid open, far enough for them to see into a dark crevice. They quickly found a piece of wood lying nearby and managed to light it, giving them light to see. They walked for hours in the darkness until finally, light started to appear on the horizon. It was faint and didn't grow any brighter as they approached, but it was enough to give them hope.

The cave went straight up for almost six hundred feet with a large staircase spiraling along the outside of it. They began climbing, seeing no windows or doors in the side of the cave. The top of it was open, which was the light that they had seen.

Far above them, it showed bright blue skies.

"We never made it to the top last time, so be prepared for anything to happen," Aaron said. The air grew warmer and slowly they felt a breeze coming down from the opening at the top.

The earth shook and the tower rumbled as the sounds of feet moving over the desert floor reached their ears. They each took a step closer to the edge of the tower they had climbed up. As far as the eye could see, black covered the land to the east. Creatures and people of every kind were gathered, not just Borags, (although there were many) like the Sorcerer had tried years earlier.

Borags, Elves, Men, Goblins, Giants, Dreeds, and even a few Dwarves marched in formation. They were scarred, deformed, and hardly recognizable as the races they had once been. He was familiar with the customs of Auzing and he knew they had been fighting amongst themselves for the past few years. Someone had united them.

Saul didn't speak as he looked to the west already seeing the massive army snaking its way into the distance. Saul couldn't see the border from here and neither could he see the front or the end of the line of troops.

"So many!" Alexandrea exclaimed.

"All sent to destroy us," Saul said.

"Why do they march against us?" Jacob asked. "We have done nothing to them."

"They've been deceived and united by a foe all too familiar in this world. The Sorcerer likely promises them freedom if they help him."

"I'm not even sure the number of troops there are here," Aaron said.

"In the end, the number doesn't matter, what matters is that we get the word out to people as fast as they can. The moment we get back to our side of the canyon, we need to raise the alarm. Alexandrea and I will get our troops ready for battle and March on the wall in a couple of days. I want you two to ride south and intercept Thaddeus and his men who are on their way back to Petrae, and get them down to Tarsus as fast as possible."

"Why Tarsus?" Jacob asked.

"Because they're the smallest town with the least amount of troops, if it was me ordering an attack I would send the first troops there and wait until all the other troops were at the wall before releasing them onto the rest of the world."

"It looks like the end of the world," Aaron said.

Alexandrea nodded. "It will be if we don't do anything. Aiden told us this day was coming."

They turned back down the tower and then through the tunnel and across the dry canyon the way they had come. In the distance, the ruins of old fortresses loomed on their side of the canyon. Remnants of the days of old. They hurried back to their horses and parted ways.

* * *

(Three Days later)

Thaddeus welcomed the sleep that had overcome him. They had ridden a great distance in a short amount of time. His men slept in their tents, which had quickly formed a small city with as many people as he had brought with him. Darkness filled his mind, as he left the world behind him, and was allowed to forget the worries of the day.

The sound of his tent being opened reached him, but he didn't sit up. He slowly moved his hand nearer to his sword, waiting for his assailant to approach. It was dark but Thaddeus could hear the man as clear as day. His footsteps were carefully placed, and his breathing was quiet. The person didn't want to wake anyone.

He kept himself calm as the assailant crept closer into the dark tent. A hand touched him. Thaddeus twisted in place, pushing the man back swinging his sword, and finding his mark. In the dim light provided by the torches, Thaddeus could see his blade catching a goblin's cheek.

The Goblin didn't yell but fell back onto the ground. Thaddeus dove on his attacker, grabbing a knife from one of the other men's armor. The other men were already up with their weapons drawn. Thaddeus raised the knife intending to strike him. The Goblin grabbed his hand and kept it from piercing his chest. Thaddeus looked to the Goblin's face, grateful he had been stopped.

"Diderus?" Thaddeus asked. His second-in-command half smiled and both of them breathed a sigh of relief.

"That's a nice greeting for you," Diderus replied. More torches were brought inside, and they quickly lit all the candles they could. "Way to scare me half to death."

"That's what friends are for!" Thaddeus exclaimed, with a smile on his face. He helped Diderus up to his feet and motioned for a couple of the aids to come and bandage his face, which was streaked with red. "I thought someone was trying to kill me."

"A little on edge are we?"

"Everyone is these days, you know that as well as I do," Thaddeus answered. "You could've just woke me up by talking or yelling my name."

"Ha!" Diderus exclaimed. "That would've been just as dangerous. I yell out, all of the soldiers are going to jump on high alert and someone would've tried to take my head off anyways. I figured this was the safer route." They both chuckled.

"Perhaps it was. Sorry about your cheek."

"I've had worse," Diderus said.

"These days grow long as the shadow in the east grows. The time is running short and with that everything that we love. I fear there isn't much time before the war will start."

"That's why I'm here General," Diderus said. Thaddeus looked up. "Saul was right."

"About what?"

"About everything. Jacob and Aaron reported large-scale movements in the northern part of Auzing and he was right. I've been keeping an eye on the wall just outside Tarsus like you ordered; a week ago there was no light of torches, nor movement or armor to be heard. Now you can hear them preparing their weapons of war. The sky on the other side of their massive wall is filled with the light of torches at night, as though it is daytime. We don't have much time."

"How much time do we have?" Thaddeus asked.

"I fear we don't even have until the sun comes up. There are thousands of Borags and filth on top of the wall. Tarsus doesn't stand a chance of defending themselves without our help. We must move now!"

"Our men are tired; we've traveled from Goshen to Ariamore in less than three days. Our steeds may have the energy, but my men cannot hope to have enough energy to fight off the evil that will flood out of the gate," Thaddeus said.

"They may not have a choice," Diderus replied. "We have no idea how many troops are inside the nation of Auzing. We have no idea of what kind of damage they're capable of. They've sealed themselves in the nation for the past four years. We both knew this day would come, and it's finally here. Aiden said that it would come like a thief in the night, completely unexpected by most people."

"I know, and I also know that it is in hours like these that we must stand strong and defend the people, but what can we possibly do against such reckless hate and such powerful ambition? They are going to come out of that nation and just like Aiden said, they are going to seek to destroy all that is good. I cannot fathom such evil, nor do I feel like we can do anything of significance."

"That's the lies of the Sorcerer taking hold of you. Aiden has believed in us enough that he's stayed with us all this time. He would not lead us astray. Do you doubt that in your heart?"

"No I do not doubt that in my heart, but my head tells me differently," Thaddeus answered.

"The greatest battle ever waged is in the heart and head, but we *know* who rides with us and we cannot be afraid."

"I do not feel fear, but I feel small in the grand scheme of things," Thaddeus replied.

"We are small in the grand scheme of things, but everything has its place. Everything has its purpose. If it does not then what are we doing here?"

"I know, and I agree with you," Thaddeus said. "Following Aiden certainly has shown me certain ironies in life. Most of the world believes that great power can hold evil back, while Aiden preaches that a kind act can do just as much.

Most generals would scold their second in command for speaking to them like this, yet I praise you for it. My soul despaired and you lifted it again. To gain life, we must risk ours and prove our love for Lathon and Sherados."

"So what do you want to do?" Diderus asked. "I realize that we are still a couple of hours from Tarsus, and I realize that we might not make it in time, but we could make it there by sunrise and hopefully give enough hope to the men in Tarsus that they can fight with the strength of twenty men!"

"Let us ride against this great evil," Thaddeus answered. "This is what we were meant to do. We were meant to take up swords and rush to help the oppressed, the wounded, and the poor. Let us do just that and make Aiden and Lathon proud! Ready the men. Tell them to prepare for war. We will ride to Tarsus in ten minutes."

Diderus turned to the other guards who were in the tent with them and nodded. The guards exited the tent and blew through their horns as they rode up and down the rows of tents telling everyone what was happening.

"So this is how the end will begin?" Thaddeus asked. "At the walls of Tarsus?"

"There are large-scale movements all across Auzing. The only thing keeping the foul creatures from crossing into Goshen is the dry river canyon. The wall that borders all the nations has become alive with activity, it doesn't seem you can move anywhere along the borders without them seeing."

"What is the condition of the other gates? Do you think they will be opened?"

"Eventually, but I don't think they will be opened anytime soon," Diderus said. "Aiden predicted that their first move would be against Tarsus and he was right."

Thaddeus couldn't hold back a smile.

"He's always right," Thaddeus said.

They stepped out into the dark night, which was lit up by torches. They all mounted their horses and Thaddeus and Diderus rode to the front of the company. "Men of the north! We ride to war and to help assist the people of

Tarsus!"

They would ride swift but casual, so as not to raise immediate alarms if spies of the enemies were watching. The horses he knew wouldn't tire like normal horses were. Where Drake and Aiden had come up with such horses he didn't know, but they were like nothing he had ever seen before.

They were swift and light and twice as fast as any horse he had ever ridden, which was the only reason why he and his men would be able to make such good time.

They moved to the east slightly, now able to see the outline of the great black wall that reached along the entire border of Auzing. From the very bottom of Ariamore all the way to Goshen, the wall stretched on. Watchtowers were posted every two thousand feet, reaching up into the sky like spears to an army.

The wall was solid rock, at least thirty feet thick and forty to fifty feet high, as best as they could measure. Thaddeus tried to get the demons out of his head, as for a moment he despaired that they were riding to their death.

They moved to the west a short while later, hoping to hide themselves from all the people on the wall. They entered a forest and were swallowed by the trees as they rode towards the city of Tarsus.

Tarsus was the first line of defense against the bigger cities further inland. If they were to have any hope of holding off their enemies, they had to hold Tarsus for as long as they could and give their allies a chance to prepare for the coming war. Atruss was ready for war and so were Drake and Saul. The foul beasts that would seek to kill them wouldn't be getting them without a fight.

The time passed and Thaddeus slipped into his thoughts, only pulled from them when they came over a slight rise in the landscape and laid their eyes on the city of Tarsus. Though the first light of dawn was filling the sky, the town lay in darkness from the large wall that stood before it.

Thaddeus and his men pushed their horses down the slope to the waiting city. He looked to the city seeing the men on the wall, ready and waiting. Their torches lit up the city. Thaddeus pulled his horn and blew through it, letting the note ring out to the world in front of them.

The people on the wall of Tarsus cheered as Thaddeus and his company of two thousand men rode towards the wall. They wouldn't be fighting in the city, they would be fighting at the wall, creating a first line of defense for the city. They moved closer to the wall, their hope, and their courage fading with each step they took.

The light was lost from them as the dark black wall towered ahead of them. The Borags on the wall watched them come closer, readying their weapons. Thaddeus halted and his soldiers filled in behind him and Diderus. They were still out of bow range.

"The wall is a lot bigger when you're this close," Diderus said. Thaddeus nodded.

"Almost too big," Thaddeus answered. "Does Amier know the plan?"

"Yes. He and his men are ready. Now it's just a waiting game to see how long they wait to attack."

"I don't think it'll be that long," Thaddeus said, pointing to move movement on the wall. Hundreds of troops appeared on both sides of the large gates. Large sickles, spears, and countless bows were at the ready. Thaddeus and his men stood in silence, as did the city behind them.

A deafening sound filled the air and shattered the silence as horns blasted from both on top of and behind the wall. The horns echoed for thirty seconds and the chanting of an army bigger than any Thaddeus could imagine began. The sound of footsteps stomping on the ground and swords clattering together brought terror to their hearts. For a moment, all hope faded from Thaddeus.

In an instant, the sound stopped and they were left in complete silence. Thaddeus watched carefully. Rumbling shattered his thoughts and then loud creaking as the massive latches on the gates were undone from the inside. Rumbling filled their ears as the gates started creeping open.

Thaddeus was blinded by the rising sun as it flooded into his eyes, acting like a spotlight on his army. Thaddeus held a hand up to block the sun, barely able to make out a sea of black slowly moving towards them. Thaddeus jerked the reins to the left, running down the line of troops that were with him. Their eyes were wide at the sight of the approaching army.

"No matter what comes through that gate you will fight! You are men of Goshen! You are men of this good Earth, and you are men of Lathon! You will not run from evil, but rather face it head-on and send these foul creatures to the abyss! Stand and fight!" Thaddeus drew his sword and thrust it into the air, letting out a battle cry. His men followed suit and so did everyone back in the city. Their cries were swallowed by the approaching army as they let out their battle cry and began running.

"Charge!!!" Thaddeus yelled. He pushed his steed forward, rushing towards the sea of enemies pouring out the wide open gates. Thaddeus looked back as far as he could, but never saw the end of the army.

His stomach churned looking at the creatures they raced to fight. Many were Borags, but just as many were citizens of Auzing. They had once been free people, now they were deformed and had destroyed all that was good in themselves. Now they sought to take away everything the rest of the world owned.

The front line of the opposing army stopped and dropped down to one knee, holding large spears and sickles out in front of them. Thaddeus pushed faster toward their enemies, determined to not be intimidated by them.

He swung his sword, pushing the sickle aside. His horse crushed his opponent beneath its powerful hooves as the rest of the line collided with the army. The cries of their enemies being trampled to death were mixed with the battle cries of both armies as they fought.

Thaddeus fought the enemies that attacked him, each one appearing more hideous than the last. He was disgusted by their appearance, but it was a good reminder of what happened on the inside when people gave their souls to something other than Lathon.

The time faded and the battle continued as more battalions came rushing out to meet them. Thaddeus looked at the Borags on top of the wall, finding it strange that they weren't trying to shoot his men.

Thaddeus searched for Diderus and found him, fighting two soldiers a couple hundred feet away. He pushed his horse through the army trampling the enemies who stood in the way.

Thaddeus looked ahead and then cried out, as a giant knocked him off his horse. He hit the ground and rolled, jumping to his feet and grabbing his sword. Thaddeus stared into the giant's eyes and stood tall and proud, hoping to intimidate his opponent. The giant hesitated for a moment and then stepped forward and opened his mouth, letting a roar travel through the land.

The rising sun blinded Thaddeus for a moment, but he managed to avoid the mace that had been swung at him. The giant spun around and swung again, this time using a sword and the mace. Thaddeus dodged the sword and narrowly missed the mace as he ducked and then turned to the left, his back now to the sun.

The giant cringed as the light blinded him. Thaddeus yelled and then lunged forward. He pulled back his sword and swung. The blade connected with the giant. Thaddeus celebrated for a moment, before being struck to the ground.

Thaddeus moved quickly, his arm struck by the mace. He stole a glance at his armor, amazed that his chain-mail had prevented serious injury. The giant raced towards him, forcing Thaddeus to run instead of fight. The giant chased him, trampling over the opposing army without even thinking about it.

"Thaddeus!" Thaddeus swung his head in the direction of the sound, seeing Diderus with twenty other men, all of them with bows. Thaddeus turned and headed towards them, the giant doing the same. He moved out of the way and the arrows were released. They struck the giant who fell moments later.

"Thanks!" Thaddeus yelled.

"Let's hope there isn't any more of them!" Diderus replied. Horns blasted from the wall, striking fear into everyone. The fighting stopped as everyone looked to the large gates. The sun was blocked out by the large shapes that moved towards them.

"Trolls!" Thaddeus yelled. The trolls ran out the gates, shaking the ground as they ran to the battle. The trolls stood taller than the giants, nearly twenty feet tall and twice as deadly. Thaddeus blew his own horn, drawing any men to him. Some were still on horseback; others like himself had lost their horses.

"What's the plan?" Diderus asked.

"What are trolls afraid of?" Thaddeus asked.

Diderus thought for a second. "Fire?"

Thaddeus nodded.

"How's that going to help us though?"

"If we can get enough fire we'll be able to direct them or steer them in the direction we want them to go. We can send them into a trap."

"We have a trap?" Diderus asked.

"We'll make one!" Thaddeus yelled. Have some of your men go into Tarsus and get some ballistae and bring them out here." Diderus gave the command and fifty of the men took off on horseback towards the city. Thaddeus motioned for Diderus and fifty more men to follow him as they fought closer and closer to the wall.

"What are we doing?" Diderus asked. "I thought we needed fire?"

"We do need fire. There's enough torches on top of that wall to light up an entire nation." Diderus and his men fell in line behind Thaddeus and they continued, eventually fighting all the way to the bottom of the wall. A hundred yards to their left was the gate, letting the troops pour out.

"Come with me!" Thaddeus urged, leading the way. They fought their way towards the gate, most of the enemy passing them by as though they weren't there finally they emerged on the other side. As far as the eye could see, the horizon was filled with the black uniforms of the Sorcerer and the fire of the torches. To their left, a staircase climbed to the top of the wall, as well as everything they needed to take down the trolls.

They fought to the stairs. Thaddeus swung and killed the first enemy that reached him, but the second caught him off guard and crushed him with a defeating blow to the side.

He stumbled and tried to regain his footing but was unable, choosing instead to launch himself off the wall, to the troops assembled below. He crashed into them, and a sharp pain entered his side as one of their swords caught him in the side. He quickly gained his footing, jumping out of the way, as a Borag fell from the stair above him.

The Borags cornered him. They yelled and charged towards him, but never reached him as Diderus came swinging down on a rope from the top of the wall. His foot connected with the first Borag and sent him flying through the air. Thaddeus quickly scaled the rope, pulling himself up with Diderus right behind.

They reached the top of the wall, assigning twenty of the fifty men they had brought with them to protect the stairs and keep anyone else from coming up. Thaddeus led the others against the Borags and other creatures that were on the wall, destroying all of them. Their enemies fell until finally Thaddeus and his men reached the far side of the wall facing toward Tarsus. Thaddeus looked over the area, seeing the numerous torches scattered along the wall. Down below the trolls still were devastating the army.

Thaddeus blew into his horn, five short notes, signaling the troops below to fire the ballistae he had ordered to be brought out of the city. All at once, weapons were launched at the trolls. The massive javelins speared the trolls in the side and the stomach. Long ropes had been attached to them and were quickly picked up by fifty men each.

The first troll tumbled down and was killed. His men quickly ascended the dead body, using it as a stronghold against their enemies.

"Sir, a catapult sits just to the side," one of his men pointed out. Together they fought towards it and then created a perimeter. He and several men pushed the catapult backwards a few feet, before turning it to face the rising sun.

They quickly loaded it and fired the projectile, which flew three hundred yards and crashed into the massive sea of black. Thaddeus felt his heart slip further into his stomach every time he looked out at the massive army. They had barely made a dent in it, and this was all the men he had.

Fear filled Thaddeus as he looked at the army, knowing that they had to hold this as long as they could. In the distance, the city of Tarsus stood waiting for

Thaddeus and his men to pull back and come rushing to help the city defend against the upcoming onslaught. They would hold out as long as they could, but eventually, they wouldn't have a choice.

Thaddeus was struck in the side, but his chainmail stopped it. He rolled to the left, avoiding the blade once again, and then sprung to his feet. He was knocked down, leaving him winded and gasping for breath. The chain mail once again saved him, but this time he thought he could feel that part of it had broken.

A Borag stood over him. Thaddeus swung his leg and swiped the Borag's feet out from underneath him. The Borag struck the ground and never got a chance to do anything else as Thaddeus thrust a dagger into the Borag's heart.

"Keep firing projectiles!" Thaddeus yelled. His men followed the order, launching projectile after projectile into the army below. A roar filled the sky, striking fear into all the men as a Taruk fell out of the sky and opened its powerful jaws.

The Taruk was red, shining in the rising sun. The powerful jaws were opened and fire spewed out, consuming three of his men. Their flame-engulfed bodies ran down the stairs and fell into the army, consuming some of them in fire as well. Thaddeus looked at the powerful red Taruk, having to acknowledge its strength and beauty. There was nothing he and his men could do against a Taruk.

The Taruk opened his mouth again and Thaddeus and his men dove for cover, behind a small tower that was constructed on the wall. The catapult was consumed and destroyed and the fire hit the bricks that were protecting Thaddeus and his men and wrapped around them, keeping them safe.

Thaddeus and his men rose out from their hiding space, expecting to be killed. Instead, they found the Taruk had turned from them and now looked over the edge of the wall at the army below. Thaddeus let a cry escape him as he raced towards the Taruk. He lunged for the tail, swinging his sword wildly.

A couple of his men did the same thing and the Taruk thrashed violently, throwing each of them off his back and scattering them among the wall. The

Taruk leapt from its spot, crushing one of his soldiers underneath its powerful feet and grabbing another one in his mouth, and tossing him over the edge.

Thaddeus tried to keep his emotions under control as he realized he was the only one left on top of the wall. Both behind and in front of him, scores of Borags stood watching, waiting for the Taruk to devour him. The Taruk roared, stealing all the courage from Thaddeus.

Time seemed to stop but the battle still raged below. Thaddeus finally pushed the thoughts of fear from his mind and stood with his sword raised. The Taruk stepped away and let a low rumble escape it. The Borags in the area backed up.

Thaddeus stood his ground. The Taruk opened his powerful jaws, releasing a torrent of fire. Thaddeus didn't flinch, trusting, hoping that Lathon would save him.

He swung his sword at the billowing flames and they split in half, making a way for him. The flames followed the path of his sword as he moved it. The heat stung his skin, but he praised Lathon for having saved him. He swung his sword again as more flames spewed from the Taruk's mouth, they were once again split and followed his sword, now trailing nearly twenty feet behind creating a whip of fire.

He flicked his sword in the direction of the large army beneath him and the whip of the flames flew spread into the army. The fire spread through the army at incredible speeds. Thaddeus stood, for a moment trying to figure out what had just happened. Thaddeus turned to face the Taruk in front of him who was eyeing him with frustration.

"You'll have to do better than fire and death to scare me off!" Thaddeus yelled. The Taruk let a low growl escape him as his eyes glowed red. "I do not fear you!" A roar echoed through the sky, but it wasn't from the red Taruk.

Thaddeus searched for the source of the sound. He dropped to the ground as a large majestic Taruk swooped out of the sky. Its color was golden and its tough skin shimmered in the rising sun.

The golden Taruk landed in front of the red Taruk, standing between it and

Thaddeus. The red Taruk opened its mouth to spew more flames but never got the chance as the golden Taruk leaped into the air, spewing flames at it. The red Taruk took flight and fled to the east, his tail and legs blistered from the heat of the golden Taruk's flames.

The Borags cowered in front of the great Taruk, whose eyes were filled with vengeance and purpose. Thaddeus studied the Taruk with fascination. The Taruk turned to face Thaddeus and bowed slightly to him, looking into Thaddeus's eyes. Thaddeus's world was once again brought to a standstill, but it was different this time, he could feel the Taruk's pleasure and see the Taruk's joy in his heart.

This Taruk was their ally.

As if the Taruk understood that he had learned the truth, the Taruk pushed off and disappeared into the sky. Thaddeus turned his attention from the Taruk to the Borags in front of him, as well as his army in front of the wall, which was shrinking. Thaddeus looked at his sword, noticing that he still had fifteen feet of fire trailing from the edge of his sword. The blade of his sword glowed red. He looked to the stairs he had come up, seeing his enemies closing in. He stepped closer to his enemies, sword in hand.

Thaddeus felt his world spin as he looked at the battle around him. His limbs ached and his muscles burned as he struggled to keep his mind focused. They had been fighting for hours and his mind was beginning to grow numb from the battle.

For every Borag they cut down, five more came out of the gate. He pulled his sword back and swung it at a Borag coming nearer to him, barely. The Borag soon joined others on the ground.

Thaddeus's head throbbed as someone struck him from behind. He stumbled forward and then spun around, impaling the man in the stomach. The man fell to the ground.

"Thaddeus!" Diderus yelled, running towards him. "We can't hold off much longer if we're going to be any good to the city of Tarsus."

"Any word from the south?"

"We sent runners there but we haven't heard back. I don't think we can hold out much longer."

"How many people do you think we still have?" Thaddeus asked. Diderus shrugged his shoulder, his face displaying fear.

"I don't know," Diderus finally answered. "I'd guess we've lost at least five hundred, maybe a thousand."

Thaddeus held his tongue, looking at their enemies, which continued to pour through the gates. "We can't win this battle on our own. We need rest; the city of Tarsus should be able to hold the defense for a little bit."

"We just have to be able to make it through the gate," Thaddeus pointed out.

"Amier and his men are on the wall, they've prepared countless amounts of arrows and projectiles to be fired at the army as they chase us. It's not much, but it might give us enough time to make it to the gate. Even if by some ill twist of fate we can't make it in the city, Amier's men will be able to give us some kind of assistance."

Thaddeus didn't reply for a moment as he watched the battle unfold before him. He wished they could hold them off forever, but he knew if they stayed, their defeat was imminent.

"There's no word from the south?" Thaddeus asked. Diderus shook his head. "Give the signal. Fall back to the city. They've done valiantly!"

Diderus nodded and both he and Thaddeus pulled out their horns blowing them and letting the notes ring through the air.

"Fall back to the city!" Diderus yelled. Thaddeus and the other soldiers spread the message as they ran towards the city. Several of his men were overtaken and killed as they tried to flee.

He looked to the wall of Tarsus seeing all the bowmen ready to fire once they were within range. The gates of the city were open and waiting for them. The first of his troops began to reach the city, making it through the gates.

A sea of black poured from the wall behind them, unchallenged. Arrows were loosed from the wall and went flying over his head striking the army of black. Countless bodies fell to the ground, trampled by their fellow soldiers. Thaddeus looked at the gate, knowing that he and fifty other men would never make it in time.

His heart skipped a beat and all time seemed to stop as a low rumbling filled the ground. The opposing army stopped in their tracks, frightened by the sound. Thaddeus searched for the source of the rumbling but didn't see it.

The intensity of the rumbling grew and began to shake the trees and the city itself. He looked to the south, his heart stirring and finding new strength as adrenaline once again began pumping through his veins. Horns bellowed strange deep notes.

His heart nearly leaped from his chest as an army of Gogs came thundering over the slight rise to the south. They rode great beasts, which were nearly as scary as the Gog's were. They were grey and nearly all muscle. Their skin was as hard as Taruk scales and spikes protruded from their heads, like a fan. A long neck allowed the beasts to do maximum damage, as they would swing their heads like a battering ram. Hundreds of Gogs and their steeds poured over the hill and flooded into the valley without hesitation.

Shavrok led the army as they collided with their opponents, running them over and pushing their way through the army. The Borags and other creatures were crushed to a pulp between the massive feet of the Gog's great beasts.

The beasts shook their heads, spearing men with the spikes from their heads and then flinging them to the left or the right where another couple of Gogs would be waiting with their swords to finish them off. Thaddeus felt his spirit soar as the city gates opened again and more men came out and charged into battle. Thaddeus found new strength charging forward with the rest of his men.

Their opponents fell and were destroyed as the battle continued. They pushed further into the battle, as still more Gogs and their beasts rushed over the top of the hill and into the battle. The sea of black was slowly pushed back as each Gog that came over the crest of the hill would move nearer to the city, cutting off the approaching army.

Thaddeus was knocked off his feet by three Borags that now stood over him.

The first Borag started to swing his sword but never finished as a huge sickle was swung through the air, collecting the soldier. Thaddeus watched in horror as the other two were crushed by a powerful arm that smashed them together with a force that Thaddeus wished was fantasy. Shavrok dove off his beast and came forward, helping Thaddeus off the ground.

"Looks like we arrived just in time," Shavrok said.

"You can say that again." Thaddeus spun around and disarmed a man who had been rushing to attack him. "Behind you." Shavrok turned on one heel and faced the man attacking him. The man hesitated. Shavrok growled at the man and then kicked him in the stomach. Thaddeus watched in amusement as the man flew twenty feet through the air before finally crashing to the ground.

"Let that be a lesson to the lot of you! Shrimp!" Shavrok boomed.

"There's too many of them for us to hold them off forever," Thaddeus said.

"How many are behind the wall?"

"There's no number high enough. This is a battle that we can't win!" Thaddeus said.

"Let the Gogs handle this battle!" Shavrok exclaimed. "Rest up and do whatever you have to in order to get the people out of this city to safety. There is a place they can go right?"

"Yes, there is!" Diderus exclaimed as he ran up to them. "Amier said there's a tunnel that runs between here and Korinth. If we can get them to Korinth they'll be safe."

"What's to keep them from following us into the tunnel?" Thaddeus asked.

"Amier said it was built to be collapsible so that no one can follow. If luck is on our side then they won't know where they went."

"There's no such thing as luck!" Shavrok said. "They'll still need people at the wall."

"Diderus and his men will do what they can. Once everyone is in the tunnel, they will abandon their posts and start collapsing it."

"Do it as quickly as you can. I'm staying with the Gogs and the few men that are still outside the wall and will fight to whatever end," Thaddeus answered.

"But sir, you're saying-"

"I'm saying get going, or we'll all die!" Thaddeus stated. He grabbed his sword Amier went running off. Thaddeus turned to Shavrok. "Shall we?"

"Let's show these slugs what defeat is like!" Shavrok moved to his large beast, which was waiting for him. He didn't climb on and instead grabbed a large sword that was strapped to its side. Thaddeus looked at the blade wondering how much it weighed.

"I thought my blade was big," Thaddeus joked, comparing the two swords in his mind. Shavrok slapped the creature on the hind end and it bolted through the battlefield, only destroying the troops of the enemy. Shavrok and Thaddeus followed in the wreckage, killing any survivors or challengers that came up to them. Thaddeus suddenly understood why the Sorcerer had once tried to hunt the Gogs to extinction.

Within a few minutes, they had sealed off the main battlefield with a line of Gogs holding the enemy at bay, creating a barrier. Every enemy troop within the barrier had been killed. Thaddeus and Shavrok stood in the middle of the valley, which had now turned into a wasteland.

Shavrok came closer as they both stared at the city walls, waiting for a signal of some kind that told them they almost had all the people in the city evacuated.

"It's sad for me to see people destroyed and hunted like animals. The Gogs once suffered this same treatment. In our hearts, we resolved to make sure that it didn't happen again."

"Why do they seek to destroy us?" Thaddeus asked. "What drives them to kill us so mercilessly?"

"We give the people hope. We follow Aiden who challenges everything the world has ever known. We live happy and content lives while they rot away because of their lust and greed. They can't stand us, but we can stand them," Shavrok answered. "I look forward to the days when the fighting is over though."

"Do you think those days are near?" Thaddeus asked. "Sometimes I wonder just how much death a person can live through in their lives."

"I do, but I don't," Shavrok answered. "I think the days of fighting will be over soon, but I think followers of Lathon will still be hunted and persecuted among the other nations. The way I see it, the heir of Lathon was just the monumental victory that marked the turning point in the war."

"Not many people would agree with that, but I do," Thaddeus said. Shavrok nodded, a sound came from the area just to the southwest. They turned and looked to the source of the sound, seeing a group of three hundred Borags rushing towards the city. They had managed to sneak around to the back of the perimeter that had been created and were now bounding toward the city.

Thaddeus and Shavrok pulled out their horns, blowing them signaling the armies. The soldiers and Gogs that weren't on the perimeter quickly took notice and gave chase. Thaddeus's heart sank as they rushed towards the gate, noticing that it wasn't closed. They frantically yelled out orders. The gates started to close, but not fast enough as the Borags poured inside, greeted by soldiers of Tarsus. The Borags pushed forward, running over anyone in their path.

"Protect the tunnel!" Thaddeus ordered. "How long until everyone is in?" Diderus came limping up to them.

"Five minutes to the west. Not everyone's in the tunnel so we can't cave it in yet."

"Say no more," Shavrok replied. He blew three quick notes into his horn. Moments later the beasts that the Gogs had been riding earlier came rushing through the gates, trampling the army beneath their massive feet.

Shavrok's beast came to him and he hopped on, reaching down and grabbing Thaddeus and Diderus as he went by. They rounded a corner and saw a few hundred people, still making their way into the tunnel.

"Get inside hurry!" Thaddeus yelled. Arrows were loosed from the approaching army, heading in their direction. Thaddeus felt his heart break as he watched a dozen people who were waiting to get into the tunnel, get shot with arrows and fall to their death. Diderus moved forward and headed towards the tunnel, where the last of the soldiers were now starting to file in.

Creaking and groaning were heard as the tunnel began to shift and become more unstable. The last of his men ran inside, and then Thaddeus also ducked into the tunnel, which collapsed in a cloud of dust.

“I wish we had been able to hold the city. Who knows what the Sorcerer will attack now,” Thaddeus said in despair.

“They'll go for Korinth next,” Shavrok stated. “There is still time.”

“As soon as we get there, via this tunnel we need to send someone to Belvanor to call for aid!” Thaddeus cried. “There are simply too many foes for even the great city of Korinth to stand against.”

Without another word, they followed everyone through the tunnel, which would take them to Korinth. Shavrok and the Gog's with him continued to fight the Borags.

Chapter 17

A GROWING FEAR

Isabel stared into the fire. There was nothing like a campfire to help her completely relax and forget the worries of her day. Looking back on how her life had unfolded she wouldn't have it any other way. She knew most people would want to skip the bad parts and probably thought that she was a prisoner of her past, but in reality, it was just the opposite.

It was in the dark moment of her life that she had learned the most about herself. It was also how she had learned on a deeper level about Lathon and what it meant to be a follower. She had certainly learned a lot in her years and with the help of Lathon, had found her purpose in this gigantic world they lived in. She had traveled to many places and seen many different people, but she knew that the world was bigger than what she even knew.

Her heart broke for the people who never found Lathon and wandered through life without a purpose. She couldn't imagine living such a life. If it wasn't for the love of Lathon raining down on her, she would have despaired and seen no reason to continue. She took off her shoes and moved her feet closer to the fire to warm them, as she rested against a large rock that they had camped by.

The plains of Ladaria reminded her of her home in Vonlaus before her parents had died. She was momentarily saddened by the fact they had been gone from the world for so long. They had been followers of Lathon; she would see them again. For her and anyone who followed Lathon, death held no sting.

The majority of the world had never really understood and she wasn't sure she completely did either, but if she had read and understood the ancient scrolls correctly death would be no match for them in the end. She closed her eyes, imagining the day when she would finally see her parents again, and the day when she would finally get to see her maker in his true glory.

She pulled out a pair of knitting needles and some yarn and began going to work as she stole a glance over to the man lying next to her. Morgrin slept peacefully.

When she had first married Rohemir, she had only imagined being married to him forever, but he had changed and it had become dangerous for her and her unborn child. She had left and never looked back and had eventually fallen in love with Morgrin. His heart is what had grabbed hers.

She looked to the east, watching as the light grew on the horizon. Finally, Morgrin began to stir as he sat up and stretched, groaning noisily as he did. She loved him more with every day that passed. He was just another example of things that she had never seen coming.

"Sleeping beauty's finally awake," Isabel said with a smile. He smiled back at her and then greeted her with a kiss on the lips.

"Yes, I'm awake. I must say I'm more surprised that you're awake. We've had a busy week," Morgrin pointed out.

"I couldn't sleep."

"Again?" Morgrin asked. "I'm starting to get worried hon; you haven't slept more than an hour a night for the past week. You can only do that for so long before you're going to have problems."

"Tell me about it," Isabel said. "For the first time in my life, I actually feel my age."

"You have to sleep sometime," Morgrin replied. Isabel nodded sadly. "Is there something on your mind that's keeping you awake?"

"There's always something on my mind," Isabel said. "There is something, but I'm hesitant to talk about it until we are in our house. I feel as though it is too risky for me to speak of it here."

"Don't worry about it hon. you can tell me when you're ready to tell me and if I need to know. You know I'm here to listen if you need to talk to someone."

"I know that, if I was to tell you everything that's been on in my head lately, I think you'd probably be dead by the time I finished, it could go quite a while."

"I'd still sit here and listen," Morgrin said. "This world has become an interesting place."

"It's only going to get more 'interesting' trust me," Isabel said. They both fell silent for a moment, each lost in their thoughts.

"Do you think Saul's scouts were right, about the movement in the south and their intentions?"

"They were right," Isabel said, with a certainty that seemed to surprise Morgrin. "We don't have much time till we'll be thrown right into the midst of war again, following Aiden into battle and having our faith tested beyond all doubt."

"Think we'll ever be able to live normal lives?" Morgrin asked. Isabel laughed.

"I don't think the word normal applies to either one of us. Besides I don't think I'd want to live a normal life."

"Why's that?" Morgrin asked.

"Because normal people don't do anything. They live their lives and go about their business and that's it. We are followers of Lathon, we have a purpose and a reason for living, we get to help people and show people that having faith in something means getting off your butt and doing something. You won't reach the top of the mountain if you never get out of your rocking chair."

"There are a lot of people that don't do anything," Morgrin said. "My own family among them. They claimed to be followers of Lathon their whole lives, yet they never proved it. They were two-faced hypocrites. Said one thing and did another."

"A flaw more and more common in the world," Isabel said. "As Aiden has said many times, the world will know that you are disciples of Lathon by the way you *love* others. Last time I checked, love didn't sit back and do nothing."

"True love can't sit back and do nothing. You can say anything you want but unless you can back it up with actions, then your faith is useless."

"Couldn't have said it better myself," Isabel said. They fell silent as Morgrin began to cook up their breakfast, which consisted of a few eggs they had bought from a local farmer. She listened to the sizzling of the eggs in the frying pan. She went on high alert as she heard muffled footsteps approaching.

She dropped her knitting needles and rolled to her feet. Two wolves came into the light and growled at her, teeth bared. She looked up at the first wolf and smiled, before grabbing her knitting needles and sitting back down. The wolf continued to growl and bare his teeth, but slowly the wolf seemed to be losing its composure.

"You might as well give up right now, you know you can't outstare me," Isabel said. The wolf finally relaxed and shook his head.

"*How can you look into the face of a growling wolf and not be scared?*" Willard asked. "*Most people freak out when we do that to them.*"

"I don't scare very easily," Isabel, told the wolf. Willard nodded his head in agreement. "If you want to catch me off guard you're going to have to do better than that!" Willard nodded in agreement and before he had finished the statement, Isabel had reached behind her and begun petting the other wolf that had been approaching while the two of them had been talking.

"*You are too good,*" Miles exclaimed, finally stepping back.

"You guys should try harder to scare me," Isabel said. "Because, for wolves, you're not very intimidating to me."

"*So we've noticed,*" Miles said. "*Maybe next time we'll just have Ellizar try and scare you.*"

"Now that would be a sight to see," Morgrin said. They laughed.

"Yes, that lovely little dwarf is going to have some answering to do when I get back to him."

"*What did he do this time?*" Willard asked.

"He gave me an orange whistling teapot," Isabel answered.

"*And the problem with that is?*" Miles asked.

"It doesn't whistle!" Isabel exclaimed. "I sat there for three hours one day and tried to boil some water and the water boiled and the stupid thing never whistled! I was half tempted to give it back to him."

"It's still a nice teapot I bet," Willard said.

"If it is a whistling teapot and it doesn't whistle then what's the point?" Isabel asked. "Plus as soon as I took it off the heat it turned to ice. It's the equivalent of me giving him an axe that doesn't cut anything." Isabel paused thinking for a moment. "Hey, that's a good idea. I'll have to keep that one in mind for the next time."

"I'm almost afraid to ask what you're going to give him," Morgrin said.

"I think that's best kept a secret for the moment," Isabel replied. "I'm more interested in what you guys found." Willard and Miles looked at each other for a moment and then sat up again.

"It's certainly worth taking a look at," Willard said. *"The entire place was deserted, not a soul to be found for fifty miles. I don't think you'll have to worry about anyone looking for you, or seeing you for that matter."*

"So it's good then?" Isabel said.

"We believe so," Miles said. *"Why is it you sent us there?"*

"Because I have to know if there's any danger or not," Isabel said. Willard and Miles both looked at each other, confused for a moment. "Morgrin I know I was supposed to join you on our way to Cos, but I think I have to make a stop somewhere else first."

"I kind of figured," Morgrin said with a smile. "Don't worry I've been to Cos before, I'm sure I can get there again. You can just catch up with me when you get the chance."

"Thanks, hon," Isabel said. "Also I don't suppose I could have you deliver something to our dear little dwarf friend now could you?" Morgrin laughed.

"Of course, I could. Just as long as it doesn't have any strange effects on me. You know, turn me into a dwarf or something like that."

"I promise that won't happen," Isabel said. The sun continued to come up over the horizon, its rays gently warming the earth. Finally, several minutes later a large black dot appeared on the horizon. Soon it became clear it was Aspen, who fell out of the sky and gracefully landed next to their fire.

Isabel got up and walked over to the massive green Taruk, whose eyes shone like diamonds. She laid a hand on the Taruk's neck and stroked it as she moved towards the saddlebag. The Taruk rumbled in pleasure as Morgrin came over and started petting her.

"You two want to come over?" Morgrin asked. Willard and Miles laughed.

"*We'll pass on this one,*" Willard said.

"*It's a Taruk for crying out loud, we would be like finger food if we upset her in any way!*" Miles exclaimed.

"Don't worry, she only eats little Dwarves that send me ridiculous gifts," Isabel said. She pulled a small package out of the saddlebag. She carefully handed it to Morgrin who gently removed the coverings, confused by what he saw.

"What is this?" Morgrin asked.

"It's a centerpiece for their table," Isabel asked.

"I thought this was a retaliatory gift you were sending?"

"It is," Isabel replied. "No harm will come to anyone but Ellizar. You see it's the combination of the table and the centerpiece together that make this interesting. I gave them the table when they moved into Cos a couple of months ago. I'll bet they never suspected that it was a setup."

"You never cease to amaze me," Morgrin said. "You have a heart like I've never seen in any other woman, yet you still love to play pranks on a dwarf."

"I think he demanded that I play pranks on him after he blew up my shop in Belvanor."

"That was over ten years ago Isabel," Morgrin said.

"It's just fun to have a childish contest going on. You screwed up our house when we were first married, but you didn't blow it up."

"I didn't screw up the house!" Morgrin replied.

"You left Aspen inside the house...with the owls. How does that sound like a good idea?"

"It was a slight oversight I'll admit," Morgrin said. Isabel was trying not to laugh. "The damage wasn't that bad."

"The worst damage was to Aspen who I don't think was back to normal for a month," Isabel replied. Aspen gently rumbled in agreement as they both looked into her eyes and then into each other's.

"Well, we said for better or for worse," Morgrin said.

"And I love you because of it," Isabel said kissing him deeply. "If the worst part is a Taruk loose in the house then we really can't complain. There could be far worse things to cause problems in a relationship."

"I couldn't agree more," Morgrin said. "Are you headed where I think you're headed?"

"Yes. It should be safe. I've had someone watching the place for a week."

"No wonder I felt like we were being watched," Miles said. *"But I didn't sense any humans nearby. Nor Rantwarts."*

"That's because there weren't any nearby. There still isn't," Isabel said.

"Sometimes it's pointless trying to get information out of her," Willard said to Morgrin.

"Don't worry. She has reasons for being mysterious. Despite all of the mystery, I must admit I find it very attractive."

"A perfect match," Miles said. *"A woman with secrets who is confusing, and a husband who loves confusion!"* They laughed.

"Now I must be going. I sense time is of the essence," Isabel stated climbing on Aspen's back. The Taruk stood to her feet, towering over Morgrin and everyone else.

"Be safe," Morgrin said. Isabel smiled and winked at him.

"Don't worry; Lathon will look out for me. See you in a few days." Morgrin waved goodbye and Aspen pushed off the ground. Isabel watched the three of them vanish from her sight as Aspen soared high into the sky.

The morning sun washed over her and the ground beneath them flew by. She had never gotten over the beauty of the land when she was flying like this. To think that Lathon had created everything and that people had slowly destroyed all that was good in the earth was something that broke her heart more with every second that passed.

She was constantly amazed by the land as she saw it as few ever got a chance to see it. Even if they did have a Taruk and flew like she did, most of them never slowed down to look at everything.

Some people looked at the world and saw the destruction and the scars of war that had ravaged the land. Although she saw those things, she couldn't help but notice the hope and the life that was on the earth. Even through all that had happened there was still hope that one day everything would be made right.

The peaks of the mountains were distant, and the land below was becoming filled with light as the day began. Her mind replayed the conversation with Willard and Miles, wondering what she would do if the rumor *was* true. Her heart trembled as she thought about the implications.

Her mind drifted to Drake, who had never seemed to be the same since Gwen had died. In some ways, he had become a stronger and smarter person, but in other ways, he seemed to look at people differently, as if they held some great secret that he didn't know. She thought about everything that had happened to the both of them in their lives, surprised that they had lived to tell about it.

Her life had been more chaotic and dangerous than she could even recall and Drake's life she knew was much the same. She tried to imagine what it would be like to wake up and never have any memory of her life before that moment.

She took a deep breath of the cool air and then exhaled, peace flooding over her like a river. Lathon had changed her life, and for that matter could change anyone's life if the person let him. Lathon would not force himself on anyone; you could follow him or not follow him, it was your choice.

Yet another thing that people didn't understand about love. Love was a choice even more so than it was an action. Although your heart did lead you in the right direction at times, other times it could lead you astray. You had to know the truth in your head and your heart, that way when one was deceived the other could lead. You had to lead your heart otherwise; you would end up in the cruel cold grasp of the Sorcerer.

Isabel shivered at the thought of the Sorcerer. She both hated and loved the Sorcerer. Wished to see him killed and wished to see him saved. Still, certain things would never be.

She looked to the distant peaks, her heart filling with mystery as the mountains grew ever closer. The air became heavy and hard to breathe, which normally would have pushed people away. Aspen and Isabel both preceded into the mountains, lost in the fog that surrounded the Dead Mountains.

Isabel walked through the Dead Mountains. She had navigated these mountains many times, but never by herself at night. Fog covered everything around her, leaving her only to see a couple of feet in front of her at a time. The mountains were quiet as a tomb as her torch cast light into the dark forest.

She had chosen to leave Aspen at the beginning of the mountains and continue on foot. She had thought twice about that one, but Isabel knew she had a greater chance of succeeding if she came on foot.

The time passed and eventually, the forest grew lighter, showing that maybe it was daytime after all. She came to a clearing. The fog was thinner now, allowing her to see twenty feet in every direction. A large shape loomed on the horizon and she moved towards it, finally able to see the outline of Enya's house. The tower rose into the sky and the rest of the house was dark and empty.

She heard rustling in the trees, grabbing her attention. She looked to the left and spotted the black featherless bird sitting silently. She stared at the bird feeling her heart stir as she looked at it. After a few minutes, the bird finally looked towards her, holding her gaze for several long seconds.

"Is it any good?" Isabel asked. The bird looked away and then appeared to lower its head before staring off into space. Isabel continued forward, walking closer to the seemingly abandoned house. Vines overgrew the house

She warily opened the door and slipped inside,

The fireplace was falling apart and the kitchen was covered in moss as water dripped from the ceiling. Isabel turned towards the cellar, finding the door was open.

She paused, thinking she heard movement in the upstairs. A few long minutes passed before she finally convinced herself that no one was there. She made her way back to the main living space and then turned to another door that she had been up only once. The door led to a staircase that spiraled up the tower.

She went through the door at the top finding the room dark. She lit a couple of torches on either side of the door. Her fears began to creep back into her mind as she noticed a large holding reservoir, which sat empty in the center of the room. Pails sat to the left in a disorganized pile. She stooped down and looked at the pail, holding her torch up to the light.

The inside was wet.

She put the pail down and studied the walls, noticing that the room was smaller than the tower looked from the outside. Finally, she noticed a dark crevice on the far side, just next to the entrance. She moved to the crevice, running her hand up and down it. She pushed her hand into it and then began pulling on the rock.

The door creaked and groaned as it slid open, revealing a sharp turn to the right and then another staircase. Isabel studied the door before moving up the staircase.

She reached the top, coming to a large wooden door. Light radiated from the other side. She pushed the door open and the light flooded out to greet her. She remained outside the room, which shone white.

A floor-length mirror stood on the far side of the room, reflecting the image of herself; except for the mirror, nothing else was in the room. She stepped in, quickly noticing blood on the stone floor. She stooped down and ran her finger through some of it before wiping it on her dress.

She looked in the mirror as she noticed a different woman looking back at her. Her normally long and flowing hair was now only to her shoulders and brown. Her eyes were blue, and the flawless complexion that Isabel had loved for so long was now older and more experienced, showing her real age.

She quickly stepped out of the room and looked back at the mirror, noticing that her appearance was back to the way it was before she had stepped into the room. She walked in again and watched her appearance change, this time looking down at herself to see the changes with her own eyes.

She pondered the possibilities, fear finally filling her as she turned and ran from the room, making it down the stairs as fast as she could. She finally broke free of the tower and then out into the foggy landscape. The questions she had been wondering about on her way here had now been answered.

Aspen took flight from the edge of the Dead Mountains. Isabel checked her surroundings carefully. The black featherless bird looked at her, holding her gaze as if waiting for her to say something.

"You know what to do." The black featherless bird took flight. Isabel moved her hand to her sword, walking into the fog, each step echoing in her head like a hammer.

She had stayed here too long.

Shapes became visible on the horizon. She stopped as they came out from the dead trees, their torches burning brightly in the dim lighting. Twenty of them circled her. She looked at each one of them, able to identify them as Rantwarts.

"Good evening gents," Isabel greeted. "How can I assist you?"

"Don't mock us with your treacherous words," the leader snapped back at her. "We should have killed you when we had the chance."

"Yes, you should've. Unfortunately for you, you didn't. You'll never succeed."

"You don't even know what we're planning," the Rantwart replied.

"I don't have to. The signs are all over these mountains. You might be able to keep the rest of the world in the dark, but not me. You can forge your weapons, and prepare your armies, but you'll never get out of these mountains."

"I'm afraid you're mistaken," the commander said. "We *will* make it out of the mountains because you won't. You'll be dead before you can raise the alarm."

"If you want me, come and take me," Isabel said. The Rantwart let a sly grin stretch across his face as he grabbed his sword. A black shape appeared in her peripheral vision. It streaked through the air unseen and unchallenged by the Rantwarts who were focused on her. She dropped to the ground and covered herself as light exploded in the air. Cries were heard and were followed by silence as she finally allowed herself to sit up straight.

Fabric and ash were strewn everywhere. Where the Rantwarts had been standing, only a burnt section of grass remained. Isabel climbed to her feet and brushed herself off. The black featherless bird, stood where the Rantwart had been just moments ago.

"You have my thanks," Isabel said, bowing to the bird. The bird took flight and flew into the trees lost from sight. Isabel stood in the fog by herself for several minutes until finally Aspen came and landed next to Enya's ruined and deserted house. Isabel climbed on and Aspen turned her head back, looking into Isabel's eyes, seeking the knowledge she had earned.

"We have to get to Avdatt as quickly as possible," Isabel said. Aspen immediately pushed off the ground, quickly rising above the fog, leaving them immersed in a sunny day, and raising both of their spirits. Isabel replayed the events that had transpired in her head and she thought about her friends and family. There was no avoiding it now.

* * *

The walls were now made of stone, offering hope that they would soon be escaping the tunnel and entering into Korinth. Diderus watched the last collapsible section of the tunnel collapse behind them, feeling both relieved and afraid as he did so. They were now in a city that could offer them protection, but that's exactly why he was afraid.

Korinth was the last known great Dwarvish stronghold in the world, and as good as Korinth's defenses were, Diderus couldn't help but wonder just how long they could hold out. The size of the army at Tarsus had been larger than he had ever seen in his life, and he could only imagine how many more troops lay behind the walls, ready to attack them.

Natural light became visible ahead of them, furthering the sense that they were reaching the end of the tunnel. Diderus slowly worked his way to the front of the crowd of people, leading them out of the tunnel to the walls of Korinth. The people looked at Korinth in wonder.

The entire city was built into the mountain with a towering fortified wall, coming out from the mountain as though it had been carved out. Flags flew at the top of the wall and the highest building before they disappeared into the mountains.

The Dwarves on top of the wall took notice of them and many people blew on their horns, announcing their arrival. The grey gates slowly began to part and the iron draw gate on the other side was raised. The wall was thirty feet thick, with large openings cut in the wall on either side of them.

They slowly filed into the city. The buildings were all carved out of solid stone and despite the Dwarves commonly being so short, the roofs and doors of all the buildings were twice the height of the Dwarves, as though they were trying to make themselves feel bigger.

Diderus stood in his spot, waiting for someone to greet them. A few more moments passed before a horse and rider came forward. The rider dismounted and bowed. Diderus returned the gesture.

"Greetings citizens of Tarsus. Word has reached our ears of the darkness that has poured out of the gates of Auzing. We gladly welcome you into this stronghold." More Dwarves came forward, their beards neatly kept and their armor glimmering in the sun, which was peeking out from behind the clouds. "Who is in charge of this great company?"

"I am," Thaddeus replied stepping forward.

"Very well. It is a pleasure to meet you, although I wish it was under different circumstances. If you would come with me, the king has heard of your arrival and wishes to speak with you."

"And I with him," Thaddeus said. He turned to the other soldiers of his. "Make sure these people find a good place to stay and help the Dwarves with whatever help they need for preparing the city." The men nodded and began carrying out the orders. Thaddeus followed the dwarf through the street.

"You speak of war as if it's eminent?" the dwarf suggested.

"The days of diplomacy are gone and Auzing seeks to destroy all that is good. Besides, even if I could, I would not attempt to make peace with them."

"You seek war?" the dwarf asked.

"No," Thaddeus answered. "I do not seek war, but I will not sell my heart and soul to a leader as detestable as theirs. I would rather be killed in battle believing that good can prevail than give in and serve the ruler of Auzing."

"Your courage is inspiring, you know what you believe and I admire that." They fell silent as he was led to a great set of gates into the mountain. The doors were opened by many Dwarfs and they made their way inside.

Diderus looked at the great hall in awe. The architecture was far beyond that of the Elves or the Men. To the left and the right, paths branched off into the mountain, some of them surrounded by similar large halls and others over open expanses of mountains. Chandeliers hung, lit with oil and sparkling off all the various diamonds and jewels that had been placed on the roof of the great hall.

If there was one reason why the gates near Tarsus had opened, first it was likely because of this hall. In this hall, so much wealth, and for some, power awaited. That was what fueled the army that sought to destroy them.

They continued forward until the great hall. In front of them, a massive structure grew in size. A column of solid granite rose out of the immense hole beneath them. It went up fifty feet above the current platform and had five other bridges connecting to it. A staircase led up to the top where the king sat on his throne waiting to welcome them. They climbed up the stairs and finally reached the top where the king was standing. Thaddeus bowed before the king. The dwarf that had led him here took his leave.

"It is an honor to house your people in this fine mountain fortress," the king said. "Though, I fear the very reason you came here in the first place."

"And you would be right to fear it Lord Naremier, for behind us marches an army greater in numbers than I can begin to imagine."

"I have heard of the situation from scouts who stopped by here on their way to Belvanor. I am confident that we will be able to hold our ground."

"Do you think so?" Thaddeus asked. "This is no little army looking to win a battle, this is an army that wants to destroy all of us and take what's ours."

"I will not have all my treasures and all my people's honor stolen by these thieves. This city will not fall!"

"I never said that it would," Thaddeus stated. "However, my lord I would request permission to bring aid into this city. I have friends that I can call on in times as these."

"I know you do, but we can defend our people. This is the last known Dwarvish-occupied city in the world, we are capable of saving ourselves."

"What if you're not?" Thaddeus asked. The king looked at him. "What I mean is what if you can't hold them back? Wouldn't you like to at least have the option to call reinforcements if you need them? Trying to face the trials and tribulations of war by yourself is never smart. Please take my advice and let me call for aid."

"Who would be in this force of people that would be sent?" the king asked.

"Elves mostly. Though I imagine there will be a great number of Gogs and humans as well. This war that is now being waged does not discriminate against race, they seek to destroy everyone not just a select group of people."

"How about this? You call your friends and they can bring their troops here, but they cannot intervene until I give the command," the king reasoned. "I will not have my people thinking their warriors are weak. We will fight as long as we can and then when we need rest we will bring them in. Are we agreed?"

"Yes, we are agreed," Thaddeus replied.

"Very good. How long do you think before the army arrives?"

"I'd say they will be here by tomorrow morning for sure. It's hard to know, we've been underground for the past day," Thaddeus replied, the king laughed.

"Indeed you have been. We will send scouts out immediately and will fortify this place beyond what it has ever been fortified. Gardule!" A Gog came forward and bowed to both the king and Thaddeuus. "Ready the hammers and help get this place ready for battle!"

"As you wish your highness," Gardule replied. He bowed and began walking away.

"And I shall join him in preparation as well," Thaddeus replied. The king nodded and Diderus left as the men spoke to his generals and other leaders that were present.

"I take it you were with Shavrok's group?" Thaddeus asked.

"Yes we were," Gardule answered. "A small group of us came by land, to scout out the terrain."

"You are one step ahead of me. I doubt the king will like it," Thaddeus said.

"I don't think the king will mind when his life is at stake. He has no idea the size and malice of the army that is approaching."

"He's running himself into a trap and there's not going to be any getting out."

"I know," Gardule replied. "I have asked everyone I could and there seems to be no back way out of the mountain. Once the wall is breached, our minutes will be numbered. Hopefully, we can take as many as we can before that."

"What does this city have for defense?"

"Besides a few catapults not much, but the Gogs have added a few things in the previous years that have added to the defense. I still fear though that it won't be enough to hold them off forever."

"So death is inevitable?" Thaddeus asked.

"I did not say that. There is always death in war, but we will stand and fight until the end regardless if we're going to win or lose. That's the commitment Lathon would want."

"Well said," Diderus agreed, joining the conversation. "Do you think help from Belvanor will get here in time?"

"I wouldn't get my hopes up," Gardule answered as they reached the large outer wall they had entered through. He followed Gardule up and looked out at the expanse of land, which Diderus knew would soon be filled with black. Diderus's mind stopped and tried to figure out what he was looking at when he noticed gaping holes in the top of the wall.

They were nearly forty feet long and ten feet wide. Massive winches and ropes were to either side. He stole a glance to the other side seeing a similar sight offset from this one slightly.

"What are these?" Diderus asked. Gardule looked at him and smiled.

"You'll see soon enough."

Chapter 18

A STAFF OF ALMONDS

Atruss climbed from his bed and pulled a robe on before opening the door. His aide stood patiently as Atruss tried to wake himself up enough to comprehend what his aide had to tell him.

"Good morning," Atruss finally greeted. "Is there some news?"

"We have received word that Tarsus was been defeated early yesterday morning."

"Defeated?" Atruss asked, his mind starting to wake up.

"Yes, they were overrun by a great number of troops."

"How do you know this?"

"A messenger, Amier, from Tarsus, sent by Shavrok and Thaddeus is waiting in the dining hall for you."

"Very good. Marshal the Calvary, be ready to depart at any moment. I'm sure we'll be headed to war after I speak with them."

"Yes sir," the aide said. He slipped away and vanished down the hall. Atruss shut the door and quickly changed into some more suitable clothes and then made his way down to the main dining hall where Shavrok and Thaddeus sat, with a few of his other generals and commanders.

"I wish I could say good morning, but the little bit of news I have heard isn't good," Atruss said as he took a seat at the head of the table.

"I'm afraid that it's not going to get any better," Amier replied.

"How bad is it?" Atruss asked.

"Worse than we thought. More troops are coming out of that gate every day. Everyone in Tarsus has been evacuated to Korinth, but I doubt that they will be able to hold off the monsters for long."

"Korinth is a very defensible city," Atruss pointed out.

"Yes it is, but we have estimated nearly two hundred thousand troops are being sent to destroy the city."

"Two hundred thousand?" Atruss asked. "I'm afraid to ask how many men Korinth has at its disposal."

"Including the soldiers and Gog's from Tarsus they don't have more than fifteen thousand, and when you're defending that only will go so far," Amier answered.

"Even if we were to empty all of Belvanor and ride to battle, do you think we could win?"

"I don't think it's not a matter of if we can win, but a matter of whether we try," Amier said. "Defeat might be certain, but are you willing to let our friends and allies die?"

"No, I am not," Atruss answered. "I have already given the order for the Calvary to be marshaled. We leave at midday. We should be there by sometime tomorrow afternoon."

"It could be too late by then," Amier pointed out.

"We have no other options," Atruss said.

"If I may make an observation," Amier suggested. "Perhaps there is a deeper level of deceit happening that we are not aware of. What if they've brought such a large force as a distraction, to get us to pull all our men and ride into a battle we cannot win? What if they have a force waiting somewhere else to destroy us?"

"Is Shavrok ready to see some action?" Atruss asked.

Amier nodded. "Whenever it is needed."

"Very good. I will send a messenger to Negev and send their fleet down the Negev River and secure the sea. If there's any threat coming over land, our scouts will certainly see it. The only other option is the sea and I'm sure Shavrok's fleet will be able to lay them to waste before they strike."

"I've never seen these Gog ships, but if they're anything like I've heard in tales and songs, then they will most certainly be victorious!"

The doors on the great dining hall were thrown to either side as seven streams of flame streaked through the air towards the table. None of them moved as the flames struck the ground. The flames gave way to a black smoke, which soon cleared and revealed seven men, each of them wearing a brightly glowing ring.

"Rade! Welcome back, we were just discussing our next move."

"What dark magic is this?" Amier asked, his face white with surprise. Rade looked at him knowingly with a look that both displayed intimidation and sorrow.

"You know not what you ask of!" Rade snapped. "We are the Korazin. Spirits from an age long past. So long ago that we cannot remember our way home."

"I thought all the Spirits were killed in the final battle at Iscariot nearly ten years ago?" Amier asked.

"The Spirits were killed; they sacrificed themselves to weaken the Sorcerer. The Korazin are separate from the Spirits though and they were not killed," Atruss explained.

"So you're on our side?" Amier asked.

Rade nodded. "We are here to right our wrongs and pay our debt. We will stand for Lathon and protect the earth until our end." Rade turned to Atruss. Everything that was hidden to be kept safe has remained so. No one knows what lies in Vernal, or that we still live for that matter."

"What is in Vernal?" Amier asked. Rade and Atruss smiled.

"Drake and Aiden have been gathering troops for the past five years and have moved them within the nation. Five hundred thousand troops are currently undetected and unknown about by the Sorcerer and his army," Atruss answered. Amier's face was nothing short of amusing. "With that being said, this meeting's adjourned. Let's go win this war!"

* * *

"You look like you haven't slept in days," Alexandrea said. Saul nodded and rubbed his eyes.

"You look the same way," Saul replied. "If we could figure out how to get our army into Auzing without killing half of them then I think we would both sleep better."

He turned to Jacob and Aaron who were standing at the doorway.

"How many men were lost trying to breach the border?" Saul asked.

"Two thousand," Jacob reluctantly answered. "We didn't get very many of their troops. A thousand at best?"

"This is in addition to the previous two attempts," Saul exclaimed, sitting in one of the chairs. Alexandrea sat next to him and put a hand on his arm.

"Maybe it's not Lathon's timing for us to attack them."

"Maybe," Saul admitted. "I feel helpless just waiting for them to come through the gates."

"For whatever reason they haven't come out yet. We pulled the army five miles south and still nothing," Aaron replied. "They seem to be waiting for their full strength to get there."

"Is there an end to the troops that are coming?" Saul asked. He had sent the two of them back to the canyon and the tower they had found.

"There doesn't appear to be, but they are splitting into six groups. One for each set of gates I'd imagine," Aaron answered.

"How can we get in the nation without them seeing us?" Saul asked. "We can't all sneak in through the canyon." They fell silent and thought for a moment.

"A thousand years ago there was a great river that flowed in the canyon. There must have been a bridge of some kind," Alexandrea suggested.

"Nice thought, but like you said that was a thousand years ago," Jacob said. The furthest east I've been is where we entered the canyon. Do we know how far east this nation runs?"

Saul and Alexandrea both seemed to come alive.

"No," Saul finally answered. "But I'll bet if we do some looking down in the archives that we can find a map or a scroll of something that might speak of the deep history and what might lie to the east."

"Or we can just ride east as far and as fast as we can and see what's out there," Alexandrea said.

"We can have horses in ten minutes," Aaron said.

"Let's do it," Saul exclaimed. "Leave Daniel in charge of the forces while we are gone. Inform him we'll be gone for nearly a week. We will ride three days east along the canyon and then we'll come back. We are already at Petrae so we'll be able to get farther." Aaron and Jacob left, carrying out the orders as Alexandrea and Saul exchanged a kiss.

"You're a genius you know that?" Saul asked. Alexandrea smiled.

"I'm your wife, of course, I'm a genius. What do you think we'll find to the east?"

"Not a clue, but hopefully we can find something that can get us into the nation. Those monsters are only going to wait so long before they march on Goshen and the other nations," Saul said.

They left the large hall and entered into the bright sunshine. Jacob and Aaron rode up on horses, with two more behind them. Alexandrea and Saul mounted their horses and the four of them started through the city.

In the streets, the effects of the past three days of battles were visibly seen. The injured lay in the streets and those that had died were covered with sheets, waiting for a place to bury them. He hated to leave them now, when they needed to be lifted up the most, but if there was any chance of winning this war then he had to leave and trust in Lathon that everything would be all right.

He watched the hope fade from people's eyes as the four of them made their way to the eastern gate and galloped from the city. Saul looked at Alexandrea who was battling the same emotions he was. This was their country, their people. They had been chosen to serve and had put their hearts and soul on the line and now they were leaving.

When he had been chosen by Aiden to lead the nation of Goshen he decided then that he was going to surround himself with people that had hearts. Who knew what it was like to succeed as well as suffer in battle. Too often, did the king and his officials sit at home and give out the orders, never picking up a sword for themselves.

Saul wasn't wired like that and he had come to believe that anyone who was a true disciple of Aiden couldn't be like that. Aiden had shown them a way of living that hadn't been seen by anyone in thousands of years since Lathon had lived among his people.

Saul often daydreamed of what it had been like to have Lathon living with him and with everyone else in Goshen. What a gift that would be, a chance to see what the world had once been like. Sadly, though, it was just a dream.

Although the stories and legends of Lathon had faded in some people's minds, as nothing more than stories for children, Saul knew better. Lathon, being the great and powerful creator that he was had found a way to come back into the very world that had deserted him. He had sent Aiden to lead the people out of the darkness and give them the chance to choose him as he had once chosen them.

The time faded and the sun slipped down deeper into the sky until finally they were forced to come to a stop for the night. They started a fire and talked as they prepared a small meal before going to bed for the night.

* * *

Drake welcomed the warmth of the fire as he held his hands to it. The forest was quiet with only a few owls to sing into the night sky. The moon was out and the stars shone down, contributing to the cold temperatures that had fallen over the forest. Drake moved closer to the fire, unsure if he would be able to get warm.

Bucklebeary lay a couple of hours to his west. His mind was filled with the memories of the first and the last time he had been there. They had been fleeing from the Spirits and had received a less than warm welcome.

His mind strayed to Gwen and then to Isabel, wondering what other secrets she held. Were they dangerous? His mind was filled with thousands of questions as he sat trying to ponder them all. If he ever answered all the questions, he probably wouldn't know what to do with himself.

Drake's hand gravitated towards his sword lying next to him as a rumbling filled the forest. The birds were woken and scattered from the trees. The sound ceased and Drake relaxed for a moment until the sound started again. Drake stood to his feet, moving into the forest and searching for the sound.

He pushed into the forest finally coming over a small crest. A clearing lay below him, where Destan lay sleeping. Drake's heart raced as he looked next to Destan and saw another large Taruk sleeping peacefully.

Drake watched as the Taruk breathed in and out, the forest rumbling when the Taruk exhaled. Drake slowly moved down the hill towards Destan who looked at him, appearing to not be afraid of the other Taruk. Drake reached Destan and laid a hand on his massive body as he looked at the large Taruk.

The light was bad, but in the moonlight, Drake could see that it was golden in color. Drake slowly moved to the right, running his hand along the tough but soft skin that covered the Taruk from head to toe. Drake was taken by the Taruk's beauty as he moved to the long neck of the Taruk, A rough patch of skin around the neck indicated that the Taruk was female.

The rumbling ceased and the Taruk slowly began to stir. Drake backed away for a moment as the Taruk sat up and then swung her head to look at Drake. He froze, not sure if he should stay or run for his life. The Taruk lowered her head to Drake and sniffed him, like a dog trying to figure out what he was.

Pleasure seemed to fill the Taruk and her eyes came alive. Drake's heart felt like it would pound out of his chest as the Taruk lowered her head and laid it on her massive front feet, like a dog. The Taruk kept her eyes open and looked at Drake for several seconds, holding eye contact.

The world around Drake faded and time seemed to stop as his mind was filled with fire and images that he couldn't understand. Drake stumbled back and fell to the ground, unsure of what was happening.

Drake gasped for every breath as more and more images filled his mind and overcame him. Suddenly as if the Taruk understood what was going on in his head the images and thoughts stopped. Drake tried to catch his breath, quickly looking to Destan who didn't seem to be alarmed by the Taruk. Despite Drake's natural urge to fear the Taruk in front of him, even he had to admit there was something familiar about her.

"Let me know if there's any trouble," Drake said. Destan looked at him and then he turned and walked back to his fire, leaving the two Taruks by themselves. He sat down next to the fire, trying to clear his head as it still pounded with thoughts and images.

Something had changed in him when he had looked at the golden Taruk. Drake couldn't put a finger on what it was, but something was different. He felt different; as though he had just solved the world's greatest mystery and had the answers to all his confusion.

Yet he was more confused now than, he had ever been in his entire life.

Footsteps grabbed his attention and he broke his stare away from the fire and into the darkness where the new sound had come from. Drake stilled himself, listening to everything around him, hoping to gather clues before the visitor revealed himself. Drake's mind was put at ease as humming was heard.

Drake listened to the notes, finding them familiar and relaxing. Drake looked harder at the forest, seeing a shadow of a man coming closer to his fire; he walked with a staff of some kind and hummed the tune that had Drake conflicted, as he tried to remember where he had heard that tune.

"Good evening my young friend," the man greeted as he approached the fire. The light was cast onto his face, revealing a grey beard and hair with aged skin and clothes. His staff was made of a dark brown wood, which had veins of gold running through it. The top of the staff was made of twisted wood, which created a small bowl shape. In the bowl, a plant grew with brown spots hanging from it. "I hope I'm not intruding, but I saw your fire and thought I might be able to join you for the night? After all, these are dark times to be wandering a forest alone."

"You are more than welcome to stay," Drake said sitting up. The man smiled and put his pack down on the ground and then slowly lowered himself to the ground, sitting cross-legged with the top of the staff lying in his lap. The man reached to the plant and pulled one of the brown spots off and stuck it in his mouth. Drake's mind was tortured by all the questions that were coming to it. The man reached and pulled off another brown spot, holding it out to Drake.

"Would you like one?" the man asked.

"What is it?"

"It's an almond," the man replied. Drake cautiously held his hand out and the man dropped the almond in his palm.

"You have an unusual staff," Drake said, eating the almond. His taste buds exploded with flavor so rich and delicious that Drake was certain he had never tasted anything like it before.

"Unusual?" the man asked, looking confused. "Don't staffs normally do this?"

"Not one I've ever run into," Drake replied. The man half laughed.

"In that case, I suppose it is rather unusual," the man agreed. "There are a lot of unusual things in the world though. Not all of them are bad, wouldn't you agree?"

"My whole life is unusual," Drake answered. The man smiled.

"Then we have something in common, you can't expect me to think that you thought that I was normal," the man replied. "Especially seeing my staff produces almonds."

"Do they grow back?"

"Yes, every hour they grow back. Unlike the ones you find in the woods, these have substance to them. They supply energy and the strength to continue when this world becomes too hard to bear. Wouldn't you agree that the taste is more different?"

"I certainly would," Drake said. "I like it better in fact."

"Most do. Not all, but most. So, what is your name my lad?"

"Drake Thomas." The man's eyes lit up.

"The famous Drake Thomas from what I've heard!" the man exclaimed. "It's a pleasure to finally meet you. I've heard stories and accounts of your upstanding character from all sorts of people."

"You have?" Drake asked, becoming interested. The man nodded. "Have we met in the past?"

"Well, not exactly. At least you never saw me, but that doesn't mean that I wasn't there now does it?" the man asked. Drake pondered it. "Think about it, millions of people walk this globe, they walk right by a thousand of them or so in their lifetime and they never think twice about it! Imagine how different the world would be if they took their passing by a little more seriously."

"What do you mean?" Drake asked.

"You walk by thousands of people and have a split second to make a good impression on them. To demonstrate that you're a follower of Lathon and are different from the lost people of this earth. You never know what difference you might make in their lives if they see you helping a widow or anyone else who needs help."

"Never thought of it like that," Drake admitted.

"One life affects so many others. You never know what might happen as a result of your kindness and generosity."

"You make a valid point," Drake said. "So where are you from originally? Where are you headed on your quest?"

"A fascinating question to be sure!" the man exclaimed. "And I shall do my best to answer both of them. Where I'm from? Well, I'm from Ancient Earth! Well, actually I'm not really from here."

"You're not from the Earth?" Drake asked. The man thought for a moment.

"No," the man replied. "Well, not originally."

"Then where are you from?" Drake asked. "There's nothing else beyond the Earth is there?"

"Well, of course, there's something beyond the earth!" The man exclaimed. "If there wasn't then how could we even be here?"

"I'm not sure I follow."

"Think about it...if Lathon created everything that is in this good earth, that means that he must have created it correct?" the man asked. Drake nodded his agreement. "If he created it, that means he must have started time and to do that he would have to be beyond time, otherwise he would be no greater than any other Sorcerer that walked the earth."

"So you are saying you are from beyond the earth?" Drake asked.

"Did I say that?" the man asked.

Drake finally let the conversation drop.

"To answer your question about where I'm going I can only say that I travel from here or there making sure things happen the way they're supposed to happen. There are many injustices in the world and I do what I can to put an end to as many of them as possible."

"Don't you have any family?" Drake asked.

"I have a lot of family," the man replied. "I believe you've met my son!"

"Have I?" Drake asked.

"A lot of people have met my son. He's done a lot for them, and the world is going to be a better place for it." Drake fell silent unsure of what the man was talking about. From what Drake could see the man didn't look similar to anyone that Drake had ever met.

"Is the golden Taruk yours?" Drake asked.

"Not that I'm aware," the man replied. "I know the greenish one is yours though."

"How would you know that?" Drake asked.

"I know many things, Mr. Thomas. I knew that because you asked if the gold one was mine, clearly indicating that it was not yours. I do know who the golden Taruk belongs to."

"You do?" Drake asked suddenly interested.

"Yes, it belonged to a Sorceress who lived in these woods, or maybe she was from a little further north. Unfortunately, the name escapes me; then again, the Taruk might not belong to the Sorceress anymore. I think if I remember…Well, I can't remember." The man laughed.

"So if the Taruk is here where is the owner?"

"The great mystery to everyone who doesn't know the answer!" the man exclaimed. "I've seen the Taruk multiple times, flying around from place to place. Never seen a rider on it before."

"So it's a free Taruk?" Drake asked.

"It appears that way, although once again things are not always the way they appear. Look at me! People have basically written me out of existence, yet I'm still here. In fact, you're the first person who's seen me in close to three hundred years."

"Three hundred years? You can't be that old." Drake looked, noticing that the man was Elvish.

"I didn't say I was three hundred years old, I said you were the first person to *see* me in three hundred years."

"How old are you?" Drake asked.

"I think I've grown tired in this fascinating conversation," the man replied, starting to stretch out on the ground. "Good night Mr. Thomas."

"You never answered my question."

"That's very true. Even if I answered it I doubt you would believe it," the man said. "However, if it puts your mind at ease I can tell you that your wife is alive and well."

"My wife?" Drake asked, hardly able to contain himself. The man looked into his eyes and nodded.

"I'm on my way to see her myself first thing in the morning. She's alive but growing weak. I'll do what I can to give her the strength to hold on a little longer."

"Where is Gwen? How did she live? Drake urged.

"Just don't hesitate. When people hesitate to do good, evil can get a foothold." Drake turned from the man and looked to the fire, wishing the man was leaving right now so that Drake could follow him. He turned back to speak to the man but found that the ground where the man had been lying was empty. The backpack the man had with him was also gone as well as the staff. Drake searched the ground for the man's indentation but didn't find any, or any footprints along the forest.

Confused and tired Drake finally abandoned his search, made his way back to the fire, and lay down. Thoughts, images, and countless questions flashed through his head making it hard for him to get to sleep. Finally, sleep came over him and he found himself lost in his dreams.

Chapter 19

A JOINT EFFORT

More ruins appeared on the horizon in front of them, offering hope, but also reminding them of the past three ruined cities, which had offered nothing of use to them. Alexandrea led the way with Saul, Jacob, and Aaron right behind. The sun was setting and they would have to be heading back in the morning, still, Alexandrea pushed, a flicker of hope igniting in her heart.

They slowed their horses to a walk until the crumbling wall of a great city lay before them. To the right was the canyon, the gap seeming to be ever wider. The southern wall of the canyon came right to the edge of the wall, leaving no room to walk around to that side of the castle. They rode through remnants of the front. The buildings were nothing more than piles of rubble. The only recognizable structure was the stronghold in the center.

"Any idea which city this is?" Jacob asked. Alexandrea and Saul had dismounted their horses and now were studying inscriptions on the wall. Alexandrea ran her hand along the inscriptions, able to read some of them.

"It's Reub," Alexandrea answered. She pointed out the text to the others. "I've read about Reub once. It was a long time ago, I think there used to be a bridge here, if I remember correctly."

"That would explain why the city wall is so close to the canyon. If there was a bridge it was probably eroded or destroyed sometime during the thousand years," Aaron replied.

"There has to be something here," Saul said. Alexandrea watched as he looked around. He finally pointed to a door in the far wall, which was open. They slipped into the darkness, feeling their way along until finally, they entered into a room complete with gates and winches. The wall in front of them faced the canyon. They looked around.

"This must have been a staging area for the army," Alexandrea said. The others nodded.

"This concludes that there must have been a bridge here at one point," Jacob replied. "They would turn the winches and open the gates and then be able to march right across the canyon, or at that time, the river."

"Genius really," Saul admitted. The area was more than large enough to hold a large army and seemed to reach deep underneath the city.

"How far do you think it goes?" Aaron asked.

"There's only way to find out," Alexandrea said. They turned north and followed the tunnel. Fifteen minutes later, they came to the end of the tunnel, finding an iron gate. All four of them pushed on it, slowly moving it until it was wide open. In front of them, the northern wall of the city was visible.

"We just went under the entire city!" Saul exclaimed.

"That's interesting, but I'm not sure it helps us out any," Jacob remarked.

"Unfortunately, I have to agree with you," Alexandrea said. "I feel silly for leading us on this wild goose chase."

"Don't feel silly, it was worth taking the risk because we would have never known otherwise what was or wasn't here," Saul reassured.

"I guess it's just not Lathon's timing for us to enter Auzing just yet," Aaron replied. The others nodded as they made their way back to their horses. They left the city behind them and rushed back to the southwest. They had to get back to the army and wait to hear from Aiden about what they were supposed to do. The time faded and so did the daylight, forcing them to stop for the night.

* * *

The pale light was starting to appear in the sky, and already Thaddeus felt his hope slipping as the unending sea of black descended upon them. He had never seen so many soldiers in one place before and with each passing minute; he knew it wouldn't be long before they were able to breach Korinth's defenses. Gardule and the other Gogs defended the wall, joining the soldiers from the city, but even with the extra help, they were hopelessly outnumbered. The army had arrived just before daybreak and hadn't let up in their attack since.

Ladders were up against the walls bringing hundreds of Borags (and other vile creatures) up them every minute. In the distance, siege towers were being pushed in their direction. Thaddeus struck the soldier coming up the ladder, he toppled backward and knocked others off the ladder as he fell.

With a final shove, Thaddeus pushed the ladder, where it fell to the ground and broke. Thaddeus allowed himself to smile for a moment, knowing full well they would come up with another ladder.

To Thaddeus, left. Diderus sprinted down the wall to the next ladder, grabbing a torch that was mounted and yelling for some oil. The oil was brought by two soldiers who weren't fighting and they threw it on the Goblins scaling the next ladder.

Diderus touched the flame to the oil and ignited their enemies. The ladder caught fire as well and quickly consumed it. They backed away as the ladder burned and finally crumbled to the ground.

"Siege towers!" Gardule yelled. "Get ready for siege towers!" Diderus ran back to his spot and looked out at the massive towers being pushed toward them by trolls.

"Aim the catapults' at them!" Thaddeus yelled. The men followed his order, moving and shifting the catapults. They were released and the projectiles hurled through the air, many of them finding their targets, shattering and destroying some of the siege towers. A few siege towers still moved towards the wall, unable to be hit by the catapults.

"Get ready!" Thaddeus yelled. Elves from the lower level, just inside the gate came rushing up to the wall. The siege tower made it to the wall and a heavy gate on the front was released, crushing the rock wall as it fell. Borags poured out of it and onto the wall. His heart sank seeing similar sights all along the wall.

Gardule sprinted towards him, jumping and rolling into the troops, killing all of them as his spikes pierced their flesh and then left them for dead. He finally made it to his feet and a couple more Gogs appeared as they grabbed one of the massive pieces of rock that the catapults were launching. They hurled the rock at the siege tower, destroying the entire structure. Thaddeus and his men couldn't help but cheer as the same thing was repeated by all the other Gogs, all across the city wall. Soon the area was free of siege towers.

"We're not going to hold out much longer!" Thaddeus yelled to Gardule who came close to him.

"Get your men to the gates; they've almost broken through."

"Yes sir," Thaddeus said.

"Make sure and don't get any closer to the gate than you have to. Don't enter the wall!"

"Why's that?"

"You'll find out, just trust me," Gardule answered. Thaddeus nodded and started running down the stairs, taking with him the men who had been fighting the soldiers and siege towers. When they came to the gate they found two hundred more soldiers waiting. Behind them, lining the streets, were thousands more. This was their last stand and Thaddeus knew it probably wouldn't end in victory.

"Whatever comes through this wall we will fight it!" Thaddeus cried out. The doors shook and pieces of rock crumbled off them and fell to the ground. Up on the wall, the Gogs were preparing something, each of them standing at large winches and cranking them vigorously.

The great doors or Korinth crumbled to pieces. Arrows were fired through the opening in both directions; soldiers on both sides went down. Thaddeus held his ground as the army raced towards them.

"Hammers!" Gardule yelled atop the wall. The Gogs pulled a large stone pin and moved out of the way as the winches were released. Thaddeus watched in amazement and horror as enormous steel hammers with spikes on the end of them slid out of the wall, then acted like pendulums, swinging up until they were parallel with the wall, and then went back the way they had come.

Thaddeus remembered now the holes he had seen in the wall and now he understood what they were for as the Borags that were speared on the end of the hammers were thrown off and sent sailing through the air. The hammers came down and swung again, driven by centrifugal force and unable to stop.

Thaddeus and his men stood. A handful of soldiers made it through the maze of death as countless others were speared and then thrown up over the wall, quickly creating piles of bodies. Thaddeus let out a battle cry and charged towards the first soldier.

The fighting continued for nearly an hour as the area became covered with bodies, making it hard to move around and fight effectively. Gardule came rushing towards him, panic in his eyes.

"Fall back!" Gardule yelled. The troops fell back. Thaddeus was pulled backward by Gardule until they ducked behind a rock wall.

"What's going on?" Thaddeus asked. "We can hold them longer."

"Look!" Gardule exclaimed. He pointed to the swinging hammers, which allowed them to see what was on the other side for only a split second. Thaddeus stared ahead.

"What is it?" Thaddeus asked. Giants and Trolls ran, pushing a wheeled device to the hammers.

"It's a battering ram, of solid rock. When it slams into the hammers it may destroy the entire wall!" The battering ram was pushed forward at a speed that only the Gogs could match.

"Take cover!" Thaddeus yelled. All the men hid where they could, while the people who normally lived in this part of the city had already been evacuated. Thaddeus watched as the army behind the battering ram began to run, sensing their victory was near.

The battering ram struck the first hammer.

The force of the hammer hitting the battering ram destroyed the hammer and vaulted the battering ram through the wall, destroying everything in its path. It flew up out the top of the wall and crashed down into another section. The first hammer, which had been thrust forward as it was shattering, ripped through the next section of the wall and destroyed the second hammer, which collided with the rock and blew out more sections of the wall. The third hammer met a similar fate as it crashed through the wall and crashed into the streets.

When the dust and debris finally cleared, Thaddeus looked to see a hole fifty feet wide with more sections of the wall heavily damaged. The army poured into the city. Thaddeus stood and drew his sword, but Gardule stopped him.

"We have to pull back. There's too many of them!"

Thaddeus and his men fled into the mountain.

* * *

Morgrin stood up in the saddle, trying to stretch and bring himself some relief. He sat back down as he raced towards Cos, slowing his horse to a light walk as he approached the gates. The guards stopped him and asked him a few questions before they finally let him pass. He dismounted his horse and walked it through the streets, relieved to be out of the saddle.

The city of Cos was one of his favorite cities. It didn't hold the splendor or glory that Belvanor or Mera Runa did, but it was a good size in his opinion. Three thousand people called Cos their home.

After a few minutes of walking, he rounded a corner and headed down a narrow little street, lined with numerous dwellings and houses. The houses ranged from the biggest and richest houses to the smallest one-room huts that he had ever seen.

It was unusual to see both together on the same streets.

Finally, Ellizar and Lily's house came into view at the end of the street. It was a modest two-story house, a happy medium between the mansions and the one-room huts that lined the street. From the outside, the house looked completely ordinary but Morgrin knew better than that.

This had been his house before he and Isabel had been married. They had only remained in the house for the first year of their marriage, so naturally, it had some of Isabel's special touches.

He tied his horse outside and couldn't help but smile as the door opened and Celine and Timothy came running out of the house, embracing him.

"Wow, you guys have gotten big!" Morgrin said embracing them.

"Did you bring something?" Celine asked her blue eyes shining in the sun.

"Bring something?" Morgrin asked with a smile.

"Did Aunt Isabel send anything for Dad?" Timothy asked. "You know, like the time she sent him the pen that played musical notes every time it touched the paper? It drove him nuts. That one was probably my favorite."

"I bet it was," Morgrin replied turning to the girl. "What was your favorite sweetheart?"

"I guess it was probably when she had a hundred mourning doves follow him around for two days. We couldn't see anything but his beard."

"That's one of my favorites too," Morgrin said. "It just so happens that I do have something for your father from your Aunt Isabel. I don't know if it does anything unique though."

"What is it?" Morgrin smiled.

"You'll have to wait and see," Morgrin replied. The door on the house opened and Lily and Ellizar came bounding down the path, embracing him. Morgrin couldn't help but hide a smile. In a world that was falling apart, love was the one thing that could unite and make people stronger than they had ever been. Ellizar embraced Morgrin and then stepped back, looking at everything warily.

"What's the matter Ellizar?" Lily asked. Ellizar looked around suspiciously.

"He's here, which means there's somethin' that's goin' teh happen teh me. I can feel it in my beard! What did yer wife plan this time?"

"She was probably going to turn all your axes into hams so we could cook them," Lily replied. Morgrin and the others all laughed at Ellizar's face.

"You know I might just have to tell her that one," Morgrin said.
Ellizar was still speechless.

"No one messes with the axes; it's bad enough that Lily did what she did with them!" Ellizar exclaimed half-laughing.

"What did you do?" Morgrin asked.

Lily smiled. "I might have changed the color of the handles. They didn't go with anything in the house, so there's a nice purple one and a blue one. They match the different flowers that grow on the wall."

"Yes, the only consolation is that the flowers that yer wife put in this house ate that axe," Ellizar told him. Morgrin laughed.

"It didn't eat the actual blade, but it ate the rest of it," Lily corrected. "It also ate half of his wardrobe."

"Yes, well that was no accident," Morgrin said. "She intentionally fed them to the flowers, to get back at you for that flock of chickens you sent her."

"Blasted elf kind!" Ellizar replied, laughing a moment later. "That flock of chickens was a good one though wasn't it?" They laughed.

"It certainly was," Morgrin agreed. "You should've seen her trying to catch them."

"What was so special about the chickens?" Celine asked.

"Every time she went near them they lost all their feathers. One big poof, and then you had all these naked chickens running around the yard. Also, every time she tried to grab one it would disappear and end up on the other side of the yard," Morgrin said.

Ellizar laughed sadistically. "I bet that one bug'ed her fer a while."

"It did, and then she finally had Aspen fly over and incinerate all of them. They made a fantastic meal."

"That's cheatin'!"

"But anyway, before I forget here's a little something for your table from my wife," Morgrin said, handing the package to Lily. Ellizar stepped away.

"A little paranoid are we?" Lily asked.

"Extremely!" Ellizar exclaimed. Lily unwrapped it and the sunlight hit the crystal centerpiece. The crystal changed colors every twenty seconds or so.

"It's beautiful!" Lily exclaimed, looking at Ellizar. "I think this is one thing you don't have to be afraid of."

"I'll still keep my distance," Ellizar replied. They followed Lily into the house, which was slightly different from what he remembered. The flowering vines that usually covered the walls, of any place Isabel owned, only hung in the corners and over the doorways.

"This is a nice place you have here?" Morgrin said. Ellizar laughed.

"Yeh would know yeh owned it."

"Well yes, but you've made some additions," Morgrin replied. "Do you like the table?"

"Very much," Lily said. "Did Isabel make it?"

"She said she found it somewhere. Who knows what that means?" Morgrin said, looking at the table. It was a large table with one center support that was a tree trunk, with roots that dug into the ground holding it in place.

The branches reached out and wove together creating a solid surface that they could eat on. It was covered in leaves, which changed colors with the seasons. Lily put the centerpiece on the table. Morgrin smiled, looking at the flowers throughout the house.

"Do you like the plants?"

"The only one Ellizar doesn't like is that one over there," Lily said. She pointed to the plant in the corner by the window.

"Why doesn't he like it?" Morgrin said. "It looks perfectly normal to me."

"If I go anywhere near it it'll try and eat me alive."

"I think you're exaggerating a little bit," Morgrin said.

"It hisses at him," Celine said. Morgrin laughed.

"Where on earth did you find a plant that does that? That seems like something Isabel would've found."

"I bought it at the market for cheap!" Celine said. "I thought it looked pretty. It only hisses at Dad though."

"Anyway, have a seat, yeh showed up just in time fer lunch. Yeh almost would've thought that was planned."

"Great! I'm starved. What are we having?"

"Ellizar's world-famous Trunchalback Stew!" Ellizar exclaimed.

"Again?" Morgrin asked. "I think you've served me that every time I've been here for a meal."

"That's because I don't cook on weekends and he does," Lily said. "And in short that means he can't cook." Ellizar started to object.

"By the way, I've been wondering what Trunchalback is? Isabel hasn't even heard of that before."

"It's a Dwarvish word for leftovers," Timothy answered. Ellizar smiled.

"Ah, I knew there was some Dwarvish in our kids."

"I knew it too," Lily said. "I was just glad they didn't have beards at the age of six."

"So you take all the leftovers and throw them in a pot and call it stew?" Morgrin asked. Ellizar nodded. "Doesn't sound like cooking to me."

"No wonder the plant hisses at him," Celine replied.

hey laughed as Ellizar turned and started walking towards the corner where the plant was. Morgrin tried to hold a chuckle back as the plant started to make a hissing sound and got louder as he moved closer. Ellizar looked at the plant and then at Celine.

"Celine, forgive me!" Ellizar exclaimed. He grabbed a pan from the counter and smacked the plant with it. Ellizar's smile soon faded when he showed them the frying pan, which was now dented.

They talked and laughed, as Ellizar made the supper for them, which Morgrin somehow got the feeling wasn't going to taste any better than it had the previous times he had eaten it. Morgrin helped them set the table and got an extra chair for himself as Ellizar brought the pot of stew over and set it on the table.

"Are you going to sit down hon?" Lily asked Ellizar. Ellizar tried to appear as though nothing was out of the ordinary as he stood at his spot at the table instead of sitting in the chair.

"Yeh know I think I'm tired of sittin' today, I think I'd much rather stand. Besides it must be better fer digestion because gravity can pull it teh yer stomach much faster."

"Ellizar, you're shorter than all of us I'm pretty sure it's going to get to your stomach," Morgrin said. "Now, why don't you sit down so we can eat this… lovely…food you've made us?"

"How about we bless the food before I sit?" Ellizar asked. They conceded and they all bowed their heads and closed their eyes.

"Lathon, may yeh bless this food teh our bodies and may nothin' blow up when I sit down!"

"Amen," they all said in unison. Ellizar smiled weakly, sitting down in the chair. At once, all the leaves that were on the table, came free and flocked to Ellizar burying him in leaves.

"Blasted elf kind!" Ellizar stood up and all the leaves flew back to the spot they had come from. Relief flooded over his face. "Glad we got that out of the way!" He sat down again and the leaves once again buried him.

"Is this goin' teh happen every time I sit down?" Ellizar asked from underneath the leaves. The front door opened.

"No I think I've had enough laughs for now," Isabel said as she came walking in the door. Isabel tapped the table twice and the leaves went back to their spot and stayed there. Morgrin greeted her with a kiss as she took a seat next to him.

Soon the meal was over and it was just Isabel and Morgrin watching the sunset in the distance.

"What's on your mind?" Morgrin asked. She had tried to pretend as if nothing was going on, but they had been married long enough that he could see through the facade she was putting on.

"Nothing."

"I don't believe you," Morgrin replied. "Something's bothering you, and I think I know what it is?"

"I've grown tired of hiding things."

"Don't worry, soon it'll be all over and then we can live happily ever after," Morgrin said. "How long are you going to wait?" Isabel thought hard, her face becoming more evident of the conflict she was feeling.

"As long as I possibly can. It might kill me, but perhaps it'll work out better that way."

"I trust your judgment. It'll be nice to finally have it all out in the open won't it?" Morgrin asked. Isabel nodded.

"Yes, it will. It's not time yet, but the time is fast approaching.

* * *

Atruss and his men thundered over the plains. Atruss had been to Korinth on several different occasions and as much as he hated to admit it, he knew Amier was right, the defense could only last for so long before they were overrun. Ten thousand men rushed towards the battle, which was likely only an hour away. No one spoke as they rode. The men were nervous and afraid for their lives, likely thinking that this might very well be the end.

"Riders from the east!" one of his men yelled out. His men took up formation as they turned and headed directly towards the small group of people coming towards them. Atruss studied the group, quickly noting a Gog riding a great beast.

"Stay your weapons!" Atruss yelled. His men obeyed his order and slowed to a walk as the Gog and the group approaching them did the same thing. Soon he could make out Gardule and Thaddeus leading a company of fifty soldiers, a mix of Dwarves, men, and Gogs.

"Good afternoon my friends," Thaddeus said. "We were hoping to meet you under better circumstances than these."

"We're too late aren't we?" Atruss asked. Thaddeus nodded. "I had a feeling we wouldn't make it in time."

"Once they breached the wall, we didn't stand a chance," Gardule replied.

"No one but us made it out of the city alive." Silence fell over them.

"These are sad tidings indeed. What of the army, what are they doing?"

"Fighting over the riches of the Dwarves, enjoying the spoils of war. They seem to have stopped proceeding for now. It's only a matter of time though before they continue and when they do it's not going to be good."

"Our time is running short," Atruss said. "The men must stay here for the night, make camp, and set watches! We must make for Mera Runa with great speed. We have much to discuss."

* * *

THE DEAD MOUNTAINS

Destan landed in the fields just outside Mera Runa. He welcomed the sight of the great city and his fellow commanders and officials who had all gathered outside the castle to greet him. Drake dropped off the side of Destan and the Taruk took off moments later heading to Cos where they would meet again.

Thaddeus and Shavrok stood at the front of the line of people, with Atruss, Diderus, and Rade standing next to them. Rade stood, emotionless and expressionless as was normal for him. Most people didn't even know that Rade had survived the attack on Iscariot years ago. The Korazin had faded into myth over the past nine years and for that, Drake was thankful. It had allowed him and Aiden to work up a surprise for the Sorcerer.

"Good morning my friends!" Drake greeted. They exchanged greetings and embraced each other before they filled him in on everything that had happened in Korinth and Tarsus.

"For reasons we can't explain, the Sorcerer's army seems to have stopped after reaching Korinth," Atruss said.

"It's hard to say why they're doing this, but the only thing I know for certain is that we can't wait any longer," Drake replied.

"What do we do?" Thaddeus asked. "Our enemy is becoming unpredictable."

"We rally all our forces and get to the border as fast as we possibly can," Drake started. "Queman has provided us with well over five thousand of his fastest horses. We will be able to make the trip in a day and a half at most. I will take my troops and head towards Athos, it's a smaller town than Malya, so it's likely going to be where most of the Sorcerer's troops end up attacking. Rade, if you could play messenger between all three of our armies that would be great."

"It would be an honor, my lord," Rade replied. "What is the third force?"

"Saul's army is camped up in Petrae, if one of the Korazin could go up there and tell him of the plan that would be much appreciated."

"As you wish. Also, I inquire, when do you want to send the men you and Aiden have been hiding in Vernal?"

"Wait until we get through the border of Auzing," Drake replied. "This will put them half a day behind us and we'll be able to offer our men rest and surprise our enemy when they show up at the next battle."

"Very well, but there is another threat that we might not have thought about," Atruss started. "We've had the Gog ships patrolling the sea just south and east of Belvanor for the past week and we have found no sign of any ships, but we all know that if there is any threat by sea, Gath will be the place they come from." Drake nodded.

"I'd like to sail to Gath and show them what a Gog ship looks like!" Shavrok exclaimed. They smiled.

"I think that would be a very good idea," Drake replied. "You and Thaddeus can head to the ships and prepare all of them for sailing for the city."

"I would warn though that our scouts have indicated that the city of Gath has been heavily reinforced over the past four or five months," Atruss said. Shavrok laughed.

"I'm pretty sure they didn't take into consideration the size and force of a Gog ship."

"Well said," Drake said. "I remember the last time we had a run-in with the Borag ships."

"Puny little things," Shavrok replied. "I'll set sail immediately."

"Stop ten miles off the coastline though, until we're all in position," Atruss started. "If we can all attack the border at one time we run the opportunity of intimidation and perhaps our enemy will slip up."

"In that case, I look forward to seeing you all once we win this war!" Drake exclaimed.

They ended their meeting and Shavrok, Thaddeus, and Atruss all departed, with Thaddeus and Shavrok making for the sea, while Atruss left on one of Queman's horses. Rade turned into flames and streaked into the sky, soon joined by six other streaks of fire as they all separated and went in different directions. Drake stood, trying to place his feelings at the moment. He wasn't sure what he should feel right now. Their enemy, the Sorcerer, was rising to power again. He felt prepared but was overcome with sorrow that Gwen wasn't here to fight alongside him.

His mind drifted back to the vision the Sorcerer had shown him so many years ago wishing he knew what was true and what was false. Never in his life had he felt more confused than he did right now. The conversation he had had with the old man was equally hard for him to understand. According to the old man, Gwen was alive.

He motioned to his second in command, Matthew. He stood, patiently waiting for orders as Drake was lost in his thoughts for another moment or two.

"Sir?" Matthew asked. "What are your orders?"

"Every soldier able to be spared must come to Cos. From there we'll march to Athos."

"Right away sir."

"I want to be leaving in twenty minutes or less. I'm putting you in charge of organizing the Gogs of Crede and the Men in Ephesi and getting them to Cos no more than a day behind me and my men. You can cut through Vernal without a problem."

"Yes sir," Matthew said, he went away and gave out the orders, which were confirmed by the sound of horns blasting. The note was long and strange, and unique enough that everyone in the city would recognize it as the war horn.

Drake quickly donned his armor. He ran out to the main courtyard where a white horse was waiting for him. He mounted and rode it down into the city, finally making it through the throngs of soldiers on horseback until he reached the open gates. He stopped and circled to face his men.

"Thank you for the speed in which you have gathered!" Drake yelled. "Now we ride to war and victory, and to the ruin of our enemies!" A great battle cry erupted from the men and horns blasted throughout the city as Drake led the way from the gates. Drake flew over the ground; behind him fifteen thousand men followed him, their horses shaking the ground with their hooves.

He had been careful over the past year to put large amounts of soldiers in the cities that were further east. He knew there were at least thirty thousand men in both Ephesi and Crede. Ahead in Phenoix, there were another twenty thousand.

They rode long into the night.

* * *

Saul and Alexandrea dismounted their horses, met immediately by a throng of his people happy to see that they had returned. Jacob and Aaron got off and led all four of the horses away. His commanders immediately came to them, hammering them with questions that Saul couldn't begin to answer.

They were silenced by a streak of flame flying through the air. Some of the soldiers took cover and prepared for war but soon noticed that the officials weren't alarmed by the sight. The flame struck the ground and gave way to the form of a man. Rade came forward.

"Welcome your Highness, I trust your trip was successful?" Rade asked.

"Not as much as I would've liked," Saul answered.

"You might be surprised at the secrets this land holds," Rade replied.

"What's happening behind the walls of Auzing?" Saul asked.

"The easier question is what's not happening!" Rade exclaimed. "As we speak, troops beyond our number have been steadily moving towards the gates after remaining stationary for three days. They will strike by nightfall I can assure you."

"We will do what we can to thwart them. I've got a few ideas," Saul said.

"I'm sure you do. The army that once camped together numbered at least six million people, but they have split up. The force that is heading towards the border is only half the people that are with the army."

"Where did the others go?" Saul asked.

"We cannot find a trace of them. They disappeared into the east further than we can allow ourselves to travel, seeing what our current mission is. Furthermore, Drake and his army have not yet reached Athos, leaving the entire nation vulnerable. We alerted the King of Edon of the threat and he mobilized his army, but I doubt he will reach there in time. Ellizar and Lily have gathered a force, should they get as far inland as Cos.

"They will have to fight their way to the wall which will take them longer, so do what you have to in order to survive and take as many of their soldiers as they can, but Aiden has made it clear that any attempt to breach the wall before it's Lathon's timing will be unsuccessful."

"We learned that one the hard way," Saul replied. "It seems I'm just too hard-headed for my own good. I thought I could do it and I was wrong."

"You are wise for being able to admit you're wrong," Rade said.

"It goes to show that everyone likes power and likes to think that they can make their own decisions and take care of themselves, yet I was still helpless without the blessing of Lathon."

"As are all who walk the earth in darkness. Lathon gives things purpose and meaning in this world if only the world would stop looking other places for purpose and meaning. The places they look can never fill the Lathon-sized hole in their hearts."

"No one here will argue with that," Alexandrea said.

"I must be off my friends; there are some people in Edon who need my help, look for my signal, and then attack Auzing at once." Rade bowed and they returned the gesture before he changed into flame and streaked high into the sky, heading southwest.

"My lord," one of his commanders said. "Forgive my pessimistic question, but how are we going to possibly hold off or defeat the army that is marching towards the gate with the men we have?"

"How many do we have at our disposal?" Saul asked.

"Nearly thirty thousand, but Rade suggested a force of three million was coming out of the gate."

"Yes he did," Saul replied, thinking for a moment. "If we draw them to the Aisles then we could hold them off indefinitely. That sounds logical doesn't it?"

"Yes it does," Alexandrea agreed. "You work them into the center and have bowmen stationed on top, they'll be able to pick them like flowers from a field. You'll need a lot of arrows though."

"I don't think that will be a problem," Jacob said as he and Aaron joined the conversation. "We were exploring the Aisles one day back about a month ago when we discovered large crates hidden in brush at the top of the large valleys.

There were hundreds of them, each filled with arrows."

"Where are they from?" Saul asked.

"We're not sure. They appeared to be fairly new, they weren't rusted or anything like that, there was a strange mark on them that we recognized though, it was three slashes."

"Three slashes?" Saul asked.

"The same as Drake has," Jacob said. "Isn't that the sign of the chosen one?"

"More accurately it's the sign of Lathon," Saul replied, thinking for a moment. "If they have the sign on them then we must be meant to use them. Station men all along the top of the valleys and get ready to use the arrows. How big are these chests?"

"Big enough that we can't lift them," Aaron replied. Saul's mind tried to wrap around what he was hearing and put all the pieces of the puzzle together. Horns echoed through the air, coming from the other side of the large wall. The entire army began to come alive.

"Aaron, Jacob, take half the men to the Aisles and get into position," Alexandrea ordered. "We will take the other half. Fire a flaming arrow into the sky when you are in position. We will lead them right to the valley, just don't hit us."

"Yes your majesty," Jacob said running off with Aaron close behind him. They moved to the north taking half the army with them. It wasn't far to the Aisles, maybe a quarter of a mile. Saul, Alexandrea, and all the commanders rushed to the army quickly telling them what the plan was.

The creaks and groans of the large gates opening sent chills up and down their spine as the army came into view. A sea of black marched towards them. Saul raised his sword and led the charge. The two sides collided in a clash of swords and shields. From behind him, the archers that had remained fired off arrows, taking out some of the vile creatures that attacked them.

Some were Borags, some were Elves, and others still were human, but they were all shadows of the creatures they had once been. Saul's mind drifted to the Sorcerer wondering if he would be destroyed this time. He may not have been involved in the battle at Iscariot ten years ago, but he had heard stories.

Had he regained physical form? Were they fighting against a physical enemy, or were they fighting against something they could not see? The effects of the Sorcerer were clearly seen and they would stand strong and fight it with everything they had in them. Lathon would not have brought them this far to have them all slaughtered by the Sorcerer.

At last, two arrows lit up the sky. Saul and Alexandrea quickly disposed of the people they were fighting and then reached to their belts, blowing on their horns, the notes rippling through the army. Their army let out a battle cry as they retreated from the opposing army. Saul and Alexandrea took up the rear.

The Borags of Auzing soon gave chase, running after Saul and Alexandrea's army. A minute or so passed and finally, the large Aisles came into view. The Aisles were a defense that had been created by a king of Goshen nearly three hundred years ago and it was still a good defense.

Narrow valleys were accompanied by towering formations of rock and dirt to either side of them. There was only one staircase on either side that would lead to the top.

Saul and Alexandrea finally entered the valley and watched as all the bowmen stood ready with great chests of arrows sitting next to them. The army reached the valley and were immediately met by hundreds of arrows, which struck them to the ground. The next troops trampled over their dead comrades only to be killed by the arrows moments later.

The rest of Saul's army moved up the stairs to the top of the ridges. He and Alexandrea finally found Jacob and Aaron firing arrows into the valley that was now filled with black.

"Where did all these weapons come from?" Alexandrea asked. "There's more here than you said!"

"I know," Jacob said. "We're not sure where they came from, but all the chests have the same mark on them. Looks like Lathon's really coming through for us now."

"Praise Lathon then!" Saul exclaimed. "It's the only way we're going to be winning this war."

"Amen to that," Aaron said. Saul and Alexandrea both grabbed two of the bows, amazed at how light they were when they picked them up. They moved to the nearest chest and grabbed a group of arrows, which were all stacked in quivers for them. They fired them off effortlessly, finding their target every time as the pile of bodies grew until they blocked the valley and the army had to climb over the pile.

"Protect the stairs!" Saul yelled. The order was repeated by everyone as it went down the ridge as they turned their attention to the small number of troops that had made it that far. Within moments, they had been killed with arrows to the neck. A battle cry was heard behind him and before Saul could react, he had been thrown to the side. He crashed into one of the chests and rolled off it, quickly landing on his feet.

All along the ridge on either side Borags and other evil creatures were crawling up and surprising his men. Saul and Alexandrea both stared in shock and confusion as deformed Gog-like creatures bounded towards them. They dove out of the way and watched in horror as their men were one by one destroyed by the hideous Gogs.

"Are they Gogs?" Alexandrea asked. Jacob and Aaron made their way over to them. Saul looked at the creature, unable to tell for sure.

"Looks like some Gogs also went east and were corrupted and mutated by the Sorcerer," Saul replied.

"How are we going to defeat them?" Alexandrea asked, Saul looked around unsure. The sun was blocked out as a cloud cast darkness on the earth.

"Form a line! Form a line!" Alexandrea yelled. The men did so, standing at the top of each ridge, a wall of warriors against a sea of evil.

"I don't think we will have to!" Jacob exclaimed. "That's no cloud!" They looked up and felt their spirits rise as they noticed the black cloud, was moving and shifting within itself. Horns bellowed in the sky above them, their notes, shaking the entire land. The battle below stopped as the mutilated Gogs on the ground looked up in confusion.

Chills ran down Saul's spine as he watched the cloud break up, pieces of it falling to the ground. The pieces came into focus as Saul realized that it wasn't a cloud at all, but instead two things that could change their fortunes in this battle. Taruks and Gogs.

Gogs rode on the back of great Taruks. Their Taruks swooped low over the battlefield with the Gogs dropping off the side. The ground shook the ground when they landed. The mutilated Gogs rushed at them but were killed as more Gogs dropped down and crushed them.

Saul looked to one Gog who appeared to be the leader as he led his troops and started attacking them. His men began fighting once again, grateful for the unexpected aid. The fighting continued for an hour as the daylight began to fade.

"In a few moments you'll see a bright light!" the Gog yelled to them. "Don't look at it. Take cover!" All the Taruks gathered in the sky and then flew towards the valley. Saul and all his troops fell to the ground covering themselves as a light brighter than any they had ever experienced came from the sky.

The light faded allowing them to look up at their surroundings. The enemy troops in the entire area had been frozen in place. Their eyes still moved, but that was all as all the Taruks raced towards them.

The Taruks swooped low, swinging their large tails at the stunned army. The tail struck the soldiers and shattered them into a million pieces. The sound of glass breaking rang through the ridges and valley until finally, not a single soldier remained. Finally, the Taruks soared off into the sky.

"That was amazing," Jacob said.

"Allow me to introduce myself," the Gog said coming up to them. "My name is Furlone, leader of the northern Gogs. We received word from Shavrok along with a note that we were to come and provide aid here."

"We're very grateful," Aaron said. "I don't think we would have survived without you."

"How much of their army was destroyed?" Saul asked.

"Every troop that had come out the gate," Furlone answered. "They have closed the gate and held off on attacking any further." Alexandrea smiled.

"That's the best news I've heard all day. What do we do now?"

Saul thought for a moment. "Wait until we hear from Aiden or Rade. I'm not about to try and attack before it's time."

"Wise choice," Furlone answered. "Doing things against Lathon's will never work out the way you think it will." They headed back to Petrae, bringing their troops with them. Saul looked to the south wondering what kind of battles the others were facing.

Chapter 20

IN THE HOUSE OF DRAKE THOMAS

"My lady, we have just received word that the king of Edon will be here in the morning, bringing with him nearly two hundred thousand troops," the messenger said. Lily and Ellizar had managed to get ten thousand people from Cos and the surrounding area who were willing and able to fight. By morning the army from Auzing would be in Cos. Messengers from other towns and villages had arrived with news them that the Sorcerer had been attacking every town they came to.

"That will be a nice bonus teh our force," Ellizar said.

"Any word from Drake yet?" Lily asked.

"A messenger arrived just an hour ago saying that he should be here by morning as well. He didn't say how many people he would have with him," the messenger told him.

"Very good, have everyone in this city ready to defend at any moment, there's no telling how long we have before the army arrives on our front doorstep."

"The enemy has just conquered the small village of Ebora, they will be here within an hour." Dread filled Lily and Ellizar as they contemplated what to do.

"How many troops?" Ellizar asked.

"It's hard to say, more come out of the gate every day. The Korazin reports that Saul and Atruss's armies have managed to get the army to retreat into their own kingdom and there is no fighting anywhere else currently."

"We need a miracle to get ourselves out of this one," Lily said.

"We need Aiden teh get here, he would know what teh do," Ellizar said. The door opened.

"How can I help?" Aiden asked as he stood in the doorway. Their spirits soared as he stepped through with the others right behind him. Isabel filed in last, seeming un-talkative and withdrawn.

"Yeh have this way of showin' up just in time!" Ellizar exclaimed. They all laughed. "How are we goin' teh hold off these troops that are comin'? We don't have anywhere near a large enough force teh hold them off."

"You're right," Aiden said. "But I have an idea. Follow me Lily and Ellizar." They got up and followed him outside where he helped them onto Elohim. Elohim lifted up into the sky as they turned and headed towards the east. They finally spotted the army, a river of black snaking its way through the grasslands. Smoke from the fires that had burned the other towns was still drifting into the sky.

Elohim dove down to the ground and then leveled out and landed in front of the oncoming army. The army hesitated, afraid of the Taruk. All three of them slid off the side of the Taruk and moved towards the frightened army.

"Greetings my fellow soldiers," Aiden started. Ellizar and Lily watched in amazement as the leader of the army, a deformed elf, got off and started towards them. He stopped ten feet away.

"Coming to surrender?" the leader taunted.

"Yes," Aiden said. "We are aware that the city of Cos has no chance of holding off such a large army, however, if you would kindly hold off attacking Cos until the morning in order for us to make right with our God, we will surrender our city with no fight."

"You have until tomorrow to surrender. If you don't, we'll butcher all of you in the streets."

"That is well understood and thank you," Aiden said. They climbed back up onto the Taruk and took flight again, vanishing into the sky.

"That was incredible, if they wait until morning Drake and the king will be here!" Lily exclaimed.

"Yep, and then we shall make our war on the Sorcerer and anyone aligned with him," Aiden replied. Elohim landed just outside Cos, where the others were still waiting. "If you have faith the size of a mustard seed, you could say to the mountains to move and they would move."

"I wish I had more faith," Ellizar said.

"You already have more than some people have their entire life, my friend," Aiden said. "Now we have to get ready for the battle that is fast approaching us. Are the Korazin nearby?" A streak of fire flew through the sky and landed in the plains in front of them. Rade walked up to them.

"Good timing," Aiden greeted. Rade smiled and took a little bow.

"The Gogs have saved Saul and his men, although I must say they were doing very well by themselves. The army has retreated into Auzing and sealed the gate. I have it on good authority the Borags have left Korinth and Tarsus and also sealed their gates. It seems our enemy is afraid."

"And so they should be," Aiden said. "What of Shavrok and Nickolas?"

"They have moved all the ships out into the sea and are currently sailing towards Gath; they will stop ten miles offshore until you march on the wall."

"Very good," Aiden said. "Have Saul move all but one thousand men to the desert plains near the ruins of Reub. Have all the Gogs gather there and bring in their siege machines."

"Why would you have them move so far to the east?" Lily asked.

"There is always a reason. Saul is about to be equipped with upwards of ten thousand horses. They should make it there in no time," Aiden replied.

"Ten thousand horses?" Ellizar asked. "Are these wild horses? Yeh don't see herds of that size anywhere." Aiden smiled.

"These are no ordinary horses, my friend," Aiden replied.

"Are they Queman's horses?" Lily asked.

"They are similar. Queman's horses are Fee-Yord," Aiden answered. "They are a breed that is untouched by today's standards, but the horses I am speaking of...are far greater."

"What deh yeh mean?" Ellizar asked. "Is there some force at work here that we can'ot see?"

"There always has been Ellizar, and there always will be," Aiden replied. "There is something in this earth that is greater than you and me. I am the heir of Lathon, who has come so that people will be able to one day see the real Lathon."

"I thought you were Lathon?" Lily asked.

"I am," Aiden answered. "I am the physical representation of Lathon. Lathon still walks this earth, but the sin and the hearts of people keep them from seeing him. Thousands of years ago, it was said that Lathon left, but in fact, that is never true. Lathon will never run out on people as long as there is still good in this world, and there still is. The people could not see him, so I was sent to lead the people back to him."

"I think I understand now just how small we are," Lily said. Ellizar nodded.

"Small, but not insignificant. I will not abandon this world to torment and judgment."

"We will follow yeh teh the ends of the earth!" Ellizar exclaimed. "Or at least as far as we can walk!" They laughed.

"Of course, we could go a lot farther if you were normal size," Lily teased.

"Blasted elf kind!" Ellizar exclaimed. "Here I was making a sincere remark and yeh have teh go make a joke out of it!"

"Seriously, I think Isabel could find something to put on you to make you tall," Lily said. Ellizar shook his head.

"Look what she did teh that table of ours! I can only imagine what she'd do to me. Besides, I'm a perfectly respectable height for a dwarf."

"I wouldn't have you any other way hon," Lily said, kissing him.

"I must be on my way. We have a lot to do and little time in which to do it," Rade said. He faded to the north almost faster than they could comprehend. They began walking back to Cos the sun starting to go down in the west. Lily pondered everything, feeling more joy than she had felt in a long time.

* * *

Drake and his army approached Cos from the southwest. They had far exceeded his expectations and had arrived earlier than he had expected when they had left from Mera Runa. His men were as alert and awake as ever.

Torches appeared on the horizon, coming from the left probably a thousand yards or so outside of the city. Drake motioned for his troops to stop and ordered his second in command to stay with the army as he rode ahead to the lone torches. Finally, he got close enough to see all of his friends, waiting to greet him.

Isabel and Morgrin stood in the back with Thaddeus, while the rest of them stood at the front. Drake dismounted as his friends came closer, Aiden approaching and embracing him first.

"Good to see you again!" Drake exclaimed as he embraced each of them. He embraced Isabel last, noticing that she seemed different to him than in times past. She didn't speak too much, seemingly lost in her thoughts.

More horses were heard to the west. Another army approached and then halted as the leader dismounted and came towards them. The torchlight lit his features as he approached, showing that he was a taller man probably in his late fifties, his hair mostly white. He walked tall and proud, a large sword was strapped to his side. His eyes were kind but his overall demeanor suggested that he had seen countless battles and wars over the years.

Drake I would like you to meet the king of Edon, Abner," Aiden said. Drake did a half bow to him and the king did the same.

"I'm sorry it took me so long to get here, we haven't had to use our military force in quite some time," Abner replied.

"You showed up right in time," Aiden said as they turned and headed into a small tent they had constructed. On the horizon, the sun was just beginning to lighten the dark sky.

"Where are we attacking?" Drake asked as they all sat down at a set of chairs and tables in the tent.

"The army has not attacked Cos yet, but they are camped out five miles away from here in the town of Ebora. Are both of you familiar with it?" Aiden asked.

"Yes," Drake and Abner both replied. Drake's blood ran cold when he realized what he had said. He *did* remember Ebora. Chills ran up and down his spine wondering how he could remember a town when he had never been there before. He had been to Cos only a handful of times in the past ten years and he had never been to any other town or city in Edon.

"It's not that large of a place and should be easy enough to take over. The army has camped out there for the night and I'm sure that they're still asleep," Aiden said.

"Taking it shouldn't be hard at all," Drake said. His mind burned with thoughts and images.

"I'll split up my army into three different sections," Abner explained. "I'll send some around to come up from behind and then also some from the north as I use the main force to come from the west. Drake if you and your army could fill in the gap and come from the south that would be perfect."

"Yes sir," Drake replied. "We'll trap them and then free the town. Do you want us to continue to the next town after that?"

"Yes, there are half a dozen towns and small villages that have been taken over from here to the border, if we can get them on the run we'll be able to defeat them," Aiden said. "Once we get to the wall we'll halt and wait until everyone is ready before we attack."

"I'm sorry to inform everyone that Drake Thomas will not be participating in the attack!" Isabel announced.

Every head turned in her direction, their eyes boring into her skull. Isabel looked at the ground for a moment before looking up. Her appearance wasn't the normal look they were used to seeing, instead of the blond hair and flawless complexion, they saw an aged woman with long brown hair.

"What deh yeh mean?" Ellizar finally asked.

"Drake is coming with me; Morgrin can lead the army in his stead. We'll be back in time for the siege on the main wall but not before then," Isabel said.

"I don't understand," Thaddeus replied.

"I do," Aiden said. "Drake, I think it would benefit you greatly if you went with Isabel. You brought your army this far and you will lead them against the

Sorcerer's army in Auzing, but right now it would be best for you to go with Isabel. Morgrin and I will lead your army against the vile creatures that are between here and the gate."

"Okay," Drake reluctantly agreed, noticing how pale Isabel was. The sight looked familiar to him.

"In three days we'll march on the border," Aiden said. Isabel and Drake both nodded as they stood up and left the tent without speaking.

"What's going on?" Drake asked. Isabel didn't answer. "Where are we going?" Destan and Aspen landed in front of them.

"You'll soon see Drake," Isabel said. She climbed on Aspen and he climbed on Destan. They soared into the sky leaving everything behind them as they flew northwest. The Taruks seemed to fly faster today than in the past and flew with an urgency and energy that Drake didn't understand. Elohim was the fastest Taruk in all of Ancient Earth but this felt even faster than what he would normally fly.

Isabel looked ahead and occasionally at him. In her eyes, he could see conflict, hurt, pain, joy, excitement, and every other emotion he could imagine. The Taruks seemed to know the way and Drake was just along for the ride, unsure of what was happening.

He watched the ground far below, trying to keep track of where Isabel was taking him. The Sea of Mar was on his left and just ahead was the northern shore of the sea, bordered by the forest that surrounded Laheer. They passed overhead and soon left the forest behind them. Another hour or two passed and more light flooded into the sky until finally, it was a bright sunny morning. The sunlight illuminated the far distant peaks of the Dead Mountains which were now to their west. Drake watched the landscape losing all concept of time and where they were.

Finally, a couple of hours after sunrise on the second day. The Taruks began descending out of the sky, eventually landing on top of a region of grass-covered hills that stretched as far as the eye could see. They climbed off and the

Taruks remained where they were as Isabel took in a deep breath, pleasure, and relief flooding over her like he had never seen before.

“This is beautiful,” Drake said. Isabel nodded in agreement.

“It certainly is Drake Thomas,” Isabel replied.

“What are we doing here?”

“We’re going to take a walk,” Isabel said, moving a few steps before looking back at Drake. A light was in her eyes that he hadn’t seen before. Drake hesitated. “Don’t worry Drake, nothing bad is going to happen.”

“I don’t understand why we’re here,” Drake said.

“I can’t begin to explain everything, but there are a few things that will soon be made clear.” He followed her down a small footpath worn into the grassy plains. The path twisted and rolled with the hills. They passed by several small farms, and some pastures of cows and fields full of crops.

Everything seemed familiar. The way the wind moved through the hills and the way the grass moved in the wind. The way the dirt moved under his foot. He stopped feeling cold come rushing over him. All the sound faded until only a voice could be heard in his heart. It was dark and eerie, stealing all hope from the world. Drake shook his head knowing that Aiden’s power was greater than this voice. The feeling retreated and he could once again hear the birds that chirped in the trees that were scattered throughout the hills.

“You alright?” Isabel asked. Drake nodded.

“Yeah I’m alright, the Sorcerer was trying to get a hold of me again.”

“He’ll never stop trying. The more you cling to Aiden and Lathon, the more he’ll try and destroy your will,” Isabel said.

“He’s weak,” Drake replied. “In the past, these attempts of his have left me crippled and unable to do anything. He’s losing his power.”

“He’s not losing his power,” Isabel started. “You’re stronger than you used to be. You’re not the same person you were. You’ve become a follower of Lathon. The Sorcerer doesn’t have a foothold on you like he used to.”

They walked for a couple of hours until finally, a house became visible on the horizon. They followed the path for another fifteen minutes as it twisted through the hills and eventually made it to the house. Drake studied it; it was a modest two-story house with a nice yard and brick path that led up to the front door.

"I thought you might like to see this place," Isabel replied. She pushed the door open and Drake followed her in. The house, although it had appeared to be two stories from the outside, now rose high above them reaching some twenty feet with staircases with strange intricate carvings on the railings.

Trees grew up through the house, but it appeared that they were supposed to be here, as though they were part of the house. The trunks were carved out with shelves and hooks to hang your hat and everything else you could imagine.

Leaves fluttered down from the treetops far above them. The sound of birds filled the house. Drake was suddenly taken to another point in time. It was perfect. The roof of the house had been made to simulate the sun, and filtered through the leaves to the rest of the house. Flowering vines covered the walls as they always did in Isabel's houses. They changed their colors every few minutes and were watered by a gentle mist, that sparkled through the air above them. Drake put his hand in the mist but didn't get wet. The shelves and walls were covered in strange but fascinating trinkets and carvings that Drake couldn't hope to understand.

"Do you like it?" Isabel asked.

"Like it?" Drake asked. "You've outdone yourself this time. This is amazing."

"Thank you," Isabel said as they continued walking through the house. "But this time I can't take all the credit. I didn't build it."

"It looks like something you would have built," Drake replied. "Who built this place?"

"You did." Drake's heart stopped as he whirled around to face Isabel. In her eyes, she could see that she was telling the truth. His mind burned with questions and confusion as he tried to figure out what this would possibly mean.

"I don't understand," Drake finally managed.

"This is your house, Drake. You built it."

"This can't be my house, look at it!" Drake exclaimed.

"Drake Thomas! This is your house. Have you ever wondered what your life was like before you woke up on the side of the river? Perhaps someone knows the answer."

"You know the answer?" Drake asked more calmly now

"I only know part of the answer, our paths have crossed each other long before that day in Belvanor. There is much that you need to be told and it is finally time for me to tell you. Trust me when I say that I wanted to tell you long before this, but I've kept these secrets for the safety of both of us."

"What kind of secrets?" Drake asked, growing afraid.

"Have a seat, Mr. Thomas," Isabel replied. She pointed to two chairs next to a fireplace. They sat down and the fireplace started. "I will start from the beginning as I know it, which takes place nearly seventeen years before you were born. I was ten years old at the time and my parents and I lived peacefully in the plains that lay between the Dead Mountains and the forest near the border of Goshen. It was a great life and I loved everything about it, I especially loved my parents. My mother was Elvish and my father was human, and they were incredible people.

"Unfortunately, they got a little too curious one day, and while I was off playing with some friends; they had an accident that destroyed the house and everything in it. I never saw them again. I felt as if my very life had been shattered. A few days later, a friend of the family, Enya, arrived and I went with her to live in the Dead Mountains. I was kind of an outcast by most people so the Dead Mountains were the perfect place to grow up. Enya was kind and I grew to love her like a mother figure.

"Eight years later I was in Punair doing some studying when I met and fell in love with a man from Revly, an apprentice of magic. He was a human named Rohemir. We were married within three months and moved to Iscariot, which in those days was not the destructive city that we later knew it to be. Rohemir was working in the dungeons in Iscariot. A very dangerous job, which is why they needed someone like him to keep things in line.

"A year passed and I became pregnant with our first child, Tremin. I loved him deeply and for a while, we had a fantastic life, but sadly, that's when it started going downhill. It was a slow fade in some ways because I only really noticed at first that Rohemir was spending more and more time at work, he wouldn't say what he was working on.

"The Sorcerer showed up one day and revealed that he was Rohemir's brother. I was suspicious at the time, seeing that Rohemir had never spoken of any brother before. I know now that they were only related by the fact that Rohemir was the one to bring the Sorcerer back to physical form. The Sorcerer was now my brother-in-law.

"I began to notice a change in Rohemir and even in Tremin who was extremely young at the time. It scared me and I wasn't sure what to think or where I should turn to. In an effort to bring us as a family closer together, Rohemir and I got pregnant again. Rohemir was much more volatile after that and I became afraid for my life. When I was six months pregnant I left Rohemir. It pained me to do so, to give up on the man I once loved but I was afraid for my life and I was afraid for my daughter's life.

"I didn't know where I should go so I went to the one place where I thought I would be safe. I went to the town of Laheer. As a child, I had often visited there and I knew a lot of the people so I stayed there until I had the baby. It was a girl and I loved her dearly."

"Gwen," Drake said.

"No," Isabel replied. Drake felt chills run up and down his spine.

"But Gwen's your daughter!"

"I lied," Isabel admitted. Drake didn't speak, his mind swimming in confusion. "I stole many things when I left Iscariot. The Seeing Stones, Rohemir's Taruk, and countless other things."

"A month after my daughter was born I made my way to the Dead Mountains. It had been years since I had been to see Enya. When I got there I was thrilled to find that Enya had also had a child, a girl named Gwen."

"Gwen was Enya's daughter?!" Drake exclaimed. Isabel nodded.

"She was," Isabel answered. "Enya would not say who the father was and her behavior had changed greatly since I had left. I began to grow both suspicious and afraid for the girl. I have now learned that the Sorcerer named Merderick was the father.

"During this time my former husband Rohemir was living in Masada. How or why he ended up there I do not know. I can only conclude that the Sorcerer had some business there. He became an advisor to the king of Masada. While he was there three elf kings arrived one night, seeking an heir of Lathon, to pay him homage. They eventually found Sherados and paid homage to their king and then helped them escape from the city. Your future stepfather, Sedric, along with Bethany and her husband Malachi also assisted in the escape effort. Marion and Joseph got away but Bethany's husband Malachi, your father, was killed. She and Sedric fled together.

"Un-beknown to them Bethany was pregnant with a boy, they named him Drake Thomas. After you were born, they met up with Marion, Joseph, and their son, Aiden, in Cos and that's the first time our paths crossed. I had heard the stories and heard about what had happened and I went to Cos to find them. I eventually did.

"I knew then that there was something special about Aiden. I could see the resemblance between you two. Marion and Bethany were sisters and I could see the connection. Sedric and Bethany had married by this point."

"Why were you in Cos?" Drake asked. "What did you want to find them for?"

"Come with me Drake," Isabel said. She stood and Drake followed her down the beautiful halls of the house. Finally, they reached a door on the left that was made of plain wood. She pulled out a key and opened the door. In front of them, a wooden staircase led down to the darkness. Isabel lit a lamp and they started down into the cellar.

The room they descended into was a small ten-foot by ten-foot cellar. The walls were covered in shelves, which were coated with dust and countless items that Drake couldn't even recognize. Despite all the beauty and elegance the rest of the house held, this room held none of it. Just dusty shelves, with dusty cloths covering whatever items lay beneath

"What is this room?" Drake asked.

"Do you recognize it?" Isabel asked. Drake nodded.

"This looks exactly like the room you took me in at your restaurant in Avdatt," Drake answered. Isabel nodded.

"That's because it is exactly like it."

Drake's eyes gravitated towards the table in the center of the room. On it stood a large object, covered with a thick black cloth, and next to it a small wooden chest, old and worn, yet vaguely familiar.

"Why did you bring me here?"

"Because I needed to bring you here. These items on the table are yours," Isabel said. She motioned for Drake to move towards the table. He hesitantly reached out and grasped the latch on the small wooden chest. He flipped it and felt excitement and anxiety rush through his veins. He raised the lid, looking inside, seeing two golden rings at the bottom of it. His hand trembled as he took them in his hand and pulled them out of the box.

The light hit the gold rings, bringing to light their unique qualities. One was more ordinary than the other but was covered in intricate carvings, which at the top of the ring formed a heart with two hands holding it. Each line that was carved seemed to sparkle and let off different colors. Drake was taken by its beauty as his mind was filled with memories. He remembered this. He looked at the plain ring, which was still covered in intricate carving. He looked on the inside seeing his name etched into it.

"Do you recognize them?" Isabel asked knowingly.

Drake was speechless. "Yes. One ring has my name on it, who does the other one belong to?" Drake asked. Isabel motioned to the object that was covered with the thick black cloth. Drake hesitated.

Isabel reached out and pulled the cloth off. The room exploded in light as the paints on the painting let off light that shone their color. Eventually, the light dimmed down and the painting came into focus.

The painting was blank at first, with a beautiful stone courtyard and palace behind them. He came into the picture a moment later and then a woman came running up to him and jumped into his arms. Her wavy brown hair came just below her shoulders and her dress was a light blue. He embraced the woman and they shared a long passionate kiss as he twirled her around, her feet off the ground. The image faded and then started again. Drake watched the scene, his mind burning with the memories that were slowly coming to him. Drake looked to the inside of the other ring.

"Rachal," Drake read aloud.

"My daughter." Drake's heart stopped. "Please allow me to tell the rest of the story," Isabel said. "I met up with Marion, Joseph, Sedric, and Bethany in Cos, and then a couple of months later I met up with them again. I hired them for a job that would have been too risky for me to carry out by myself. I hired Sedric and Joseph to kidnap Gwen from Enya's possession. I was scared for the child and I didn't think it was safe for her to stay with Enya.

"They managed to kidnap her and then I took both of the girls and fled with them. I took them to Laheer, where I had many conversations with Quemen about what my options were. An old man with a staff showed up that eve, he offered to put protection on both of the girls to hide their identity so that they would not be recognized. To Gwen he made her hair forever brown, to look more like me, when mine isn't affected by magic. To Rachal he put a spell that would make her hair black with green highlights in it…sound familiar?"

"It does. Nickolas was courting a woman matching that description a few years ago."

"It was her," Isabel replied. "I left Rachal in Laheer with Quemen and a kind-hearted couple who had been unable to have kids. I took Gwen as far away as I could so she would be safe. I left her on the doorstep in Fiori, where she lived undetected by Enya. I did whatever I could to make sure they both lived normal lives. I settled into a house a couple of hours north of Fiori and kept an eye on both girls."

"How did you manage that?" Drake asked.

"Have you ever wondered where that black featherless bird came from?" Isabel asked. Drake nodded. "He appeared to me right after Rachal was born and he's remained with me ever since. I don't know where he's from or why he came, but I believe he came to help me. He kept an eye on one girl while I would be watching the other.

"I visited Laheer often and was very close with Rachal and the people there. No one besides the people I left her with and Quemen knew I was the mother and it was best if it was kept that way. Later on, the couple I had left Rachal with were able to have children of their own, a girl and two boys. The years passed and eventually lo and behold you came to work for Queman as one of his ranch hands, tending to some very *special* horses.

"While there, you found a way into Rachal's heart, and she into yours. I remember the first time I saw you together I couldn't help but notice how happy you made each other and I couldn't help but be glad that a person like you was interested in my daughter. You won each other's hearts and decided to get married.

"As is tradition, once you were engaged you started building this house and of course when the house is done then you could marry. So you spent every minute working on the house and a lot of the people from the town pitched in, especially your brothers and sister-in-law."

"Who are they?" Drake asked. "Are they still alive?"

"The two brothers are. You remember Jacob and Aaron right?" Isabel asked.

"They are her brothers?" Drake asked, memories flooding back to him.

"I was a friend of the family and had the privilege of being hired to do a painting of the two of you to hang in your new home. Hence the painting on the table. Also as a special gift to the, would be, newlyweds I gave an egg to the two of you."

"An egg?" Drake asked.

"A Taruk egg. It was a golden Taruk."

"Golden Taruk?" Drake asked, stunned, hardly knowing what to think anymore. His mind burned with questions as he tried to wrap his mind around everything that he was hearing. "I saw the golden Taruk just a few days ago."

"I know. I sent him," Isabel replied. "Enya had never given up searching for her daughter and during the search; she found you and noticed the mark on your hand. How you got the mark I do not know. She contacted Merderick who gave the order to terminate you in whatever way she wished. You had just finished the house and it was the eve of your wedding when you were kidnapped in the dead of night.

"Enya hired men to snatch you out of Laheer and kill you. The event did not go unnoticed though and was witnessed by three people. Jacob and Aaron and myself. I fled, knowing that it was too dangerous for me to stay, and I knew more things had to be done. Jacob and Aaron told the story of what happened, but no one believed them. The entire family was outcast. Each of them went their own way looking for you.

"The men who had been hired to kidnap you took you all the way to the Charenella Falls in Epirus and threw you over. No one has ever survived before. You were the first and the last to do so, but you lost your memory in the process. I doubted the rumor at first, but when you came through my doors in Belvanor I could see that there was no lies in your eyes. For some strange reason, your memory had been taken."

"I don't know what to say," Drake said, looking at the rings in his hand. "Why didn't you tell me earlier?"

"I doubted Enya's apparent death when we were in the Dead Mountains five years ago. I know now that Enya has never stopped looking for her daughter, she never found Gwen. However, she has at last discovered Rachal and I fear her true identity. If you remember on the day we left Avdatt five years ago Nickolas said that Rachal had left, that she didn't want to go with us. That's not entirely true.

"Rachal was captured the night before and taken away. Where she was taken I did not know, but now I have learned that Enya captured her and took her back to the Dead Mountains."

"Is she still alive?" Drake asked.

"Yes, but she's not well. There was a room I found in the ruins of Enya's house that takes away all 'magical' spells. I believe she took Rachal in the room and her real identity was revealed. Now I fear she is held captive in the heart of Megara, imprisoned and tortured by Merderick.

"As far as why I let Rohemir believe that Gwen was his daughter, I did it to protect Rachal. Gwen and yourself were already hunted, so it was easier for me to keep my eye on one thing as opposed to two."

"How did you know Rachal had been captured?" Drake asked.

"The golden Taruk that I gave you stayed with her for many years, but when she went missing the Taruk came back. As of right now the Taruk still has no name because you were going to name him when you were married."

"So Merderick has my fiancé, your daughter, held captive?"

"Yes," Isabel answered. "I know how this must be shocking to you, but unfortunately there's no time to waste. Someone we love is in danger and in just a couple of days all the armies will be ready to storm the wall."

"How long do we have?" Drake asked. "What if the Sorcerer kills Rachal before we get there?"

"I think he'll keep her alive to torture both of us. Maybe even try to tempt us to join him. We'll free her though and the Sorcerer will be defeated."

"I wish we could storm into Megara right now and be done with this war."

"So do all who live through war," Isabel said. "However, there is still one stop we have to make before we join the army at the wall."

Drake got up and they left the house. He slipped his ring on his finger and put the other one in his pocket. His mind burned with the memories trying to sort out everything that had been said.

The Taruks once again exceeded all strength and speed that Drake had previously thought possible. They had been flying east for hours and had covered twice the distance they normally would have. They had flown over

Cavil and after that, Drake recognized none of the landscape below them.

He had never traveled this far east before and as they traveled farther east, he concluded that there wasn't much to see in the east. The land had flattened out an hour ago and although it was lush and green when they had first started, the vegetation had thinned until finally, they flew over nothing but hard red rocks that stretched as far as the eye could see.

They passed over old fortresses and castles and other various towns that were nothing but ruins. Drake studied each one with interest and fascination wondering what great civilizations had once lived there.

Most of the time during the flight he had replayed the conversation Isabel and he had shared back at the house. Drake stopped, reminding himself that it was *his* house. He remembered the painting in his mind. Memories came to his mind, but slower and more incomplete than he would have liked.

He could now feel the warmth of Rachal's smile, and remember the sweet smell of her perfume, the taste of her kiss. He remembered how they had met and the first time they had talked. But still, the rest was shrouded from him.

He struggled with himself, wondering why he had lost his memory. Had Lathon planned for that to happen? He finally gave up trying to solve the great mysteries, reminding himself that there was a reason for everything, even if he couldn't see what it was.

All the years that he had wandered within the darkness of his mind, he had always felt abandoned, and alone. He was a man without a past. Only now did he realize that he had never been alone. Lathon had always been there, silently working in Drake behind the scenes, and now saw fit to restore at least part of his memory. Drake praised Lathon.

His attention was drawn to the land in front of them as a sea of black became visible. Just beyond the sea of black stood more ruins, these ones larger than any of the others they had passed up to this point. The Taruks began descending and the ruins and the sea of black came into focus. A great army, made up of a combination of Gogs and Elves stood assembled in formation.

Drake looked to the north where massive Taruks were flying through the sky, their size making Destan and any other Taruk look small. Objects hung underneath them but from the distance they were at Drake couldn't tell what they were. They flew in closer to the ruins and landed a few feet from where the original wall would've stood when the castle was first occupied. Drake and Isabel both slipped off and the Taruks sat down and minded their own business as Isabel led the way to the large tent that was in front of them. They stepped inside, everyone looking their way.

"Are we late?" Isabel asked with a smile.

How could you be late when we didn't know you were coming?" Saul asked.

"Aiden sent me, he said you needed some help."

"More than you know," Alexandrea said. "Rade informed us that Aiden wanted us all to come here and then cross over into the Auzing. It's just the crossing over part we're having problems with."

"How so?" Drake asked.

"There is no good way to get the entire army down and up the canyon and into Auzing," Rade said. "We have found multiple deadly traps in the canyon and have deemed it an unsafe way to cross. With all the traps, it explains why the border on the other side is for the most part unprotected."

"We've searched miles of the canyon edge and have found no bridges that cross," Furlone said.

"I remember several bridges used to stretch across here, but that was many years ago," Rade said. "No one has lived in this castle for over a thousand years."

"It's in remarkably good shape for being that old," Drake replied.

"It was once a Gog stronghold; it was conquered and destroyed in the campaign by the Sorcerer to wipe out all the Gogs."

"So there were Gogs this far east?" Drake asked.

"In the deep history, it is said that a great number of Gogs went east and then went their own ways. My group moved further to the north, far beyond the maps of your people."

"This world is turning out to be a very big place," Drake said. Furlone nodded.

"What city is this?" Isabel asked. "If Aiden sent us here he must have had a reason. He must have known a way to get across."

"Perhaps I can be of assistance," a voice said from behind them. Drake and Isabel turned around and looked to the entrance but no one else did, acting as though the man didn't exist. Drake recognized him immediately as the old man who had visited him by the campfire. He still carried his unusual staff and seemed to be invisible to everyone but them.

"This is the city of Reub," the old man told them. "I think you will find something helpful beneath the castle. Or at least, beneath the main part of the castle." Drake and Isabel both started to speak to the man but before they got a chance, the man had vanished.

"This is the city of-"

"Reub," Drake and Isabel both interrupted. Saul looked surprised that they had figured it out so quickly.

"Does that help any?" Alexandrea asked.

"Maybe," Isabel answered. She paced for a moment, every eye watching her. "Are there any tunnels beneath the city?"

"Yes, there is," Saul answered. "They don't lead anywhere though."

"Take me to these tunnels," Isabel said. Saul led the way with everyone else following behind. Drake looked to the north seeing the gigantic Taruks still flying through the sky. He could now see what it was they were carrying. They held ropes with their claws that wrapped around various structures. Catapults, ballistae, and siege towers were all being flown into the city.

After a few more minutes of walking, they finally made it to an underground tunnel that ran under the city. From the one end, Drake could see light and from the direction they were heading they could only see darkness.

They lit torches and continued forward until they reached the end of the tunnel. Isabel fell to the ground and brushed some of the dirt away. He watched her as she methodically checked the floor. She blew away some of the dirt, and a thin gap appeared on the floor. Isabel cleared some more dirt away and blew again and the gap grew longer.

Drake looked around, noticing winches on the far side of the room. They moved to the wheel with spokes on it and each grabbed a position on one of them. Furlone called in some more of his men and they took up the wheel on the other side as they began pushing and walking in a circle, turning the giant wheel. Slowly the ground they had been standing on started to shift and slide out from its place.

The set of doors that bordered the canyon opened and the rock floor slid out. They stopped a few seconds later, moving to the exit and walking out five feet. They were now suspended over the canyon by a land bridge that had begun to slide out from the tunnel beneath the castle.

"Land bridges!" Alexandrea exclaimed. They looked to their left and their right seeing two more bridges coming from the castle. "Getting an army across here shouldn't be a problem at all."

"No it shouldn't," Drake replied. "It's incredible, after all this time the bridges are still here."

"Just don't cross until the other armies begin their attacks."

"When will that be?" Saul asked. Isabel shrugged.

"I'm not entirely sure," Isabel answered. "We're heading back to Edon immediately and if everything goes according to plan, we will attack tomorrow. I'm sure Rade can keep an eye on things and let you know when it's time to cross over."

"I can certainly do that," Rade answered.

"Very well," Alexandrea said. "We'll make sure all the men can be ready to move out in five minutes or less. After we cross we'll head to Megara and meet up with everyone there."

"Sounds good," Isabel replied. "Just be careful." They said their goodbyes and headed to their Taruks, the city disappearing into the distance as they flew away. Drake's mind was filled with thoughts of hope and victory.

His heart went out to Rachal who he knew was being tortured right now. In just a little while, they would be reunited. He took a deep breath and kept his emotions in line as he imagined falling in love with Rachal all over again.

Chapter 21

THE SORCERER

Aiden and Drake led the army. They had sent Lily and Ellizar ahead last night with a group of sharpshooters to take out the scouts between Athos and the great wall. They had been taken out without anyone being alerted, giving them the upper hand. The Taruks flew above them, undetected by the Sorcerer and his army.

The Taruks had informed them that the majority of the troops were at the gate near Athos. Drake was sure the Sorcerer knew of the defeat of the towns and cities he had occupied days before, and he likely knew of the numbers they brought with them. More Gogs had arrived from the south reinforcing their large army. They pushed their siege machines and weapons over the land.

The land sloped upwards for the next two miles and then it would drop sharply and place them at the foot of the great wall that stood between them and the rest of the Sorcerer's army. Drake knew that originally the upward slope hadn't been there, but that the Sorcerer, when he was first uniting the people had transformed the land to give them an advantage. By forcing them downhill the soldiers on the wall would be able to do just about anything to their men.

The Sorcerer's defense would now become his demise as plans had been drawn up to get them through the gate and the defense faster than ever before. It was an ambitious plan, but Drake was sure that it would work; after all, it was Aiden's idea.

Aiden never ceased to amaze him and somehow Drake got the feeling that as hard as he would try to be exactly like Aiden and demonstrate the same kind of love and compassion that Aiden had shown, he would never fully succeed.

Drake wasn't discouraged though, it was a challenge to him. He would spend the rest of his life trying to help other people in whatever way he could. His mind drifted to Rachal, now able to recall all the time they had spent together.

They would serve Lathon together.

Drake wondered for a moment what it would be like when Rachal and himself were reunited again. Would they immediately feel the love that they once felt? Or would they be like strangers to each other?

He remembered Rachal as she once was, but he was interested to see how she had changed. Drake now knew that Jacob and Aaron had likely told her about him, but how badly had she been wounded by the information? Did she know that he had been abducted, or did she think he had run off with Gwen?

Aiden stopped and the entire countryside became as silent as a tomb. Up ahead of them, the crest of the hill waited, and on the other side was the wall and the gate that they needed to get through.

"You ready for this?" Aiden asked.

"As ready as I'm going to be," Drake said. The Gogs stood at the ready with their war machines, ready to push them into position as soon as the word was given.

"Don't worry about anything Drake. Everything that's going to happen will work out exactly the way it was meant to play out," Aiden encouraged.

"I know, and I believe," Drake said.

Aiden looked back at the men with them and waved to the Gogs in the back. The sea of soldiers parted and a company of fifty Gogs began pushing a large battering ram forward. It was similar in design to the one that had defeated the defense of Korinth, except this one was twice as big. The Gogs pushed it into position. The army filled in behind them.

"Are your men ready?" Aiden asked.

The Gog shook his head. "They know what to do; we'll be through this gate in no time."

"Rade," Aiden started. "As soon as we get over this crest, send word to your brothers. They must signal for everyone to begin their attacks."

"Yes sir, although I must remind you that there will be a delay between their attack and your own," Rade said.

"That will be fine, it might even work to our advantage," Aiden replied.

"Why's that?" Drake asked.

"It might draw more of them to our gate, and force our enemy to pull from the other gates, making it easier for them to get in." Aiden quietly drew his sword and slowly started to creep up to the crest of the hill. The soldiers behind him did the same. Drake drew his own, moving up next to Aiden.

Drake and Aiden halted, barely able to see the top of the wall. Aiden moved back and motioned for Drake to do the same. Aiden walked back to the Gogs, giving them an order and then coming back to Drake.

Drake watched as the Gogs scurried off to the left and right, heading to the next set of Gogs and relaying the message. Aiden looked at Drake and smiled.

"Let's do this!" Aiden said. He spurred his horse forward, letting a battle cry escape him. Drake and the rest of the army followed suit as they all flooded over the top of the hill and began the steep downhill to the wall below. Drake winced as arrows came from the wall and landed on the hillside. The entire area was shaken by the rumbling of Gog horns. Drake and everyone else in the army looked behind them making sure they were clear of the oncoming obstacles.

The battering ram had now been pushed over the crest and was freewheeling to the wall below. It was flanked to either side by three more battering rams of similar size, all of them rushing towards the wall. Gogs rode on the back and sides of them, steering before jumping off just before they struck the wall.

The sound of the rock battering rams striking the wall was beyond anything Drake could have imagined as the first ten feet of the thirty-foot thick wall was destroyed. The debris flew high into the sky and then crashed down on the other side of the wall destroying their enemies. The doors had been destroyed, leaving only the iron drawgate between them and success. The army filled the gate, for as far as the eye could see. Drake was momentarily pulled back into a state of despair.

The feelings subsided and adrenaline rushed through his veins once again. Massive javelins soared over their heads and struck the walls. Each one of them was spaced two feet apart and each one rose from the previous one.

Drake watched in amazement as the Gogs that had been riding on the battering rams, mounted to the first of the javelins and sprinted up them like stairs. They flanked both sides of the gates getting to the top of the wall and engaging the troops. Other Gogs loaded themselves into the catapults that they had brought and launched themselves to the wall. Drake and Aiden led the rest of the army to the wall, another javelin being fired. This one struck the wall with a rope hanging from it.

Aiden climbed up the rope with Drake right behind him. They reached the top and pulled themselves over the wall, forced to defend themselves as the Borags attacked them. More of their soldiers poured over the wall allowing Drake and Aiden to break away from the main battle to where the Gogs were fighting to their left.

In front of them stood a tower, which was mirrored by a tower forty feet away bordering the gate on either side. Aiden jumped into the fray letting his sword find its target. They broke through the wooden door, and they all stormed inside, with Aiden and Drake behind them. Up above, a staircase circled around the entire structure, clinging to the outside wall. In the middle, cables, and weights were hanging from a winch system that controlled the iron draw gate keeping their army out.

"Where's the winch?" Drake asked.

"It doesn't matter," Aiden said. "Watch." Drake looked three stories above where some Gogs had already fought their way up. They leapt from the staircases, onto the counterweights.

The chamber above them was filled with an explosion as they all dove for cover. The winches that held the counterweights in place and the gates shut had been destroyed. Drake looked to see the Gogs and the counterweights go plummeting to the ground below. Horns echoed outside. Drake followed Aiden back out, seeing that the iron draw gate had been lifted and then blocked up with a large piece of stone.

They swung their swords, defeating the first people to attack them. Drake pulled back his sword swinging at his next opponent. His sword struck the man who fell back and then smiled as he turned into dust and floated away with the wind. Drake's mind struggled to comprehend what was happening as the entire enemy army turned into sand and fell to the ground. Within moments, the only thing that accompanied them was a deep silence.

"What just happened?" Drake asked.

"The Sorcerer turned into a wimp," a Gog replied.

"He thinks he has a better chance of holding us off at Megara," Aiden started. "He's keeping focused on us, but I don't think he knows about Saul or Shavrok and their armies yet. We have a long journey in front of us and I'm pretty sure it's not going to be as easy as we think, after all this is the Sorcerer we're talking about."

The army snaked its way into Auzing, the silence pounded in their heads threatening to drive them insane. They walked for miles and miles past villages and small towns finding every one of them empty and abandoned. They pushed forward determined to defeat their enemy. Rade landed in front of them, taking form a moment after he struck the ground. He bowed to Aiden.

"The same that has happened here has happened everywhere else. The Sorcerer seems to be afraid like we've never seen him afraid before."

"And so he should be," Isabel said walking up next to them. Drake couldn't help but look at her feet, seeing she had no shoes on as they trekked through the desert.

"Atruss's men have easily gotten through the gate at Tarsus. No word yet on what is happening with the Gogs at Gath but I think that's one battle they will have to fight."

"Why do you say that?" Morgrin asked joining his wife.

"Because he doesn't know about the Gog navy being offshore. He has been focused so much on the border he may have overlooked the sea."

"Let's hope you're right," Drake said.

"What should be done about the people in Vernal?" Rade asked. "The army of five hundred thousand is ready to depart at any moment."

"Matthew has orders to come a half day's march behind the last of our troops," Drake reminded.

"When we reach Megara, the Sorcerer will think this is all the men we have and will likely try to trap us with a force from behind. He should be surprised by the revelation," Aiden said.

"Yes, I'm sure he will. There is also activity to the east which seems to be promising," Rade said. Drake's mind came alive.

"To the east?" Drake asked. "What's happening? Is there something to the east?"

"We must continue moving. Our time has come and the Sorcerer's demise is inevitable," Aiden told them. "He may be able to take physical form but that's where the extent of his power ends. He will not even come close to winning the battle that lies ahead, let alone the war." They walked into the desert and Rade took off into the sky.

* * *

Horns blared through the ruins of Reub. The first of the army entered into the tunnel beneath the city. Saul and Alexandrea led the way with Furlone, Jacob, and Aaron right behind. They walked until they reached the large winches and then they came to a stop. Five Gogs moved to each winch, each turning them at once. Slowly the doors at the end began to part and the land that they were on began to slide out over the canyon. Light flooded into the dark tunnel, which thankfully was tall enough for the great siege towers that the Gogs had brought in.

Saul glanced to his left and then to his right seeing two other land bridges being extended as well. The land on the other side of the canyon was empty and deserted, with no life form seen for miles and miles, instead only the tough desert floor greeted them. Finally, the land bridges reached the other side and they were able to set foot in Auzing. More horns were blown and another great cheer erupted from the army as they began marching into the unknown.

* * *

Nickolas had never been on a Gog ship and if the size of them wasn't enough of an intimidation their speed definitely would be. They had covered hundreds of miles of ocean in an amount of time that almost seemed unreal. Now they raced towards the shoreline having been given the go-ahead to start attacking.

The coastline was rough, a large black cliff stretched as far as the eye could see. In the distance they could see the spires of Gath, reaching into the sky. Strange and twisted carvings sat on the top of each, complimented by large statues along the main wall.

"What are those?" Nickolas asked pointing to the horizon of their stern.

"Where?" Shavrok asked.

Nickolas pointed and Shavrok remained quiet for some time before his face seemed to wash white.

"White Ships!" Shavrok exclaimed, almost in a whisper.

"White Ships? What does that mean?" Nickolas asked.

"But they're just supposed to be legend!"

"What does that mean?"

"They're on our stern sir, they can't possibly be targeting us!" another Gog called out.

"Towers, off our bow!" Another Gog yelled.

They turned their attention to the bobbing towers in front of the first wall that stood in their way. Small boats were being rowed between them, scores of Borags and other twisted creatures going from one tower to the other.

Rade had flown over and told them exactly how the city was laid out. The main wall at the city jutted up against the sea and then farther out into the water another wall had been built. This one is not as tall or intimidating as the main wall, but certainly enough to do damage to other ships.

"They're towers alright," Shavrok confirmed. "That's new, but not hard to get by."

"Is anything hard for these ships to get by?" Nickolas asked. They both chuckled.

"That first wall will be the test. We have to get through that one unscathed to breach the second one with ease."

"How are we going to do that?" Nickolas asked. Shavrok grinned.

"Carefully. Teverin!" the captain of the ship came running to them. "Prepare operation iron shield and have all the harpoons ready to fire at those towers. Carry this order to the other ships as well.

"Yes sir!" Teverin replied sending messages to the other ships. The ships came alive as Shavrok moved Nickolas to the side as a large compartment in the deck of the ship was opened. Two large steel plates were lifted out of the compartments and carried to the bow of the ship. Nickolas watched as the Gogs carefully attached a winch system and lifted the metal plates up and over the edge. Down below small compartments were opened in the side of the ship and other Gogs leaned out and latched the steel plates to the wooden beams. The process was repeated on all the other ships.

Harpoons were placed on the front of the ships, one pointing in each direction as they raced towards the floating towers. Shavrok stood at the bow with Nickolas soon joining him as the floating towers grew closer.

"Go in full speed!" Shavrok yelled. Fear trickled through Nickolas as they raced forward reaching the first of the floating towers. The towers were filled with Borags, all of them firing their arrows until the massive bow of the ship was nearly on top of them. The towers were crushed beneath the massive ships, their enemies washing away into the sea. Some of the Borags managed to grab onto the ship and begin climbing to the main deck, but all of them were picked off by the Gogs. They continued forward, crumbling dozens and dozens more of the towers as all the Gog ships lined up in formation with the rest of the fleet behind them.

The harpoons were fired, shattering the top of some of the towers, and latching into the woodwork. The ships continued forward, pulling the floating towers backward into the next set of towers, destroying both of them. Finally, the lines were cut and the debris was pulled underwater by the undertow of the ships.

Nickolas was amazed as they laid waste to all the towers and then rushed full speed towards the first wall. They crouched down and backed away from the bow of the ship moments before they struck the wall.

The sound was beyond anything that he had ever experienced before as the first line of Gog ships all hit the wall at once. Rock and water flew up in front of them and the screeching of metal on wood could be heard. Finally, the noise stopped, telling them that they had made it through the wall without destroying their ships.

The Borags on the wall showed the fear on their face as arrows came streaming from the wall. Most of them splashed harmlessly into the water but a few of them found their targets.

"Return fire!" Shavrok yelled. The Gogs pulled out their bows and fired them into the sky. Fire flashed through the sky, igniting all of their arrows. The fiery arrows dropped into the city setting it ablaze. The golden Taruk flew overhead and all of them cheered as the people on the wall fled from the wall.

"Keep the ships full speed!" Shavrok ordered. Nickolas's heart rate picked up as they raced towards the now empty wall. "Hang on!" Everyone ran to the back of the ships, holding on wherever they could find room. The ships struck the wall, crumbling it effortlessly.

The ships freefell as the water shoved them into the city. The water cascaded over the wall and crashed into the city pushing the bow of the ships back up. The lower half of the city, which was below sea level, began flooding and was buried in seconds.

The lower half of the city was submerged and destroyed as the fires that had been started were put out. The ship bounced and ground through the middle of the city as it was flooded. Up ahead a twenty-foot tall cliff jutted up to the highest level of the city.

"Weapons ready!" Shavrok yelled. On all of the ships, everyone drew their swords or clubs and remained at the back of the ships. They clashed with the cliff, the fronts of the Gogs ships finally being pulverized by the rocks. They covered themselves as wood and metal flew up into the sky and then came crashing down. The ships rocked before finally becoming grounded on the buildings they were sitting on.

Nickolas and everyone else stood to their feet looking out on the large army that was standing on the shore. Shavrok lifted his sword in the air and let a roar escape him. The rest of the Gogs and Nickolas let out a battle cry as they sprinted from the ships into the battle.

* * *

It had been two days since they had breached the wall at Athos and never in his entire life had Drake ever felt so defeated. The sun beat down on the army mercilessly; even the Gogs seemed to be slower than usual. They trekked through the desert, the hot dry wind on their faces, and bits of sand in their mouths. The day wore on and finally, they came to a stop, Aiden appearing to be the only one who didn't feel the fatigue.

Isabel came and sat down next to him, joined by all the others that he had considered his family over the years, Morgrin, Ellizar, and Lily. If Drake had ever felt alone he needed to only look around and realize how many people he had in his life that he loved.

"The Sorcerer must be running out of tricks," Isabel said.

"What makes you say that?" Lily asked.

"Remember back when we marched to Iscariot…it was uncomfortably hot then too," Isabel said.

"I'm not sure how long I can go on without water," Ellizar said. "Everyone's water has evaporated in this blasted heat."

"I'm sure Lathon will work something out," Drake said. "Right, Aiden?"

"That depends," Aiden replied. "What are you willing to do?"

"What do you mean?" Lily asked. "We're marching to Megara, what more can we do?"

"Never expect anything to be handed to you. If you do, you can easily fall into the Sorcerer's trap," Aiden replied. "Get some shovels. We'll fill this entire place with ditches, large ditches. In the morning they'll be full of water."

"They will?" Ellizar asked.

"If they aren't then what hope is there?" Aiden asked. "I'm not just talking about ditches that you can dig with a shovel, I'm talking about taking chances, acting in faith; taking that first step even if you don't know where your foot is going to land. If you don't dig some ditches in your life how can you expect to grow, or accomplish great things?"

"Let's get some shovels," Isabel said, being the first to get up off the desert floor. She led all of them over to the supply wagons, grabbed shovels, and handed them out to all of them. Drake and everyone else spread the word to the rest of the massive army and soon they were spread out over the desert floor digging ditches.

"Looking forward to tomorrow?" Morgrin asked. Isabel and Drake both exchanged glances.

"Yes," Isabel answered. Morgrin nodded and then looked to Drake.

"How about you?" Morgrin asked.

"I'm scared."

"So am I," Isabel answered.

"You don't show it," Drake said.

"Believe me Drake I'm terrified inside. The last time I was face to face with the Sorcerer I lied to all of you. He knows Rachal is my daughter now, there's nothing more I can do to protect her. It's out of my hands. So believe me I am terrified, but I am also filled with hope because of who leads us into battle! The Sorcerer has no real power; he only has power if you let him take hold of you."

"In some ways, it's not the battle that I fear it's what will come after the battle," Drake admitted. "Will Rachal still love me? Will she look at me differently, knowing that I have married another woman? I just don't know what to think."

"Then don't," Isabel said. "My daughter is a wise woman and she's never stopped loving you, I can feel that in my heart. She wouldn't have sent Aaron and Jacob running all over the hillside five years ago if she hadn't still been holding out hope that you were alive."

"I suppose that's true. I just can't help but have a little doubt. I guess I'm only human," Drake said.

"Don't worry about it, Drake. Worrying won't stop the bad stuff from happening, it only keeps you from enjoying the good," Aiden said.

They talked and worked long into the evening until finally the desert had been filled with several hundred ditches each of them at least three feet wide and at least three feet deep.

They collapsed on the desert sand and then set up their tents and laid their blankets on the ground welcoming the sleep that would soon take them. Thunder ripped through the sky and the dark night was lit up with flashes of light. The sound of rain was the last thing that Drake heard before he fell to asleep.

They woke the next morning to find desert sand beneath them. Drake moved his stiff body, slowly climbing out of his tent. He stretched and stared in amazement. Every ditch that had been dug was filled to the top with water. Drake cupped his hands and drank the water, feeling renewed energy rippled through him.

Aiden stood next to him smiling as he looked over the entire area.

"This is amazing," Drake cried.

"Dig some ditches and Lathon will do the rest," Aiden replied. Drake took another sip of the water.

"This water tastes different. Purer somehow."

"You didn't think Lathon would send ordinary water, did you? This water will give new life to every part of you."

Everyone else was awakened and drank and filled as many canteens as they could, all the while the water level in the ditches never went down. The army assembled and stood, refreshed, finding new energy in the water.

Three hours later the city of Megara came into their view. He could feel a sense of awe come over his men and Drake couldn't even deny that he was overwhelmed by the size of the city.

If only the city wasn't one of destruction.

Megara jutted out of the desert landscape looking as though it had been part of the desert, the entire fortress was made out of the same type of rock and dirt that the desert floor consisted of, giving the appearance that it had been carved from it.

The city consisted of seven levels, each one filled with Borags and war machines, ready to destroy them. Each level had a gate, which would then lead up to a courtyard three thousand feet wide around the next part of the city, that reached further up into the sky. A small wall wrapped around each level of the city.

Around the entire perimeter of the city was a wall, nearly forty feet high and at least twenty feet thick from what the Taruks had told them. The wall was filled with Borags and Drake was sure it was the same story on the other side of the wall. His eyes drifted to Isabel, noticing how she walked with purpose and fear at the same time. Rade came flying through the sky and then struck the ground in front of them, taking form.

"It's going to be a great day," Rade said a smile on his face. Aiden and the rest of them smiled.

"Yes, it will. What news do you bring from the other armies?"

"Saul's army-" Rade was interrupted as horns echoed out to the north. "Is here."

"What deh yeh think the Sorcerer has up his sleeve this time?" Ellizar asked. Rade shrugged.

"He has an army of three hundred thousand Borags that is wrapping around behind your army. He hopes to trap you. Matthew's army of five hundred thousand that was being hidden in Vernal is now three hours behind you and will entrap and trap the Sorcerer's army. Shavrok and his army however have not been sighted anywhere. I'm not sure where they are."

"He might be trapped, but this battle is going to take more than one day,"

Lily said.

"This day will not end before we have taken all seven levels and defeated the Sorcerer," Aiden said.

"There's no way we can take all seven levels before nightfall!" Lily cried.

"Are you saying the sun's not going to set?" Morgrin asked.

Aiden nodded. "That's exactly right. The sun will not move in the sky until this battle is over."

"That's impossible," Thaddeus replied. Aiden smiled.

"Is it?" Aiden asked. "With Lathon anything is possible. We will have victory today my friends."

Rade flew back up into the sky, joining the other Korazin who were hidden in the clouds. To their north, Saul's army was growing in size, the war machines now clearly visible. All the war machines in Drake and Abner's army were pushed to the front, their catapults loaded. The Gogs also loaded theirs with massive boulders, which then had spikes driven into them. Aiden and Isabel stuffed something into the cracks that were created and then joined the others at the front of the army once again.

The two armies rustled in their armor as they mentally prepared for the battle that lay ahead of them. Aiden stepped forward, the entire region fell silent. He walked out fifty feet in front of the army and thrust his sword into the ground.

The breeze that had been lightly blowing through the desert stopped, the only sound that was heard was the beating of one's heart. The opposing army turned from them and looked up towards the top of the fortress. The highest spire reached into the sky, a red Taruk perched on it. Distant roars filled the sky. Elohim, Aspen, and Destan will be here shortly.

The Borags on the wall parted for a person Drake wished he didn't recognize. The Sorcerer came into view, his bald head exactly the way it had been the last time Drake had seen him. He was dressed in a black cloak and his eyes were cold and dark. Isabel moved closer to Drake.

"Say hello to your former father-in-law," Isabel whispered.

"Give yourself up Merderick!" Aiden exclaimed. "You know you can't win."

"And why can't I?" Merderick asked. "You can't stop me!"

"I can stop you."

"*Plan* on stopping me!"

"Not plan; I *will* stop you!" Aiden corrected. "Give yourself up and perhaps mercy will be granted to you."

"That's just what I want, to be handed mercy by the one who cast me out."

"You brought that on yourself."

"Did I?" Merderick taunted. "I think you need to examine yourself you fool! Why are you here? I'll tell you why you're here; you are here because you're jealous."

"Yes I am," Aiden replied. Drake's mind swam in confusion. "I am a very jealous person, I cannot stand the thought of anyone not having the chance to know me, and I know them. I am jealous to win their hearts and transform the world."

"It's useless trying to reason with you!" Merderick snapped. "You hear nothing of what I say!"

"I hear what you say and I know the condition of the heart that speaks the words," Aiden said.

The Sorcerer cursed.

"Kill them all, leave none alive!" Merderick paused and looked at Drake and Isabel. "If you wish to save your wife to be, and your daughter you'll have to get to me. With each second that passes, she will feel more and more pain until she will finally be brutally and miserably killed. That's what I do to people who are nothing more than diseased slime." Without another word, the Sorcerer turned and disappeared into the citadel. The Sorcerer's army let out a battle cry.

Aiden held his sword in the air. The army roared, shaking the city.

"Where's Saul?" Aiden asked. Saul came ridding up moments later.

"Spread the word that we'll fire the catapults first and after we're done with them we'll send in ladders. When we do we'll need your sharpshooters to aim wherever the ladders are perched to keep away the enemy."

"Yes sir," Saul said. He ran off to where his men were stationed.

"Fire the catapults'! Bring down the walls!" Aiden yelled. The army roared as the adrenaline began flowing through their veins. Abner's men released their catapults, the rocks, and projectiles finding their targets, sailing over the wall and crushing buildings and Borags.

"Do not move from your spots!" Aiden said. "No harm will come to us." Drake shook in his armor as the catapults mounted on top of the wall were released. Projectiles streamed through the air rushing towards them.

Roars echoed out behind them. Drake looked behind as black Taruks swooped out of the sky and caught the projectiles in their massive claws. They lifted them back into the air and then dropped them on the other side of the wall. Gog's came forward with torches and touched them to the large rocks they had placed in their catapults'. They fired the catapults. The boulders sailed through the air, exploding when they reached the wall.

"How did that happen?" Drake asked.

"I created a special formula," Isabel replied. "That's what Aiden and I were putting in the large cracks."

"I'm sure glad you're on my side," Drake said. They both laughed.

"Let's go!" Aiden exclaimed. He turned to face the army. He yelled out and the army repeated his cry. "Charge!"

The roar of the army, shook the city of Megara as they sprinted towards the wall. Saul's men, just like planned, followed suit. Ladders were brought to the front and set up against the walls as Aiden and Isabel were the first to climb on. Drake followed behind them as hundreds of ladders were set up along the wall. Siege towers were also being pushed forward. Drake bounded over the edge of the wall swinging his sword at the first enemy that raced at him.

The battle raged on as the dead bodies began to pile up, covering the ground in blood. Drake was sickened by the amount of death that was taking place, but he also knew that compared to the Sorcerer's army they had lost hardly any people. The Borags fought as if they were slow and tired and hadn't expected to be attacked. Their army on the other hand seemed to be moving faster than he would have expected for having marched three days through the desert. It was almost like a brand-new army.

The red Taruk sat atop the spire at the top, unmoving, also seeming to have fear in his eyes. Drake slayed another Borag, keeping a watchful eye on the red Taruk, knowing that it was going to attack sooner or later.

The whole fortress was shaken by a deafening roar as the golden Taruk came flying up from behind the fortress. It collided with the red Taruk ripping off part of the roof as it did. The golden Taruk latched its powerful claws into the flesh of the red Taruk and then pushed toward the ground.

The red Taruk was released, but before the red Taruk could get flipped right side up the golden Taruk had spewed white-hot flame from its mouth. The red Taruk was consumed as it tried to fly away. Moments later the flame engulfed Taruk and plummeted into the assembled enemy army, letting off thick black smoke as its flesh was consumed.

"Where's Shavrok?" Drake asked; an hour more had passed. Isabel shrugged as she fought off another Borag.

"He should've been here by now," Isabel answered. Aiden came running up to them.

"We're about to get some company," Aiden said. "When the Gogs get here, be ready to pull back the entire army!" Horns echoed to the west, grabbing their attention. A massive army appeared on the horizon.

"There are the Sorcerer's reinforcements," Aiden said. Their army created a line to match the opposing army, which was larger than Drake could even hope to count. The Borag army charged towards them, while their army remained where they were. All four Taruks swooped down out of the sky spewing flames into the opposing army. The bodies were consumed in fire, their bones were the only thing to survive the intense heat of the Taruks. Most of the Borags staggered a few feet until they fell to the ground. The few troops that weren't destroyed by the fire rushed forward and were fought off by Drake's men.

Aiden led them further into the city. The gates of the city hadn't been opened, but thousands of their men had made it over the wall and now engaged the troops between the wall and the entrance to the second level of the city. The ground was shaken as a rumbling came from beneath the ground. Drake stopped, fear pounding through his heart.

"What was that?" Drake asked. Aiden stood a few feet away.

"Pull back!" Aiden yelled. "Pull back!" Drake sprinted up the wall and the order was repeated as the army moved back a thousand yards. Horns echoed to the west and the south. From the west came the army that had been hiding in Vernal. Matthew led the army of five hundred thousand, which came to a halt. To their south, a low rumbling was heard, shaking the city. Shavrok's army appeared over the horizon.

"Get back!" Aiden yelled. Drake and Isabel did as he said. The enemy troops on the other side of the wall stood, looking confused by Drake's army, which had pulled away. Aiden held his sword up to the sky. Lighting came from the blade and arched up to the sky. He swung his sword down and the lighting was drawn to the ground, creating a shockwave that ripped through the army that surrounded the fortress. Only enemy troops were harmed as they dropped over dead. Shavrok's army roared and began their charge towards the wall. Aiden turned around and sprinted down the stairs. Everyone else followed with them.

"Take cover!" Aiden yelled. Their men dove for cover as the Korazin appeared in the sky. They streaked to the ground and tunneled underneath the wall, following the path of the wall all the way around the fortress. The wall was obliterated and chunks of the wall flew through the air and crashed down on the opposing army. When the dust and debris finally settled, Drake's spirit soared as he took up arms once again.

"Into the city!" Aiden yelled. The army roared and followed behind Aiden as they met the onslaught of troops between them and the second level. They fought their way to the second level, unable to tell how much time had passed due to the sun remaining in the same place since the battle had begun.

Drake had never had any doubts about Aiden, but if he had, they would've been chased away by the sun standing still.

There was only one who could command that kind of power.

Chills swept through Drake as they finally laid their eyes on the gate to the second level of the city. Drake looked up and saw four people in robes standing on the second level. The army didn't seem to notice them. The figures were dressed in white robes with gold sashes and stared out into the battle. Drake stopped fighting, and Aiden followed his gaze.

"Don't worry about them," Aiden said. "They won't harm us."

"What are they here for?" Drake asked.

"Many things will happen as we press up to each level of the city," Aiden explained. "Terrible things, but none of it will affect us. Even members of the Sorcerer's army won't be harmed if they decide to join Lathon."

"Who are they?" Isabel asked.

"Friends of mine," Aiden replied.

They rushed towards the gate to the second level of the city, finding that it opened when they rushed towards it. They clashed with the troops on the other side, fighting their way in, easily destroying the Borags, Elves, and Men that made up the Sorcerer's army. Isabel looked at her hand and held it to Drake, on her palm was a mark just like he had, three slashes.

"You have one too?" Drake asked.

Morgrin came running up behind them.

"Everyone has one," Morgrin said, holding out his hand for them to see.

"No harm will come to anyone who has the mark of Lathon on their heart and their hand!" Aiden exclaimed. They continued fighting noticing that the army in front of them seemed to be more uncomfortable with every second that passed. Soon blood began to come out from underneath the armor of the Sorcerer's armies. Boils covered the Sorcerer's army from head to toe. The Sorcerer's army grew weak and was destroyed with ease as they reached the third gate of the city.

The gate crumbled in front of them allowing them to pass to the next level, which was once again filled with Borags. Thunder rumbled through the sky and green fire began to fall to the ground. Drake watched as it crashed into the ground far beyond the armies that were present. Dust from the impact filled the sky and then smoke slowly started to rise from the craters.

The sky was filled with black as the smoke became thicker and thicker. The sound of countless wings fluttering in the distance became the sound of hornets or bees as the black continued to come towards them.

"What is this?" Drake asked.

"A demon of the underworld!" Aiden exclaimed. "They are called the Revule. They will not harm us!" The black covered the sky and spread to the city at a speed Drake couldn't comprehend. Within seconds they were all immersed in darkness as the creatures consumed the world around them. The sound of their wings and the cries of their enemies being killed and destroyed was all they could hear. In twenty seconds, it was over, and the black creatures, which Drake never did see clearly, lifted up into the sky and vanished to the craters they had come from. The ground swallowed them up and then the holes were sealed off.

The third level of the city had been destroyed with buildings leveled and the bodies of their enemies as nothing more than skeletal remains. Drake and the entire army slowly moved to the fourth level, almost afraid to see what destruction would befall their enemies this time. Aiden stopped at the gate.

"You cannot keep me out!" Aiden exclaimed. The gate shook and then finally opened allowing them to pass through to the next level, which was filled with troops as the others had been. The Korazin flew through the sky colliding with each other in a clash of light. The light spread through the sky and a moment later was followed by darkness. Drake looked around and could see as clear as day despite the darkness. Their enemies groped in the darkness, disoriented.

"They can't see, but we can?" Isabel asked. Aiden nodded.

"Anyone who believes in Lathon can see, while the lost are left to wander the darkness of their hearts." They passed by the troops, not killing them this time, but instead leaving them to wander the darkness. The fifth gate towered in front of them, this one made out of black rock with strange markings along every side of it. Storm clouds had now formed overhead.

Aiden drew his sword and touched the tip of it to the large gates. The gates opened immediately and they passed to the fifth level. More troops awaited them and rushed to attack them. They defended themselves as thunder rolled overhead. Hail began falling from the sky, larger than any Drake had ever seen. Their enemies were crushed under the boulders which when they melted was a mixture of water and blood, which dripped down to the previous levels. Within minutes, they reached the gate of the sixth level.

They reached the sixth gate, surprised to see that it was already open and that the entire level was empty of people. Buildings stood, empty and unoccupied, like tombstones in a cemetery. They walked through the vacant level and finally reached the tower in the center, which reached higher yet. Drake felt his courage slip from him.

"Who's coming in with me?" Aiden asked. Drake and Isabel stepped forward immediately. Morgrin stepped up beside them, holding Isabel's hand. The others remained where they were.

"Lily," Aiden said. "Make sure everyone is out of the city. I'm not sure what the Sorcerer has up his sleeve, but better safe than sorry."

"His power is almost gone isn't it?" Isabel asked. Aiden nodded.

"He has grown weaker with each one of his troops that we have killed. His strength is almost nothing. This will not be our end but his."

"Is there any hope for him?" Drake asked. "Do you think in his heart he would ever realize the truth?"

"He knows what the truth is Drake Thomas, but he is far too proud, vain, and arrogant to admit it. Pride is always the worst enemy. He won't be turning from his evil ways now, or ever."

Lily and everyone who wasn't going into the tower left and started getting all of their soldiers out of the city until finally, the entire area was like a graveyard. The door of the tower called out to Drake who was both terrified and excited about what lay behind the door. The gold ring in his pocket burned in his mind.

Aiden opened the door of the tower and they began climbing the winding staircase that was inside. The stairs were covered in dried blood; cobwebs hung everywhere. Drake and Isabel pushed on, their courage and determination returning to them. They reached another door and it was opened for them as a guard let them into the room. The guard wore no weapons, just a plain black robe.

"Well, well, well, look who it is!"

Enya stood at the far end of the room; looking weak and battered as though she had just marched through the battle. Merderick was on his knees, his skin ghostly white, appearing to gasp for every breath. Drake's eyes were drawn to the middle of the room.

A brown-haired woman lay motionless. Her dress was torn and tattered, her body scraped and cut. Blood covered the floor. Drake slowly moved forward, making his way around until he could see her face. Her eyes were closed and her chest rose and fell with hard labored breathing.

Drake bent down to one knee, reaching out with his hand and gently brushing the brown hair away from her face. Her eyes fluttered open and focused on him. A moment later they closed again.

"She's alive," Drake managed. Isabel breathed a sigh of relief.

"She needs to die!" Enya screamed. "I can't kill her! We've used thousands of spells! She won't die."

"It's not her time to die," Aiden said. Isabel moved towards Rachael.

"Don't touch her!" Enya yelled. "You must pay for all the crimes you've committed. If you touch her, or help her, so help me I'll slice you from head to toe."

"Stop me!" Isabel yelled. Enya rushed forward, drawing a knife from her side. Isabel twisted out of the path of the knife and pulled it from her hand before thrusting it into Enya's back. Isabel threw her to the floor. Enya rolled over and looked up, struggling for every breath.

"I've been separated from my daughter for all these years; you're not stopping me from being with her now! Die knowing that," Isabel cried.

Enya struggled to speak before finally dying. Isabel moved back to Drake and Rachal. They carefully moved her away from the center of the room as the Sorcerer managed to pull himself to his feet. He stumbled forward, hardly able to keep upright.

"I will defeat you!" The Sorcerer yelled. Aiden remained calm and looked deep into the Sorcerer's eyes until finally, the Sorcerer looked away.

"No you won't," Aiden said. "You see, you've had it all wrong. All these years, you've focused all your attention on destroying me…which is what I wanted you to do. However, you would've never been able to defeat me, because you don't understand what a true follower of Lathon is."

"You are Lathon!" Merderick exclaimed. "If I beat you, I win. Your followers would lose faith without you. They would curse you."

"No," Aiden corrected. "A true disciple of mine would not lose faith, because they see the goodness that has been poured out from my example. True followers of mine will push themselves to be a carbon copy of me and display the love and grace that I have shown them. The more you attack us, the more this kind of love will be clear to the world, it will spread like wildfire. People would be united and the world would be restored. Even if you had killed me, I would still be with them. They would still be in the world they would still love people. Love Lathon, Love people."

"No!" The Sorcerer yelled. "I can't lose like this!"

"You already have," Aiden replied. "In the end, every knee will bow and every tongue will confess that I am Lord."

"Never!" The Sorcerer yelled. He ran forward drawing his sword but stumbled and fell to his knees, his sword falling from his hands. Each second that passed the Sorcerer's condition worsened. Drake could now clearly see his skull through his fading skin.

"You know this is the end for you," Aiden said. "You cannot win."

The Sorcerer cursed, struggling for every breath. "I know what you are, but I cannot say it," Merderick replied.

"In that case, there's nothing else to say," Aiden said. Aiden drew his sword and held it to the Sorcerer's neck. The Sorcerer didn't move or try to grab his weapons. Aiden pulled the sword back and let a yell escape him as he thrust it into the ground just in front of the Sorcerer.

Light flooded from the point of impact, overwhelming everything. The Sorcerer and Enya both vanished in the light, which obliterated the walls of the tower. The roof was blown away as the light thundered out, chasing away all the storm clouds and killing the remaining troops in the Sorcerer's army. The light shone down on all of them as they looked out over their armies. Everyone breathed a sigh of relief.

Chapter 22

THE DAYS AFTER

Drake collapsed on the top of the ruined tower. Isabel sat down next to him, gently feeling for Rachal's pulse.

"She's alive but very weak," Isabel reported.

"Can you heal her?" Drake asked. Aiden looked at the three of them long and hard. "You healed all of us in the Dead Mountains before."

"I would like to heal her right now, but I fear that sometimes, even though it is beyond our knowledge; it is best to wait and be patient. I cannot heal her now." Isabel and Drake looked at Rachal, sorrow overcoming them.

"I'm not sure what to think," Drake admitted. "I'm overcome both with sorrow and fatigue."

"I imagine that's so," Aiden said. "Look around, the Sorcerer's armies are defeated. If you find no other comfort today, know that you have both done valiantly. And I'm proud of both of you for the people you have become."

Drake and Isabel felt their spirits rise as they looked over the horizon. Where the Sorcerer's armies had stood mere minutes ago, now only a sea of corpses remained. Drake breathed heavily as he looked first to Isabel and then to Rachal.

Her eyes were still closed, and her breathing was hard and labored. Drake stared at her, lost in his thoughts as he tried to sort through everything that had happened. Parts of his past were slowly starting to filter into Drake's mind, but as of yet, he was unable to put the pieces together.

Aiden watched Drake and Isabel intently as if he was trying to guess their thoughts. Drake and Isabel didn't speak and instead wandered about the top of the tower mindlessly.

"Let your hearts be eased, she will recover from her injuries, but it will be a long road for everyone," Aiden told them. Drake breathed a sigh of relief, his eyes once again moving to the woman lying in the middle of the tower

Aiden moved over next to Rachal and stooped down. He held a hand up to her forehead and muttered something under his breath. Drake watched in amazement as her breathing became steadier. Aiden stood to his feet.

"What did you do?" Drake asked.

"Let's leave this tower. I have put a blessing on her. We can move her now, but not far. It'll be a long trip back to Cos."

Drake and Isabel made their way down the tower, leaving Aiden with Rachal at the top. Slowly they sifted their way through the battlefield, which looked more like a graveyard than a field of victory.

Thousands of bodies littered the group and puddles of blood mired some parts of it. Neither of them spoke as they carefully picked their way through and reached their armies, which had fought against the Sorcerer.

"That was what I call a victory!" Ellizar declared as Drake and Isabel walked towards him. Drake and Isabel forced a smile. "Why are yeh not as joyful as yeh usually would be in this case?"

"Our hearts are indeed happy for the Sorcerer's defeat," Isabel replied. "But there is a person on the top of the tower that we are concerned about."

"Is the Sorcerer still alive?" Lily asked.

"No, it seems Isabel's daughter. Her real daughter is at the top of the tower…and it seems I was engaged to her at one point." The others remained speechless. "I'm still trying to take it in myself." Silence still lingered until finally, Ellizar started laughing hysterically.

"Yeh know Drake Thomas? If it was anyone else tellin' me this I might be surprised. But because it's Isabel, I believe yeh without a doubt!" They all laughed and breathed a sigh of relief.

"She's in bad shape," Drake said. "I hate to ask this of you Ellizar and Lily. Would you be able to lead the army back to Cos? I'll get there as soon as I can, but I feel like I need to be with Rachal."

"We agree," Lily said. "We'd be concerned if you didn't stay with her, we'll meet you as Cos and then figure out everyone's next move."

"Thank you, my friend," Drake said. "Also send word for Nickolas to also meet in Cos."

"Thanks," Isabel said. She remained silent looking at the ground.

"We need a couple of people to help get her. Something to lay her on would probably be good, we have lots of stairs to go down," Drake said. Within minutes Morgrin had gathered the supplies and made something to put Rachal on. A few soldiers came with them and they began the long trek back to the tower, which now stood silent, a reminder of the horror that had transpired just hours earlier.

They reached the top of the tower where Aiden was patiently sitting next to Rachal who was still unresponsive. They brought their makeshift stretcher alongside and carefully lifted the fragile woman onto it.

"Isabel and Drake please remain behind," Aiden said, breaking his silence. The others started making their way down the tower, vanishing from sight. Drake and Isabel sat down next to Aiden.

"Do you guys have any questions?" Aiden asked. "Do you have any questions for me?"

"How is it that the Sorcerer was able to appear in physical form again?" Isabel asked. "I thought he had already been defeated and couldn't come back."

"He was indeed defeated the first time and by all natural means, he should not have come back. However, he is a master of evil and has twisted the minds and hearts of many people over the centuries. Through unnatural ways, he returned, and take note he was not strong, he was weaker than ever.

"Through unnatural ways, Enya was able to bring him back but for a moment. But through the process it destroyed her, leaving her weak and easily defeated. When people try to do things against the will of Lathon it never works out. The Sorcerer will never again gain physical form, but his spirit has not lost its malice and will show itself in new ways in the future. Do you have any questions, Drake?"

"More so I have insecurities," Drake admitted. "I'm not sure what to do. I remember some of what Rachal and I once shared, but I don't remember everything. I'm not sure what I'm supposed to do. I feel guilty for having been married to someone else."

"I understand, but do not let that guilt get the better of you," Aiden said. "Trust me when I say that Gwen had a far better life with you than she would have otherwise. Your marriage accomplished far more than you are aware."

"Perhaps," Drake answered, slipping into his thoughts for a while. "Still, with the current state of things, I'm not sure I can just feel the way I once apparently did."

"That's okay," Aiden said. "She isn't going to feel the way she once did either. You have both grown much since you were thrown over the falls ten years ago. Love is not a feeling, it's an action. And sometimes it's best if it comes slowly, rather than love at first sight."

"Are we meant to be together after all of this?" Drake asked.

"I'm not going to answer that," Aiden said. "I encourage you to take the time to get to know each other as you are now and look forward to who you will become. People don't stay the same as time passes." Drake nodded and fell silent. "How about you Isabel?"

"I look back on my life…I see how Lathon has brought me to this moment. Yet I fail at times to see that I have done well in Lathon's eyes. I have stolen many things, and hidden many things. Did I do well? Have I helped Lathon's cause in any of this, or have I merely made a mess for myself that finally caught up with me in the form of my daughter getting tortured within an inch of her life?"

"Your question is a common one, but a hard one to live with," Aiden said. "Lathon has a plan for all of our lives. He wishes for us to follow him. Sometimes we do, sometimes we don't. Lathon doesn't choose our path for us but lets us choose. But no matter our choice he is always there ready to help us come back to him. The choice is ours alone. Just because one is doing the will of Lathon, it does not mean that life will be easy, in fact, it will likely be just the opposite.

"Your life may seem like a series of disasters, but your heart has stayed true, and Lathon smiles upon you today. You have shown love and devotion on so many levels, and not the least of which, was doing your best to give Gwen and your daughter a better life."

"Your words are welcomed," Isabel said with a slight smile. "Still I am not at peace."

"Time will be the best remedy for the both of you," Aiden said. "You are weary now, and emotions can hardly be trusted when one is weary. We will rest here tonight and catch up to the others tomorrow. It will be very slow traveling back to Cos."

They started early the next day, eager to leave the quiet tomb behind them. Before long it had become nothing more than a dot on the horizon before vanishing altogether. The air was silent and a light breeze moved through the open desert.

As Aiden had said, they caught up to the company that was traveling with and caring for Rachal. They walked until sunset and then made camp in the open wilderness. Isabel wandered from the camp for some time before returning with a flask in her hand.

"What's that?" Morgrin asked. She handed it to him and he smelled it, cringing.

"It's *Yon ula*. A rare juice that comes from the *Airndu* flower," Isabel replied. "It used to be a common plant in this part of the world. Now it is hard to find. The trick is to pick the flower and then immediately boil it for thirty minutes."

"What does it do?" Drake asked.

"It's a stimulant of sorts," Aiden said. "It will replenish the vital nutrients that Rachal needs to stay alive in case she does not wake for a long time. It is indeed hard to find."

"I had to walk five miles to find it. I picked as many as should last for several months if need be."

"Several months?" Drake asked. "Certainly she can't stay asleep that long. Can she?"

"It is not for me to say," Aiden said. "She will sleep until the time is right for her to wake up."

They fell silent as Isabel slowly tried to pour some of the liquid down Rachal's throat. She swallowed some as a reflex but didn't show any other signs of life as her body soon relaxed into the same state she had been in all day.

They worked long into the night, tending to her numerous injuries and treating them the best they could. Her tattered clothes were thrown to the fire and she was wrapped in cloaks and blankets so they would easily be able to redress the wounds as they needed to.

Drake lay on the ground, unable to sleep, staring mindlessly into the fire. The scene from the tower playing out in his head again and again. Such darkness had come over him when they had reached the top. Drake still struggled to process everything he had seen and experienced.

Morgrin was keeping watch and himself appeared to be lost in his thoughts. Drake sat up and then moved over to Morgrin who smiled weakly through his sleepy eyes.

"Quite a turn of events eh?" Morgrin asked. Drake chuckled.

"I'm still not sure what to think."

"She's a good woman Drake. You are a lucky guy."

"I suppose you knew all along. That she was Isabel's daughter."

"Actually I didn't know. At least not for a long time. My wife has had many secrets over the years and I always trusted that when the time was right she would trust me enough to at least tell me. I was right, but so was she. All of her secrets would have come to terrible ends had she told the wrong people at the wrong time."

"Doesn't it bother you that she kept all those secrets?"

"We all have secrets Drake, even if it's only in our thoughts. The only question that you have to ask is does the secret bring you closer to Lathon or further away? Isabel kept secrets, but each one was set on the demise of the Sorcerer and the glory of Lathon."

"Never thought of it like that."

"Few do, and as a result, they keep secrets that should not be kept. They deliberately shipwreck their faith for a dark secret that they're unwilling to part with." Drake pondered his words far into the night, mulling them over in his head.

A week passed and finally, the company stepped out of the desert and into grasslands. Cos appeared in the distance, a faint dot in the distance. They walked for several hours more, feeling their spirits rise with each mile they covered. Soon the large walls of Cos loomed before them, while to the south a large sea of tents had been formed. Matthew rode up to them.

"Good day my Lord and lady," Matthew greeted. He wore the crest of Rhallinen on his horse.

"Good day Matthew," Drake greeted.

Matthew stopped his horse and dismounted. "We are glad to see you have returned from the desert. Some of the men were starting to wonder if you were coming back."

"We had many delays, but nothing too exciting," Drake replied. "Please spread the word that we're back and nothing's wrong. I have some business to attend to in the city, but I will join the men at nightfall. Tell the men that in three days we will be headed back home."

"I'll let you tell them yourself tonight." Matthew mounted his horse. "Welcome back once again."

"Thank you."

Matthew turned his horse and headed in the direction of the sea of tents, blowing loudly on his horn. Returning calls came from the tents as well as from the city."

"Morgrin," Isabel started, breaking her long silence. "Please find Nickolas and have him come to Ellizar and Lily's house as fast as possible. He may already be there, but look for him elsewhere just in case."

"As you wish my dear. I'll see you tonight." Morgrin quickly ran off into the distance, leaving the company behind.

"Don't worry my dear," Isabel said to Rachal, who was still unconscious on the stretcher. "We will be in a safe place soon." They walked for many more minutes and miles before the city became large before them.

"Looks like news of the victory has certainly reached the king of Edon's ears," Aiden observed. "They came over the last slight hill that slowly descended into a shallow valley. Thousands of people lined the last half mile that led up to the main gates, and beyond that, they could see streets lined with more people than they could count.

"Looks like everyone in the city is out to greet us," Isabel observed.

"Everyone may not know exactly what happened, but they at least understand that a great evil has been broken," Aiden said.

A company of horsemen rode up and flanked them on either side, blowing their horns joyously. The notes rang clear and strong through the air and everyone who had been anxiously talking fell silent.

"A great victory has been achieved!" the lead horsemen cried. "By order of the king, a great feast will be held in honor of the great victory over Megara. All hail Drake Thomas of Rhallien! And Aiden of Rhallien!"

The city erupted in cheers as they were paraded through the streets. Drake fell back alongside Isabel who was now glued to the side of Rachal's unconscious body. Isabel studied Rachal closely as they walked.

"Is something wrong?" Drake asked.

"I don't know. Even in the state she is in, all this noise that is around us now ought to get some reaction out of her unless I've mixed the medicine wrong."

"You've done everything right," Aiden told her. "Take your daughter and go to a place that is quieter than this. We'll find you later."

"I want to go too," Drake said.

"I'm sure you do," Aiden said. "But I have a feeling we're going to be unable to get away for several hours, seeing that the king is throwing a feast in our honor. Don't worry, Rachal will recognize Isabel if she wakes. They have known each other many years."

"Does she know Isabel is her mother?"

"No she doesn't," Aiden said. They both glanced back at Isabel who was looking over Rachal intently. "But Isabel will be a welcomed face to her when she wakes." Isabel and the men carrying Rachal disappeared.

It was late in the night before Drake was finally able to steal away from the great feast. The city was alive and full of energy even at the late hour. He stepped into an empty street, accompanied by nothing other than silence.

He walked for almost an hour before he stepped into the street of Ellizar and Lily's house. A single light shone in most of the houses as he silently passed them. From some houses came laughter, while others remained silent, but even still there was a sense of peace about everything. His spirits were high as he pressed forward, coming into view of Ellizar's house.

Everyone sat on the front porch, a single lantern lighting the space. The rest of the house was dark, except for one small lamp in the front window.

"Sorry I'm so late," Drake said as he walked up.

Ellizar just laughed. "Yer not late! Everyone else is just early. Dwarvish saying! Usually said teh justify every kind ov laziness that might overtake a dwarf at a time or two. How was the party?"

"Lavish and beautiful. Like it was meant for a king."

"That's good, seeing that you are a king," Isabel said. "Though I understand your humility about the situation. I've never been a particular fan of parties or feasts that have been thrown in my honor."

"Well Drake, what have yeh been thinkin' since we saw you last? Been nearly a week!"

"I was at first scared and unsure what to do, with Rachal making a reappearance. Part, but not all of my memory is returning. It was a lot to take in.

I long to speak with Rachal and get to at least know her again. Being ten years removed I imagine we're very different from what we once were. I'm a bit torn right now between my duties as a king and leader of Rhallinen, and a normal person who wants to be with the people he loves."

"I understand that struggle," Isabel said.

"I'm sure you do," Drake started. "What I think I should do, is return to Mera Runa in three days as I said I would with my army. I hope Rachal wakes by then, but if she doesn't then I could return every second weekend. With Destan, I could certainly make good time as far as traveling is concerned. I would only be able to stay for a couple of days at a time."

"Sounds like a decent plan," Morgrin said. "Isabel and I aren't planning to leave the city until she wakes, whether that is one week or six. We'll certainly send word as soon as she wakes."

"Then it's agreed then." They all nodded their heads. "Has anyone spoken with Nickolas?"

"I found him and brought him here," Morgrin started. "Seeing that you were held up, I took the liberty of explaining the situation. He gives you his blessing to pursue Rachal again. He did thank you for being courteous, but many things have changed in five years."

"I guess that's settled. Lily and Ellizar, please allow me to compensate you for having her in your care."

"No Drake we couldn't!" Lily cried.

"I insist, and as a king, I can probably do that every now and then."

"Don't argue with the king!" Ellizar exclaimed.

They continued chatting for a few more minutes before heading to the various beds and couches that had been prepared for them. Drake closed his eyes and looked at the visions that flooded into his soul. Most of them were about Rachal; bits and pieces of the memory that he had lost slowly returning.

***

Drake took a deep breath as he settled back into his throne. People lined the halls, each of them patiently waiting their turn as he settled disputes of the people. Although most things were solved in the lower courts of justice, some things were still undecided.

This part of the job had scared Drake more than any other when Aiden had first appointed him to lead Mera Runa. Through much prayer and encouragement, he had been granted the wisdom and guidance that he had come to ask Lathon for every night.

"I can only take one more dispute, Matthew," Drake said. "I am weary and my heart is on edge for whatever reason."

"I understand my lord," Matthew said, motioning to the guards to let the next people come forth. "I'd say you're doing remarkably well for a king whose heart is in anguish."

"More like suspense. It's been four weeks and still, Rachal has not awakened." Drake disappeared into his thoughts for only a moment. He looked up and saw two women on the floor in front of him. One's face was filled with rage, while the other was filled with tears. A guard that had escorted them to the front carried a young baby.

"What is the dispute?" Drake asked. The women glared at each other before the one on the left spoke.

"Please my Lord, judge wisely in this matter," the woman began. "This woman and I live in the same house. It so happened that we both became pregnant. I gave birth to a baby while she was with me in the house. That was a week ago. Three days later this woman also had her baby.

"Her baby died during the night when she rolled over on it. Then she got up in the night and took my son from beside me while I was asleep. She laid her dead child in my arms and took mine to sleep beside her. In the morning I tried to nurse my son, only to find that he was dead! But when I looked more closely in the morning light, I saw that it wasn't my son at all."

"It certainly was your son, and the living child is mine!" the woman on the right cried.

"No," the woman on the left said. "The living child is mine and the dead one is yours." Drake drew a big breath as he listened for several minutes as the women screamed at each other, tears streaming down both of their faces.

Lathon help me, Drake silently prayed.

"Silence, both of you!" Drake finally yelled above the screaming. Both women fell silent. "Let's get the facts straight. Both of you claim the living child is yours and each says that the dead one belongs to the other. Despite you both needing to go back and read the ancient scrolls and adjust your moral compasses accordingly, there is only one action that makes sense. General, bring me a sword!" Matthew drew his sword and handed it to Drake.

"Bring me the baby." The guard carrying the young baby came forward. "Put the baby on the ground. We are going to cut the living child in two." The people fell completely silent. "Each of the women will get half of the child. The baby was placed on the ground and Drake raised his sword.

"No, my lord!" the woman on the right cried. "Give her the child- please do not kill him!"

"It seems fair to me," the woman on the left screamed. "He will be neither yours nor mine; divide him between us and let this woman suffer as she should."

Drake pulled the sword back and handed it to Matthew.

"I'm not going to kill the child, but I will give the child to the one who wanted him to live. Only a mother who truly loved her child would willingly offer him to another person, to spare him from death." The woman on the right took the baby in her arms, tears of joy streaming down her face.

"That is all for today." They left and the palace was emptied as Drake sat down until everyone was gone. Finally, Matthew approached.

"If I may say so Your Majesty you do not seem yourself these past weeks. Is it only because of Rachal or is there something more that I should know about?"

"It's partly just because of Rachal," Drake started. "I've been doing Lathon's work here and leading this nation as I was asked to. Nonetheless, now that Rachal is in the picture I'm not sure how everything is going to work out. The uncertainty is slowly starting to eat away at my soul."

"I think I understand," Matthew said. "You told me previously that you had expected to see Gwen at the top of the tower. Perhaps you are grieving her loss in a new way? Perhaps in a way that you didn't grieve the first time?"

"That's probably accurate," Drake replied. The door opened on the far side of the room and a messenger was ushered in. He sprinted to the front of the room and handed a sealed envelope to Drake, who quickly opened it. "She's awake." He quickly read the letter that Isabel had sent him.

"That's wonderful!" Matthew cried. "You should go to her immediately. I can take care of things while you're gone."

"I'm not sure I want to go," Drake admitted.

"You're going, if I have to push you out that door. I see your thoughts, and I can see that you think that if you do not pursue this woman your unease will leave you. It won't. There are some things in life you cannot escape, outrun, or leave behind forever. They will find you and consume you if you do not put them to rest. Go to her. Talk to her. Get to know her. Who knows? Maybe there's more here to be healed than just your heart." Drake nodded.

"You speak wise words. I will go in the morning and we will see what will happen."

***

Destan landed in the stables that housed any Taruks should they be coming or going from the city of Cos. Drake dismounted and patted Destan on the head.

"All the battles I've been through, and all the times I've been moments away from death and now I find that I'm more afraid than ever."

The Taruk rumbled in response. Drake exited the stables, where Morgrin was waiting for him, two horses already saddled.

They started through the city, only talking briefly about things that had been going on the last month. They rounded a corner and Ellizar and Lily's house came into view.

"I'm nervous," Drake admitted.

"So is she," Isabel said, coming out onto the porch. "I almost couldn't get her to agree to see you."

"Besides nervous to see me how is she doing?"

"Pretty well all things considered. I think she appreciated seeing a friendly face when she awoke. Can you imagine waking up to Ellizar's face?"

"You'll have to ask Lily how she does it," Drake replied.

"Come, time is precious, let us not waste any more of it." Isabel motioned for him to get up and follow her. They walked down the halls until they reached a room with the door closed. Isabel looked up and down the hall.

"She doesn't yet know that I'm her mother. The time is not right to trouble her with that." Drake nodded and Isabel carefully opened the door. Rachal lay in the bed asleep. Her hair had been neatly combed and done up nicely. Drake struggled with himself and eventually backed out of the room.

"I can't do this," Drake admitted, holding back tears.

"Yes you can," Isabel said. "It's perfect really. She is unconscious, you can take your time, and get comfortable. Talk to her. Unconscious people can hear you when you speak. With her unconscious, you'll speak to her heart, and her heart needs that more than anything." Isabel pushed him into the room and closed the door on him. Rachal shifted at the sounds of the door but didn't wake.

Drake slowly moved over to a chair that was set next to her bed and took a seat. He looked into Rachal's face getting lost in it as memories flooded back into his head at a rate that he could hardly comprehend. Still, they were distant and confusing. Several hours passed and soon the light had faded leaving him and Rachal in the light of lanterns. Finally, Drake spoke.

"I don't know what Isabel has told you, but I can only say, and I know it may sound ridiculous, but my memory was taken from me. I have not remembered you for the past ten years. Not until the end. I'm not sure why, and that's why I'm having such a hard time right now. I don't understand why I was meant to lose my memory.

"I'm grieving right now. If not for my lost memory, then it's for the love that we were not able to share because I had lost it. I was married to another woman, and now I wonder to what purpose did it serve when I had been promised to you?

"I'm not sure how we're supposed to move forward with everything that's happened. My heart feels so much turmoil I'm being eaten alive. What do I do?" Silence lingered as Drake wept.

"Forgive," a faint female voice said. Drake's heart stopped as he looked to see Rachal stirring. Drake held his breath as she looked at him through her groggy half-closed eyes.

"Forgive is all you can do in a situation like this. Forgive yourself for the things you had no control over. Isabel told me what happened and though I once thought I would be angry, how can I feel anything other than joy when my love is sitting by my bedside at last? You did not take your memory away, therefore you are not guilty of any sin. And even though we may not see it, there is some greater power at work here."

"You're not angry that I was married to another woman? In some places of the earth, it would be unthinkable for you to marry me."

"When I saw you in Avdatt five years ago, I was deeply hurt. Then I was kidnapped in the night and held in a dungeon. Tortured for five years. They questioned me every day, and sometimes they assaulted me for no reason. I didn't even know who they were. I grieved for us for a long time."

"How did you get through it?"

"One day as I was being whipped, the pain was so bad that I didn't think I would live. It was at that moment that I looked up and said, "Lathon! I will do whatever you want me to. Please help me." Somewhere next to me, I then heard a voice speaking in a gentle whisper… '*I can work with that.*' I looked and a man was standing next to me. I asked who he was.

"It was Lathon. He had come to me! My heart was so overjoyed that I hardly remembered the rest of the torture. When my captors had left he walked over and touched my body. My wounds were not cured, but the pain subsided.

"In my brokenness, I came to understand fully what it meant to lay down everything, all my dreams and desires, and seek only one dream and one desire. Lathon's. He never promised to save me from the torture or to see you again. He asked me to be faithful.

"I still feel the pain for the years that we didn't get to spend together, but I am at peace with it. And now at last we have been reunited! My heart is filled with joy. Do you remember any of our past?"

"I'm slowly starting to remember some of it," Drake said.

"From what I remember of our past, I think we were focused on the wrong things. We did love each other, and we were getting married but I feel like something was missing from that equation. Something that we now have."

"Faith in Lathon," Drake said. Rachal nodded.

"Whatever happens with us, we need to put Lathon first. Whatever that may look like." Rachal smiled weakly, tears running down her cheeks. "Let's start over. Do it right this time. It may take years for us to get to the place we were, but I've not stopped loving you. Do you feel the same?"

"Yes," Drake managed, struggling to get the words out. "I would like that very much."

The night wore on until at last daybreak came. Isabel entered the room finding Rachal asleep in the bed and Drake asleep on the floor. Rachal stirred and smiled when she saw Isabel.

"Good morning my dear," Isabel greeted. "How is everything?" Silence hung in the air for several moments before a small smile tugged at Rachal's lips.

"Perfect."

***

"My Lord! My Lord!" Drake stirred in his bed to see Matthew standing by his bedside, two other guards were with him, lanterns in their hands.

"What is so important that you needed to disturb me at this unearthly hour?"

"Aiden is here."

"Now?"

"Yes, he sent for you as soon as he and Elohim landed twenty minutes ago. He waits for you in the throne room!"

"Strange tidings must be at hand," Drake stated, throwing off his covers. "Tell him I'll be there in five minutes."

"Very well my Lord," Matthew went off and Drake got ready as quickly as possible. He stepped into the dark halls, grabbing a torch from the wall as he walked towards the throne room. Matthew and all the other guards on duty were waiting for him.

"Do you have any idea what he could want?"

"No your majesty," Matthew answered. "He would not say. He only said that he wished to speak with you and with you alone. Normally of course we wouldn't do that, but it's Aiden, how can you refuse right?"

"Indeed," Drake said. Matthew moved to the side and Drake stepped in, squinting as his eyes adjusted to the abundance of light. Every candle, lantern, and torch was lit, making it nearly as bright as day inside. Aiden casually sat on the steps to the throne, standing when Drake appeared.

"Good to see you Drake, come on in!" Drake briskly walked forward, embracing Aiden.

"I'm glad to see you. A lot has happened since the last time we saw each other."

"Yes indeed. It's been five months! How is everything in your life going?"

"A lot better recently," Drake admitted. "I think I've finally grieved for everything that I needed to grieve for and come to understand things in a new light."

"I'm glad to hear that. How's Rachal doing?"

"She's doing well. We have plans to get married next spring."

"That's wonderful!" Aiden cried. "I had better get an invitation."

"You kidding? You're going to be the guest of honor." They both laughed. "Why are you here at this hour?"

"It's the only hour I had," Aiden replied. A long silence fell between them.

"What do you and Rachal intend to do after you get married? Is she going to move here?"

"We're undecided on that. We've had many discussions, we just can't quite put our finger on what we're supposed to do. You appointed me to lead this nation and I am, but is there something more you would like us to do? We're willing to do anything."

"I'm going to put that to the test," Aiden said. "I would like for you and Rachal to step down from leading this nation. I want you to sell everything you have and travel east."

"Who will lead this nation?" Drake asked.

"I will choose someone. You have done very well Drake, and Lathon is very proud of you. You have become a new person. But this nation's purpose is to raise leaders and then send them out into the world, not keep them here."

"And you want to send us east?" Drake asked. "What are we going to do?"

"Go east," Aiden answered. "There are many nations in the east who have not heard the name of Lathon, or the ancient scrolls. They need to know about Lathon, about me."

"Where in the east are we to go?"

"To your home," Aiden said.

Drake's blood ran cold. "My home?"

"Have you ever wondered how you got that scar on your hand?"

"I suppose I did at one point. I haven't given it much thought lately."

"You are from the east. In that region, prophets deliver messages for Lathon. By Lathon's leading a prophet named Sarule came to your parents' house and anointed you."

"Anointed me for what?"

"To be a leader."

"How did I end up working for Queman?"

"You were running."

"I see." Drake fell silent, immersed in his thoughts. "I haven't talked to my parents in many years. I know they moved east, but I've lost touch with them."

"They never made it back," Aiden said. "I have only recently learned of this. Willard and Miles have reported many things that are concerning."

"Can you tell me anything else?" Drake asked. Aiden shook his head.

"No, I cannot. Only by going east will you find answers. You probably think it's cruel to ask you to leave it all and go somewhere far away. But it is what I'm asking. You don't have to do anything yet, nor do I seriously expect an answer until the wedding. It's a big decision and you need to figure it out together." Aiden got up and walked towards the door, stopping to look back at Drake. "This is what Lathon wants you to do. Will you?" With that, he turned and left. Drake pondered everything, his heart filled with joy and fear.

The Story Continues...

DRAKE THOMAS: PART FOUR
IDOLS & TRINKETS

MAPS

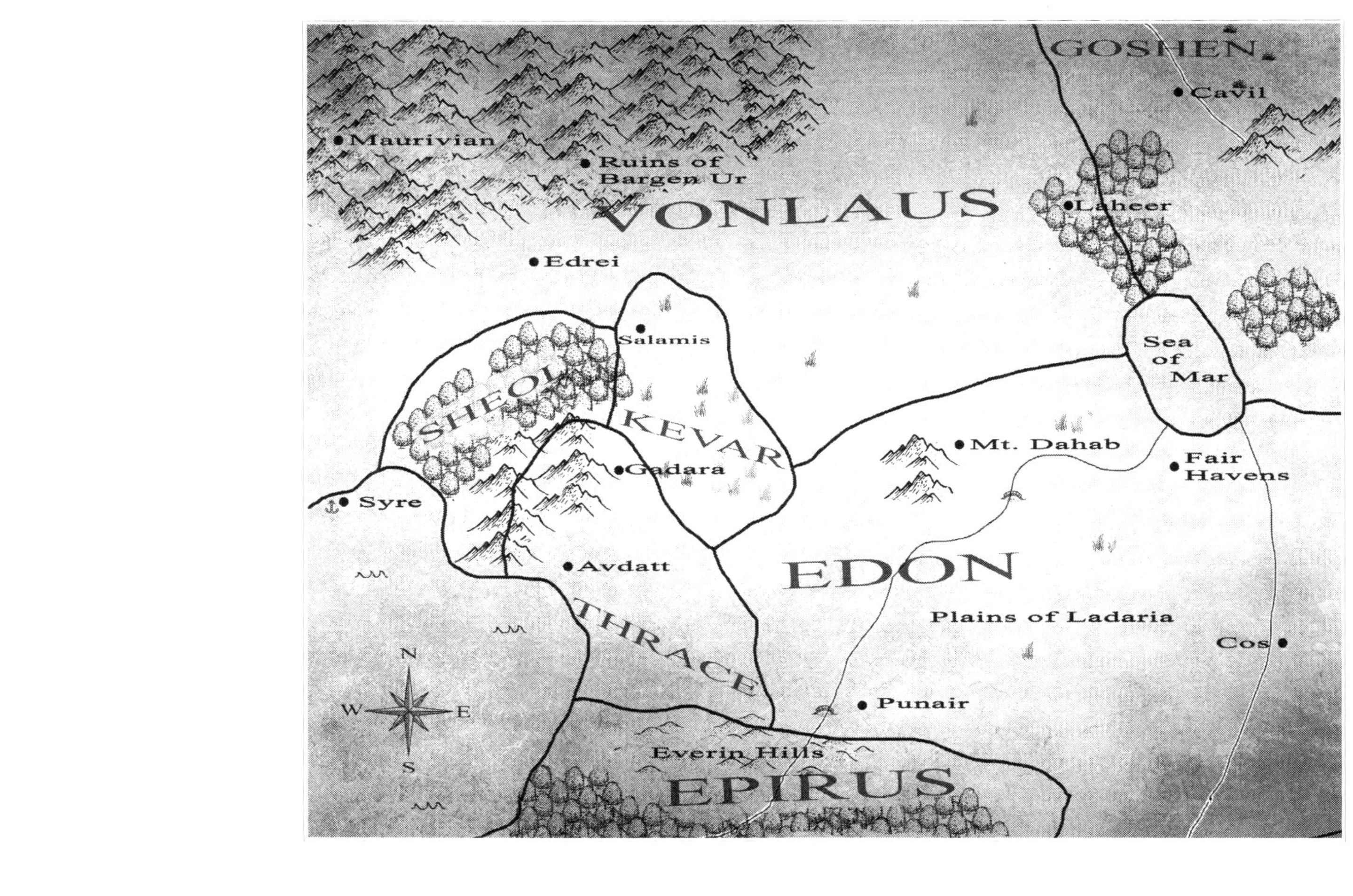

GOSHEN
Cavil
Maurivian
Ruins of
Bargen Ur
VONLAUS
Laheer
Edrei
Salamis
Sea
of
Mar
SHEOL
KEVAR
Mt. Dahab
Fair
Havens
Gadara
Syre
Avdatt
EDON
Plains of Ladaria
THRACE
Cos
N
W
E
S
Punair
Everin Hills
EPIRUS

EPIRUS
VERNAL
RHALLINEN
ARIAMORE
Farndor
Idumea
GIAHON
CALAMAR
Tyre
Erdok
Buckleberry
Latm
Nariven
Nathon
Korizinth
Somur
Phenoix
Crede
Mera Runa
Gibend River
Tel-Amor
Negev
Negev River
Ephesi
Bronk Lake
Rock of Petron
Dav
Omar
Urdik
Remnda
Maril
Revly
Belvamor
Ruins of Temnar
Havren
N
W
E
S

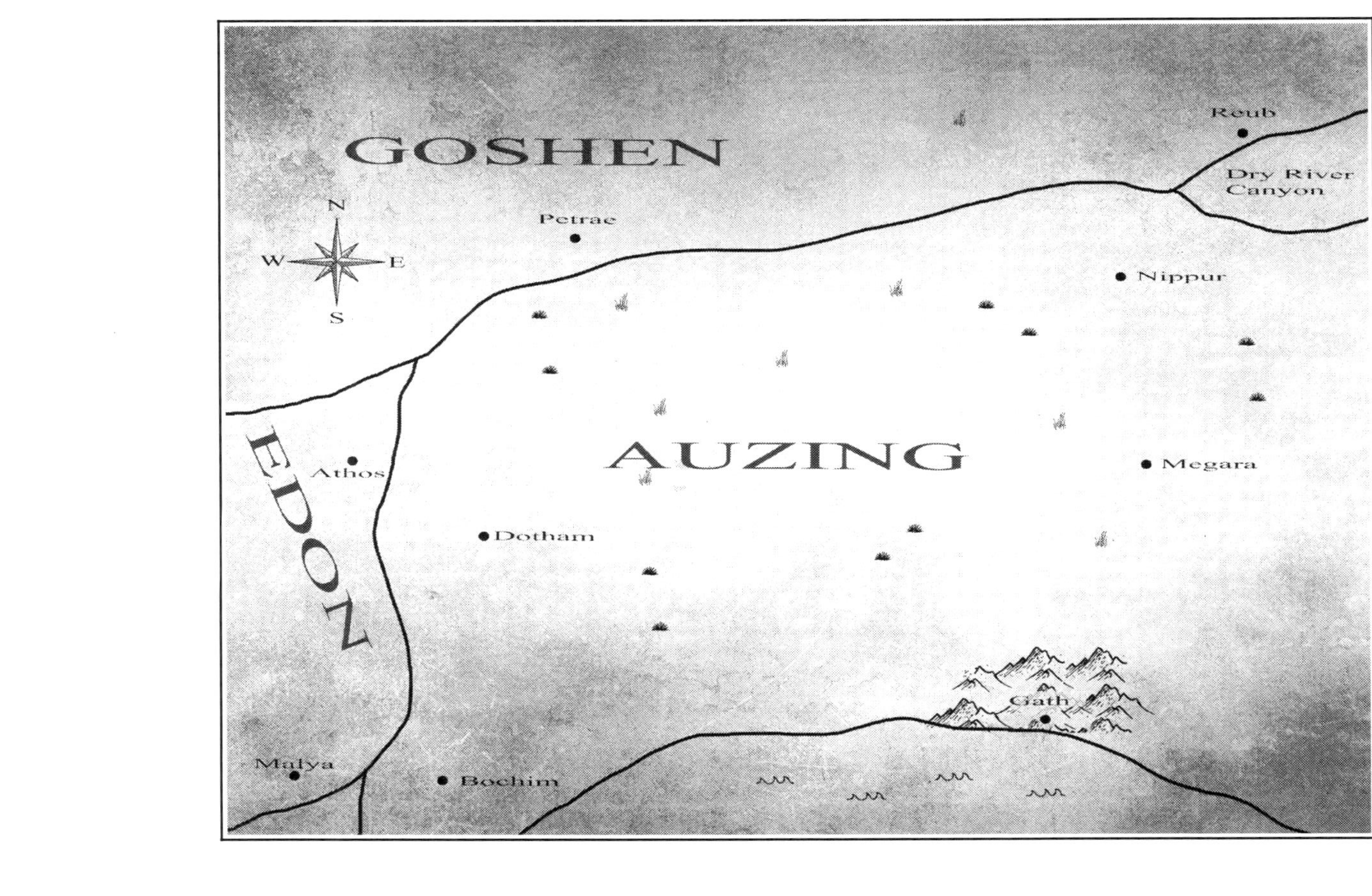
GOSHEN
Reub
Dry River
Canyon
N
W
E
S
Petrae
Nippur
EDON
Athos
AUZING
Megara
Dotham
Gath
Malya
Bochim

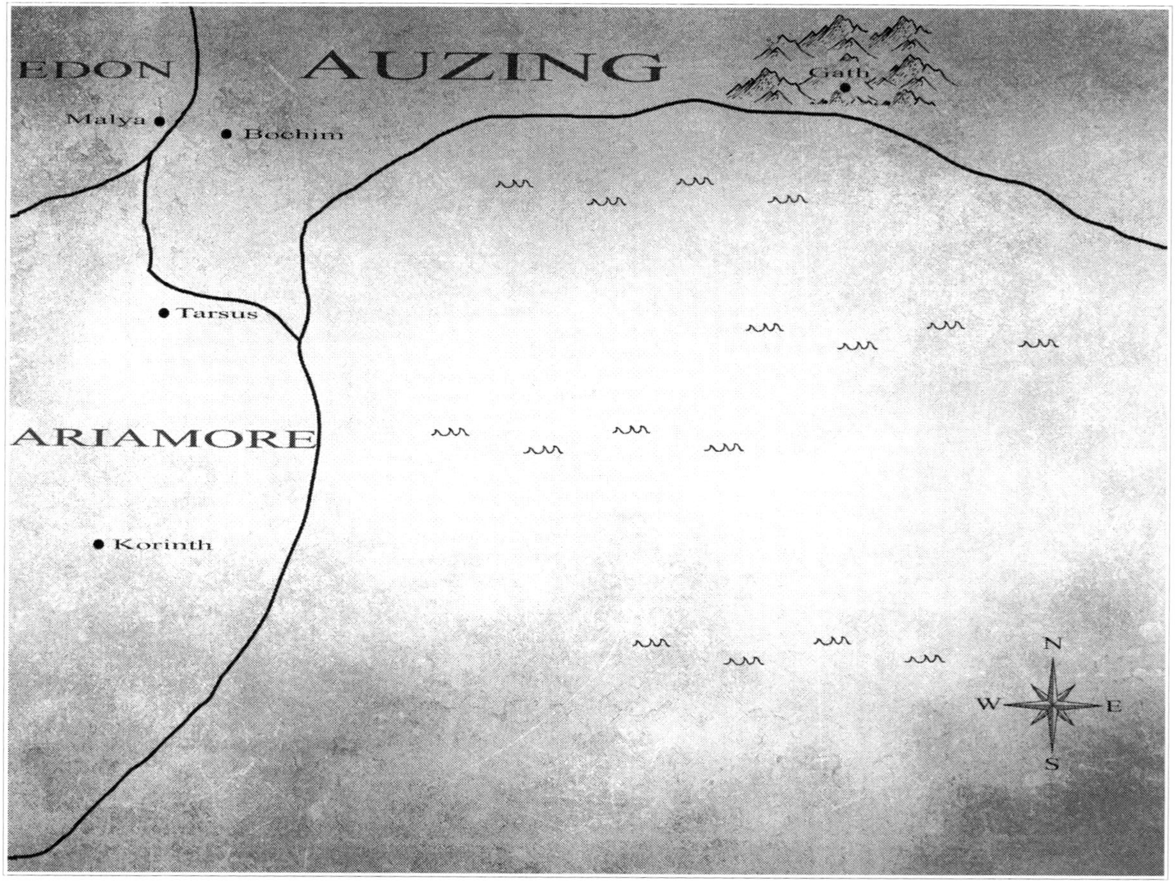

EDON
AUZING
Gath
Malya
Bochim
Tarsus
ARIAMORE
Korinth
N
W
E
S

Stories & References

Pg: 42-43 – Mark 11:15-18

Pg: 58-61 – Jesus and Nicodemus. Based off John 3:1-21

Pg: 64, 71 – Matthew 9: 9-17

Pg: 67-68 – John 8:1-11

Pg: 69 – 1 John 2: 15-17

Pg: 70 – Based off Matthew 4: 18-22

Pg: 90 – Matthew 22:15-22

Pg: 102 – Based off Mark 4:13-20

Pg: 154 – 2 Peter 3:8

Pg: 164 – Genesis 19:23-26

Pg: 176 – Saul's Background based off Moses. Exodus 2:3-15

Chapter 13 – Contains several plagues mention in the bible as well as 10 commandmants. Exodus 7:14-11:10, Exodus 20:1-17

Chapter 14 – Taken from Red Sea crossing. Exodus 14

Pg: 245 – Jezebel's Death. 2 Kings 9:30-37

Pg: 303 – Staff that sprouted Almonds. Numbers 17:8

Pg: 362 - 2 Kings 3:15-19

Pg: 365 – Joshua 10:9-14

Pg: 370-371 – Contains many elements from Revelation.

Made in the USA
Columbia, SC
21 October 2023

d7c4fa9b-ac9f-4855-a37d-b673ec8114dfR01